Tyger, Tyger, Burning Bright

Acclaim for Justine Saracen's Novels

"*Mephisto Aria* could well stand as a classic among gay and lesbian readers."—*ForeWord Reviews*

"Justine Saracen's *Sistine Heresy* is a well-written and surprisingly poignant romp through Renaissance Rome in the age of Michelangelo. ...The novel entertains and titillates while it challenges, warning of the mortal dangers of trespass in any theocracy (past or present) that polices same-sex desire."—Professor Frederick Roden, University of Connecticut, Author, *Same-Sex Desire in Victorian Religious Culture*

"...the lesbian equivalent of Indiana Jones. ...Saracen has sprinkled cliffhangers throughout this tale. ...If you enjoy the History Channel presentations about ancient Egypt, you will love this book. If you haven't ever indulged, it will be a wonderful introduction to the land of the Pharaohs. If you're a *Raiders of the Lost Ark*-type adventure fan, you'll love reading a woman in the hero's role." —*Just About Write*

"[*Sarah, Son of God*] is a charming venture into the world of, not only the transgendered, but the charisma of Venice itself." —*Out in Print*

"Saracen's wonderfully descriptive writing is a joy to the eye and the ear, as scenes play out on the page, and almost audibly as well. The characters are extremely well drawn, with suave villains, and lovely heroines. There are also wonderful romances, a heart-stopping plot, and wonderful love scenes. *Mephisto Aria* is a great read."—*Just About Write*

Visit us at www.boldstrokesbooks.com

By the Author

100th Generation

Vulture's Kiss

Sistine Heresy

Mephisto Aria

Sarah, Son of God

Tyger, Tyger, Burning Bright

Tyger, Tyger, Burning Bright

by

Justine Saracen

2012

TYGER, TYGER, BURNING BRIGHT

ISBN 10: 1-60282-652-8
ISBN 13: 978-1-60282-652-6

This Trade Paperback Original Is Published By
Bold Strokes Books, Inc.
P.O. Box 249
Valley Falls, NY 12185

First Edition: March 2012

Credits
Editor: Shelley Thrasher
Production Design: Susan Ramundo
Cover Design By Sheri (graphicartist2020@hotmail.com)

Acknowledgments

While there is an ocean of information available on Nazi Germany—in print, film, video, and documentary—it is also useful to check with someone who's been there and remembers. I'd therefore like to thank Dr. Jacqueline Nolin for providing her personal accounts of living as a child in war-torn Berlin.

I am also thankful to Marion Hoffmann and Irmgard Löffler for their help in the fine points of German terminology, and to retired surgeon Radclyffe for medical information on stab wounds.

My deep gratitude is ever and always to Shelley Thrasher, my editor and trusted friend whose scrutiny has saved me over and over from error and cliché. Thanks also to Susan Ramundo, for the equally important task of setting it all up in perfect form, and to Sheri for the ingenious cover, which tells the whole novel, if you know how to "read" it.

Most of all, of course, my deepest gratitude must go to Radclyffe, who keeps the whole ship sailing, week after month after year.

Dedication

To

Denise Block, Cicely Lefort, Violette Szabo

British agents killed at Ravensbrück

Tyger, Tyger, burning bright
In the forests of the night,
What immortal hand or eye
Could frame thy fearful symmetry?

In what distant deeps or skies
Burnt the fire of thine eyes?
On what wings dare he aspire?
What the hand dare seize the fire?

And what shoulder, & what art,
Could twist the sinews of thy heart?
And when thy heart began to beat,
What dread hand? & what dread feet?

What the hammer? what the chain?
In what furnace was thy brain?
What the anvil? what dread grasp
Dare its deadly terrors clasp?

When the stars threw down their spears
And water'd heaven with their tears,
Did he smile his work to see?
Did he who made the Lamb make thee?

Tyger, Tyger, burning bright
In the forests of the night,
What immortal hand or eye
Dare frame thy fearful symmetry?

William Blake

PART ONE

SEPTEMBER 8, 1934

NUREMBERG, GERMANY

CHAPTER ONE

The air over the Nuremberg stadium radiated with patriotism. One hundred fifty thousand uniformed men, the flower of Germany's manhood, stalwart and true, stood at attention waiting for command. But for the fluttering of the five-story banners behind the dais, all was silence.

In the tiny elevator platform on the flagpole stanchion overlooking the field, two cameras recorded the scene. While the senior cameraman panned the entire stadium with the wide-angle lens, Katja Sommer knelt beside him and captured the formations below.

Slowly, she turned the crank on the single-lens Bolex, focusing on each huge phalanx in the panorama. The *Arbeitsdienst* with their spades, the far-larger *Sturmabteilung* in brown uniforms, and the elite *Schutzstaffel* all in black. They had left a wide avenue down the center of the field and now they waited for command.

"Rechts UM!" One hundred fifty thousand men snapped a turn toward the center and presented arms. On the hard-packed stadium ground, three hundred thousand booted feet sent up a dull double concussion, *whomp-WHOMP*. An instant later, a thousand standards, topped with gilded swastikas, pivoted to salute the three celebrants who marched along the avenue: Heinrich Himmler, head of the SS; Viktor Lutze, head of the SA; and between them, Adolf Hitler, Führer of Germany.

The three leaders paced in solemn steps past the endless ranks of men, and both cameras filmed until they became tiny specks in the distance. Lowering her camera, Katja absorbed the spectacle: blocks of men as far as she could see, Germany in microcosm, paying tribute to its martyrs.

After a solemn moment, the leaders did an about-face to return along the same wide avenue and the cameras resumed filming. Still Katja heard no sound but the fluttering banners and the soft whirring of the camera mechanism. The field of men seemed a single organism harboring a vast primordial will that waited to be unleashed.

Katja was awestruck. Such manifest power had to come from something deep and wonderful. She forced away a tiny spark of doubt. Adolf Hitler, the one man who harnessed that will, had alleviated Germany's poverty and ended its humiliation. To be sure, his Brownshirts sometimes became violent, and the boycotts of Jewish shops seemed an overreaction. But she could not forget the sight of the burning Reichstag building, proof that Germany had dangerous enemies in its own cities. Even the concentration camps in Oranienburg and Dachau seemed reasonable if they held people intent on destroying the nation. Germany had endured so many hard years, and this government had begun to deliver prosperity and hope.

Katja had felt the same euphoria the day before, when they filmed the arrival of the flags. In the dusky light, countless thousands of men had paraded in, bearing the banners of the new Germany. Filmed from above, the crimson flags seemed to pour into the stadium like the blood of a people.

Then the Führer had walked onto the field before their holiest relic, the "blood flag," soaked in the gore of the men killed in the failed putsch. It bore the mystic spirit of the National Socialist movement, and in a solemn ceremony, he had touched the bloodied corner of it to each of the new standards, suffusing them with the patriotic "memory" of their comrades' first sacrifices.

The military bands struck up another march, drawing her from her reverie, and she watched Hitler return to the dais.

"That's it for now," Marti announced, to Katja's relief, and they descended to the base of the stanchion. She looked at her watch; the ceremony had taken two hours. Her back hurt from crouching the entire time, and she was cold. Marti probably was too but, as the oldest member of the camera team, he would have suffered frostbite before admitting it.

She hoped she had filmed some good material. She wanted to please not only Marti, but also the director of the whole enterprise and the bright star that illuminated Katja's every aspiration: the amazing, brilliant, beautiful Leni Riefenstahl.

CHAPTER TWO

Katja caught up with the senior cameraman and his young son, and together they crossed the Adolf Hitler Platz. "It's so quiet now," Katja remarked. "It's hard to believe that twenty-four hours ago, this square was bursting with people all screaming for the Führer."

Marti nodded and ruffled his son's hair. "Yes, it was pretty exciting, wasn't it, Johannes?"

"I liked the soldiers," the boy said, producing an awkward imitation of the goosestep. Marti smiled with paternal pride. "He's a little scrapper, and even though he's only five, he can't wait to join the *Hitlerjugend*. I think he likes the dagger. Frankly, my wife and I wish he'd go back to puppies."

They arrived at the Schlageter Platz and the building that had housed most of them during the filming. A stately structure in reddish concrete, it had three wide, arched windows on the ground floor and ornamented pilasters flanking the three arches on the floor above. But Katja always focused first on the enormous sign between the floors that announced in block letters: REICHSPARTEITAG—FILM 1934.

"I'm going to miss this place," Marti said.

"I will too. Even if I did have to sleep in a dormitory and eat in a cafeteria. I learned so much."

"You could sleep and eat? Lucky you. I barely remember doing either one. Another few days of that pace would have done me in."

Once inside, Katja saw that most of the other cameramen had already arrived. She immediately recognized Sepp Allgeier, the head of operations. She knew most of the others by face, but particularly liked cameramen Koehler, Vogel, and Gottschalk. All the men in the crew greeted each other with backslapping and mild ribaldry and smiled courteously toward her. They seemed exhausted, simply waiting for their director to declare the job done so they could go home.

Leni Riefenstahl was nowhere in sight. To Katja's disappointment, she'd never gotten to talk to her. In the turmoil of the week's events, the busy director had never stayed in one place long enough for Katja to even approach her. A shame, because Riefenstahl was half the reason Katja had applied to work on the project. Of course she also wanted to learn filming, an infant industry in which she hoped to make a career. But Katja had watched Riefenstahl act in the mountain-climbing thrillers *The White Hell of Pitz Palü* and *Storms over Montblanc*, and by the time she saw *The Blue Light,* she was starstruck.

The door to the large conference room opened and the crowd of people in the corridor filed in. The conference table had been moved to the back and rows of chairs placed in a semicircle before a portable screen. Behind the chairs, a projector was mounted on the table, and Gottschalk stood by it with some half-dozen cans of film.

Leni Riefenstahl appeared at the front of the room. In a rumpled jacket, she was visibly tired and the face Katja knew from the movie screen was somewhat haggard. Her stylishly short hair looked as if she had run her fingers through it in lieu of combing. For all that, she was still attractive, the sort of woman men both feared and lusted after.

Katja had considered cutting her own dark brown hair in the same fashion, but decided against it, keeping it pinned in a roll at the back of her neck, the way her fiancé liked it.

"Thank you all for staying an extra day," Riefenstahl said. "I know you're all anxious to leave and I promise I'll release you in just about an hour."

During the murmurs of approval one or two people actually checked their watches.

"I've already thanked the City of Nuremberg for the lads who built our observation towers and bridges, camera tracks, and, above all, the electric elevator on the mast in the Luitpold stadium. But that was them, and this is you. Bravo to you."

Another rumble of cheerful agreement.

Riefenstahl scratched her barely combed hair. "For your information, we have 130,000 meters of film and a couple of hundred stills from Rudi Lamm and myself. I've had a few important scenes developed, and I edited just a little, to see what's possible. I think we've done a terrific job, but you can judge for yourselves." She signaled for the light switch and the projector began to run.

An airplane emerged from the clouds and flew low over Nuremberg, casting its cruciform shadow over the city like a benediction. Below, long columns of people marched in formation toward the stadium. Ingenious. The Führer arriving from on high, about to descend to the adoring multitudes who streamed to greet him.

"Fantastic scene, someone said. "How did we get that?"

"We had both an airship and a small Klemm single-engine up there at the same time."

"That's the material I took from the Klemm flying alongside," Richard Koehler said. "Glad you like it."

"Don't worry," Riefenstahl said. "We'll keep it, no matter what else we cut."

"That's good news." Koehler slapped his hand on his knee. "Why don't we cut the speeches? They're all drivel."

"Don't let anyone hear you say that, Richard," Sepp Allgeier said. "The propaganda ministry already has some kind of blood feud with us."

Riefenstahl declined to comment and instead called attention to the screen where the scene had jumped to the Führer's motorcade through Nuremberg. "I did some experimental splicing here, just to show what I have in mind." The camera shifted focus repeatedly, from Hitler's car, to the crowds, to the city itself, as though its ancient edifices also welcomed him.

"It works beautifully," Vogel said. "I see some of my segments here, but those overheads look like they're from Marti."

Katja smiled to herself, recognizing some of the shots she and Marti had done together to highlight the beauty of the city. Deep in Bavaria, Nuremberg was a gem, the obvious choice for a political party that claimed the soul of a people. A born Berliner, Katja did not know much about Nuremberg beyond what she had learned in school, that it was an early center of humanism, science, and painting, and that two of its famous sons were Albrecht Dürer and Johann Pachelbel. But she found its medieval look intriguing.

A good thing, because she was engaged to a young Nuremberger, Dietrich Kurtz, and would probably end up living here.

Leni Riefenstahl's voice penetrated Katja's thoughts. "There's a moment coming up that's just perfect. We filmed hundreds of meters from directly behind the Führer with the sunlight delineating him. But look here, how the morning sun radiates around his head and shoulders like a halo. Fortunately, we were also filming from the front, and with a little splicing…right here…we shift to full sunlight blazing off his face." She pointed to the screen. "Did you see his raised hand? Light leaps from it like something divine. Great effect. We'll keep that and cut back on the crowd scenes."

"I hope we keep *some* of the crowd scenes," Rudi Lamm said, "but filmed against the backdrop of the medieval buildings. The city should be part of the story."

"I agree, Herr Lamm," Riefenstahl said. "The propaganda minister seems to believe we are making a political document, but that was never my intention. It's to be a work of art, like Nuremberg itself."

The conference room door opened abruptly and a man hurried in to take a seat. "Sorry for being late," he said, but offered no excuse. Katja recognized Erich Prietschke, one of the assistants, she wasn't sure to whom. He was tall, with blue eyes and blond hair brushed up on one side and tumbling down on the other. The film crews had worn SA uniforms to blend in with the crowd, but all the others had turned theirs in the evening before. Only Erich had kept his uniform another day, she suspected because he knew it made him look the perfectly dashing Aryan soldier.

The light went off again. "This is one of the reels from the next morning." The camera "eye" began before an opening window then glided over the water of the canal, past ancient houses hung with long NSDAP banners, as if the swastikas were as much a part of Nuremberg's history as its painted façades and medieval sculpture. The camera cut to the tent cities of the Arbeitsdienst and the Hitlerjugend, where the boys were just emerging.

Richard Koehler spoke up. "We got those overheads from the airship. But I think Sepp got better shots from below."

"We did," Sepp Allgeier said. "Lots of pretty faces, naked chests. There's some of it now." The camera panned from one shining face to another, then withdrew to show the young men shirtless and in trousers, scrubbing arms and feet under a dripping pipe.

"The *Volk* in its glory," Koehler commented. "Attach that to the scenes of the Führer kissing children and old ladies in native costume, and no one will remember he's not German."

Katja noticed Erich frowning at the banter. When the reel ended and the new one was threaded in, conversation resumed.

"What about the Hitlerjugend scenes?" someone asked.

"There's plenty of that. We had six cameras on it," Riefenstahl said. "Plus, we got all the blood-flag ceremony. That's coming up now."

The projector clattered as the scene unfolded. At screen center, Hitler strode forward holding the corner of a stained National Socialist flag borne by a soldier in *Stahlhelm*.

Stepping from standard to standard, Hitler touched the flag's corner to the fabric of each banner. He took his time, solemnly clutching each swastika panel to the holy relic, passing the sacred blood-magic to the new banner, and the camera revealed each *Gau* name—Hessen, Paderborn, Spessart, Rhineland—as it received the Führer's touch.

"Great filming, Sepp," Marti said. "The Nazis love their flags, don't they? Did we get any good stills of them?"

"We did," Riefenstahl answered. "Rudi and I were both on the field right after the ceremony. I got a couple of wonderful shots, of a Hitlerjugend holding a flag over his head with sunlight filtering through it."

At that moment, the door to the conference room opened again, interrupting them a second time. Annoyance briefly crossed Riefenstahl's face, then faded. "Oh, it's you, Frederica. What is it?"

"It's the *Reichsminister*, Frau Riefenstahl. He just sent over a note." The young woman held out an envelope, and from where she was sitting, Katja could see the insignia of the propaganda ministry.

"Don't tell me. Dr. Goebbels is sending his congratulations, is he?" Riefenstahl perused the letter, shaking her head. "The same old nonsense. A reminder that it's his prerogative to monitor the film for its 'value to the Volk.' He also requires that I come to his hotel this afternoon to discuss when he can review the films."

She took a breath. "For godsake! It's the party congress. Does he think I'll smuggle in a mountain-climbing scene?" She slapped the letter closed and shoved it into her pocket. "What crap," she muttered. "The Führer said I had carte blanche for this project, and Goebbels just hates that I'm the only person in the German art world he can't control." She sighed. "I suppose I'll have to go and soothe his ruffled feathers."

"This afternoon?" Allgeier asked. "Weren't we going to have a last meal together before everyone leaves?"

"Oh, that's right, I'd forgotten." Riefenstahl nodded. "Well, Herr Reichsminister will just have to wait." She turned back to her secretary, who had sat down next to her. "Please stay after the film showing, Frederica. I'll write him a note that I'll be happy to come to the ministry at his convenience, when I'm back in Berlin. That'll irritate him, but not enough for him to do anything about it."

Riefenstahl stood up in front of the group again. "All right, everyone. That's all we've got for now. I've got a lot of editing ahead of me, to reduce those 130,000 meters to about 3,000, so count yourselves lucky to be able to stop working now. I know some of you are leaving immediately, but for those who can stay a few more hours, we've asked the kitchen staff to put together a final meal at two o'clock. I hope to see you there."

The departing team members gathered around to say good-bye to their boss, and Katja migrated toward the corridor. Just by the door, Frederica was conversing with Erich Prietschke, tall, blond, and in uniform, like an image on a political poster.

He bent over Frederica with one hand on the wall above her head and the other hooked on his military belt. Katja chuckled to herself. Even when he flirted, he swaggered.

Frederica, for her part, was harder to fathom. Even physically, she was a curious mixture. Under her amber, almost-blond hair, she had an oval face with a wide mouth and full, well-formed lips. Her large eyes seemed to squint back at her admirer, either with amusement or skepticism, Katja couldn't be sure which.

Statuesque, even beautiful, she had a distinctly un-German look. The features were finely chiseled, and Katja couldn't possibly imagine her in a dirndl dress or with a coif of twisted braids. What was it, then, that attracted Erich?

"He's really pouring it on, isn't he? Do you think she's falling for it?"

"Rudi!" Katja glanced sideways to see one of her best friends on the team. "Hi there. I haven't seen you for days. What have you been doing all this time?"

He pecked her on the cheek. "Working my pretty fingers to the bone. Every time Frau Riefenstahl went out for a shot, I had to go with her so we'd have both film and stills of it. I could have had my camera glued to my head and no one would have noticed the difference. Where did she assign *you*?"

Katja stood back to study him, trim yet muscular, like a dancer. She had liked him from the first moment she met him. His lighthearted banter and genuine warmth always cheered her. He posed, though not the way men posed—to assert authority. Rather it was as if to say, *Look, I'm posing. Isn't this fun*? He was handsome in a more delicate way than Erich. His features were finer, and his brown eyelashes were as long as a girl's.

"I was Herr Kraus's assistant. I mostly carried his equipment, but they let me film now and then, when they wanted extra coverage."

"Ah, yes, I saw you up on the pole once, squashed in behind him. That can't have been so nice." He chuckled.

She smiled along with him. "It was a tight squeeze, but I didn't think much about it. I was too intent on getting the picture. I want so much to live up to Frau Riefenstahl's vision."

"I know what you mean. I'm not thrilled about the political message, but I love what she's doing for cinema. Cameras on the ground, cameras on tracks, cameras in dirigibles. Absolutely brilliant. You can't help but be in awe of her."

"I am, but I've never really talked to her. Herr Kraus engaged me. We're both from Berlin and he knew I was studying film, so he took me on."

"I'm from Berlin too. Neukölln. I live just down the street from the Alte Post, if you know that district. I got my job because I know Frederica, her secretary."

Katja's attention had wandered as she glanced again toward Erich, who still hovered over Frederica. "They'd make a nice couple, don't you think?"

"Erich? He *is* a beauty, isn't he? But Frederica's much too smart for him. She doesn't go for *blond beasts* like that."

"How do you know what she 'goes for'?"

Rudi allowed himself a slight smirk. "We were once engaged."

"Really? What happened?"

He waved his hand, as if brushing a fly away. "Long story. Let's just say we were well matched, but not for marriage. I love her to pieces, but we realized in time that we were much better off as best friends. What about you? Is there a Mister Sommer?"

Katja chuckled. "Yes, my father. But I'm engaged to a man in the *Wehrmacht*. We haven't set a date yet, and I'm not in a hurry, but I suppose it will happen eventually."

"You make it sound like gray hair. You're not in a hurry to get married?"

"No. I want to do so many other things first. But Dietrich, my fiancé, is patient. Brave, kind, hard working. He was on the field yesterday, with his unit, in the middle of all those other thousands. I'm sure he was wildly proud to stand there for Hitler."

"'Brave, kind, hard-working, proud to stand for Hitler.' I guess that's what every German woman wants in a man." Katja detected the faintest note of irony in his voice, which she didn't know how to respond to.

"Ah, Katja! Finally, I found you," someone said, and Katja turned around. Of medium height, with light-brown hair tending toward red, and the faint remainder of childhood freckles, Dietrich Kurtz looked slightly out of character in his Wehrmacht uniform, like a boy dressed up as a soldier.

"Dietrich! I thought you had marched off to the train station yesterday with twenty thousand others."

"I did. But before we even arrived for the rally, I applied for leave. They gave me twenty-four hours, isn't that great? I thought I'd surprise you."

"Oh, yes, it's great," Katja said, forcing cheer into her voice. His sudden appearance reminded her of her life outside the film project and diluted the excitement of the last hour of the great adventure.

Most of the others from the camera team were leaving, and he slid his arm around her waist. "Let's go for a walk then," he suggested, guiding her toward the door.

They passed Frederica and Erich at the doorway and, for a moment, Katja locked eyes with her. Frederica's eyes were gray-green, her glance intense before she shifted her attention back to Erich. Yes, Katja confirmed inwardly. A perfect Nazi couple.

Then Dietrich pulled her from the warm film-crew building into the cool, sobering air of the Schlageter Platz and her previous life.

Chapter Three

Dietrich looked at his watch. "My father will be at work and my mother does her shopping in the middle of the day. We'll have the house to ourselves," he said pointedly.

Katja was not enthusiastic. "I shouldn't be away too long, Dietrich. Herr Kraus might need me for something."

"Oh, come on," he said with obvious disappointment. "Frau Riefenstahl said herself that the work was all done. We've been engaged ever since last summer and you've never seen our house here in Nuremberg. I got leave especially to spend a few hours alone with you. It's not the wrong time of the month, is it? I thought I knew your 'safe' times."

Katja was not particularly in the mood for the sex he was alluding to, even if this was a time when she couldn't get pregnant, but it wouldn't take long to satisfy him. His parents were genuinely good people, and she was sure the house was lovely too. So why did she feel like she was being dragged away from something? Then she reminded herself, the film project was a one-time adventure; Dietrich would be her life.

"All right. We can spend an hour at your house, if you'd like, but I want to be at the supper the film team is having."

Dietrich hugged her to his chest and kissed the top of her head. "You're a very strong-willed woman, you know. That will be good when it comes time to raise the children."

"Children," she repeated. "Yes, I suppose so."

She walked alongside him, wondering what had brought her and Dietrich together. Perhaps because he was the first man who courted her instead of the prettier schoolgirls with their round, soft faces and pink cheeks. Her slightly angular features always made her look older than her years, and her single-mindedness about her studies made her unsociable. Dietrich's attentions were enormously flattering, and before she knew it, she was engaged.

"We can catch the *Strassenbahn* right here at the Adolf Hitler Platz, and see? One's already coming." He grasped her hand and drew her along in a gentle jog.

❖

Dietrich's family house on the Schwalbenstrasse could have been in a children's story book. The exposed-beam construction was medieval and, even without the swastika flag, represented traditional Germany. Geranium-filled flower boxes decorated all the windows, red at the street level, pink on the floor just above, and white on the top floor. The front door was oak, with a wreath of walnut shells and dried thistle at the center.

"Oh, drat. The light's on in the kitchen. My mother's still there. Well, maybe she'll take the hint and leave," Dietrich said as he shoved the heavy oak door open and they entered the foyer. On a series of hooks just inside the doorway, hats and a woman's green *Loden* jacket hung next to a carved walking stick.

"Mutti, look who's here!" he announced, standing in the doorway of the kitchen.

A woman in her sixties looked up from where she was sitting and writing. "Ach, Dietrich!" she exclaimed, and hurried toward him. "And Katja! How wonderful. Dietrich, I thought you had to stay with your unit after the congress."

"I do. I've only got a few hours' leave but look, I was able to convince Katja to come."

"That's splendid. I was just making a list of things I need to buy at the market in the square. I'll pick up some beef and make *Tafelspitz* for dinner. Your father will be so pleased." She cupped her slightly plump hand under Katya's chin. "We'll have a nice family meal with our future daughter-in-law."

"Uh, I'm afraid not, Mutti. Katja has to be back at work later this afternoon."

"Yes, I'm sorry, Frau Kurtz. The team has another meeting and of course I have to be there. For the party congress, you know." It was only half a lie.

"But maybe we can have some coffee before you go shopping." Dietrich's emphasis on the word "shopping" made it clear that he expected her to leave them alone.

"Ja, natürlich," she responded with maternal understanding, and set about grinding the coffee beans. While Dietrich assisted his mother in preparing the ritual snack, Katja surveyed the room.

The walls and ceiling were pine supported by pine beams, and the floor was oak. But not merely the preponderance of wood gave the room its heavy Bavarian atmosphere. The table in the corner had wooden benches attached to the walls on two sides, and the tall green-tiled *Kachelofen*, which over-warmed the kitchen, held tiles painted with edelweiss and acorns. On the wall over the table were both a statue of the Virgin with the infant Jesus and a crucifix with the vividly painted dead one. The other wall sported three trophy heads of mountain goats. The cloying, overheated coziness hinted of mortality and guilt.

"Can I help?" Katja asked, but Frau Kurtz waved her away. "Oh, of course not, dear. Just sit yourself down. The coffee will be ready in a moment."

Katja studied a gray stoneware pitcher and cups on the counter nearby and next to them two picture frames. One held a family portrait. Against the backdrop of a dusty curtain, Konrad Kurtz stood in a suit with stiff paternal pride next to his wife, who was seated on an ornamental chair, her long skirt draped artistically to cover her feet. Between them, in lederhosen and white shirt, a very young Dietrich posed with his hand on the arm of the chair. A paternal hand rested on his shoulder, as if to hold him in place.

The other photo, obviously more recent, was of Dietrich in his Wehrmacht uniform, posing with the same stiffness as his father.

The solemnity of his expression belied the sweet, playful boy she knew was hidden inside.

"Here we are, my dear." Frau Kurtz swung around with a painted porcelain coffee pot and three matching cups. Dietrich followed with a plate of small cakes. Katja braced herself for the inevitable question of when she and Dietrich would marry, but Frau Kurtz was stealthier than that. "How exciting that you've been invited to do this wonderful film for the Führer. Did you actually get to photograph him?" Frau Kurtz asked, pouring the steaming coffee into all of the cups.

"Yes, several times, but I was only an assistant to one of the cameramen."

"That's exciting" she repeated. "I watched the parade when the Führer arrived, but it was hard to see in such a big crowd. You know how the Bavarians adore him." She served the cakes. "Did you actually speak with him? I think I would have fainted."

"No, he was always at a distance. But we made some nice films of Dietrich standing at attention with thousands of others on the field. If it makes the editing cut, you'll be able to see it in the cinema."

Dietrich laughed. "Yes, and you can be sure she'll be looking for me. I'll be the one on the right side, nine hundred rows back, eighty-seventh man from the center."

"Perhaps by the time the film is in the cinema, you'll be home on leave again with your new bride. Have you set a date yet?"

Katja looked away. She should have seen it coming. Dietrich, bless his heart, fielded the question with finesse. "I can't be a husband when I'm in training, Mutti. And Katja has to finish her film studies. But don't worry. We love each other and we'll get married when the time is right for both of us."

"I know, my dears. It's just that your father is nearly seventy, and we both want grandchildren. Is that so selfish?"

Dietrich took her hand. "No, not at all. But don't worry about grandchildren. We're working on that," he said pointedly. Katja blushed at the obvious hint of what they planned that afternoon, but Frau Kurtz understood immediately.

"Yes, that's lovely," she replied ambiguously, and gathered the empty plates and coffee cups. "And that reminds me, I do have a lot of shopping to do before the market closes at two. Please excuse me, Katja, dear."

With a peck to the cheek of her son and her almost daughter-in-law, Gertrude Kurtz gathered her various nets and sacks and was off to the market square.

"Should we wash the dishes?" Katja asked, stalling. "She would probably appreciate that."

"She would be horrified." Dietrich laughed "The kitchen is her realm and she takes offense if anyone lays claim to any of her responsibilities. No, I think she will be quite content for us to have our little hour to ourselves." He took her hand. "I've been thinking about you all week."

He kissed her palm. "Come on, I'll show you my room in all its simplicity. I don't want to have any secrets from you." He drew her from the table and up the narrow wooden staircase to the next floor. His room was at the far end.

It was friendly, orderly, and meticulously clean. Katja had no doubt that Frau Kurtz dusted it every day, even when it was empty. A narrow bed was in the corner, and the wallpaper, she noted, bore a pattern of tiny hunters with old-fashioned shotguns alternating with rabbits under bushes. A bookcase held books on its lower shelves and toys on the top one: lead soldiers and a tin castle with tiny knights positioned against a raised drawbridge. An open shelf on another wall held folded sweaters, well-worn lederhosen, presumably the ones in the photograph, and a balsa-wood airplane. Below it stood a pair of hiking boots and wooden shoes. On the far wall, in a wooden frame, hung a poster for the Hitlerjugend.

"Come, sit down." Dietrich drew her to him on the edge of the narrow bed. "You make me so proud to be a soldier," he said, sliding his lips along her cheek to her neck.

"You should be proud to be a soldier for everyone, not just me." She was not really in the mood for intimacy, but he was gentle, and although she never felt the thrill that other people apparently did, she didn't especially mind. It would occur eventually, she was sure.

He slid off his military boots and set them together against the wall. Standing in front of her, he unbuttoned his military tunic to his undershirt. A few blond hairs showed in the V of the neckline. He draped the tunic carefully over the only chair in the room, then, undoing his suspenders, he snapped open his *Gott mit Uns* belt buckle and dropped his military pants.

To save time, Katja unfastened her skirt and drew off her stockings. In a moment, both were naked from the waist down, and she lay back on his bed.

Unlike the first time they were together, he spent little time on foreplay, merely stroking her sex long enough to create a bit of moisture. Katja wished he would have done it longer; she was just beginning to warm up to the idea of him, but he was impatient, and he lay on top of her before she was really ready. Nonetheless, she held him tight, feeling his hardness on her belly, and sensed a slight tingling. If he were just not in such a hurry.

But obviously he could not hold himself back and so, moaning against her throat, he spread her legs with his knees and, after a few tentative pokes, he plunged into her.

She murmured back at him because she knew he liked it, and he began his motion. She matched his grunts of pleasure with her own, and though they were not feigned, she knew she was not experiencing what he was. She had imagined ecstasy differently, not at all like this. But she did like his warmth and the protection of his arms while he thrust into her; she was lucky to have him rather than any of the brutes some of her friends had married. His lovemaking would get better, she was sure.

In just a few moments he was finished and rolled off, breathless. "It's so good with you, Katja," he murmured into her ear. "I can't wait until we're married and we can do this every night. And have children come from it, lots of them. Being an only child is no good. We might have to live here with my parents for a little while, until my military service is over, but then we'll have our own little house. Won't that be fine?"

Cradled in his arms, Katja felt the sticky pool of fluid beneath her. What would Dietrich's mother think when she came to clean her son's room and make up his bed—which she surely would do. The idea of having Gertrude Kurtz monitor her marital sex disturbed her deeply. And Katja had not even considered the question of living arrangements after marriage. The thought of living under the authority of both her husband and her parents-in-law, benign as it was, suffocated her.

"We can also keep being together like this while you do your service. We don't have to be in a hurry to have children. I would like to accomplish a few things first."

"I know you're ambitious, Liebchen. We all have dreams when we're young. But eventually you have to grow up and accept your responsibilities as a woman." He spoke gently, as was his nature, softening the reproach. "And just as a man's duty is to fight for the Volk, a woman's duty is to raise a family. Both are noble in their own way."

Suddenly the room seemed smaller. She sat up from his embrace and swung her legs around to the floor. The floorboards felt cold under her bare feet.

Dietrich curved around her, grasping her playfully around the hips as she bent to pick up her skirt and underpants. He cajoled her. "Are you sure you want to get up already, *Schatz*? I think I'll be ready again in a few minutes."

"Please, Dietrich. I'd like to wash before your mother comes home. And all this talk about children has put me off. A woman should be able to do more than have babies and clean house. Look at Frau Riefenstahl."

"You can't compare yourself with her. She's serving the Führer in a unique way. Besides, you don't know her. She may have a man some place. I'm sure dozens of good German men would like to make babies with her."

"I don't want to talk that way about her." Katja stood up with her clothing in hand. "Is there a sink upstairs?"

"I'm sorry, no. All the plumbing is downstairs, next to the kitchen." He was sitting up now too, obviously resigned to their "little hour" being over.

She crept down the wooden staircase clutching her clothing to her chest, hoping frantically that no one would come through the front door while she was in sight. Passing the cozy Bavarian kitchen, she imagined herself living with the little corner table and benches, next to the Kachelofen, the crucifix and the picture of the Virgin Mary, and she shuddered.

Chapter Four

How many are you?" the *Hausmeister* asked, his upraised finger twitching as he counted. Twelve?"

The cook, standing next to him, confirmed the number.

"Thirteen, counting Frau Riefenstahl," someone added from the doorway.

"Good, because that's all we have food for."

With all of its trestle tables but two dismantled and stowed away, the temporary dining room looked cheerless, and the voices of the gathering team members rang slightly hollow. Still, in an effort to be festive, someone had put the two tables end to end and covered them with a long white tablecloth. Plates and silverware had also been laid out.

The diners filed in, taking places more or less randomly, and Katja glanced around to see who out of the team had stayed. Riefenstahl sat at one side, with Sepp Allgeier and her secretary, and across from Erich Prietschke, Marti Kraus, and young Johannes. Cameramen Richard Koehler, Walter Vogel, and Hans Gottschalk joined them at the other end of the table, near Dietrich. Only one person was unfamiliar, the rather striking young man who had come with Rudi and who sat now between him and her. He wore spectacles, and the dueling scar on his chin suggested he had been a cadet at university.

Rudi glanced to the left and to the right and observed the layout of the table. "We're a little Last Supperish here, aren't we?" He laughed.

Katja enjoyed the image. “Yes, you’re right. And look who’s in the middle.”

“That can’t be a good omen,” the spectacled stranger remarked, then twisted around toward Katja. “Hello. I’m Peter Arnhelm, and you, I know, are Katja. Rudi has told me a lot about you.”

“Really? I’m sure I’m not as bad as he said.”

“No, you’re just as charming.”

Katja felt out-quipped but amused. “He told me nothing at all about you, though. How do you know Rudi?”

“We met ages ago, when he photographed a stage play I was working in.”

“You’re an actor?” She could easily imagine the slender man posturing onstage.

“No, costume designer. In the Deutsches Theater.” He blinked as he cleaned his glasses on his shirt. “I worked on the costumes of a couple of Schiller plays, *William Tell* and *Maria Stuart*. But that was a few seasons ago, under Max Reinhardt. I don’t think they’re performing them this year.”

“Max Reinhardt, I know that name.” Katja frowned slightly, trying to recall him.

Peter threaded the wires of his glasses back over his ears. “You should. One of the great geniuses of the stage. But he was Jewish and had to leave last year.”

“That seems…I don’t know…a mistake. To get rid of geniuses.”

“Yes, it was a big mistake,” he said neutrally.

The food arrived, a sort of stew made up of an assortment of meats and vegetables that might not have belonged together, but were well enough seasoned and served with enough bread and beer to satisfy.

People were conversing in clusters of twos and threes, but as the plates were cleared, they turned their attention to the director.

“Frau Riefenstahl,” Walter Vogel called. “What was our biggest accomplishment?”

Riefenstahl folded her napkin while she gave the question some thought. “Hard to say. We did a lot of things that hadn’t been done before. But I'm proudest of our convincing Nuremberg to build us an elevator on one of the flagpoles. I'm not sure how high—"

"Thirty-eight meters," Marti Kraus sang out. "I was up there every day and I can tell you it was thirty-eight bloody meters. And me, afraid of heights."

"*Now* you tell me." Riefenstahl laughed. "But that little elevator gave us some of the best filming opportunities. That and the airship."

"What was the *worst* thing we did?" someone else asked.

After the general laughter Riefenstahl answered immediately. "That would have to be the torch fiasco."

"Fiasco, oh, I like that word," Erich Prietschke said. "This is a story I want to hear."

Riefenstahl leaned forward on her elbows. "Well, you all remember the nighttime ceremony with the diplomats in front of Hitler's hotel? We tried to film with spotlights, but Hermann Goering ordered them shut off because they were too bright. I didn't know the order came from him, so I ordered them turned on again. But a minute later, they went off again, and we were in a panic. Then *someone*, who shall remain unnamed," she looked tellingly down the table toward Hans Gottschalk, "suggested using the magnesium torches the SA had stocked nearby." A few at the table remembered the outcome and tittered.

"So, we did. But no one warned me about the smoke. No sooner did we have them lit and were filming away, when the air became thick with greasy clouds. Everyone started coughing and the diplomats fled like the place was on fire."

Allgeier laughed, slapping his hand on the table.

"Did anyone get in trouble for it?" Vogel asked.

"Not yet," Riefenstahl said. "I think they're still trying to figure out who to blame. And of course none of you are planning to talk, are you?"

"Us?" Vogel looked around with feigned innocence. "We wouldn't *think* of it. We're a team, after all."

Allgeier raised his beer glass. "To the team. To us!" Everyone seconded the toast, and during a moment of quiet, beer flowed quietly down thirteen throats. Then Erich Prietschke stood up, still in his SA uniform.

"Frau Riefenstahl, I just want to say how proud I am to have worked with you making the party congress into a great drama for the world to view. Seeing the German Volk through your vision has been an inspiration."

On the other end of the table, Dietrich Kurtz stood up as well. "I wish to echo that sentiment, Frau Riefenstahl. Although I was on the field, amongst the thousands of my brother soldiers, my fiancé was with your team and I was damned proud of that. You've done a great thing for the Fatherland."

Johannes Kraus, Marti's young son, looked back and forth between Erich in his SA disguise and Dietrich in his Wehrmacht tunic with an expression of the purest adoration.

Riefenstahl raised both hands. "Oh, for God's sake, sit down, you two. I'm glad to hear you're so enthusiastic, but you must understand, I intend this work as a piece of art, a spectacle. Of course we want to satisfy the wishes of the Führer, but the work is *not* a propaganda statement or a newsreel. Art is not political. This film, like an oil painting, should be its own glory, and you should all be proud of making it." She turned then to her chief of operations. "Sepp, you feel the same way, don't you?"

Sepp Allgeier pursed his lips. "Frankly, I wouldn't worry about it. I've filmed with you on glaciers and mountainsides, and I think your message is always a bit more poetical than mine. Me, I just want to record the most truthful moment."

Rudi Lamm, the youngest of them all, spoke quietly. "I think I'm among friends here and can speak freely. I joined this team in the belief that we'd make a masterpiece. I would not have signed on with Dr. Goebbels to make a propaganda film. We saw so much power and idealism on the field this week, but that power can be abused, as it was when the SA threw our sound cart into a ditch. That spirit of the 'Volk' is beautiful but it's also explosive. I hope it continues to be directed toward raising Germany up, building roads and planting forests and creating jobs." He glanced over at Peter, who sat beside him. "And not on boycotting Jewish shops or beating up Social Democrats."

A moment of uncomfortable silence followed. Katja watched the mysterious Frederica for a sign of her political position, but saw only a carefully composed face that revealed nothing. Riefenstahl broke the silence.

"So, who is going with me to the propaganda ministry to face down Herr Goebbels? You'll come, won't you, Sepp?"

"I'm sorry, Leni. "I'm not even returning to Berlin. I've got a contract in Munich for the next two weeks."

"Marti, what about you? I just need someone to be there so he behaves himself. If he doesn't get his way, he can become very disagreeable."

"Unfortunately, I can't go either. I have to take my son to his grandparents."

"Frederica, at least you'll face him with me, won't you? It's logical for me to show up with my secretary. He'll control his temper if there's a witness."

Frederica winced. "I would love to stand by you, Frau Riefenstahl, but in this case, I can't. My family has…um…other business with the ministry and I can't show up there as an antagonist. I'm sorry."

"Business? What 'other business' do you mean?" Riefenstahl seemed affronted.

"Stop tormenting the girl, Leni," Richard Koehler said. "If all you want is for him to mind his manners, why don't you take someone he doesn't know? Someone like…" He looked down the table. "Someone like Katja."

"What?" Riefenstahl said aloud what Katja thought.

Hans Gottschalk agreed. "If he's like any politician, he has to keep a certain public image, and what's more public than a complete stranger? Take her along and say she's your assistant, or your secretary. You'll have your little confrontation, which will be necessarily polite, and then it'll be over."

"I suppose you're right. Katja, do you mind?"

Katja glanced around the table, wondering if she'd been selected for slaughter, but before she could voice any reservations, Dietrich spoke up. "What a wonderful idea! You'll have the chance to meet one of the most important men in the country."

"Uh, yes, I suppose it's all right."

"Bravo. Here's to our Katja!" Marti Kraus raised his glass, and the entire table thumped on the table as applause.

Leni Riefenstahl stood up. "Would you look at us? A table full of cameramen and no one has a camera to record our last supper."

"I have one." Rudi held up his camera case by the strap. "And by chance, I've got a wide-angle lens on it."

"Splendid. Come on, everyone," she ordered in the directorial voice everyone recognized. "You six, slide down with me to the other end of the table, and you six, come around and line up on this end. Herr Lamm, if you will do the focusing, we can ask the Hausmeister to snap the photo."

She called over the portly man who had been standing in the doorway to the kitchen. "Would you be so kind, Hausmeister?"

"With pleasure, Frau Riefenstahl." He took the camera from Rudi's hands, listened to the explanation of focus and trigger, and waited for him to retake his seat.

"Oh, look," Rudi exclaimed, as he sat down. "I'm in the middle. Does this mean I get to be the Son of God?"

At the sudden surprising remark, everyone looked away from the camera and at each other. At one end of the table, Erich Prietschke and Marti Kraus stared in amazement at Rudi. Riefenstahl herself was resting sideways with one elbow on the table laughing, while Sepp Allgeier leaned past her to whisper something to Frederica. Only Rudi Lamm, at the center, looked somberly at the camera, while Peter held his arms outstretched, as if to embrace him. Katja could hear the other cameramen at the other end, in private conversation. At that disorganized and unposed instant the shutter clicked and caught the image.

Chapter Five

Berlin, Two days later

"So that's it, then," Katja said. "The Ministry for Popular Enlightenment and Propaganda." Katja recognized the old Leopold Palace with its stripped-down classicism so favored by the National Socialists. "Where they decide what's German and what's not."

"Yes, it is," Riefenstahl confirmed. "And woe be unto him who has a different vision," she said as they entered the wide entry hall. The interior still had some of its original murals, its painted ceiling, and its chandeliers from the previous century, reminding Katja of the way monarchy used to look.

An SS guard led them to the door of the Reichsminister's office, leaving them to wait outside while they were announced. Several minutes passed and, though she said nothing, the hard set of Riefenstahl's face revealed her exasperation, both at having to appear in the first place and at being made to wait. The day's newspapers lay on a long table against one of the walls, and most prominent was a small pile of *Der Angriff*, Goebbels' own newspaper and the platform for his articles. Several copies of the party instrument, the *Völkischer Beobachter*, were next to it, as well as a sampling of *Deutsche Allgemeine Zeitung, Das Schwarze Korps*, and the tabloid that even Katja recognized as a rag, Julius Streicher's *Der Stürmer*. Presumably, one was expected to inform oneself while waiting for the propaganda minister.

Finally the door opened from within and another SS guard stood back to admit them into Goebbels' office.

"Welcome, ladies," he said, rising from his seat behind a wide, well-ordered desk.

Katja was taken aback. Joseph Goebbels was much smaller than he had seemed at the party congress. His face had something fairy-tale ugly about it. His bulbous skull was rendered even more so by the way his hair was combed straight backward and rose in a mound across the top of his head. But below his brow, his face tapered off, for his cheeks narrowed suddenly. On a small jaw, his mouth seemed extraordinarily wide so that when he smiled, as he did now, it appeared predatory. He was immaculately dressed, but even in a carefully tailored suit, he looked like a gnome.

He seemed surprised to see a second person enter the room, but kept his cold smile as he motioned them to the chairs in front of his desk. When he sat down again, he appeared to increase in height, and Katja realized his chair was on a platform a few centimeters above the floor.

"Well now, I am glad to see you were able to find time in your busy schedule to visit me, Frau Riefenstahl," Goebbels said with unmistakable condescension.

"Thank you for receiving us," Riefenstahl replied, unperturbed. "This is my assistant, Katja Sommer."

Goebbels nodded acknowledgement and came to the point. "Have you brought some of your film for me to review, Frau Riefenstahl? I believe I made my message to you clear in that regard."

Riefenstahl shifted slightly in her seat before throwing down the glove. "No, Reichsminister, we haven't. I am still in the process of developing it and selecting the most telling segments of over 130,000 meters of film. It is not subject to review, and no one outside my team will be able to see it until it's edited."

The battle lines were drawn. Hitler's filmmaker had said no to Hitler's propaganda minister. For several seconds, a vapor of wrath wafted between them like poison gas. If one could have ignited it, it would have burned blue.

The minister's voice was ominously soft. "Do you know to whom you are speaking, Frau Riefenstahl?"

Riefenstahl's reply was equally calm. "Yes, I do. I also know that the Führer has given me full artistic control over this film and has allowed me to bring my own artistic vision to the party rally. When it is completed, you will be invited to see it."

The minister's lips pressed together in a wide, flat line that slashed across his face. "I remind you that you are *not* entitled to your private 'artistic vision,' least of all in a work relating to the party and created on the party's money. We have spent years transforming a nation's spirit from sloppy liberal thinking to a sense of the Volk. German culture no longer has room for decadent *individualism* of the sort that brought us Kirchner and Matisse, or a Picasso, and even Jews like Chagall. He spat each name out as if it were poisonous. "Nor for the self-indulgence of an actress turned filmmaker."

Riefenstahl would not be lectured to. "Who defines German 'culture' if not the German artists themselves?"

"I define it, and do not forget it. I measure all forms of public expression as to how they affirm and revere the German people."

"Herr Goebbels," Riefenstahl said. "You cannot negate the genius of individual expression and replace it with slogans."

He was beginning to squint, which should have been a warning. "Don't come to me with your 'genius of individual expression.' All art is political, and you are either with us or against us."

Katja seized her courage. "Herr Reichsminister, surely a concerto does not carry a political message. Some things are beautiful in themselves."

Both heads turned. Riefenstahl looked pleased by Katja's unexpected burst of support, while Goebbels looked as if a roach had scurried across his desk.

"You are mistaken, Fräulein…" He obviously had forgotten her name. "Music also belongs to the Volk. It must please the ear or embolden the spirit. The Führer himself listens to Wagner and Mozart and Beethoven. Under my jurisdiction, you will not hear the ridiculous atonal noise of a Schönberg or Hindemith. These decadent and intellectualized works reveal the *judifying* of our culture and will no longer be permitted."

Riefenstahl brought the argument back to her film. "Since a National Socialist Party Congress can scarcely be *judified*, I see no reason to subject it to your judgment."

"*All* work produced in Germany is subject to this office," Goebbels reiterated, like a child who had run out of arguments.

Riefenstahl stood up. "Herr Goebbels, I have paid you this visit because I promised the Führer to remain in contact with your office. I have honored his wishes, so if you will excuse us, we have a great deal of editing before us, to meet his deadline." Riefenstahl did an about-face and took a step toward the door.

Katja stood up to follow, but the enraged Reichsminister came from behind his desk to have the last word. In his rush, he made no effort to control his stride and Katja witnessed what only his closest acquaintances saw. The Reichsminister had a clubfoot and limped like a cripple.

They were outside now, and Goebbels stood in the doorway. Like a troll crouched under a bridge, he drew his wide mouth into a grimace and snarled, "I caution you, Frau Riefenstahl. Do not cross me."

Riefenstahl kept walking and declined to reply, though the words seemed to echo down the corridor. Behind her, Katja nodded a polite greeting of departure and hurried after her employer.

Riefenstahl, obviously fuming, was in no mood to talk, and Katja was simply stunned. What now? A project that had seemed so glorious, so utterly supportive of the nation and the Volk, now seemed jeopardized by the hostility between director and minister.

They were about to turn the corner toward the great entry hall when Riefenstahl glanced to the side and halted them both. There, through an open door to an office, they saw two SS men conversing with a woman. Though the woman was three-quarters turned away, there was no mistake; it was Frederica Brandt, Leni Riefenstahl's private secretary.

"I should have known," Riefenstahl muttered, and touched Katja's elbow, urging her along toward the exit.

"Should have known what?" Katja asked, once they were outside.

"I should have remembered that Joseph Goebbels is a philanderer—and has a powerful allure for young women. My secretary has obviously fallen under his influence. Now I'll have to dismiss her. Who knows what information she's given him about me?"

"I always thought Herr Goebbels had a perfect marriage. I've seen so many pictures of his family with the Führer.

Riefenstahl snorted. "The man's a womanizer, I know from experience."

"Oh?" Katja was careful not to sound overly interested, but Riefenstahl was obviously ready to talk.

"After I returned from filming in Greenland, Herr and Frau Goebbels invited me for dinner several times. It was all very proper. But Goebbels began to telephone me at home, then visit me. It was obvious that he was inventing reasons to call, and everything I did to discourage him just seemed to stimulate him. At his last visit, he behaved like a schoolboy. He went on about Nietzsche and poetry and then suddenly blurted out that he had loved me for years, and life would be a torture if he couldn't have me."

Katja was aghast. "What did you do?"

"I pushed him toward the door and called the elevator. I know it was humiliating for him. We've met since then several times at public events and he's always polite, but at the same time, he's started a power struggle between us. I'm sure that's what's behind this ridiculous meeting."

"And Frederica? You really think he's won her over?"

"If he hasn't, he will. She's already much too cozy with him. I can't trust her now. I don't like being exposed to the minister's scrutiny, even less through one of his spies. No, I'll have to let her go. It's a pity. She was a very good secretary."

Katja gazed back at the ministry where Frederica was still engaged in some mysterious business with Joseph Goebbels and his agents, and she thought the same thing. A pity.

Riefenstahl kept up a rapid, angry pace until they reached the Kurfürstendam, where she glanced at her watch. "Well, I've lost half a day for this nonsense. Thanks for being a good sport about coming along. If you hadn't been there, his tirade would have been much worse and lasted much longer."

"Does this mean I have to worry now about repercussions?" It suddenly struck home how vengeful the Reichsminister could be.

"No, I don't think so. I doubt he even remembers your name. And as long as you are in my employ, you also have the protection of the Führer."

Katja was confused. "Am I still in your employ? I thought the filming was finished."

Riefenstahl brushed back wild hair. "It is, but now I need a secretary. Are you interested?"

"Uhh, yes. Of course. When can I start?"

"How about right now? Rudi Lamm promised me a set of still photos but called this morning to say he couldn't get away until tomorrow. You can save me a day's delay if you go pick them up."

"I'll be happy to. He lives in Neukölln, I think."

"Yes, here's his address." Riefenstahl scribbled on a notebook page and tore it out. "Bring me the photos this afternoon and I'll show you the business."

Katja hurried to her task, trying to absorb the fact of her sudden promotion. A few days before, she'd been a lowly camera-equipment holder, and now she was secretary to Leni Riefenstahl—actress, film director, and friend of Adolf Hitler.

Chapter Six

There it was, the Old Post Office, in all its red-brick, German-Renaissance architectural excess, onion-shaped dome and all. On its side wall was the street sign, Bergstrasse, and walking south from the corner, she found the Heldengasse.

Rudi met her at the door with cheerful enthusiasm. "So you're Frau Riefenstahl's 'enforcer' now. I'm delighted. Come in."

"Yes, I feel sort of guilty replacing Frederica like this. For some reason, Frau Riefenstahl doesn't trust her. I have no idea why." She followed him in.

"Don't worry about Frederica. She's nobody's fool," he said over his shoulder. "If she's no longer working for Frau Riefenstahl, it's by her own choice, you can be sure."

As they entered the living room, two young men stood up from the sofa.

"You remember Peter, don't you, from our dinner in Nuremberg?" The young man with the glasses and dueling scar stood up to shake her hand.

"And this is Yevgeny Khaldei." A boy who couldn't be more than seventeen or eighteen, with a broad Slavic face and dark hair, didn't speak but offered his hand as well. It was a meaty hand that gave a firm handshake.

"Here, sit down." Rudi motioned to the sofa while Peter swept gracefully away toward the kitchen. The sound of porcelain cups and saucers suggested he was making coffee.

Rudi said something in Russian to Yevgeny and the boy laughed.

"I didn't know you spoke Russian? When did you learn that?"

"There are all kinds of things you don't know about me. I learned Russian the year I studied in Leningrad. I wouldn't try to read Pushkin, but I can converse and take care of business in it. Speaking of which, I've got the pictures for Frau Riefenstahl right here." He picked up the thick manila envelope that lay on the side table. "These are just a few good ones I'm sure she'll want to use." He slid out some dozen photographs in A4 format.

"She asked to see the portraits, though some are more dramatic than others." He flipped though photos of Bormann, Ley, and Himmler, by daylight, and Hitler, Hess, and Speer by the more dramatic nighttime lighting. "Some good banner shots." He shuffled through photos of Party flags, SS standards, and Hitlerjugend banners, forming various geometrical patterns across the frame.

He held up the last photo. "And this one is really good. She took it herself, and it shows you what a fantastic eye she has."

Katja studied the image. The swastika flag, held up by a Hitlerjugend with the sun behind it. The boy stood in profile, his chiseled face almost silhouetted, and the afternoon sun shone through the flag so that it seemed incandescent.

Rudi snorted. "I think all this posing with flags is pretty kitschy, but as a photograph, it's very successful. Frau Riefenstahl will love it, and the Nazis will love it, and they're paying our salaries." He passed the photo to Yevgeny, with some remark in Russian.

Yevgeny studied it, tilting his head and nodding. "Yes. Is good one," he said in thickly accented German with the hard *R*s of Russian. "Very, very good one. Bravo. This is my inspiration and challenge. One day I make a flag photo good like this one. Better. You will see."

He handed it back and turned to Katja. "You are from camera team? Such big event and chance to use a high-quality camera." Peter returned and set down a tray of coffee cups and hard cookies.

Katja shrugged slightly. "I was just an assistant and got to do actual filming only a few times. And of course I got the *old* camera. Are you a photographer?"

He lowered his glance in what appeared to be genuine modesty. "Apprentice photographer. But is great passion of mine, since I am small child in Ukraine."

"Oh, me too. I wanted to take pictures when I was little, but I couldn't get my hands on a Brownie until I was sixteen."

"Same problem for me, and you can imagine. In little town in Ukraine, where would a poor boy get camera? So I make one with box and lens from grandmother's eyeglasses and took pictures of my sisters." He chuckled. "Not very good ones. When I got job, with my first money, I bought good camera and took pictures of my comrades in steel factory. Finally, paper in my town printed some, and after that I was like a man in love." He dipped a hard cookie into his coffee and bit off the wet corner. "After that, I never stop."

"Yevgeny is a photographer with TASS," Rudi interjected. "And he's being much too modest. He's the youngest photographer on the paper." Katja imitated the cookie-dip and found the dry ginger cookie greatly improved by the coffee.

"Are you here on assignment from Moscow?" she asked.

Yevgeny nodded. "My boss come to Germany for article on new government. I convince him to take me along. And I have own camera now."

Katja was intrigued. She'd never spoken with a Russian, or a Ukrainian, before, had heard, in fact, that they were brutish. How did Rudi meet such interesting people? "So, what do you think of our National Socialism? Does it bear any resemblance to Soviet socialism?

The Russian's open, friendly face took on a cartoonish frown. "No, not at all. Germany and Soviet Republic both have strong leader, yes. Stalin has great power like your Führer, but Communists struggle for all workers, not just Russians. Factories owned by state, but state means workers."

"I think the catchword is justice," Rudi added. "Economic justice primarily, but justice in all other things is supposed to follow. That's the theory at least. Am I right, Yevgeny?"

"Yes, is heart of Communism. Each one gives their ability, each one receives their need." He tilted his head and curled up one side of his mouth. "Problem is how to make this happen."

"Don't National Socialists have a similar ideal?" Katja asked.

Rudi shook his head. "No, not at all. You haven't listened closely enough to Dr. Goebbels. If Communism is about forced sharing, National Socialism is about seizing power. Whoever is strong enough to claim something is entitled to it. The exact opposite of justice and equality. You have to admire them just a little for their romanticism. They have this image of themselves as the noble beast, nature's perfect creature and highest creation. I wonder which vision will prevail."

Yevgeny suddenly jumped up from his chair and grabbed a canvas satchel he had obviously left by the door.

"Conversation becomes serious, so is time to open." He drew out a bottle of vodka. "For my new friends, while we discuss Soviet ideals, we drink Soviet coffee." He carried the bottle back to the sofa and poured a generous portion into each empty cup. "Please to add coffee and maybe little sugar."

Peter refilled all their cups and brought out a saucer of sugar cubes. Katja tried the mixture, and it was like a slap in the face. It burned her mouth and throat slightly, but after she swallowed it, a warm feeling spread through her chest. She exhaled some of the warmth and the sensation was pleasing, so she took another drink. It got better with each swallow.

"Actually, we were discussing Nazi ideals before the vodka arrived. About the German 'blond beast.'"

Yevgeny poured another shot of vodka into each cup. "Is insane. 'Beast' is what civilization fights to be free of. You can admire lion for eating lamb, but always one day bigger beast comes and eats lion."

"What beast eats lions?" Katja asked, feeling a bit giddy.

"He's speaking metaphorically. Aren't you, Yevgeny?"

"Yes. Beast morality is no morality."

"I'm not keen on either system. My personal choice is to just do my job, not hurt anyone, and stay out of the fight." Rudi studied his coffee.

"But the fight may come to you. I mean us." This time it was Peter who spoke. "What about the Jewish Question?"

Yevgeny joined in. "Your Führer is little bit crazy on subject of Jews."

The remark brought Katja up short. It was almost as if he had heard the tirade of Joseph Goebbels that very morning. She felt herself sliding toward agreement with him. "Um…" She nodded vaguely, not ready to criticize the man her entire country worshipped. "The party has done a lot of good things for Germany. I just don't understand why there's so much talk about the Jews."

Yevgeny pressed her. "So you *don't* think the Jews cause all German problems?"

"No. I mean, I suppose not." Katja hadn't given much thought to the question before.

Rudi packed up his photographs and sealed the envelope. "Yevgeny, stop testing Katja and tell her you're Jewish so she doesn't embarrass herself."

Katja felt suddenly defensive. "I'm not embarrassed at all. I don't know much about what goes on in politics or in business. I only know what I read, and what I learn from my friends. But, I admit, I don't have any Jewish friends."

"You do now," Peter said, offering the plate of cookies again. "Well, half Jewish. Mother was Jewish, so my name is German, but Jewish law says I'm a good Jewish boy." He laughed. "Though I think it's all a bit silly, the praying and the towels on the head."

"Two Jewish friends," Yevgeny added, offering his hand again to Katja. "Two photographers. Maybe we both have famous photos some time."

"I will drink to that, and to all my new friends." Katja raised her vodka-enriched coffee cup.

Giggling now, Peter made another trip to the kitchen, returning in a moment with two more trays of tidbits in an impromptu supper.

Katja felt a sudden affection for all three men, as if she had been adopted into a family with three brothers. "How is it that you know Rudi?" she asked Yevgeny.

The two men exchanged glances.

"We…uh…meet in club, Yevgeny answered, glancing away. "Sports club."

"I don't think we have to worry about Katja." Rudi caught her eye. "Do we have to worry about you? You don't care about Berlin's bars and special 'sports clubs,' do you?"

It suddenly all crystalized. They were talking about homosexual meeting places. And Rudi and Peter, at least, were homosexuals, criminals in the eyes of German law.

Though slightly befuddled by the vodka, Katja grasped that Rudi had just confided something important, a fact that could land him in jail. It was a gift, of sorts. "Of course you don't."

Rudi relaxed visibly. "We met just yesterday in a bar in the Nöllendorfstrasse. We got talking, and when we found out we both were photographers, I invited him home to meet Peter. You happened to arrive while he was here."

Peter took her hand. "So you see, dear Katja, you have landed in a very dangerous place. With homosexuals, Jews, and Communists. But we're not so bad, are we?"

Katja thought, as much as she could focus her thoughts at all, that they were not so bad at all.

"No, you're charming, all of you, but I should go now." She stood up on uncertain feet.

"Maybe you should have some regular coffee before you leave," Rudi said, placing the envelope of photographs in her hand.

"No, I'm fine. The cold air outside will clear my head. I…I just have to deliver these to Frau Riefenstahl before the end of the day. If I don't, then by tomorrow she'll be looking for a third new secretary. Thank you for everything."

Having shared alcohol, they had passed the line of demarcation between handshakes and cheek kisses, and she leaned happily in for her departure pecks.

The cool afternoon air did sober her as she walked the three blocks to the stop and boarded the Strassenbahn. But then she brooded, barely noticing the crackling of the overhead electric pole or the clank of wheels on the track joints. Three good men had invited her a little into their lives, had shared their meal and their secrets. She thought them engaging, even fascinating, but the new thoughts did not fit together with the old ones.

She had never quite understood the "Jewish" threat, and the recent great purge of the SA on the grounds that Ernst Roehm and many of his officers were homosexual had troubled her. But she had always thought of herself as a good German, and when the Führer spoke, she never considered disagreeing. Not to mention that she was engaged to a man in the Wehrmacht. What would he think? It was bewildering. On one side were the heroic Aryan images they had so artfully captured on film and, on the other, the despised Jews, Bolsheviks, and homosexuals, three of whom now felt like her brothers.

She shrugged inwardly, then concentrated on preparing herself for the meeting with Frau Riefenstahl, who surely would have no sympathy for her dilemma.

Chapter Seven

January 2, 1935

As Katja arrived at the Königsplatz, Leni Riefenstahl was obviously in a foul mood. "I hate this sort of thing," she grumbled. "More speeches telling us what we already know and killing a whole day of work. How am I going to finish editing *Triumph* for the March premier if they keep summoning me to these events? I'm not even a party member."

Katja responded with caution. "I suppose Hitler sees you now as an honorary party member. But you're right. Why would he need you, without a camera, at a Reichstag meeting?"

"It's not really a Reichstag now, since they don't act like a parliament any longer. They just cheer him when he speaks."

Ahead of them, at the end of a wide drive, stood the handsome complex of Italian-Renaissance-styled buildings that made up the Kroll Opera House. Katja was struck with a brief nostalgia. "I remember when the Kroll was still the seat of the State Opera. I spent a lot of nice evenings there. Before they went bankrupt."

"It was very sad, wasn't it? But at least the Reichstag then had a suitable building nearby for their meetings after the fire. If the Communists thought they could launch the Great Revolution here with a single blaze, they got the exact opposite. They made the entire party illegal and so lost the Communist deputies from the Parliament, which gave the Führer absolute power."

Katja glanced back at the soot-stained shell of the Reichstag edifice at the other end of the Königsplatz. "It's hard to imagine they could be so stupid."

They were in the lobby of the Kroll now, and Katja saw with regret that much of the opulent furnishing of the old opera house had been stripped away. Where there once were gentlemen in white tie and ladies in evening gowns, now there were only business suits and uniforms. SS men stood everywhere.

They took seats on the aisle at the back of the main hall, and Katja noted that the entire stage area had been reconstructed. In place of the raked stage was a series of levels surmounted by rows of desks, with a speaker's dais at the center. She recognized Rudolf Hess at one end and Hermann Goering, plumper than ever, on the other. Over their heads the stylized eagle stretched its wings from wall to wall, its wide claws grasping a wreath that contained the swastika. Lines like rays of sunlight emanated from the wreath and filled the entire wall. Was it Albert Speer or one of the set designers of the Kroll opera who was responsible for the ponderous emblem? The effect was certainly operatic.

At the last moment, Joseph Goebbels arrived and strode toward the podium, signaling silence in the hall. After some preliminary remarks, he announced that the party had prepared an oath of loyalty to the Führer, which would be required of all government officials and armed servicemen.

An oath, not to Germany, but only to the party leader. How curious.

After the corps of deputies had dutifully taken the oath, the Führer himself came to the podium. Thanking the assembly for the fealty just sworn, he began his speech, which sounded much like the speech he had given in Nuremberg, about unification and race.

At its conclusion, when the entire assembly rose to its feet and raised the full-armed salute, Katja glanced sideways at Riefenstahl to see if she joined. But she kept her arm firmly by her side, and the sudden tilt of her head signaled they should leave. At the door, where the shouting was no longer deafening, Riefenstahl said, "Now comes the worst of it. We have to smile and pretend we approve."

People were already streaming into the foyer. One or two of the deputies recognized the actress-director and made polite conversation in passing. Gradually they edged toward the outside doors.

"Frau Riefenstahl! I wondered if I might see you here."

Katja followed the voice to its source, the wide, unpleasant mouth of Joseph Goebbels, who was threading his way through the crowd toward them. Behind him was a man in a brown pinstriped suit, and behind both of them was Frederica Brandt.

Katja saw anger flit across Riefenstahl's face, then disappear.

"Good evening, Herr Reichsminister. Very nice to see you this evening," Riefenstahl said lightly. Katja had to admit, the woman had style.

The minister responded with a frigid smile. "Frau Riefenstahl." He offered his hand first to Riefenstahl, then turned to Katja. "Fräulein…?"

"Sommer."

"Yes, Sommer." The gargoyle smirk appeared again. "Please allow me to introduce my stenographer, Otto Jakobs. I believe you already know Fräulein Brandt, Herr Jakobs's assistant."

A moment of awkward silence followed, then Goebbels spoke again. "How's the work coming on our propaganda masterpiece?"

Ignoring both the words "our" and "propaganda," Riefenstahl replied. "Very well, thank you. Though every political event I am requested to attend robs me of a day's work."

"You must not think of the two occupations as separate, Frau Riefenstahl. Both are of historical importance. You do not want to neglect the nation itself while you sew its flag, do you?" The minister smiled at the metaphor he'd apparently just come up with.

"Is that what I'm doing? Sewing a flag? It feels more like a patchwork quilt right now, for which I must select two dozen panels out of thousands."

"Oh, I'm certain you are up to the task. But you must admit, this event was an important step."

Riefenstahl was having none of it. "What is the purpose of this loyalty oath, Reichsminister? Haven't the deputies, the various militias, and the Wehrmacht already sworn loyalty to Germany?"

"Yes, that's so. But the Führer feels that meeting a thousand different opinions on things cripples the advancement of his vision. Now, having sworn a loyalty oath to the Führer, each man understands himself as a part of that single great vision."

No one else in the group seemed convinced, and Otto Jakobs changed the awkward subject, admiring the Kroll Opera House. "A veritable palace of beautiful music," he said, clasping his hands.

Goebbels laughed. "Beautiful music, to be sure. But once, after a performance, I went backstage to visit a stunning Violetta, only to find that without her costume and makeup she was as ugly as a horse. But of course I am too much of a gentleman to reveal her name."

Jakobs laughed obligingly, but Katja ignored the vulgar remark. "I remember the backstage as being sort of magical. A place of transformation. I'd love to see it again."

"I'm sure I can arrange it, Fräulein." Goebbels raised himself up a few millimeters in height. "I believe I have some authority here."

Frederica spoke up for the first time. "I'd love to see it too."

"Who can resist an appeal from such charming ladies?" Goebbels waved over one of the SS men standing guard along the periphery of the hall. "*Scharführer*, these two ladies wish to go to the backstage area. Would you see to their admittance?"

The SS man saluted cleanly and stepped back to allow her and Frederica to precede him.

Riefenstahl's scowl indicated she did not enjoy being left alone with the Reichsminister, so Katja raised a placating hand. "Ten minutes, at most. I promise," she said, and hurried after the SS man.

He led them to a double door, unlocked it, and returned to his post.

A few steps into the corridor, Katja could already see how the magic had vanished. Every dressing room was now an office, and every door held a neatly printed cardboard sign identifying its new occupant or function. All of them were stultifying.

They strolled to the end of the corridor to a large room with chairs along two walls and file cabinets along a third. "This used to be the orchestra room," Katja said with melancholy. "My father played in the orchestra, and I was here for the final performance in 1931."

Frederica brightened. "I saw that! It was *The Marriage of Figaro*, with Klemperer conducting. That was always one of my favorites."

"I loved it too. I was as smitten with the soprano as Dr. Goebbels was. But unlike him, I found her lovely."

"Who was it?" Frederica asked as they did an about-face and retraced their steps.

"Jarmilla Novotna. A delicate, fragile beauty."

"I agree, Novotna was exquisite. Funny you mention being smitten. You know who I was crazy about? Anny Helm. She sang in *Tristan und Isolde*. Not so beautiful, but she was very kind. She chatted with me seriously, not like the silly Wagner-struck girl I was."

Extraordinary. Frederica Brandt loved Mozart and Wagner, and had crushes on opera singers. Katja rapidly reassessed her.

"Why did you go to work for Dr. Goebbels?" she asked abruptly. "Do you like his politics?"

"Heavens no." Frederica answered too quickly, then caught herself. "I needed a job with a future," she added blandly. "Work in the arts is just too unstable for me."

"Why do you care so much about stability? You're young and on your own. Why not be adventurous?"

"A rebellion against the past, I suppose. My mother was always looking for adventure and she basically destroyed our family. I'd rather be a little more secure and know where my next pay envelope is coming from."

"I'm sorry to hear about your mother but, in principle, adventure isn't such a bad thing. Unless, of course, you hurt other people."

"The problem was, she did. My mother was a failed actress. British, by the way. Her name was Vera Humboldt. She met my father while on vacation here and they got married, apparently on a whim. By the time she decided it was a mistake, she had me. After a few more years she'd had enough of domesticity and left my father for some firebrand Communist who wanted to change the world. She took me back to London but then dumped me with her sister so she could travel with this guy. That lasted for a few years, but then I came back to live with my father. I never really felt like I had a home, so at this point in my life, I want something solid under my feet."

"If that's the way you lost your mother, I'm terribly sorry. I lost mine to cancer a few years ago, but at least she was there until I was an adult." Katja studied Frederica's chiseled oval face and wide expressive mouth, full of character. She could see how a woman with that face might try for the theater. "Did she look like you?"

"A little. But our taste in jobs and men is certainly different. The man in my life has mostly been Rudi Lamm."

"But Rudi is…" Katja stopped. "Rudi seems quite happy as a bachelor."

"And I'm happy for him to *stay* a bachelor. He's like a brother and that's all I want right now. But we were talking about my leaving the film project. You, obviously, are committed to staying."

"Yes. I want to be a filmmaker, so I'll stick with it as long as I can and see where it takes me."

"And if it doesn't take you anywhere, do you have a second career plan?"

Katja chuckled. "Oh, you *are* a cautious one. But, yes, I do. My father has friends at the Charité hospital and is always encouraging me to study nursing. That would definitely be permanent employment, though I don't know if I'm cut out for it."

"How lucky we are when we can do what we're cut out for," Frederica said, then glanced at her watch. "Oh, oh. I think we've gone past our ten-minute mark, and we both have employers we don't want to antagonize. Let's go back."

In the car on the way to the film-cutting studio, Katja watched the rain pelt the windshield. "Days like this make me glad I know someone with a car," she remarked.

Leni Riefenstahl swung onto the Kurfürstendam. "It does make life easier. But if I didn't have the advance for the documentary, I wouldn't be able to afford it. So, what did you and Frederica talk about on your little backstage tour?"

"Opera, actually. She likes Mozart and Wagner."

"Did she say anything about the Reichsminister?"

"No. But I didn't ask her. Why does Dr. Goebbels have this Otto Jakobs, his own personal stenographer?"

Riefenstahl snorted. "Herr Reichsminister not only writes for his own newspaper, but composes endless speeches and addresses. As if that were not enough, he also dictates a report of what he thinks and does every day in a sort of diary. Imagine that. Even the Führer wrote only one book and got it all off his chest. Goebbels just never shuts up."

"Maybe once you start propagandizing, you just can't stop." Katja laughed.

"Well, speaking of propaganda, we've got to start making some advertising for *Triumph des Willens*. As we get close to release time, we'll need to send out press materials and photos. Can you coordinate that with Rudi? It'll take a lot off my mind so I can concentrate on editing."

"Yes, of course. Whatever you like." Katja stole a glance at Leni Riefenstahl's handsome profile. What an enigma the woman was. She obviously had no interest in the Nazi program, yet she was creating a masterpiece to further it. She hated Joseph Goebbels, had only contempt for Goering and Himmler, yet seemed entranced by Hitler. How did she feel about Jews?

❖

The spacious house on the Brahmsstrasse seemed cheerful in spite of the early evening darkness. Katja changed out of work shoes into slippers and began preparing supper for two.

Five minutes later, Karl Sommer arrived home from his orchestra rehearsal. As was his habit, he stood his violin case in its cabinet and went to the living room to put a disc on the record player. This evening it was the one of the Brandenburg concerti. Then he joined Katja in the kitchen carrying his souvenir chest and smoking his first cigarette of the evening.

She pecked him on the cheek, wrinkling her nose at the cigarette smoke, and resumed slicing the boiled potatoes. "I do wish you'd smoke less, Vati. I hear you coughing every night."

"Don't worry about me, dear. Let me have my little pleasure. Smoking is my only vice, and I'm sure I'll die of something other than that."

She roasted the potatoes with onions and a handful of sausage chunks, turning them frequently. "Well, this cough of yours never goes away. What do your friends at the Charité say?"

"Oh, they're no good. They just suggest I take a rest cure in Bavaria. What nonsense."

"Why don't you go see Dr. Mandelbaum? He treated mother's lung cancer. Surely he can handle a little chronic coughing."

Karl opened one of the window panels and brought in two bottles of dark beer that had been cooling on the windowsill. "He won't be staying much longer. The Nazis want to make it illegal for hospitals to employ Jewish doctors. It's not the law yet, but it looks like it soon will be."

"Insane," Katja muttered. "Can't the hospital make an appeal?"

"No, darling. We'll manage. There are Christian doctors just as good. The same is happening in the orchestra. We're losing people from the strings and the woodwinds, but others will replace them. It's not wise to get involved in politics." He set the table for two and poured the beers into glasses.

Katja added an egg to the potato and sausage mix, which hissed appealingly as it reached the hot grease. "I thought this anti-Jewish thing was just a small part of the party's plans for the future, one they'd stop obsessing over after they got into power. But it just gets worse."

"That's not our concern, Katja. The Nazis are a little extreme, I know, but Germany is finally on its feet again, and if all it costs is a few Jews their jobs, it's a small price to pay. I don't worry about those things. I just care about my music and you. And this, of course." He patted the little oak chest he had brought in with him.

"Your opera souvenirs?"

"Yes, these are some of the high points of my musical life. I treasure them, and…" He paused dramatically. "I have a new one." He reached into the briefcase at his feet and withdrew a large dagger.

Katja carried the frying pan to the table and scooped the contents onto their plates "Oh, my. That *is* impressive. It's even made out of metal. What opera is it from?"

"Verdi's *Macbeth*. Yesterday evening was the last performance. It's an old production and they don't plan to do it again, so I convinced the prop department to let me have this. What do you think?" He handed the weapon across the table to her.

Katja held the dagger up in front of her. Its pommel was coated with some sort of reflective green paint and its metal blade tapered to a mean point. She tapped it lightly on the table. "I thought they were supposed to use collapsing blades on these stage daggers, or wood. Someone could get hurt."

"No one gets stabbed with this one. It's from the scene where Macbeth sings about a dagger hovering in front of him. The prop people made it so that it would reflect light even on a dark set. It's quite a moment on stage."

"Vati, you get so excited about the melodrama of opera. Meanwhile, all over Germany, *real* drama's going on, but you don't want to talk about it."

"Of course I don't. I can't do anything about all those real dramas. I'm a musician. I have nothing to say about politics."

Katja didn't respond. Was she any different, after all, making a propaganda film without really thinking about its influence—simply to further her own career? The thought troubled her, so she let the subject drop.

They ate in comfortable silence, attending to the music. It had been that way since Gerda Sommer died. Dinner in relative silence, as if out of respect to her. But this time Katja sensed another absence. What would it be like to have Rudi and Peter at supper? Or Frederica Brandt?

Would she ever feel the sense of family again? She had been hoping for that with Dietrich, though at the moment, the image of sitting in a quaint Bavarian kitchen with his parents seemed less appealing than the memory of vodka coffee with Jews, Communists, and homosexuals.

Chapter Eight

Peter answered the door with a needle and thread in one hand. "Hello, Katja dear. Rudi is just finishing some pictures, and I was doing the mending. Rudi goes through socks like a mountain climber," he said with feigned despair as he led her into the living room.

Rudi was just emerging from the corner he had made into a darkroom. He greeted Katja while drying his hands on a cloth. They were lovely hands, she noticed. Unusual for a man. Someone with hands like that could do only gentle things, creative things. It fit that he was a photographer. He drew her toward the sofa.

"Frau Riefenstahl said we'll be coordinating press releases to the venues that will be airing the documentary in May. Is that right?" she asked as she sat down.

"Yes, that's the plan. And this…" He indicated the living room. "This will be her Press Office."

Katja let her glance sweep around the room. With a third of it curtained off into a darkroom, and the other third a dining area, the Press Office amounted to the sofa and coffee table. "I love it," she said with sincerity. "Until we get famous, this will be fine."

"Glad you like it." He crossed his legs and made a little tent with his pretty hands. So, here's how we'll proceed. I've got a set of my best photos from *Triumph des Willens*. Using those, you'll write clever and inspiring texts to market the film. Frau Riefenstahl will choose her favorites from among those, and we'll send them off to the venues. It will be a challenge, though. Your descriptive material mustn't sound like something from the Ministry of Propaganda."

"Yes, I know. Art, not propaganda. But doesn't the Führer *want* it to be propaganda?"

"Of course he does. But we're going to let Frau Riefenstahl ski that slalom herself. From our side, we'll promote the film as a work in its own right."

"I agree. No politics. So, show me your photos, and I'll jot down a few artistic remarks."

The morning passed quickly as they discussed the merits of each photograph, and within three hours and two cups of coffee, they had a substantial folio of material to present. A little after twelve, Rudi looked at his watch.

"I think we need to stop. I don't want to rush you out of here, but I'm meeting with Yevgeny Khaldei again to photograph Goebbels giving a speech at the exhibit on The German Woman." Rumors have been circulating about how the Nazis want to regulate marriage, but this will be the first time we've heard it from the dwarf's own mouth."

"That sounds fascinating. Would I be in the way if I joined you?"

"Not at all. You're welcome to come along. Yevgeny is photographing for TASS and I'm doing it for my personal archives. It starts at two this afternoon."

"That's perfect. I'll have plenty of time afterward to drop off our notes and photos at the studio. Frau Riefenstahl's overwhelmed with editing right now and won't even look at them until tomorrow." Katja stood up and moved toward the door. "All right, then. Women's Exhibit just before two."

❖

Rudi and Yevgeny stood just outside the exhibition hall as Katja arrived and the doors to the hall opened. As the crowd flowed in, journalists took up strategic places with their cameras and microphones. Yevgeny went along the side wall as close to the podium as possible with a microphone and bulky recording machine hanging on a strap over his shoulder. Rudi took a series of photographs of the Reichsminister when he entered, then remained at the rear with Katja.

"German women. German men," Joseph Goebbels sang out over the buzzing crowd.

Katja glanced around at the audience. All in civilian clothes, they were very different from the uniformed audiences at the party rallies. These were "polite" Germans, women and men one met all over Berlin, who claimed to be apolitical. But Magda Goebbels, the model National Socialist woman par excellence, sat in the front row.

Did she know about her husband's flirtations?

Katja moved her eyes along the rows from head to head, first row, second row, third row. Ah, there, at the far end of the fourth row, the familiar sweep of Frederica's not-quite-blond hair. She chuckled inwardly. It seemed slightly sordid for a man to lecture on the role of women to an audience containing both his wife and his next conquest.

Goebbels' opening remarks had passed right over her, but now his voice penetrated the fog of her thoughts.

> *Although men make history, women make the boys who are the men who make history. You know that the National Socialist movement has kept women out of politics, but that is not because we do not respect them. It is because we respect them too much.*

Katja shifted uncomfortably. The words could have come from Dietrich or his mother. But perhaps the Reichsminister could justify that view more effectively than Dietrich had.

> *Looking back over Germany's decline, we come to the frightening conclusion that the less German men were willing to act manly in public life, the more women attempted to fill the role of men. Yes, the feminization of men always leads to the masculinization of women. An*

age in which the values of hardness and determination have been forgotten, it should be no surprise that men have lost their authority to women.

Was it true? Katja asked herself. Had Dietrich's gentle nature made her too aggressive in the pursuit of her own goals? It was a troubling thought.

The first, best, and most suitable place for the women is in the family, and her most glorious duty is to give children to her people and nation, and thus guarantee the immortality of the race.

Katja's thoughts wandered back to Nuremberg to a warm Bavarian kitchen and a room filled with Hitlerjugend memorabilia. Was that her duty, to live in that room, waiting to be impregnated? So far, by choosing the days to allow sex, she had managed to prevent that, but marriage would presumably end her right to do so. She glanced toward the back of Frederica's head and wondered what she was thinking.

German women have begun to see they are not happier being given more rights and fewer duties. They now realize that the right to be elected to public office at the expense of the right to life and motherhood is not a good trade. The German birthrate is declining precipitously and we must halt this impoverishment of our blood. The liberal attitude toward the family and the child is responsible for Germany's rapid decline. Germany has a great mission in the world and calls upon German women to let their sons join in the reawakening of the nation.

He gave a signal and some dozen Hitlerjugend came along the rows of listeners and handed out a flyer. Katja took one as a lad passed by. It was a diagram of racial purity, with colored bubbles—clear, quarter black, half black, and full black, next to various "marriages" with tags labeling them "encouraged," "permitted," and "forbidden." She looked back toward the podium for explanation.

> *This is the beginning of a new German woman, who proudly and freely chooses motherhood to save the race. It goes without saying that women must bear children only of their own race, and that racial mixing is mongrelizing. The diagram we have passed around to you is a clarification of our thinking. Let it be your guide and reminder.*

He raised his gavel and brought it down smartly onto its pad. "I now declare this exhibition open." At that moment, Magda Goebbels stood up and went to embrace her husband as he came from the podium. A carefully choreographed moment, Katja was sure, to illustrate the model German woman. Faithful, fervent, and fertile.

Frederica did not move from her seat.

Katja declined to visit the exhibit and noted that Leni Riefenstahl had not been invited for the opening speech. Obviously, as both ambitious and childless, she presented an embarrassingly attractive alternative to the National Socialist model.

Katja glanced down at the "racial-purity" chart in her hand. Behind her, Yevgeny said, "Is disgusting, no?" He pointed to the column where a black Jewish bubble linked with a pure Aryan bubble was underscored and labeled "forbidden."

"We have some like that in Russia, but not so bad. But plan for women to have sons for homeland is same in Russia."

"Everyone wants me to have a baby," Katja murmured.

"I don't, Katja, dear." To her surprise, Rudi linked his arm into hers. "I just want you to be happy. So why don't you ask her to lunch?"

"Ask who to lunch?"

"You've been staring at one person through the whole lecture, and it wasn't Herr Reichsminister."

"I wasn't staring at anyone," Katja insisted.

Rudi didn't argue, only touched her shoulder. "Ask her to lunch."

Chapter Nine

The usual SS stood guard at the Ministry for Propaganda and Education, but Katja's papers identifying her as assistant to Leni Riefenstahl got her past the first phalanx. Confronted inside by two more guards, she told half the truth, that she had no appointment but that she was in the process of preparing the documentary of the party congress. She did not need to bother Dr. Goebbels himself, but only one of his assistants, Frederica Brandt.

Obligingly, the guard departed without question to seek the requested person while the other guard remained at his post. She waited some fifteen minutes, feeling more and more foolish. She had rehearsed what she was going to say, but now it sounded like complete nonsense. People simply did not—

"What a surprise." A familiar voice pulled her out of the squalor of her doubts.

Frederica looked stunning. In fact, she was dressed much the same as she had been at the Women's Exhibition, in a skirt and matching jacket of forest green. Her not-quite-blond hair was no better coiffed than before, but her smile, this time, was directed at Katja, not Joseph Goebbels. She leaned toward Katja and brushed a light kiss of greeting on her cheek.

"I was in the middle of transcribing something and I can't stay long, but I'm delighted to see you. How is everyone? Frau Riefenstahl? Sepp? Marti? The others?"

"Sepp is on some other film project, and so is Marti. I never see any of them. Only Rudi. We were at the Women's Exhibition the other day, in the back of the hall."

"Oh, I was there too. How could I have missed you?"

"We left early. I'm sorry." Katja regretted hurrying away now; they might have talked.

"Um, what brings you to the ministry, then? The guard just said you had business related to the film."

Katja's face grew warm; she was about to be caught in a lie and be humiliated. It felt a little like putting a gun to her own head. "Well, no. I was simply wondering if you were free on Sunday," she blurted.

"Free? What do you mean? Like to do something?"

"Yes, to…um…go to the Tiergarten. There's ice-skating, and we can drink hot wine afterward."

"I'm sorry. I can't."

"Oh, that's too bad." Inwardly, Katja came crashing down. Yes, this is what humiliation felt like. "I should have known you'd be busy. It was just a thought," she mumbled, looking away.

"No, no. I'm not busy. It's just that I can't ice-skate. I hurt my ankle a few years ago doing just that, and I'll never put on ice skates again. But what about the zoo? I heard there are new lion cubs. If that sounds appealing, I'm free after ten o'clock."

Katja jerked back from despair. "Oh, the zoo would be fun. Let's say just after ten by the entrance."

"Perfect," Frederica said softly, but then added more urgently, "Listen, I'm sorry I can't stay here long. I'm doing a transcription and the deadline is in an hour. But I'll see you on Sunday." Frederica leaned near for a departing kiss and Katja felt the quick softness on her cheek. A faint whiff of perfume and Frederica was away, waving behind her while she hurried toward the stairs.

As Katja all but danced down the stairs leading from the Ministry of Propaganda, she muttered to herself. "What are you doing?" But the other half of her was not listening.

❖

Katja stepped off the Strassenbahn at the Tiergarten-Zoo stop a bit early. Even the leaden winter sky that seemed to suck color out of every object could not affect her. Neither did the bitter cold, though on her own, she would never have considered wandering around the zoo. The ice-skating she had suggested was intended to be short-lived, with them ending up huddled together inside a warm café.

But even in the cold zoo, they'd have the morning all to themselves, with no one listening, and they could still end up in a warm café. She realized suddenly that for the past two years, she had spent such intimate time only with Dietrich. The zoo meeting felt faintly like betrayal.

The zoo entrance had changed little since her last childhood visit. Even the kiosk a few dozen meters down the street was still selling newspapers and sweets, and she remembered the lemon drops her father always bought for her there before they visited the animals. For years, she had associated the zoo with the taste of lemon candy.

The entry fee was a bit higher, which was no surprise after twenty years, and as she passed through the gate, she looked at her watch. She was prepared to wait but then saw Frederica at the distant kiosk and wondered, with slight amusement if she was buying lemon drops. Katja watched, bafflingly happy, as Frederica approached. She wore a long gray coat, nearly shapeless, over slacks. Brown shoes laced up to the ankle gave her a faintly British-explorer look.

"Oh, There you are," she called, the steam of her breath wafting upward. They embraced quickly, their cold cheeks touching.

"It looks like we're the only ones here. I suppose the children don't want to come out in this weather."

"Very smart of them." Frederica laughed. "I hope you don't mind. If it gets too cold, we can leave." Dropping her still-folded newspaper into a bin, she took hold of Katja's arm and drew her along in a slow stroll.

"So, how are you? Are you getting on with Frau Riefenstahl?"

Even through two layers of coat sleeve, Katja felt Frederica's warmth. Chatting came easier. "She's working like a dog, twelve, fourteen hours a day. I don't envy her the fame one bit. She's got the success or failure of the whole project hanging over her head. Sometimes she even sleeps in the studio," Katja poured out in a stream.

"The devil's a hard taskmaster," Frederica said enigmatically, and the subject fizzled out.

They strolled, unhurried, becoming comfortable together. "I like the zoo," Katja volunteered. "I don't know why I don't come here more often."

"I love it too. It's a little like humanity in microcosm, and you can find most of our vices and virtues in one species or another. They act out our urges and tell us a lot about ourselves."

"You mean like when monkeys throw feces?" Katja teased.

"Well, yes. I've seen a few exchanges of verbal feces in my life. Haven't you?"

Katja chuckled. "Yes, but now I'm going to have that image in my mind the next time I hear a political speech attacking our enemies."

"I have it all the time," Frederica said, turning them both toward the Gorilla House.

The double doors to the building effectively blocked the icy air, and the temperature inside was pleasant. In the first cage, two gorillas squatted lethargically in their cages, scratching themselves like old men. They gazed at them with slight curiosity, as if waiting to be engaged in conversation.

"Gorillas look at you with so much understanding," Katja said. "You can't help but wonder what they're thinking."

"A bit like men," Frederica muttered.

Katja giggled. "Except, we know what *men* want." Then, after a moment's thought, she said, "It is amazing, isn't it, how they simplify things." I mean, I just heard Dr. Goebbels speak about the role of women in Germany, and while I could see he had a point about keeping Germany strong, the whole baby program depressed me. I mean, I don't want to live like Magda Goebbels, being subject to her husband's sexual whims and existing to produce children for the Reich."

They wandered out of the Gorilla House back along the winding path that led past the big cats.

Frederica crossed her arms, keeping warmth against her chest. "What is it you didn't like? The thought of having babies or the sexual whims of Joseph Goebbels?"

Katja glanced sideways. "Both, I suppose. My fiancé, his family, and my father are all pushing me to have children to 'carry on the bloodline.' But it sounds so much like cattle breeding. As for Joseph Goebbels and his sexual tastes, the thought makes me cringe."

"Really? Oh, I wouldn't attribute that much potency to him. Men like him make a big show of their manliness, but they're pretty easy to lead around. At heart, they're teenage boys who need to keep proving that they're wild animals deep inside."

"Do you lead him around?" The question was presumptuous, Katja knew.

"Ah, here we are at the Lion House," Frederica said, ignoring it. She opened the door and they entered the same warm air as in the Gorilla House, but with the stronger odor of carnivore defecation. They strolled down the central corridor past the smaller cats, to the lion cubs. They cooed at them for a while, but the cubs were curled up asleep close to the lioness, so the spectacle soon lost its interest. A bit farther along, the male lion also lay dozing on his side. They strolled past him to the cage with the tigress.

"Have you read Nietzsche and Schopenhauer?" Frederica asked suddenly.

Katja had to think for a moment. "Yes, in my last year in school we had to read *Will to Power* and a summary of Schopenhauer. You're not going to quiz me on them, are you?"

Frederica laughed. "No, of course not. But they explain a lot about the notion that Germans have, that the 'blond beast' lives in their souls."

"The 'blond beast'?"

"It's from Nietzsche's *Genealogy of Morals*. He uses the image of the lion or tiger to refute what he sees as the Christian idea, that nature is evil and must be tamed. Nietzsche says that wild beasts are not evil, merely natural, even noble. I think Nietzsche was just being the philosophical bad boy and would not have wanted to live in a moral jungle himself. But the Nazis jumped on the idea of the 'blond beast,' since they fancy themselves as blonds, even the ones who aren't."

Katja was intrigued, but remained silent.

Frederica continued. "Those 150,000 men on the field, in perfect columns, standing at attention and waiting for the Führer's command. Didn't you feel something ominous under that orderly exterior? It seems to me that was the Nazi version of the 'beast.'"

They found themselves before the main tiger cage. The big cat, a Sumatran male, stared at them through expressionless eyes, panting, its breath steaming slightly.

"But is the 'blond beast' good or evil? According to you."

"According to me, it's the wrong question. Nietzsche was playing with the difference between 'evil' and 'dangerous,' and in glorifying the savage urges, the Nazis have overlooked that point completely. Even if you throw away the concept of 'evil' you still have something destructive." She pointed with her chin toward the tiger, who turned and padded to the back of the cage, as if the discussion of Nietzsche bored him.

"He's thrilling to look at, but would you like him strolling down the Kurfürstendamm? Of course not. They're beautiful, but destructive to civilization."

"You didn't answer my question about Joseph Goebbels," Katja said abruptly.

Frederica frowned at being thrown off her philosophical track, then looked away. "I told you, I keep him happy because it's a good job, with good pay, and I need the money."

"Your father can't help you?"

"No, he died of diphtheria when I was eighteen. But look, I'm freezing. Let's have something warm at the zoo café and then come back."

Katja was a little disappointed by the direction the conversation had gone, or not gone, but the thought of hot wine appealed to her. They fell back on the subject of animal intelligence as they made their way to the café, and in a few moments, they both held cups of steaming *Glühwein.*

They clinked cups and Katja took a careful sip, gauged the temperature as safe, and took a long swallow.

Frederica set her cup down. "Look, I'm sorry if I was a little sharp out there. I just don't want to talk about the ministry. So tell me more about yourself."

"There's not much to tell. I live with my father now but will move in with my fiancé's family once we're married. That will mean going to Nuremberg, which I'm not happy about, but I suppose I have to accept my responsibilities some time. At least that's what Dietrich says." She finished her Glühwein and signaled the waiter for two more.

Frederica ran the tip of her finger around the rim of her cup. "Are you in love with this Dietrich?" The way she said "this Dietrich" seemed faintly contemptuous. But it could have been Katja's imagination.

"I suppose so." She sipped from the new cup, feeling pleasantly light-headed, and giggled. "He's the only man I've slept with, so I can't really compare."

"So it's the sex then." Frederica started her second wine.

"No. You couldn't say that, exactly. But that will change, I'm sure, once we're living together. Do you know what I'm talking about?"

Frederica's gray-green eyes stared across the table for a moment. "I think so. It sounds like you're putting up with boring sex hoping it will get better." Before Katja could reply, Frederica stood up, ending the conversation. "Finish your wine. I want to show you the newest exhibit, something rather nice for a zoo."

Outside, Frederica tugged her by the arm toward a small building with a sign over the entrance. NIGHT CREATURES.

After the heavy entry door, they passed through a wool curtain into a dark corridor. Katja halted, letting her eyes adjust to the diminished light.

"The exhibit starts with twilight hunters," Frederica said. "Then, each section we go through gets darker."

"How do you know about this place?"

"I came a few months ago, out of nostalgia, and discovered it. But look, here are the owls. Beautiful, aren't they?" She tapped softly with a fingertip on the glass covering the chamber that held two owls and both turned their heads.

"Over on the other side are rodents and ferrets," she added, urging her along with a gentle hand, and Katja felt a prickle of pleasure at being guided through the darkness.

The second section of the corridor led past glass-protected displays with other nocturnal mammals, a hedgehog and a slow loris.

They groped along the wall as the corridor turned at a right angle and they were in almost total darkness. "Just stand for a few moments right here and your eyes will adjust," Frederica whispered, unnecessarily, for there seemed to be no other person in the exhibit.

"Oh, I see them now," Katja said softly. Bats. Four, no, six of them." They watched together in silence as the creatures furled and unfurled their soft leather wings. "When you see them that way, they're sort of beautiful." She could smell Frederica's perfume again now, or was it her hair?

"And then there's this," Frederica said, touching her elbow and leading her through a final curtain. Katja saw nothing at first, but waited, her heart beating against her breastbone for Frederica's hand was still on her arm. Then she saw them, fireflies. They did not light all at once, but intermittently, glowing with a soft yellow light, then disappearing, only to glow again a few centimeters away.

"Lovely," Katja whispered.

Frederica did not reply and there was no sound in the darkness. Only Frederica's fragrance told Katja she was at her side. It was an almost intolerable intimacy, an embrace without contact, a kiss without touch.

"Mutti, I can't see!" A child's voice rent the air and the moment passed.

The family that came in behind them bumped into them and apologized. "Quite all right," Frederica muttered, and led Katja by the arm through the final curtain and the exit.

In the freezing cold again, Katja turned up her collar and looked toward Frederica for a sign. She was not sure of what. She would have given anything to be back inside in the warmth and the darkness, surrounded by fireflies and Frederica's sweet smell.

"I'll walk you to the Strassenbahn stop," Frederica said, calling an end to their afternoon. "I go in the opposite direction, unfortunately."

Walking, they linked arms again, as they had in the morning, but now it seemed a new sort of trust united them. On the walk back to the stop, they chatted about the animals, the weather, nothing at all.

"There's my Strassenbahn already," Frederica remarked. "So good-bye, then, and thank you for the invitation." She gazed at Katja for a moment, then seized her face between gloved hands.

For a stunned moment, Katja felt Frederica's lips on hers, slightly open, a tiny hollow of moist warmth between their two chilled faces. Then Frederica broke it off and turned away, just as the Strassenbahn pulled up to the stop.

Chapter Ten

Katja typed the last line of promotional text and pulled the page over the platen along with its carbon copy. She perused it briefly, then glanced up to ask for another job to do.

On the other side of the room, Leni Riefenstahl sat stooped over her cutting table peering at one of the countless film segments to be evaluated and spliced in or set aside. Her posture said, "Don't bother me now."

Katja studied her back, bent from exhaustion.

Who did Leni Riefenstahl kiss? Katja wondered. Had she ever kissed a woman—that way? Katja imagined Leni Riefenstahl's kiss and was unmoved. The director of *Triumph des Willens* was too much of a locomotive, driving relentlessly toward her goals, and she had never shown any emotion but anger. No, Katja wanted to kiss only one woman.

What did that mean with respect to Dietrich, the stalwart, ever-accommodating man she was about to marry? She loved him, in the simple way she had always, but the kiss befuddled her. It suggested an unknown country, one that was safer not to think about.

Dietrich had obtained a short leave, in preparation to being shipped with his battalion somewhere in the East, and she would see him that evening. That thought also left her unmoved.

"Have you spoken with Frederica Brandt?"

The sudden question came as a shock. It was as if Riefenstahl had been reading her mind.

"No," Katja lied. "Why do you ask?"

Riefenstahl looked up from the eyepiece of her Lytax cutter. "I've got to make up the guest list for the reception after the premiere of the film at the UFA Palast. It goes without saying that Herr and Frau Goebbels will be there. But I need to know which of his current entourage of mistresses will also be coming."

"Why?"

"It's not wise to put his conquests at the same table as his wife. So, if your friend Frederica is one of them now, I need to know."

"She's not. I mean, she couldn't be. He's so repulsive."

"Not to women who need him. Power is an aphrodisiac, and he's a very powerful man."

Someone knocked at the door.

"That's probably Erich," Riefenstahl said, rubbing her eyes. "He's bringing some film material I sent to another editor for help. It's more than I can handle alone."

Katja opened the door to Erich Prietschke, dashing as ever, even without his SA costume. He greeted her cordially and dropped a canister of film on a side table.

Riefenstahl offered a tired smile. "Thank you, Erich. One task done, four thousand remaining." She glanced toward the empty typewriter. "Katja, do you have the text?"

"Yes, I finished it just now." She crossed the room and presented it. Riefenstahl scanned it quickly and nodded approval.

"Would you please deliver it to the Ministry of Propaganda. Herr Goebbels will be pleased that I'm finally sending him something to judge for its German correctness. I won't let him touch my documentary, but he's welcome to poke around with the advertising material. It will make him feel important."

Erich stepped forward. "I can take it along, if you'd like. Save you some time."

Katja reflexively held the typed page to her chest. "No, I'll deliver it to the ministry. I know someone there. She'll see to it that the minister reads it right away."

Erich looked perturbed. "You mean Frederica Brandt. I know her too. Perhaps I could accompany you."

"That won't be—"

"Excellent idea," Riefenstahl declared. Two of you arriving together will make the message seem important. Now, please get moving, both of you."

Disgruntled, Katja gathered the pages and photographs she had been preparing while Erich stood by the door. Once outside and on route to the ministry, he seemed to notice her irritation.

"Look, I'm sorry if I'm being a nuisance." He slowed his pace so she could keep up with him. "But the truth is, I'm sort of hooked on Frederica Brandt. I can't get her out of my mind."

Katja felt a stab of jealousy. How dare he.

Erich plunged the blade in deeper. "Ever since the party rally, I've wanted to get to know her better. I think she could be the right person for me."

"You don't know anything about her," Katja snapped.

"I know enough. She's beautiful and clever, and she showed a real interest in me in Nuremberg. Of course, she has to be pure Aryan, but if she is, I could get real serious about her."

Katja fell silent, hoping Frederica would find him a fool and reject him. But another, more authoritative voice reminded her that a single wild kiss on the street was nothing against the full-frontal courtship of a confident, attractive man.

A different set of SS guards was on duty when they arrived, but obviously Riefenstahl had called ahead and they were admitted with little delay to the outer office of the Reichsminister.

The minister himself received them, and Katja handed over the document for his perusal. Frederica, alas, was absent. Erich, too, seemed disappointed and inquired whether Fräulein Brandt was in the office. "She is tied up at the moment," Goebbels replied brusquely. "Please tell Frau Riefenstahl I will contact her tomorrow with my judgment of the text." He twitched in a faint suggestion of clicked heels and turned away without further acknowledgement of them.

Rebuffed, they turned to leave, unsatisfied. But a bit farther down the corridor, Erich stopped in front of another door. "I know the layout of this ministry. That's the door to his actual office. I wonder if it's open."

"Give it a try." The minister's rudeness had momentarily united them in resentment.

Erich turned the handle quietly but firmly. The door was open only a crack before he stopped and they both peered in. The heavy door had made no sound and so Frederica, standing at the window with her back to the room, had no idea she was watched. Nor did Joseph Goebbels, who went to her side and whispered something in her ear. He faced toward the window as well, and his hand touched her back, then slipped down slowly to caress her buttocks.

Erich recoiled. "That's it. He's had her," he whispered. "The pig," he said louder, and stormed away alone down the corridor.

Katja drew the door gently closed again. *Yes, he is,* she murmured to herself and left the ministry stunned. She felt like a complete fool.

❖

Katja opened the door and embraced Dietrich as he entered. "I'm sorry I don't have long, darling," he said, kissing her.

"That's all right. I've made a nice dinner for us. It's on the table now." Guiding him by the arm, she drew him into the kitchen where her father was just setting down a wide wooden trencher with a roasted goose.

"Welcome, Dietrich. Good that you could get leave for a few hours." Karl Sommer shook his hand. "Katja has made you a festive meal this evening, though she hasn't said why. Maybe she'll tell us while we're eating." He drew out a chair and gestured for his guest to sit down.

"It's always a pleasure to be here," Dietrich replied, sitting next to Katja and taking her hand. "Unfortunately I can't stay long past dinner. I guess Katja told you, my battalion is being sent east in three days, so I have to be back at the barracks tonight."

Karl turned the corkscrew into a bottle of *Riesling Spätlese* and tugged out the cork. He poured first into his own glass, tested, then served them. "Let's drink to friends and family, then," he said, raising his glass.

"No, Vati, I have a better toast," Katja said, standing up. "Let's drink to our wedding. I have decided to accept Dietrich's proposal and want us to get married right away, before he leaves Berlin."

Chapter Eleven

March 28, 1935

It was the night of the world premiere of *Triumph des Willens* at the UFA-Palast theater. Dietrich Kurtz, in the dress uniform of an *Obergefreiter*, descended from the Strassenbahn car and reached back to offer his hand to his wife. Katja took it and stepped down carefully in her evening gown. As soon as she touched the sidewalk, she recognized the Strassenbahn stop and her knees went slightly weak. How stupid of her not to remember. Of course, the UFA-Palast-Zoo was also the Strassenbahn stop for the zoo, the place where Frederica had kissed her.

She tightened her grip on her husband's hand and turned her attention to the façade in front of them. The UFA-Palast, the largest movie theater in Germany, was lit up garishly. A spotlight illuminated the circular arch above the marquee with the film title *Triumph des Willens*, while block letters the size of a man ran along the marquee edge forming the word TRIUMPH.

Dietrich presented their tickets at the door and they shuffled along with the crowd down to the three rows of reserved seats. Leni Riefenstahl had so far not yet arrived, though a seat with a cardboard tag DIRECTOR was being held in the middle of their row.

Katja twisted around to gaze up at the loge. The Führer was already in place, with a number of guests, presumably diplomats. In a loge off to the side, Goebbels sat with his wife Magda. Katja looked away, repulsed.

In the rows nearby, she identified Sepp Allgeier, Richard Koehler, Hans Gottschalk, and Walter Vogel. "I wonder where Marti Kraus is. Oh, I see him, down there, on the left. With his wife and son."

At that moment, a tall man marched into the hall in a full dress SS *Sturmmann* uniform. The blackness of his tunic contrasted splendidly with his blond hair and handsomely etched face. Only after focusing on him for several seconds did Katja realize it was Erich Prietschke. She had to admit, the look suited him. Now, where were Rudi and Peter, she wondered, then spotted them two rows behind her. She twisted around to wave, and both waved back.

Katja checked her watch. Eight o'clock exactly. Where was Riefenstahl?

Just then, the door at the top of the aisle opened and the manager of the cinema guided Leni Riefenstahl, in a dark-blue evening gown, to her seat. No sooner was she seated, when the lights went down and the buzzing of the audience died. A live orchestra in front of the stage played march music for a few minutes, then the curtain parted, revealing an illuminated screen.

Katja watched, hypnotized, as the title appeared in elaborate *Fraktur* lettering, then lines of text with a sound track of Wagnerian fanfares in the background.

> *On September 5, 1934, 20 years after the outbreak of the World War, 16 years after Germany's Suffering, 19 months after the beginning of the German Rebirth, Adolf Hitler again flew to Nuremberg.*

March music followed as a cloud bank appeared and gradually, through the mist, the towers and spires of the ancient city of Nuremberg came into view. For a brief, dizzying moment, Katja seemed to float in free air, wafting slowly downward toward the city. But the camera's eye shifted, revealing an airplane, a Junker 52, swooping low from out of the clouds and casting its cruciform shadow on marching columns below. An entire city on the march, perhaps an entire nation, and she was caught up in the thrill of it.

The scene fragments that she had previewed after filming now were part of an inspiring narrative. Scene followed scene, of uniformed men, of joyful blond children, of monuments to German history and culture, of Beethoven and Bach: a compelling testimony to the beauty and the truth of the movement.

A brief, subversive thought percolated up from somewhere deep in her mind. Of Yevgeny Khaldei, the Communist Jew, and of Rudi and Peter, secret homosexuals. Her forehead tightened in an involuntary frown as she struggled with the contradictions plaguing her. Then Dietrich in his handsome Wehrmacht uniform took her hand again, and his warmth was a comfort. She closed off the critical part of her mind and recalled the teamwork in Nuremberg, when they had all worked together like madmen. She'd never forget the taste of the canteen food in the Schlagater house, the gritty eyes she had at the end of a fourteen-hour day of work, the hilarity of some of the cameramen trying to film while on roller skates, the tobacco smell of Marti Kraus in the film elevator high on the flag stanchion, and, of course, the last supper with the Berlin crowd.

After tonight, would she see the twelve of them ever again?

PART TWO

SEPTEMBER 3, 1939

BERLIN, GERMANY

Chapter Twelve

It seemed like ages since Katja had visited Rudi and Peter, and so when Rudi Lamm greeted her warmly at the door, she embraced him energetically.

"Come in, our little angel of mercy. How's the nurse's training coming along?" he asked between pecks on both her cheeks.

"Long story," she said, taking his arm and walking with him into the familiar living room. Peter emerged from the kitchen with a dishtowel tucked into his belt.

"Hellooo," he sang, wiping his hands. "Just in time. I'm making *Knödel* soup." He repeated the greeting kisses and then returned to his post.

"Sit down, please. And tell me about the nursing 'story.' Peter's soup won't be ready for a few minutes, anyhow."

Katja dropped onto one end of the sofa and crossed her arms, a story-telling posture. "Well, as you know, after the two *Olympia* films, Frau Riefenstahl went back to doing feature films, starring her. For that she needed a whole different kind of staff and had no more apprentice work for me. The only other film jobs were with the propaganda ministry, and I couldn't stomach that. So, I did the nurse's training at the Charité hospital.

"So, have you got your certificate and a position?"

"Certificate yes, job no. But that's because Dietrich is on duty in Austria. Oh, sorry, I mean the *Ostmark*."

Rudi touched her wrist with his fingertip. "You don't have to use Nazi language in this house."

"Yes, Austria. Well, I thought I would apply for a position in Vienna, to be near Dietrich. But he told me his battalion is being sent to Poland. It's too bad because things are not going all that well in Nuremberg."

"What do you mean? Is your mother-in-law tyrannizing you?"

"No, nothing like that. It's just, it's bad enough being a bride with nothing to do, but Dietrich is hardly home. He's on duty most of the time and loves the army. He's just been promoted to *Feldwebel*, by the way. But we still don't have our own house, and this will be our fourth year of living with his parents. I'm suffocating there."

"In a little Bavarian house in Nuremberg? I can imagine," Peter observed as he added a third place setting on the table and returned to the stove.

"Yes, and they keep going on about having babies to continue the race, soldiers for the Fatherland. It's as if they'd memorized Goebbels' speech on motherhood. Fortunately, I've convinced Dietrich to avoid that until we have our own home."

Peter came from the kitchen again, this time carrying a porcelain soup tureen in a towel. The steam from the soup was still on his spectacles. He set the tureen down and wiped them with a napkin.

They took their places and passed around bread while Peter ladled out the steaming broth into their bowls. "Oh, it's really good," Katja said.

"Yes, I know," Peter replied. "My mother's recipe. The trick is to add ginger. "But speaking of Goebbels, Frederica seems pretty happy working there, because it's been ages since she's visited. I saw her by accident about a week ago, buying a paper at a kiosk near the zoo. We chatted for a while, but she seemed nervous, so I let her go."

"Frederica? Oh, I'd forgotten all about her," Katja lied. "How did she…uh…look?"

"Beautiful as ever, though a little shopworn. With her boss traveling around, keeping the party line going and the Führer happy, she must be pretty busy."

"Or maybe she's busy keeping the propaganda minister happy," Katja said, then regretted the catty remark. That it was probably true made it even more regrettable.

Peter collected the empty soup bowls. "Why don't you apply for a position here in Berlin? Dietrich can visit you here just as well as in Nuremberg, and you'd be near us."

"I thought about that. I could live at my father's house and probably get a job at the Charité. It's just that I've never stopped wanting to film. All the time I was studying bandaging and disinfecting sores, I was wishing I was somewhere else with a camera in my hands."

"I know the feeling," Rudi said. "Why don't you ask Leni Riefenstahl if she has any other projects in the works? She might know of a film someone else is doing."

"Isn't she in the US, promoting her *Olympia* film?"

"Not any more. She came back yesterday. She called me and asked if I would be available for some portrait photos, but I had to tell her no, I've got a project starting in Vienna."

"She's back?" Katja was suddenly buoyant.

"Yes. Give her a call now. I even have her number."

"How was the America trip?" Katja asked, stepping into Leni Riefenstahl's apartment.

"A little bit of it wonderful, and a lot of it terrible." Riefenstahl moved aside some half-unpacked boxes and motioned her to sit down. "It started off very well in New York and Chicago, but in Los Angeles, things began to deteriorate."

Katja took a seat, noting how little Riefenstahl had changed in four years. She had a different hairdo, a slight filling out of the face, but still the same nervous energy.

"Did you meet any big Hollywood names?"

Riefenstahl bustled around her, unpacking, laying things out on a table, talking as she worked. "I did, or was supposed to, but then the strangest things happened. Gary Cooper invited me to dinner, but then suddenly he cancelled the invitation. Even Walt Disney, who was charming and enthusiastic about the *Olympia* film, said he couldn't watch it because it would get him in trouble with powerful people in Hollywood. It was schizophrenic, with some people wining and dining me, and others condemning me and preventing people from buying or even seeing the film. As it turned out, it was the anti-Nazi league that hounded me wherever I went. They insisted I was somehow responsible for the attack on Jewish businesses and synagogues in November. Mr. Sheehan, one of the big MGM producers, finally informed me that, no matter how good the *Olympia* film was, because of anti-German sentiment, it could never be shown in the United States."

"So the trip was a loss?"

"Oh, no. Not a loss. I had lots of good experiences, but it was not profitable either. The press seemed uniformly against me, and when the time came to leave, I was fed up."

"So, now you're back, what do you plan to work on?" Katja tried to sound casual.

"Everything is at loose ends right now, but I'm hoping to form some of the unused *Olympia* film material into short sport films. Then there's *Tiefland*, which keeps dying and being reborn. Why? Are you looking for work?"

"In fact I was, though—"

There was a knock at the office door, and Riefenstahl called, "Come in".

It was an assistant of some sort, a young woman. "Frau Riefenstahl, I'm sorry to interrupt, but the Reichsminister just telephoned."

"Tell him I'll call him back later."

"No, Frau Riefenstahl, he's already hung up. He just said to turn on the radio."

"What? Whatever for?" Nonetheless she strode to the corner of the room where a wooden cabinet radio stood and she turned the knob. It took her a moment to tune it sharply, but then they stared at the radio, hearing the familiar shrill voice addressing the Reichstag:

Last night, Poland has for the first time shot at us with regular troops in our own territory. Since 5:45 this morning, we have shot back. From now on, bomb will avenge bomb, poison gas will meet poison. I will lead this war against any and all and as long as necessary until the security of the Reich and its rights are vouchsafed.

Leni Riefenstahl's voice was a whisper. "Germany's at war."

Chapter Thirteen

Katja was pleased with the speed at which she had put things in order. She had written Dietrich to say that she was working again for Leni Riefenstahl, carefully crafting her letter to suggest she was merely filling the time until he could return and they could settle down together in Nuremberg. It would be a week before she would get a reply, but even if he disapproved, the move would be a fait accompli. She had already informed her parents-in-law of her decision, and while Konrad and Gertrude Kurtz were disappointed at losing her, they acknowledged that she could wait for her husband in her own house as well as in theirs.

In a matter of days, she had packed her belongings and transferred them back to Berlin to her old room, to her father's enormous delight. They had a celebratory dinner together, and the next morning, Katja reported at eight o'clock at Leni Riefenstahl's apartment in Westend Berlin.

Riefenstahl was packing two large suitcases, one of film equipment and the other of clothing. "Things have changed," she announced. "I've contacted officials with the Wehrmacht and have proposed working as a battlefront film journalist. Sepp Allgeier and a few others will be joining me in a few days. If you're game, you can come with us to Poland. Obviously, you have to decide immediately."

Caught off guard, Katja watched mutely as Riefenstahl crisscrossed the room, dropping items into one or the other bag. A string of good reasons raced through her mind of why she shouldn't go. It was dangerous, it would horrify her husband and father, it was madness. On the other hand, she couldn't resist the novelty and adventure of it.

"I'd love to. Can you give me a couple of hours to prepare my baggage and tell my family?"

"Certainly. An officer from the Wehrmacht will pick us up tomorrow morning for training with gas mask and pistol. Be here before nine and you're part of the photojournalist team. Bring your own camera. We'll try to get you something better, but if not, you'll have something to start with."

Katja turned toward the door, excited to be doing something both useful and slightly shocking. Only when she reached the street did she recall that Riefenstahl had said "pistol." With a shock she realized there would be shooting.

An officer from the Wehrmacht appeared in a car before the Riefenstahl apartment precisely at nine o'clock, and by ten, they were at a base at Grünewald. After an hour of verbal instruction, an officer led them to the quartermaster's building.

"We have to wear uniforms?" Katja asked as someone handed her a folded pile of clothing.

"Yes, Fräulein. In civilian clothing, it's too easy to be confused with enemy partisans and get shot. These uniforms will be issued to all military reporters." He pointed them toward a supply room where they could change clothes.

With slight misgivings, Katja tried everything on: shirt, trousers, jacket, all in blue-gray. The trousers felt awkward at first, but when she paced around the room, she began to appreciate the freedom they allowed her. Finally she could open her legs when she sat down.

Once they passed through the quartermaster's barrack, they began gas-mask and sidearm instruction. Both filled Katja with equal measures of fear and excitement. It was the first time she had actually touched the instruments of war, the one that could save and the one that could kill.

The next day, they left Berlin in a small military plane for Poland. At noon, they reached the headquarters of Army Group South and reported to Major general von Rundstedt who, preoccupied with a brand-new war, greeted them indifferently.

"*Unteroffizier* Hartmann will look after you. Good luck," he said before returning to his maps.

Unteroffizier Hartmann saluted smartly, then directed them toward an open half-track personnel carrier. Eight men already sat in the open vehicle. Katja and Riefenstahl climbed onto two seats in the rear and piled their suitcases on a third. Hartmann climbed in next to them, and the vehicle started east.

Katja studied the backs of the soldiers sitting in the seats ahead of them. They wore steel helmets, field gray uniforms, and had half-a-dozen objects strapped to their backs: a mess kit, canteen, gas-mask canister, shovel, and bread bag. They all held rifles, and she had already seen the black cartridge belts they wore in the front. She wondered if their thoughts wandered as hers did, with mixed anxiety and pride, toward the battlefield. A great drama was about to unfold, one that the ordinary dull people at home would have no idea about, and she would be part of it.

After some two-and-a-half hours, the half-track stopped outside a village.

"What is this place?" Riefenstahl asked the Unteroffizier.

"Konskie. We've just captured it. General von Reichenau has his command center over there." He pointed toward the railroad station.

Suddenly they heard gunfire in the distance. "Are they still fighting?" Riefenstahl asked, with apparent alarm.

"They shouldn't be," he said, leaping from the half-track and signaling the men to follow him. "It's coming from the center of the village."

With barely a second thought, they left their suitcases and ran after the soldiers, with only their cameras in hand.

In a few moments, they arrived at the edge of the market square. "What's going on?" Hartmann asked.

A soldier stepped forward. "Yesterday, some of the Poles killed an officer and four men. The bodies are laid out in the church, and the troops have some of the men from the village digging a hole. But anger's running high. We fired off a few shots to keep them in line."

"Sounds like our first story," Riefenstahl said, drawing Katja into the square to get a closer look. A circle of German soldiers was training rifles on six Polish men digging the pit. The soldiers were shouting, and it was clear from the faces of the Poles that they didn't understand German and believed they were digging their own grave. A few dozen other villagers hung back fearfully at the edges of the square. The *Feldgendarmerie* arrived, declared that the Poles had nothing to do with the murder, and ordered them released.

Riefenstahl took up her camera and began to focus on the scene, but the soldier next to her slapped the camera away. "No pictures!" he snarled, but his voice was drowned in the general shouting of the soldiers. Katja had just taken hold of her camera, but under the angry glares of the men she returned it to its case.

When the pit was dug, the grave diggers stood together in the center, eyes wide with terror. Still with no idea what was being shouted at them, they tried to climb out of the pit, but the soldiers kicked them back in.

"What are you doing? Didn't you hear what the Feldgendarmerie said?" Riefenstahl shouted.

One of the soldiers swung his rifle around and pointed it directly into her face. "You get the hell out of here, bitch, or we'll shoot you too."

"Don't cause trouble!" Unteroffizier Hartmann took her by the arm and dragged her to the back of the crowd. Katja followed, confused. Then from behind, she heard the crack of rifle shots, screams, then another volley.

The shots started a panic and the Polish onlookers in the square began to flee. But the enraged soldiers were in a frenzy now and pursued them, shooting randomly. Katja saw a man fall and crouch on the ground cringing, both hands clutched in front of him.

The soldier—it seemed to be the same one who had threatened Riefenstahl—fired point-blank into his chest.

Riefenstahl and Katja ran headlong from the carnage, while the gunfire continued behind them. At the far end of the square they stopped, panting. Katja dropped to her knees. "I can't do this," she said. "I'm sorry. I don't have the stomach for it."

Leni Riefenstahl leaned against a wall next to her. "Me either. This is not what I came to film. Let's get out of here."

❖

It was, by all definitions, a massacre, perhaps the first of the war. By the time it concluded, Riefenstahl had appealed to the general to release them from the assignment and provide transport back to Berlin.

General von Reichenau was exasperated, both by the rioting of his men and by the inconvenience of having two witnesses. After making sure they had no photographs of the event, he sent them back to the main headquarters in a supply truck and left them to their own devices. At headquarters, an equally annoyed commander informed them that the only aircraft scheduled to go out was a small Henkel, but it was fully assigned and the only space was on the floor. They accepted.

The tiny aircraft came under attack immediately upon being airborne, and while it took evasive action, they were thrown about wildly. The air was filled with shouting, the *rattatat* of flack fire, and the screaming of the engine as the craft dropped nearly vertically.

Clutching the back of one of the seats, Katja fought nausea until the plane leveled off and climbed again. For the rest of the trip, she was silent. So this was war. No flags or heroes. No ceremonies or Sieg Heils or defense of the Fatherland. Only murder and fleeing from murder.

❖

At her desk in the propaganda ministry, Frederica Brandt assessed her new position with guarded satisfaction. It had been a long slow advancement, a huge investment of time, with no certainty of there being any point. But finally the order had come down from Goebbels himself, and she received the most important assignment of her life.

She was nervous, of course. So much was at stake, but it felt good to be trusted with something so important. It made all the lonely years worthwhile. Not that she felt sorry for herself for being alone. She had, after all, chosen to stay in Germany after her father died rather than return to England where her mother had already abandoned her. The abandonment had hurt deeply, but she realized now it was less because of the loss of love, than for not being taken along on the adventure, whatever it was.

In spite of her "need for stability" excuse, which she used to explain to Goebbels why she wanted the job, Frederica had never feared adventure. When she was orphaned at eighteen years, she had finished raising herself without complaint, living on her father's inheritance until she passed the *Abitur* exam. Then she found a job. She had proved herself, though she could not have said to whom she was proving it. Perhaps to the last image of her mother that still shimmered in her memory.

The bleakness of the first year was also alleviated when Rudi re-entered her life. An old school friend, he arrived at her door one day in full courtship mode and swept her off her feet. But after a few weeks and tentative kisses they both realized that romance between them would simply not flower. Instead, something more wonderful emerged—complete sympathy. They loved the same things: opera, Expressionist art, the poetry of Rilke. They made the rounds of museums and concerts and exhibits like young lovers, but without desire or plans for the future.

When Peter appeared, it became a comfortable constellation of three. The occasional outings and suppers that Peter created sustained her for years while she sorted just exactly who and what she wanted.

What she wanted, she decided, was adventure and purpose, and those came with the unexpected telephone call from her aunt.

Who she wanted was much harder to decide. At some point she had concluded it would have to be a woman, but that realization had merely replaced one puzzle with another. Where did one go to find the woman of one's dreams? Certainly not to the noisy, smoke-filled bars and cabarets of Berlin, even when they were still open. The feeble overtures she had made to female friends had been rebuffed. And she did not even allow herself to think about her reckless flirtation with Katja Sommer, now the fully domesticated wife of a military man. She shook her head. That could have ruined everything.

But Germany was at war, something more important than her pathetic emotional life had presented itself, and she was satisfied.

Drawing her sweater closer around her shoulders, she went back to work transcribing the personal journals of Joseph Goebbels.

Chapter Fourteen

Katja could see how happy her father was to have his only child safe at home; he'd even cooked the *Bratkartoffeln* for their dinner while she unpacked her bags. He asked no embarrassing questions about her sudden return from the front and all through dinner just kept patting her on the hand and talking about music.

After washing up, she retreated to her room where she composed a letter to her husband, putting as good a face as possible on the whole misadventure. Once again she explained that she planned to stay in Berlin until he returned home. She would do odd clerical jobs for Frau Riefenstahl while, with her new nursing certificate, she would look for a job in one of the Berlin hospitals.

In fact, she was not at all certain she would find a job so quickly. She was frankly a little up in the air at the moment, since the Riefenstahl project had fallen through and there was little left for her to do. But she was determined not to go back to a little boy's bedroom in Nuremberg. She had just written his military address on the envelope when her father knocked at her door.

"There is a gentleman to see you. Peter Arnhelm. Do you know him?"

"Peter? Yes, of course I know him." She looked at her watch. "I wonder what he wants at this hour."

Peter stood just inside the door tapping his hat against his leg. He shook hands with Katja and glanced nervously at her father. "Well, I just wanted to welcome you back home again from the front. Can I invite you out to a café? There is one just a few streets away." The lie was transparent, but it was also clear to Katja that he urgently needed to talk to her. It had to be serious for him to come at night all the way from Neukölln.

"Of course. I'd love to. Vati, Peter is one of my friends from the film project," she said vaguely. "We'll be back in a little while." She reached for the jacket that hung by the door.

"Nice to meet you, young man," Karl Sommer said, but Peter merely nodded and was already backing through the doorway.

Once on the street, Katja clutched his arm. "How did you get out here to Grünewald? I didn't even think you knew where I lived."

"We had your address. I took the Strassenbahn as far as I could and then walked."

"For God's sake, Peter, what's wrong?"

"They've arrested Rudi." He choked. "In Vienna. I just got a telephone call from our friends."

"Arrested? Why? What did he do?"

"You know why. Paragraph 175. Homosexuality. He was in Vienna to work on a project with a postcard company. He was staying with friends, you know, people like us. Someone must have denounced them and when the police came to arrest the others, they took Rudi too. Of course the police have his address and they came to his apartment in Berlin. Fortunately, I wasn't there when they arrived." He broke into tears. "And now I can't go back."

"Where did they take him?" Katja linked her arm in his and leaned against him as they strolled like a love-struck couple.

"I don't know, exactly. There are camps in Austria now too, but they could just as easily bring him back to Dachau or Sachsenhausen."

She embraced him, overwhelmed. The massacre in Poland the day before, and now this. "Oh, Peter. I wish I could do something."

Peter disengaged himself and held her by the upper arms. "You can. Rudi worked for Leni Riefenstahl and she always liked him. You know as well as I do, she's friends with Hitler. She can say she needs him for her next project, or something like that. People do that all the time for their friends."

"But we don't even know where they took him."

A car came along the street, its headlights reflecting for a brief moment in Peter's spectacles.

"That doesn't matter. The Nazis have everything systematized and Himmler has a record of where everyone is, at least the ones who stay alive. It's just a matter of a few telephone calls."

"I can try. I don't know if she'll do it. Right now she's pretty rattled about something that happened when we were in Poland. And I have no idea how much influence she has with Hitler." Curious, for the first time, she felt no urge to use the worshipful title of "Führer."

"What will you do now?"

"I'm on my way to Frederica's place. She'll put me up for a few nights, but then I have to move on. It's too dangerous for her to keep me longer. Her neighbor's a big Nazi."

"Why can't you go back to Rudi's place?"

"Because with his arrest, they will have cancelled his residency permit and the apartment will be listed as empty. The neighbors know I live there, and if the Gestapo shows up again, at least one will denounce me. Even if they don't, the Gestapo will want to know who I am, and my papers show I'm half Jewish."

"It's not illegal for half-Jews to live in Berlin, is it? You're only a *Mischling*." The Nazi word sounded stupid and hateful when she said it.

"I don't know how safe I am. But I promise, I will not creep into a cellar. I want to get Rudi out, and then I'll find some way to fight them."

"Fight them?" They were still on the street with no one near, but she dropped her voice nonetheless. "You mean the government?"

"Yes. How can you support it? They've just invaded Poland for trumped-up reasons. Dachau is full of their political enemies. They butchered their own in the SA purge, and they've been smashing Jewish shops and synagogues everywhere. And now they've taken Rudi."

Katja felt as if the ground were falling out from under her. She didn't know what she supported, except she knew she supported Rudi.

"I'll talk to Frau Riefenstahl tomorrow. How can I reach you?"

"I'll come by tomorrow evening around the same time. Do you think your father will be suspicious?"

"Not the way you mean. He's not a Nazi. He'll just want to make sure I'm not doing anything illegal."

"Illegal? I don't even know what that means anymore." Peter kissed her on both cheeks and hurried away, hunched inside his jacket.

❖

Leni Riefenstahl shook her head. "I can't just walk into the Reich Chancellery and demand to see the Führer. Martin Bormann guards him like a Doberman, and what's more he dislikes me."

"Even if it takes a week for you to get near Hitler, we've got to try. Rudi was on your film team. He served the party as a photographer. Surely that's worth something. We can't just abandon him."

Riefenstahl's hands came up in front of her, as if she were fending off blows. "Look, Katja. I liked Rudi too. He did very good work and was a sweet person, but you know—"

"Don't talk about him in the past tense. He's not dead! He's a living person, an artist, just like us. We have to help him."

"We *can't* help him. Rudi is not 'just like us,' and you know as well as I do that the Führer has strong ideas about homosexuality. Goebbels even more so and looks for any excuse to slander me. Getting involved in his situation could get both of us in trouble."

"Does that mean you wouldn't lift a finger for Sepp Allgeier or Marti Kraus either?"

"Don't use that tone with me. I'm trying to survive too, and to keep my business going. I'm not responsible for everyone who's ever worked for me. We all find our ways to coexist with a harsh regime. I trust the Führer and his vision, even if some others in his government go to extremes. Now, if you'll excuse me, I have to finish this article for *Völkischer Beobachter* this afternoon."

She sat down again and resumed writing but snatched up her fountain pen with such vehemence that a drop of blue-black ink formed at its nib, and as she held it up, the ink flowed backward onto her fingers. "Damn!" she muttered, standing up and striding angrily toward the tiny sink in the corner.

Riefenstahl looked back over her shoulder. "Why don't you ask your friend Frederica if she can cajole the Reichsminister to help you out? She's got much more influence on Goebbels than I have on the Führer, and you know why that is." Letting the innuendo hang in the air, Riefenstahl busied herself with scrubbing the stain off her hands.

Katja had not moved. "So this is what it means to be a good German. To sacrifice a friend so as to not fall out of favor with the Führer, no matter how abhorrent his policies are."

"Don't talk to me that way. You have no idea what plans the Führer has for Germany. The future of a nation is more important than one sexual misfit."

"That's what you think of Rudi? Just a 'sexual misfit'?"

"He was an employee, not a friend. I can't put myself at risk for everyone I know who falls afoul of the law." Riefenstahl returned to her desk and resumed writing.

Katja made an about-face toward the door.

"To hell with you, then," she said, and stormed out of the studio.

❖

Even in the twilight that blurred all features, Katja recognized the graceful stride of Peter Arnhelm. When he reached the empty doorway where she was waiting, she stepped out and embraced him. "I'm sorry, Peter. She won't help him," Katja said, getting to the point. "She doesn't want to risk her own neck."

Peter's shrug showed he had not really expected otherwise. "That's too bad," he said, glumly.

"Do we know where he is? Can we write him? What are the rules in a case like this?"

They walked with shoulders pressed together to keep warm. "I don't know. I think sometimes the prisoners are allowed mail, but of course the SS monitors everything. A letter from Leni Riefenstahl would be safe and would probably reach him. But it would be very dangerous for anyone else, and impossible for me. By now, he may have been forced to give my name. And even if the Gestapo isn't looking for me, as a Jew, I can't draw attention to myself."

"Yes, I understand. You're staying with Frederica?"

"Just one more night. But I have a few good friends, people like me, and if I keep moving, I should be all right. The problem is food coupons. They're issued to a household, so I can't get them now."

"I'll help you out. And we should meet every couple of days so I know how you are. But what are we going to do about contacting Rudi? Can't his parents write him?"

"I don't think they will. His father all but disowned Rudi when he found out we were together, so he's not going to share any information with me."

"Do you think you can trust Frederica? I mean, I know she and Rudi were close, but now she's cozied up to Goebbels." Katja liked talking about Frederica, even if she all but slandered her.

"I trust her completely. And it's precisely because of the Goebbels connection that I can't endanger her."

"I see," Katja said, though she didn't see at all. "I should talk to her. Maybe together we could come up with an idea that she hasn't thought of. Why don't you meet me here again on Thursday evening and I'll tell you what happened. In the meantime, take this." She handed him a bundle of Reichsmarks.

"I can't take money from you, Katja."

"Of course you can. It's not even that much. The bills are small, but there are some food coupons there. They should be enough for a few days. By Thursday, maybe we'll know a little more."

"Thank you, dear. Who would have thought, when we met at that silly supper in Nuremberg, that it would turn out like this?" He dropped a brotherly kiss on her cold cheek and made an about-face.

Katja watched him walk away, reassessing her future. She had another mouth to help feed now and had effectively left the film business. What was left for her?

Obviously, it would have to be the Charité.

Chapter Fifteen

The wind whistled around the corners of the Ministry of Propaganda while Katja stood huddled inside her coat, each exhalation an expulsion of steam.

She had timed it as carefully as she could and, fortunately, she didn't have long to wait. At six ten exactly, Frederica came down the steps of the ministry. Katja greeted her shyly, pressing their two cold cheeks in a superficial kiss, wondering if Frederica remembered the other one, four years ago. Probably not.

"Thank you for agreeing to see me. How have you been?"

They fell into step, marching shoulder to shoulder, as Katja and Peter had done, but not touching. "I'm fine, thank you. You know, with the war, it's been very busy. But I've been promoted."

"Oh, really? No longer a simple typist?" Katja feigned interest. She didn't want to dwell on Frederica's advancement in Dr. Goebbels' domain.

"Oh, I'm still that, but after five years, I guess they trust me and they've given me a higher security ranking. I used to do general work, proclamations and so forth. But now I get to transcribe more personal documents." After a moment's silence, she added, "But you didn't come to see me about that, did you?"

"No, I've come about Rudi, of course. I know Peter's staying with you, and I admire your courage. But can't we do anything else?"

"I think we've got Peter sorted."

"Good to know. But Rudi's situation is more dire. What can we do for him?"

Frederica seemed to sink farther into her winter coat as they hurried along the street toward nowhere in particular. "I know what you're thinking, that I should approach Dr. Goebbels and ask him to intervene, but I absolutely can't do that."

"Why not? You could argue that he's an artist who has worked on the Führer's own documentary."

Frederica shook her head. "First of all, whatever makes you think Dr. Goebbels will do something against his own program of ethnic cleansing just for me? And secondly, if you think you can argue for him being an artist useful to the Reich, ask Frau Riefenstahl to make that argument to the Führer."

"She won't. She's afraid to endanger her position."

"So you want me to endanger mine?"

"Endanger you? No, of course I wouldn't do that. But the subject was Rudi. I thought the two of you were close. How can you simply abandon him?"

Frederica stopped short. "Don't accuse me so lightly. You have no idea of the circumstances."

Katja faced her, the steam of her breath mixing with Frederica's. "Then explain the circumstances to me. Please, don't just become paralyzed. What about some of the other department heads in the ministry? Isn't there one for photography? Maybe we can approach him."

"Look, I'm doing the best I can for both Rudi and Peter, and all your naïve passion for them will only make things worse. Please, just stay away from the ministry and let things take their course. There are bigger issues at stake that you simply don't understand."

"Bigger things at stake. That's what Leni Riefenstahl said. I had expected more from you." They came to a corner with a stop for the Strassenbahn that went toward Grünewald. Katja halted; she was not accomplishing anything and might as well go home.

"Thank you for helping Peter, but if that's all you're willing to do, it's not enough. We're going to have a glorious new Reich, but half of our friends will be dead."

Frederica winced at the remark, but as she walked away, her reply was, "My regards to your husband. I'm sure you wish him great success in his battle for the new German order."

Katja looked away abruptly. It was like a slap in the face.

❖

Peter stood at their usual spot as she walked toward her own street. Katja embraced him and took hold of his arm. "My father has a late rehearsal. Come in for awhile. I'll make us something to eat."

As soon as they had taken off their coats, Katja drew him into the kitchen. "Sit down. I'll warm up some *Erbsensuppe*." She fetched a bowl of something yellowish-green from the windowsill.

Peter stretched out his legs. "I love your house. Cozy, in good taste. Your parents must be nice people."

She scraped the paste from the glass into a pot, sprinkled some pepper onto it, and turned the stove on low. "There's just my father now. He plays in the orchestra of the *Staatsoper*, like his father did. He inherited that talent as well as this house in Grünewald so I got to grow up almost in the country. But I don't want to talk about me. I want to hear how *you're* managing. Are you still with Frederica?"

Peter pulled out his shirt and wiped the steam from his glasses onto the fabric. "I moved out yesterday, for both our safety. A friend of hers has connections at the zoo and they're letting me work 'discreetly.' I can sleep in the supply room and no one's likely to come looking for me there."

"Really, why not?"

Peter chuckled. "It's in the Lion House. I clean the cages of the big cats. I also ride a service bicycle delivering the crates of food, hay, tools, and so forth, around the zoo, but mostly I'm able to blend in. Nobody wants to have a conversation with a janitor. I like it. It's much better than hiding in someone's cellar all day."

She laid out bowls and oversized spoons for both of them. "What about food? You'll still need ration cards, won't you?"

"Yes, but friends are helping me with that. I get a little here, a little there. Plus, I can sneak food from the canteen sometimes. I just worry constantly about Rudi."

"Do you have any news of him?" Katja asked from the stove.

"Yes. I finally got the courage to call his father yesterday. He was pretty nasty to me, but at least he told me he'd got notice that Rudi's in Sachsenhausen. Then he went into a tirade and blamed me for ruining Rudi's life. You know, that I turned his son into a pervert. He said if I ever called him again, he'd denounce me. I told him, 'Too late, old man. I'm already running.'"

"I'm glad to know where he is. Now I wonder if there's any way to get word to him." She carried the pot to the table and ladled the steaming soup into their bowls.

"Who would dare contact him? I'm a criminal, his father wants nothing more to do with him, and you'd only draw suspicion to yourself if you tried. It kills me to think he's there, maybe starving, maybe sick, and I can't even tell him I'm thinking about him."

"I'm sure he knows. And people *are* let out of Sachsenhausen sometimes. You just have to hold onto that hope and concentrate on taking care of yourself. If…*when* he gets out, he'll need you to take care of him."

Peter shrugged half agreement and continued spooning up the hot soup, taking off his glasses, which persisted in collecting steam.

Sitting across from him, Katja studied his face, worn now from a week of dread but still handsome. She decided her initial assessment of him was correct. He did look like a cadet, yet he had nothing in common with her husband, an active soldier.

"Were you together long?"

"We met at university when I joined a dueling fraternity he was in."

"Ah, I wondered about the scar on your chin. So it's a *Schmiss* after all."

"Yes, though I just got it to impress Rudi. In fact, I dueled only twice before the other boys found out about my Jewish mother and threw me out. Rudi was so upset, he quit too. Our relationship just developed naturally from there."

"You never had any desire to marry?"

"Is that a polite way of asking if I've always preferred boys? Yes. Always. The same way, I suppose, *you've* always liked them."

Katja chuckled, "Well, I *don't* always like them. But it's the way things have to be if you want children."

"I don't want children. I just want to make pretty things. My family had a small factory in the district of Wedding. After university, I worked there designing clothes. You can imagine, all that pretty fabric. I was in heaven. And all the while I was seeing Rudi. When we decided to live together, my father told me I had to choose: marry a nice girl and stay in the family business or leave. I was really in love, so I chose Rudi. I've never regretted it. Not even now."

She considered for a moment whether she would have accepted expulsion from her family and from respectability to live with Dietrich. Except she had done the opposite; she had left her freedom to marry *into* respectability, and it was stifling.

His bowl empty, Peter stood up and settled his glasses back on his nose. "I'd better be going before your father comes in. Much better if you don't have to explain me."

"Yes, you're right, of course." She helped him put on his coat. "Wait. Take these with you." She snatched a net bag from the kitchen wall and filled it with whatever was at hand. A dried salami, some winter apples, the two rolls left from lunch.

She handed him the net and took hold of his arm. "I know how angry you are about what happened to Rudi, but please don't think about anything subversive. Just stay low until things get better. I'll help you as much as I can."

Peter looked away. "No, you *don't* know how angry I am, but I thank you anyhow for your help. I promise not to do anything to endanger you."

"Or yourself either," she added, and embraced him warmly. "I want us both to be here when Rudi comes out." It sounded like a lie, but they both needed to hear it.

Then he disappeared into the night.

Chapter Sixteen

Rudi Lamm had been amusing his three friends with tales of his work on the two Riefenstahl projects when the Viennese police arrived. It made no difference that he was German. The *Anschluss* had united Germany and Austria into one Reich, and he was subjected to the same humiliating interrogation as the Viennese men to establish that he was homosexual. Doctors examined his anus and demanded that he name at least two women with whom he'd had sexual relations. He could provide no names, and certainly no one in Vienna would lie for him, so his only possible defense evaporated.

The Gestapo separated him from his Viennese friends and put him on a prison train that took thirteen days to travel from Vienna to Salzburg, Munich, Frankfurt, and finally to Berlin-Oranienburg. Those thirteen days gave him ample time to reproach himself for his obtuseness.

The Nazis had never concealed their loathing for homosexuals, even while some of their leaders in the SA and the SS actively pursued boys. The party leaders tolerated the homosexual behavior of the widely popular Ernst Roehm and his coterie only so long as they continued to increase the numbers of Stormtroopers. When that moment passed and the party no longer needed its Brownshirt leader, his homosexuality provided the justification for his murder.

Rudi could scarcely bear the irony. Not only had he not fled Germany when he had the freedom to do so, out of excitement at working with the great Leni Riefenstahl, he had helped produce the party's powerful propaganda documentary. The party that clamored now for his death.

His prison train was divided into tiny cells, each with a wooden bench. But he had no water and no place to relieve himself until nighttime, when the prisoners shuffled in leg chains to the local prisons where they slept. For thirteen days he suffered hunger and thirst, but the real torment was the constant fear of what might happen to Peter. The Gestapo had his Berlin address and it was only a question of time before they would seize his apartment. Would Peter know in time to escape? And where would he go? Lovely, gentle Peter, who cooked and sewed and whose only experience with police was the sewing of costumes for *Carmen*. And a half-Jew. How could he possibly hold out against the Nazi machine?

On the thirteenth morning, the prisoners were led out of the train cars and trucked to a camp. The sign overhead said SACHSENHAUSEN.

The several hundred arriving prisoners gathered on the open parade ground of the camp, where men forced them with shouts and blows into rows. A roll call began in which each man had to announce his name and crime. Rudi had called out his name but for his crime said "robbery," as the two men before him had done.

The camp commandant checked his transport list and shouted back, "Don't lie to me, you filthy queer. Get over in that group, you butt-fucker!"

He stumbled over to join a group of some two-dozen men huddled together. But as soon as he reached them, the SS guard knocked him to the ground with his cudgel. "That's for lying," he shouted into his face. "Stand at attention, you scum. Show some respect." Rudi struggled to his feet and stood with his head ringing until the roll call was complete.

His group was marched off to their block where they had to strip for showers, shaved heads, and camp clothing. Rudi held up the uniform shirt and noted the badge sewn on the left side of the chest. The rumors were true. They all had pink triangles.

Block nine, his block, was the barrack for homosexuals. At first he was optimistic; perhaps he might meet inmates like himself, sensitive, reasonable people. But every man was exhausted and fearful, and the block senior prohibited talking.

Fear and pain and cold kept him from sleeping at first. His head pounded and all his muscles hurt from the assault and the thirteen days on the train. But finally exhaustion overcame discomfort, and he passed out for a few hours on the thin, pillowless mattress.

At 6:00 am, a buzzer sounded over the public-address system, waking the entire camp, and Rudi lurched from his platform to his feet. The others were making their beds, so he imitated them and followed as they shuffled toward the latrine. He relieved himself and washed in the icy water that trickled from a pipe running across the room over a metal trough. The others seemed to be hurrying, so he hurried too, and then he saw why. Just outside, on a trestle table, something hot was being ladled into bowls and handed out with a slice of bread, and no one wanted to be last.

Breakfast was brief and in a few minutes he had to line up in the place assigned to him at the end of the fifth row. He huddled with shoulders drawn up, trying to conserve warmth, and watched as two men carried out the body of a third and laid him at the end of their row. The nearest man called out his own number and then that of the dead man.

When roll call was completed, the camp leader counted off groups of men for assignments. Rudi waited patiently, with no idea which were the "good" assignments and which were dangerous. "Block nine, clay pit!" the camp leader announced. "Dear God," his neighbor muttered, sending a wave of fear though him.

The appeal to God was justified, he found, for the clay pit of the Klinker brickworks was a scene of damnation. It seemed to be worked solely by pink triangles, and it seemed to be a death sentence. In the dead of winter, the old snow had frozen to gray ice in and around the pit. The *Kapo* explained that a fixed number of carts had to be filled with clay from the bottom of the pit and dragged up toward the brick-making machines and ovens. The molding of bricks depended on the flow of clay from the pit, which had to be constant so that the ovens would not have to stop and be reheated.

Rudi was issued a shovel and assigned to hack through the ice and fill his shovel with clay, then fling the shovelful of clay into the cart. The lack of food and sleep had weakened him, so after only three hours, he fell to his knees. The Kapo was on him in a second.

"Get up, you scum. You fuck up the system here and get me in trouble, I'll cut your faggot balls off. Now get up and dig."

Rudi hauled himself to his knees, but the pain in his arms from the repeated motion was too great, and he couldn't heft the shovel again. "I can't any more. Can you give me another job?"

"Another job?" The Kapo's voice was full of derision. "I'll give you another job." He hauled him up by the shoulder and shoved him against the cart he had just been filling.

"You can help your sissy-ass friends push the cart to the top. You there, you do the digging."

The speed with which the other prisoner relinquished his cart and snatched the shovel told Rudi that things would get worse, not better. He soon saw why. The slope that led up to the rim of the pit was steep and the track was slick with ice. No pulley system had been installed, so only brute force brought the cart each time up to the surface. Under the icy conditions on that day, it seemed almost impossible.

Yet terror and constant beating drove them on, four men pushing the car, each one in turn slipping and falling to his knees and struggling to his feet again while the other three strained to keep the full cart from rolling back down.

In the following days, he fell into a sort of toiling stupor, and a dumb-animal resistance kept him going through the pain and exhaustion. Like King Sisyphus, he thought, though he was in too much agony to appreciate the irony. Almost every day, carts fell back, crushing someone's fingers or feet, and once fracturing a skull.

"What's to keep someone from sacrificing a finger, to get to rest in the hospital barrack?" Rudi asked someone when he was back on shovel duty. "At least you'd get a day off while they bandaged you up."

"Don't be a fool," one of the older men growled. "Don't you know what they do to queers here? Us and the Jews. We're the lowest of the low. If you get admitted to hospital, that's the end of you. They use you for experiments, and you know why? Because no one gives a shit what happens to queers and Jews. No one wants to know. Even our parents have disowned us. No. You just put your back to it and try to stay alive."

Day after day, Rudi marched with his blockmates to the clay pits, and ten hours later the columns of men followed their Kapo back into the camp. They marched in darkness until they came to the spotlight-lit entrance gate, and always Rudi stared numbly at the man in front of him. Once he found himself just behind the Kapo, and when they neared the gate, the spotlights illuminated him in the front and the fierce glare radiated around his head and shoulders like a demonic halo. It reminded Rudi of a frame in Leni Riefenstahl's film.

When he reached the entry of the camp he glanced up at the familiar cruel message over the gate. It said *Arbeit macht frei*.

Chapter Seventeen

January 1940

Katja strode through the public entrance with the dozens of visitors into the Lion House. In the January cold, the big cats stayed indoors, so one could see them all at once simply by marching down the center aisle of the house.

The leopards and the cheetah were curled up in their corners, and the panther paced. Though Katja was late, she stole a minute to look over the heads of the schoolchildren toward the wrestling lion cubs, then spotted Peter working in the next cage, where the lioness was temporarily blocked outside.

Katja watched as he hosed down the newly scrubbed concrete floor and then climbed down out of the cage.

She caught his eye and he nodded, padlocking the cage door, then reached overhead to open a connecting door with the turn of a key. The lioness bounded in from outside and sniffed at the soapy water that still ringed the drain. Then, to the huge merriment of the children, she squatted on the newly washed floor and urinated.

Rolling up the hose, Peter withdrew to what was apparently the storage room and signaled Katja to come after him. She followed to find him washing his hands in a small sink between two iceboxes. On the wall beside him, crates were piled high with cleaning products, and on the other stood a table with a cutting board.

"An interesting job. Do you feel safe here?" Katja asked.

"Not completely. The zoo director is an old pal of Goering, so I stay far away from him. But the assistant director is a friend of Frederica, and she gave me the job, so I have at least one ally here."

"Where do you sleep?"

"Right here. I roll out a mattress on the floor. It's a little lonely, but I have the animals as company. And I can usually get food in the canteen. I go there just as they're cleaning up, and no one asks questions."

"So, you're in charge of the big cats?" Katja asked, impressed.

"No, Herr Riedel is actually in charge of them. He measures out the food for each species and puts it in the right bowl. Then, at feeding time, I simply deliver the bowls to the correct cages. I also carry food over to some of the other houses on a freight bicycle."

"Is that dangerous? Getting in the cages with the big cats, I mean."

"Well, I don't get in *with* them. Come back with me into the corridor and I'll show you how the system works."

They stood together in front of the lion cage. "You can see that every cage is double, with an inside and an outside part. The dividing wall has an opening that I can control electrically with a key, from here." Peter pointed overhead to a locked box.

"I start by luring them with food to the outside cages. While they're eating, I lower the connecting doors and enter the inside cages from here and do the cleaning. When I'm done, I reopen the connecting doors and lure them inside again."

"I guess you have to be careful to keep track of which doors are open and which are closed."

"Yeah, but you develop a system after a while."

Katja let her eyes sweep along the line of cages. "Do they ever threaten you?"

"Yes, all the time. But that's their nature. The Nazis are a bigger danger, since I don't know how to recognize them. Fortunately, no one seems to notice a man who cleans cages."

"Good. Then I can stop worrying about you for a few days." Katja laid a hand on his sleeve, surprised to find the arm beneath as muscular as Dietrich's. She looked at her watch. "I've got to be back at the Charité in half an hour, so I can't stay. Do you need anything? Food, a little money?"

"For the moment, I'm all right. Just take care of yourself. I don't know what I'd do if I lost you too."

"You won't lose me, I promise." She embraced him hurriedly, slipped from the storage room, and threaded her way again through the crowd of people admiring the great predators.

At the entrance to the zoo, she peered down the avenue for the Strassenbahn. Nothing in sight. Damn. She hated to be late, even by only a few minutes. She paced like the lions she had just seen and gazed dully at the buildings all around her. Then something brought her to a halt.

What? She could almost feel the word form in her mouth. Frederica Brandt was coming toward the zoo. Was she going to visit Peter? For a fleeting instant, Katja felt a charge of electricity at the thought they might have a pleasant encounter and talk again. It had been so long.

But Frederica was not going to the zoo, only buying a newspaper from the kiosk a hundred meters from the entrance. She folded it under her arm and walked away from the kiosk, across the street in the opposite direction.

Katja had an instant recollection of the same gesture. The day they had met here, five years before, Frederica had bought a newspaper and then discarded it.

As Katja stared into the distance, another recollection surfaced, of waiting with Leni Riefenstahl in the office of the propaganda ministry, where Frederica had just been hired. A table was covered with the day's newspapers. Frederica did not need to buy a paper, and she certainly did not need to come all the way to the zoo to do it.

There had to be more to the story, so she strolled toward the kiosk, glancing with forced casualness inside it as she passed. An old man, balding and spectacled, was arranging his piles of papers. He wore fingerless gloves and a wool scarf wrapped high around his neck, but otherwise he was unremarkable. What had she expected? She was baffled.

She returned to the stop, and when her Strassenbahn came, she boarded it, scarcely aware of paying and finding a seat. Wheels were turning in her mind and, inexplicably, her mood lightened.

Chapter Eighteen

Katja let several days pass while she ran through her mind all the possible meanings of the kiosk transaction. None of them made sense. The only thing that seemed certain was that the newspaper was a prop and Frederica had either given or gotten something at the kiosk. And whatever it was, she had been doing it for five years.

Finally, Katja was able to get off her hospital shift early and, at six o'clock, she stood waiting in the twilight outside the Ministry of Propaganda. When Frederica appeared, Katja confronted her. "Can we talk some place? I have something important to discuss with you."

Frederica was clearly caught off guard, but seemed pleased to see her. "Well, yes, if you wish. There's a café only a few streets from here. We could have some coffee."

Katja shook her head. "I'd rather we just kept walking."

"What's gotten into you?" Visibly perplexed, Frederica allowed herself to be pulled along.

Katja wasn't sure what sort of tone to take, or even what she was doing. Her suspicions could be all nonsense, so she began cautiously. "You know that Rudi is in Sachsenhausen. You care for him as much as I do, so why haven't you tried to use your influence with Dr. Goebbels to get him out?"

Frederica stopped. "I told you I don't *have* any influence with the Reichsminister."

"But you *do*. I've seen him put his hands on you like someone who owns you. I don't care what's going on between you and Goebbels, but *he* might care that you have some regular business with a kiosk near the zoo."

"What are you talking about?" Frederica's voice was steady, but her sudden drop in volume showed Katja she had struck a nerve.

"I was there yesterday and saw you buying a newspaper you didn't need. Just like you did the day we went to see the gorillas. Peter saw you do it too, some time ago. You've been buying and throwing away newspapers from that kiosk for five years. What's going on?"

Frederica took a breath and answered softly. "Why are you doing this to me?"

"I'm just trying to get you to help Rudi."

Frederica stopped walking, in spite of the cold. She faced Katja, boring into her with gray-green eyes. "You have no idea what you're doing."

Katja wanted to press her lips on those eyes, and the urge made her angry. "No idea? Maybe not. But I know what I want to *stop* doing," she said. "For seven years, I've been swept along with the lies. I've helped *sell* the lies, about what it meant to be German. I didn't much care when the Brownshirts killed each other for some trumped-up reason in 1934, or when they dragged out hundreds of "un-German" books we've been reading for years and set fire to them. I didn't even really object when they smashed all those shop windows of the Jews and burned their synagogues. I looked away when the deportations started. Then we declared war on Poland, and I was prepared to believe that we only "shot back." But it's come home now. Someone I care about is in a concentration camp, for the crime of loving someone. I've had enough."

Frederica shook her head softly. "Stop, Katja. Your heart's in the right place, but you can't help things from where you are."

Katja pulled her along again. Too many people on the street who could overhear. "Listen, you said something just like that the last time we talked. That 'there are bigger issues at stake,' and that I just didn't understand them. What are they? Why are you sneaking around? What are you hiding? Are you passing out information or receiving it?"

Frederica looked around nervously. "Don't talk so loudly. You'll get us both arrested."

Katja drew her into an empty alleyway. "You *are* involved in something against them, aren't you? What is it? Are you stealing something? Is it sabotage? I've seen it, so you can't lie."

Frederica closed her beautiful eyes for a moment. "I can't tell you anything."

"Why not? Why don't you trust me?"

"Why should I? You're married to a nice Nazi soldier and have a nice Nazi father- and mother-in-law. I trust you least of all."

"That's not fair. That's not who I am. Not any more. What can I do to make you trust me?"

Frederica looked down at the hand that held her. "Nothing."

"Not even this?" On a sudden impulse, Katja pressed Frederica back against the wall and kissed her full on the mouth. A kiss that did not invade and might have been innocent, but for its force and the long moment Katja held it.

Frederica did not resist, nor did she kiss back, as if she were waiting for some third entity to arrive and arbitrate.

But none came and when Katja broke the kiss, Frederica stood for a moment, as if dazed. Then she said, "That was reckless."

"No one's here to see us. Everyone's gone." Katja glanced around to confirm. "I'm sorry. Not for the kiss, only for endangering you. But I have to show you that I'm on your side."

Frederica looked exasperated. "You don't even know what side I'm on."

"I think I do. It's the side I've finally come to myself. Look, we need each other. We're both already committing a crime by helping Peter. I'm willing to go further. A *lot* further. Do you—"

Frederica touched her lips with a gloved hand, silencing her. "Come home with me."

❖

"I'll make us some coffee," Frederica said, hanging both their coats up on hooks in an alcove by the door.

"Anything to take the chill off." Katja gazed around the room while Frederica busied herself in the kitchen, a little surprised at the modesty of the apartment. Surely the Reichsminister ought to have taken better care of one of his mistresses. The modest sitting room held only bookshelves, a floor lamp, sofa, and narrow coffee table. A table in the corner served as a dining area, and the door on the opposite wall presumably led to the bedroom. Only the carpet seemed of good quality.

"You read a lot in English," she observed, walking along the bookshelves.

"Are you surprised?" Frederica brought in cups, saucers, sugar bowl. "Most are from my university days."

"Where did you study?"

"Here in Berlin. But I was no longer a student when they burned all those books in the Opernplatz. I've still got copies of some forbidden books—Brecht, Sinclair, Hemingway."

Katja glanced along the shelf. "Also Shakespeare, Milton, Marlow, Blake, even a translation of Julius Caesar. This is not the library of a 'good German.'"

"I studied British literature. But you'll find some good Germans there too. Goethe, who's really a bore, Schiller, less so, Thomas Mann, and even the *Nibelungenlied.* It doesn't get any more Germanic than that." She returned to the kitchen to pour the boiling water over a filter into a porcelain pot. "What about you? What do you read?"

Katja stood in the doorway while they waited for the water to filter down. "Nothing as poetic as what you've got. I studied at a technical institute—film, photography—and mostly I read about that. I wanted to be a filmmaker like Leni Riefenstahl, and was thrilled to work with her. *Triumph des Willens* is a masterpiece, but I was slow to grasp its real message. I even went with her to film in Poland at the beginning of the war. But what we saw was not the Germany we filmed in Nuremberg. Or maybe it was. That's an even more depressing thought."

With the hot porcelain pot in hand, Frederica led them back to the tiny table and filled both their cups. The smell of the fresh coffee was intoxicating.

"Sorry. I digressed. Since filmmaking never came to anything, I did what my father encouraged me to, studied nursing. Now my bookshelves are full of medical books."

Frederica sipped her coffee, holding Katja's glance, and Katja's face warmed at the scrutiny. "Please trust me," Katja said. "I never would have de—"

"Sssssh!" Frederica stood up abruptly from the table and went to turn on the radio. It was the state news station broadcasting reports about Polish crimes against Germans. She turned the volume up high, then sat down again and leaned in, inches from Katja's face.

"Before we go any further, you have to know, you're leaping off a cliff here. If you survive the rocks, the water is very deep, and there are sharks."

Katja couldn't resist a smile. "Okay, I think we've gone about as far as we can with the cliff metaphor. Please, stop all the obfuscation and tell me what you're doing. Is it black market, extortion, sabotage?"

"You can leave now without my answering that question and everything will be as before. And you won't have put yourself in mortal danger."

Katja ignored her. "Who are you doing it for? What do you do? How can I help?"

"Answer this question first. What about your husband?"

It was a reasonable question, so Katja took a long drink of coffee while she composed her answer. "What *about* him? He's a good, decent man, doing what he believes is right. But it's *not* right. When he comes home, I'll…I don't know what I'll do. I'm not his puppet. I have a mind of my own, and I'm past the point of worrying about what he thinks of what I do."

"Are you willing to betray him?"

"What do you mean? Commit adultery?" Katja felt herself blushing again at the thought of adultery with Frederica.

Frederica appeared to blush too. "There are other ways to betray him."

Katja paused to consider, to answer truthfully. "My husband never cared much about racial purity before, and he didn't hate Jews or Gypsies, or Communists or homosexuals. This new Germany has changed him and I don't like it. I can't make his decisions for him, but I can make my own. Tell me what you were passing to the kiosk man. Or what you got from him."

Frederica stirred her half-drunk coffee and seemed to study the little whirlpool she made. "I told you my mother abandoned me when I was young. To be more precise, she handed me over to my aunt when I was six, and after that I only saw pictures of her. When I was ten, my aunt sent me back to live with my father."

"What has this got to do with the kiosk at the zoo?"

"Be quiet. I'll get there. Anyhow, when my father died, I stayed in Germany, of course. I had been here for eleven of my eighteen years. I was getting by and felt no need to contact anyone in England. Obviously no one there cared much about me. But suddenly, in 1934, just at the time I was working for Leni Riefenstahl, I got a call from someone in England offering me a job. An organization called the Special Operations Executive, or SOE, was recruiting people to integrate into the new German government. They offered to pay me a stipendium to simply apply for a job in any of the ministries. The higher the job, the higher the stipendium. I agreed and applied for the secretarial pool at the propaganda ministry."

"Wait, I don't understand. Who hired you for the SOE?"

"My aunt made the call. But I reported to the organization in general, then later to someone called Handel—obviously a code name. I had to report to him once a month, just to assure him I still held the position. I didn't have to deliver anything, just stay in contact."

"How long did that go on?"

"For years. Until the war started, in fact, when the SOE promoted me and gave me my own code name, Caesar."

"Caesar?" They must have been expecting great things of you."

"It *is* ridiculous, isn't it? They never told me why. In any case, my job was anything but imperial. I just plodded along, month after month making myself valuable. I did a few things I'm not proud of, but finally I got the position I needed to really be useful as typist and transcriber to Otto Jakobs."

"Who is he?"

"The principal stenographer at the propaganda ministry. You met him at the Reichstag speech you attended with Frau Riefenstahl. Anyhow, I type the finished copy of the dictations that he takes down in shorthand."

Katja was losing the thread that now seemed very far from the newspaper-kiosk question. "What's so special about working for Jakobs?"

"Goebbels dictates his diary entries to him every day. I get to type them."

"His private diaries?" Katja's amazement grew like a rising sun.

"Which contain his private conversations with Hitler, military reports from the front, gossip about Goering and the rest of the inner circle. He goes on endlessly."

"And you make a copy of everything for the SOE?"

"Summaries. He writes thousands of words, so I have to decide what might be of interest."

"Who do you deliver it to?"

"The kiosk, of course. Roughly once a fortnight. But that can't go on. It's obviously become too repetitive. If both you and Peter have noticed me, then others could have also."

"Who do you talk to? Who gives you orders?"

"I don't talk to anyone. If I'm caught, I can't betray anyone other than the drop, and I don't know him. He sees to it that the coded text is sent by wireless to someone named Handel. I almost never hear from Handel directly, usually through a message left at the kiosk, or an encrypted telephone call, but that's rare."

"So you are passing Goebbels' reports to this Handel. But who is Handel?"

"I don't know. Somebody important in British Intelligence."

Katja sat back, the full import of the remark finally sinking in. Frederica was a spy.

Chapter Nineteen

June 14, 1940

"Deutschland Sieg! Deutschland Sieg!" The hooligans behind Katja were shouting and pounding their fists against the air, as if it disagreed with them. But no one disagreed with them. Everybody was cheering. Holland, Belgium, arrogant France, all defeated in a week. And England in full retreat. It was breathtaking.

She hurried along the Hardenbergplatz toward the zoo, still trembling with the accomplishment of her first act of treason. She willed herself to walk more slowly, to smile like the others celebrating in the street, but her heart thudded so violently she was dizzy. She had delivered the little package of papers. The balding, spectacled little man had looked alarmed when she slid it toward him under the *Völkischer Beobachter*, but she gave the code phrase, "A nice day to be home listening to music," and he replied, "Myself, I prefer Handel." Obviously accepting her replacement of Frederica, he casually slid Katja's packet toward him and let it drop on the floor before turning away to wait on another customer.

She had expected to be afraid, but had never anticipated having to make the drop on such a day as this, plowing her way through triumphant crowds. She forced a cold smile as people passed her, waving their flags. Shame on them. The British, Dutch, Belgian, and French soldiers who fell on the battlefield were one thing. They had declared war. But innocent Germans, men and women who wanted only to live, were in the camps now in their thousands. And the victory in the West increased the power of the regime that held them. Every cheer sickened her.

A few years ago she would have cheered as well. *Did* cheer, at the hollow ceremonies. How could she have been so blind? What else that she took for granted would prove to be false?

She was through the zoo entrance now and away from the cheering crowds, so she quickened her pace. No one was visiting the Lion House since everyone was outside cheering, so she went immediately to the storage room and knocked.

The door opened to the pale, sun-starved face of Peter, and without a sound, he drew her in and closed the door behind her. "You've heard the news, of course," he said glumly.

"Yes, of course. But I refuse to believe it's the end." She sat down next to him on a crate and laid a package in his lap. "I know you get food in the canteen, but it can't be very good."

He laughed. "It's all right. A lot of soup. And now and then I steal a tiny bit of the lions' meat. It's horseflesh and I roast it over a candle. It's not so bad with salt."

"Ah, I never thought of that. Very smart. Just don't let them catch you."

"Who? The zoo directors or the lions?"

She chuckled softly. "I don't know which would be worse. But I've brought you something you can't steal from the animals." She helped him unwrap the package. "There's sausage and cheese, of course. But my father loves prune cake, so I made a double portion, one for him and one for you. He never noticed."

"Oh, God, I love prune cake." He broke off a large corner and bit into it. "You have no idea how I've been craving sugar," he mumbled through a full mouth.

"I'll try to bring you more when I can get sugar again. Unfortunately, I've used up this month's ration." She hesitated for a moment, not wanting to suggest what she was thinking. "Now that the Nazis seem to have won the war, have you thought about trying to leave Germany?"

"Strange that you should ask. A number of people besides you know that I'm here. People on my mother's side, who are members of a Zionist organization. They're still managing to get Jews out of Germany. Mostly to Palestine."

"Have they offered to help you?"

"Yes. My cousin Günther knows an expert forger who'd made a passport for a man who looks a lot like me. He died of pneumonia before he could use it, so Günther offered it to me. I told him no. I asked if they could make me a ration card instead."

"Why didn't you take it? Things are bound to get worse and it could save your life."

"Because I don't want to go to Palestine. I don't believe a word of the Old Testament, and no one in my mother's family has been to a synagogue in a generation. I'm only a half-Jew because the Germans say I am. Let them give that passport to a real Jew to go and live in the Jerusalem of their dreams. They've suffered enough and thousands of them would love to go."

"That sounds very noble, but I don't understand how you can pass up a chance to escape."

"Well, the real reason is Rudi. I refuse to leave him here alone. I only wish I could do more to reach him. When I hear the thugs outside celebrating their victories, I get sick to my stomach."

"Me too. But I've started working against them. I won't tell you how, it would just put you in even more danger, but finally my conscience is clear."

Peter threw his arms around her and kissed her on the cheek. "Oh, my brave Katja. I'm terrified they'll arrest you, but I'm so proud you've finally seen what a monster Germany has become."

"I'm terrified sometimes too, but I'm also relieved. I don't underestimate what's out there. I know it's powerful and lethal. But it feels good to stand up to it."

"I'm sure it does." Peter looked at the clock over one of the iceboxes. "You'd better stand up *now*, in fact. Herr Riedel will be along in about ten minutes to measure out the food, and I don't want to have to explain you. Will you come again in a few days? I need to see you from time to time so I don't give up hope."

"Of course. I'll come as often as I can. I promise." After a quick embrace, she slipped out of the storage room and into the corridor. It was still empty of visitors, and the only sound other than her own footfall was the low rumble of the big predators.

❖

Katja worked a morning shift at the hospital and so was able to arrive at Frederica's apartment shortly before she returned from the ministry. She stood at the top of the staircase waiting until the double clack of the handle on the downstairs door told her that someone had entered the building. She peered over the bannister and relaxed when she saw the familiar navy-blue beret over amber hair.

Frederica's face also brightened when she saw who waited, though neither of them spoke until she had unlocked the door and admitted them both to the apartment. Katja started to speak, but Frederica pressed a finger to her own lips and pointed at the radio. It was set to the state-radio broadcast frequency, so it needed no tuning. On that day, the Ministry of Health was discussing the widespread success of the Strength through Joy program, which brought the youth of Germany together for patriotic woodland hiking. With the volume on high, Frederica beckoned Katja into the apartment.

"Nosey neighbors?" Katja asked, as she took off her coat.

"Of course," Frederica said, *sotto voce*. "Especially Herr Dehbus upstairs. A real Nazi, that one. The other families, across the hall and downstairs, seem decent enough. They say 'Guten Tag' when we pass on the stairs instead of that ridiculous 'Heil Hitler.' Dehbus says it so often it comes out 'heitler'! If he saw you arrive, I wouldn't be surprised if he was lying with his ear pressed to the floor right now, trying to hear us."

Hanging up both their coats, Frederica led Katja to the table next to the radio. In order to hear over the din, they had to sit close and speak directly into each other's faces, which Katja found very agreeable.

"So, how did it go?" Frederica's eyes bored into her with interest and concern.

"Oh, it worked just fine. The vendor seemed a little thrown to get the delivery from someone new, but otherwise it went smoothly. Do we know his name?"

"No. He doesn't know mine either. We only acknowledge each other with the code phrases. If he doesn't reply with his, we don't exchange anything."

"It's a strange phrase. Why not remark about the weather or request a paper he doesn't carry?"

"First, because anyone might remark about the weather or ask for another paper. And second, because Handel is the man in charge of the Berlin circuit."

"That's right. Did you ever meet him, or talk to him?"

"No, never, but after all these years, he feels a little like a sort of fairy godfather. Someone invisible who cares about what happens to me. Otherwise I work alone and anonymously."

"It must be awfully lonely operating in a vacuum." Speaking the word "lonely" so softly, and so close to Frederica's cheek, felt less like a question than a flirtation.

"It's the price one pays. When any two people meet, each one is a liability to the other, and that includes us now too."

"I wouldn't betray you," Katja murmured with utter sincerity, then realized the subject was torture. "I mean, I would try very hard not to."

"I'm sure you would. But it's difficult to hold out until the end if you know any names. That's what happened to three SOE agents, Cecily Lefort and Violette Szabo and Denise Bloch. They were in the French circuit, and Cecily was the only one I knew personally. I made a brief trip back to London in early 1939, just before the war started, and met her. She was very young and had just signed up. In between training sessions we did girlish things like shop for shoes. That was before I was assigned to Handel. Anyhow, I didn't think much about her until a few months ago, when word filtered back that she had been captured along with the other two, after parachuting into occupied France. I told you I don't hear much from Handel, only when I have to know something important. But this message was the first sign I got that Handel was worried personally about me. In any case, the capture of the three women caused a change of policy."

"Does anyone know where they are?"

"No. They just went silent. The theory is that an agent captured earlier knew their names and betrayed them to the Nazis. Since then, none of us knows any of the others."

"Do Rudi and Peter know that you're 'Caesar'?" Katja asked.

"No, and I've taken pains to keep them out of it. But when I left the Riefenstahl project, Rudi came to see me and I hinted I was starting something dangerous. I asked him not to quiz me further and he honored that request. It breaks my heart that I can't help him in Sachsenhausen, but I think he knows by now I'm working for him in my own way. Peter also suspects, of course. By the way, have you seen him?"

"Yes, and he's safe for the moment. He even turned down a chance to escape. Zionist friends of his mother offered him a forged passport so he could emigrate to Palestine, but he said he'd rather wait here for Rudi. Love makes people do reckless things."

"And heroic things," Frederica murmured.

"Yes, heroic ones, too."

They both fell silent for a moment and let the radio broadcast drone on, extolling the joys and benefits of girls joining the *Bund Deutscher Mädel*. Frederica's fingers slid softly across the table to barely touch Katja's. "Who would have thought, when the thirteen of us were eating our little supper in Nuremberg, that some of us would be committing treason?"

The electricity of the touch shot up Katja's arm to her heart, which began to pound. How unutterably sweet was the first touch that connected them. More precious than their two combative kisses, their fingertips, reaching each other across the abyss of fear and the fog of Nazi propaganda, signaled a pledge.

Frederica took Katja's hand and held it like a little bridge over which their talk flowed. "It's terrible when you think of what we did there in Nuremberg. We contracted with the devil. We all added our voices, talents, even genius, to the creation of this state, this Vaterland intoxication. And look what it's doing to us now."

"What's happened to the rest, I wonder," Katja said softly. "The thirteen from that table. I know that Leni Riefenstahl and Sepp Allgeier are still filming as if nothing were happening."

"Well, Rudi's in Sachsenhausen and Peter's in hiding, Dietrich and Marti are in the Wehrmacht, and Marti's son by now is in the Hitlerjugend. Who else is caught up in it?"

"Erich Prietschke for sure. He's in the SS."

"Hans Gottschalk joined the navy. Last I heard he was on the Battleship *Bismarck*. Vogel and Koehler? I don't know."

Frederica held Katja's hand in both her own, but seemed to look deep inside herself. "It's going to last a long time, you know. People are saying Germany will win and it will be over by Christmas, but they're wrong. I've read the ravings of Goebbels and I know what's in his mind. He's both servile and ambitious, and he burns to follow Hitler to the end. They'll keep pushing east and they'll probably get far. But Russia and the United States are sleeping giants, and who knows what will happen after that."

Frederica brought the hand up to her own face, brushing her lips softly over the palm, then laid her cheek on it.

"I'm with you in this until the end, whatever it is," Katja said. "I love you, you know."

"I know. But your husband loves you too."

Hurt by the remark, Katja drew her hand away. "What's that supposed to mean? You're trying to bring down the Third Reich, but about Dietrich you suddenly have scruples?"

"You don't? He's on a battlefield right now and he thinks he's fighting for you." She paused, forming her thoughts. "I shouldn't have to tell you how precious you've become to me. I think about you day and night and can't imagine carrying on without you. But don't you see? How terrible it would be to tear you away from the man who loves you the same way that young Communist tore my mother away from me."

Katja stood up and took a step away from the table, exasperated. "The situations are not parallel. Dietrich is not a child," she said in full voice.

Silently, Frederica stood up as well, took Katja by the hand, and guided her back to the table and the protection of the radio noise. Caressing Katja's cheek, she murmured, "You must believe me. I want you more than I ever realized I could want anyone, but it is possible to love someone without claiming them. Please, let that be enough for now."

Katja took hold of the gentle hand, started to speak, then shook her head, resisting the retort she was about to make. She exhaled. "All right, for now. So, what's next?"

"I carry on stealing information from the Goebbels diaries and you carry on passing them to Handel. Until the tide turns, or they catch us. I can't live any other way."

The radio broadcast ended and they no longer had protection from eavesdropping neighbors. There seemed nothing left to say, anyhow. Wordlessly, Katja stood up from the table and fetched her coat from the hook by the door. "I should be going, shouldn't I?"

Frederica helped her on with her coat, then encircled her with her arms from behind. Katja relaxed into the embrace, close to tears with longing, until Frederica stepped away. "Until next time," she said brightly, meaninglessly, for whoever was listening.

"Yes, next time," Katja said, and cringed at the sound of the door closing behind her. She forced the first step away from the apartment, then the next one and the next. But by the time she was outside on the street, the magnitude of the day's events struck her.

Within twenty-four hours she had committed treason, for which she could be executed, and she had fallen in love.

CHAPTER TWENTY

June 22, 1941

At eight in the evening Katja returned home bone weary from work at the hospital. She was also depressed, since on her way home, she realized it had been a year since she had joined Frederica in their biweekly act of espionage, and nothing seemed to have changed.

Rudi was still in Sachsenhausen, Peter still hiding in the Lion House, Dietrich was still reminding her of the children they were going to have, and Frederica was still physically unavailable.

The love and loyalty they had implicitly pledged was deeply satisfying in every way but one. Something new had arisen in her that she had never known before, and that was lust, the overwhelming desire to learn every part of Frederica's body and to engage in carnality of a sort she had no idea how to carry out. Its suppression was an engine that drove her, week after week, to risk her life, to carry out their mission, as much to be a part of Frederica's world as for the redemption of Germany.

Yet the war hammered on, calling on ever more of Germany's reserves, ever more of its young men. Bafflingly, the increasing hardship did not elicit resentment among the people, but rather a growing fervor to enact the roles the party created for them. Just two days earlier, Germany had violated its non-aggression pact and attacked Russia, widening the war by a continent, and all Katja heard was the call to greater, nobler patriotism.

She hung her coat on the hook, grateful that her father cooked on the days she worked late, and was about to go to the kitchen when she saw Dietrich's letter. The poor man had been home only twice in the past year, and each time for so short a period she didn't need to lie to him about the work she did or the life she led. He was always so grateful to be near her that he never talked about anything but their future.

She was in no hurry to open the letter, and only after she had greeted her father and set the table did she read it, expecting the usual regrets and platitudes. But they were absent. Dietrich was in Russia now, and it was clear that Russia was changing him.

My dearest Katja,

It is a filthy job fighting the Russians, but finally I see why we must do it. The pitiful mobs that descend on us are lowlife criminals fueled by vodka and fear of their own commissars' pistols at the back of their heads. The Bolshevik hordes really are animals, and finally meeting them has made a lasting impression on me. If I ever had any doubts about the importance of this war in the East, they are gone now. These sub-humans have been whipped into a frenzy by the Jews and our standing up to them came just in time. The Führer has saved Europe from chaos.

Katja set the letter aside as her father sat down across the table from her. "Anything new?" he asked, as he always did, serving out the eternal potatoes without listening for an answer. "We've got mushrooms tonight," he added. "Our neighbor was in the woods this morning and I bought some from her."

"The war is hardening him." Katja returned to the letter. "Before he always talked about fighting for me and our children, but he's beginning to sound more bloodthirsty."

"It's the nature of warfare, dear. Things were just like that in the Great War. The soldiers went out as nice boys and came home hardened men."

"It didn't happen to you."

"No, but I was a bugler and nothing really terrible happened to me, as it did to thousands of others. It's the same now, I'm sure, and I'm only glad that I have the dispensation of age and a seat in the Staatsoper orchestra."

"Some people in Germany are opposing the war and Hitler," she said casually before taking a bite of potatoes and mushroom gravy.

"Subversives and saboteurs. They should be hanged," Karl Sommer blustered.

"But if you disapprove of the war, there is a certain logic, I suppose," she said lightly, as if half in jest.

"There's no logic in treason. Subversion threatens the whole nation. Even if I don't go in for all that flag-waving, I never forget that our troops are fighting right now, and for us. We have to support them."

"Yes, of course," Katja said. "We have to support the troops."

❖

August 1941

The Hauptsturmführer barked, "Fall in!" and Erich Prietschke and eleven other men lined up for the special detachment, SS *Einsatzgruppe* 4.

He knew a speech was coming, but he was surprised to see the man who was about to give it. It was *Obergruppenführer* Reinhard Heydrich himself, easily recognizable by his height and his impressive Nordic features. An elongated face with a high forehead, emphasized by thinning blond hair, gave him the haughty look of nobility that so many of his colleagues envied.

> *You all know why we're here on foreign soil. The invasion, Operation Barbarossa, is a battle forced on us by the Bolsheviks to prevent the Soviet attack that we know was planned for July 1941. But it's more than a strategic battle; it is a war of civilizations, a racial*

> *war between German National Socialism and the more primitive culture of Soviet Communism. We all know who the Bolsheviks are, and who sent them, and who drives the brutes and peasants who are sent out to kill us. Jewish Communist Party commissars.*

Standing in formation, Erich could not nod, but he permitted himself a sudden decisive blink of the eyes in agreement.

> *It is therefore the task of all four Einsatzgruppen to secure the offices and papers of all Soviet commissars and to liquidate all of the cadres of the Soviet state. That is, to execute all Soviet officials, all captured Red Army political commissars, all members of the Cominterm, members of the local and provincial committees of the Communist party, and all Communist party members of Jewish origin.*

Erich did not know any of the men who stood on both sides of him, but he was confident that not a single one among them disagreed with that assessment. He'd heard a similar speech the week before, on his first Einsatzkommando, when they entered Konitz.

The Communist committee was easily identified, as well as the Jewish mayor and a dozen other city officials. The *Sturmbannführer* had ordered a trench dug outside the city and the Jewish-Bolsheviks were lined up within it. He and nine other SS men executed them, and, after the men had all dropped, an armored truck with a plow attached in front covered the trench with dirt. It should have been a clean job, but he could see that not all of the twenty-seven men were dead. Some of the shots had been sloppy, and two of the wounded men even tried to climb out of the trench. One of the SS men took his rifle butt and forced them back in as the field vehicle plowed the dirt over them.

Erich turned away so he wouldn't see, and afterward, when he was off duty, he got drunk. For his service, he was promoted and given an increase in pay. That part he liked, so he volunteered for the next commando.

The speech was over, and the detachment snapped to attention. They had their assignment. The condemned, whoever they were, had already been arrested that morning and trucked outside of town. By now, the trench would have been dug and all that remained was for the Einsatzkommando to carry out the order.

In half an hour they were there, the twelve of them, eight SS men and four from the Security Service. They scrambled from the truck and fast-marched toward the site where the prisoners were being held. It was a larger group this time. He counted forty-two. They would have to be shot in groups. Well, he could do that. Just blank out his mind and fire, reminding himself who he was shooting and why he was doing it.

He lined up in place with the other eleven marksmen before the first row at the edge of the trench. A squad of twelve rifles for twelve prisoners. At the commands of the Sturmbannführer he raised his weapon and took aim, and at the final command he fired. Twelve of the condemned fell, from clean shots. The marksmen marched farther along the trench and took aim at the next twelve. This time there were both men and women. Crap, he hated that. Worse, some of them stood facing their executioners. Fortunately, his own target was turned away. Command: "Raise rifles." Command: "Aim." Command: "Fire!"

When they took position for the third group, it was easier. Raise rifles, Take aim, Fire. And it was done. He never looked to see if all the shots were clean. Not his problem.

The last six waited and he took final position with the first five rifles in the line. Erich cursed to himself. His target, a young woman, was facing him. Worse, she looked familiar. Her face…oh, shit, her face was identical to one he knew. His mouth was suddenly dry. It was the face of Frederica Brandt.

"Raise rifle." He obeyed.

"Aim." He peered down the line of sight toward his target, and in the split second before the last command came, a revelation came to him and his nausea turned to rage. If this Jew looked like Frederica, then Frederica must have been a Jew. That explained why she had rejected him in favor of the vile little propaganda minister—for his money and power.

"Fire!"

He heard the concussion of his own rifle, as if someone else had fired it. To his horror, the woman didn't fall. She clutched her chest with crossed arms, as though she embraced something, and continued to stare at him until he shot again. She fell to her knees, and he shot a third time, knocking her back against the wall of the trench. Then the order came to march away, and he didn't look back as the armored truck started its engine and plowed the wall of dirt into the pit.

Chapter Twenty-one

September 1941

Katja covered her ears against the roar of the bulldozers as she hurried past them toward the zoo. Berliners knew, vaguely, that a flak tower was being constructed on the corner near the bird sanctuary, but only a few knew how large it would be and that it would serve in part as a command center, hospital, and bomb shelter.

Katja knew. Joseph Goebbels had recorded his conversation with Albert Speer in his diary, and Frederica had transcribed it. Now Katja was in the process of delivering the summary of the transcription to the kiosk drop.

The flak tower was ominous in every respect. Germany was now so threatened by air attack that Hitler had ordered the building of such towers in every major city. Moreover the location of this one meant increased visibility for her own work.

Frederica had also grown more cautious. She no longer attempted to smuggle material copies of the transcriptions, however small, from the ministry. Discovery would have meant her certain and immediate death. Instead, she tried to memorize the most important sections and summarized them each evening, then hid the tiny notes until she could code them for Katja's delivery.

There it was, the kiosk, just a hundred meters away. Katja slipped one hand around the tightly wrapped bundle in her pocket and approached casually, waiting for a customer to pay for his paper and leave. Finally the space in front of the kiosk was empty and she stepped up to the piles of newspapers.

Her heart sank. An old woman tended the newspapers, someone she had never seen before, and there was no sign of the little bald man.

Katja forced calmness on herself. “A nice day to be home listening to music,” she said loudly over the sound of the bulldozers, and laid her free hand on a copy of the *Deutsche Allgemeine*, as if to buy it.

The woman looked at her, puzzled, then grunted indifference. “You want the paper or not?”

“Ah, yes, of course.” She lifted her empty hand from her pocket to drop the necessary coins into the dish. Then, with a frozen smile, she hurried away.

❖

Katja turned on Frederica’s radio to loud polka music and dropped onto Frederica’s couch. “I couldn’t make the drop,” she said. “Someone else was there, an old woman, and she didn’t know the code. So I came right back.” She tossed the cigarette-sized packet of notes on the coffee table.

Frederica dropped down beside her. “I guess they’ve caught him. Now he’ll just disappear, like Cecily and Violette and Denise.”

“What about *us* now? If the Gestapo interrogates him he can describe us both. What are we going to do?” Before that moment, Katja had never seriously thought about being arrested, and she was close to panic.

“No, I think we’re all right. First of all, the kiosk agent is no fool. He’s not going to give them every detail about your face. But secondly, we’re both of medium height, with nothing distinctive about our hair, and I’m guessing he never saw our eyes. Even if he gives a true description, it will match that of several thousand Berliners.”

“You’re not afraid the Gestapo will break the code and trace the transcription back to you?”

"Rather unlikely. It's coded, against a base in Caesar's *The Gallic Wars*. The Edwards translation, to be exact."

Katja calmed slightly. "Ah, that explains why you have the book. Maybe that's why they gave you the code name Caesar. In any case, what do we do now? How do we get word to the SOE about the new flak towers?"

"I don't think we have to worry about that. I got a message from Handel some time ago with an alternative drop site, a 'dead drop,' in case we lost the kiosk. I guess he was already worried about it."

"A 'dead drop'? What's that?" Katja obviously had more to learn about espionage.

"A drop where you don't know who is going to pick it up, or even when. It's more precarious, but it's where we are now. Our new 'dead drop' is the Hotel Adlon."

"The Adlon? Good Grief! Hundreds of big Nazis are there all the time. Why don't we go all the way and just drop things at Gestapo headquarters?"

"Don't joke. I wouldn't put it past the SOE. After all, they've got an agent in the propaganda ministry, haven't they? The Adlon is a good site to place some sensitive ears. It's not so hard for people with vague documentation to get menial jobs like kiosk vendors, waiters, dishwashers, that sort of thing. In any case, they've got someone in or near the kitchen. Since we missed the drop this week, they'll be waiting for us."

Katja exhaled slowly, calculating the risks. "In for a penny, in for a pound. All right, then. So how, exactly, do we 'drop' the material?"

"In a bottle," Frederica said, and went to the kitchen. She returned with a red earthenware Steinhäger bottle. "See? Opaque, so you don't notice the paper inside. We're supposed to drop one into the trash on Friday. One or both of us is to eat dinner there and order a bottle of Steinhäger. Then, when we're done, we exchange our loaded Steinhäger bottle for the one on the table. When it goes into the kitchen, whoever separates out the trash will pick it up. That's the plan, anyhow."

"What happens if it's not picked up? What if he misses it?"

"I presume it goes into the trash, forever. It shouldn't endanger us. No one would have any reason to look inside an empty schnapps bottle. If they do, the coding still protects us. Of course, the loss would be a big waste of my work, but let's not think about that, shall we?"

"Won't we be conspicuous, two women alone, having dinner at the Adlon? Besides, Dietrich will be here on leave Friday. He's been promoted again. What should I do with him?"

"It looks like the second problem is the solution to the first. We'll have a celebratory dinner. Tell him I've been given a bonus for my work for Goebbels and that I invite you. That should please him. We'll toast his new promotion with a lot of Steinhäger."

❖

The main dining room of the Hotel Adlon was chandeliered and palatial. Dressed in his new uniform, Feldwebel Dietrich Kurtz guided Katja and Frederica to a table for three in one of the corners. A chamber orchestra played something from Schubert, and the air of the dining room held a curious mélange of women's perfumes and the fragrance of meat sauces.

For a few moments, at least, Katja forgot the danger they were placing themselves in and enjoyed the thought of an expensive dinner paid for indirectly by British Intelligence. She had been worried about Dietrich's reaction to the suggestion of a dinner threesome, but she needn't have been. He was so bedazzled that it never occurred to him to question it. She also felt a twinge of guilt thinking about Peter having to steal bits of raw meat from his lions, and Rudi, who might have had nothing to eat at all.

The dining room, reputed to be the playground for the Nazi upper class, in fact held a preponderance of SS and Wehrmacht officers in uniform. The women, in formal or semiformal gowns, were obviously the pampered wives and mistresses of the men in power. For the briefest moment, Katja wondered if Frederica had ever dined at the Adlon with the Reichsminister, then forced the thought from her mind.

In the gold-trimmed green evening outfit she usually wore to her father's opera performances, Katja was suitably dressed for the Adlon, but Frederica, in a black satin gown with décolleté, outdid her in her simplicity. She felt no jealousy, however, rather a persistent craving to touch some part of Frederica's upper body. A single item that did not quite fit with Frederica's glamor was the large handbag she carried, and Dietrich had remarked on it. But Frederica explained that it carried urgent work papers she would have to return to the Reichsministry after dinner, and she did not want to make a special trip back. A curious tale that Dietrich blithely accepted.

"Shall we order champagne?" Dietrich asked, but Frederica took charge of that part of the menu right away.

"The ministry has just concluded a contract with the city of Steinhagen for a…uh…documentary about the traditional craft of making German schnapps. The minister signed a contract with Steinhäger yesterday, and for my part in creating the contract I got a bonus that allowed me to invite you both this evening. Since Steinhäger is paying for our dinner, it seems fitting we order a small bottle. Don't you think?" She glanced coyly at Dietrich.

"If you're brave enough to drink it instead of champagne, I am too." He laughed and cast an obvious let's-see-who-gets-drunk-first glance at Katja.

The stoneware bottle arrived with the dinners and it immediately became obvious to Katja that she herself would be the first one drunk. Even the heavy pork meal was not enough to offset two drinks of the potent gin. Dinner-table conversation had been light banter, about life in the Wehrmacht, life in Berlin, the shortages of sugar and coffee, and the meaning and history of all Dietrich's medals. But by the time they finished eating, Katja found it hard to concentrate or even pronounce some words. Fortunately, the chamber orchestra at the far end of the dining space was playing music, and five or six couples were already on the dance floor in front of them.

"Look, why don't you two lovebirds go dance a bit while I order dessert," Frederica suggested, catching Katja's eye.

Obviously pleased by the suggestion, Dietrich took Katja's hand and led her on slightly unsteady feet to join the other couples.

It was strange to be in his arms again, looking up into his open, slightly freckled face. She felt no desire for him, but had rarely felt it anyhow. His awkwardness dancing was endearing, and in her intoxicated state, she sensed a wave of affection for him. But she no longer felt like his wife. She almost wished he had been born her brother, or that they were already divorced and moved to the category of old friends. She assumed he would want to make love that night, his first night away from the battlefield, and she would allow it the same way she always did, with patience and the desire to please him rather than herself.

What did excite her was the thought that while they danced, at the other end of the room, Frederica, in her stunning dress, was committing treason. For better or for worse, she was connected with Frederica—unto death, perhaps—and all she could think of was how lovely she looked in black satin and décolleté.

The tune ended and they broke apart. Dietrich stood for a moment holding her and looking slightly bleary-eyed into her eyes. "How nice it is to be home, Liebchen. When I'm home for good, we'll come here often, I promise."

"Yes, dear," she said mechanically, and led him back to their table where dessert was already laid out alongside real coffee. Frederica gave the faintest of nods to indicate the drop was done, and, in fact, the service had cleared away the Steinhäger bottle along with the dinner dishes, but Katja was dizzy now from the alcohol and the motion of dancing.

Dietrich sounded disappointed. "No more schnapps?" he asked but was interrupted by the dreaded sound: the deep buzz that rose immediately to a high-pitched oooooooooaaaaah and after a full thirty seconds dropped again to a growl, only to rise again to the high whine of the air-raid siren.

The diners stood up, the regular patrons heading immediately for the air-raid shelter stairs, while the waiters called out, "This way, ladies and gentlemen, this way."

Both of them uncertain on their feet, Dietrich took Katja by the hand and she in turn made sure she had hold of Frederica, so that they moved together with the crowd down the stairs into the hotel cellar.

They entered a long corridor with benches on both sides and, arriving among the last, they sat close to the entrance. Several bombs fell close enough to cause a tremor in the earth and to dislodge plaster from the ceiling. Katja still held the hands of both Dietrich and Frederica, but with every detonation, she squeezed only Frederica's.

"Bastards," someone nearby said. "The Luftwaffe will pay them back for this."

Katja shuddered. A year before it had seemed the Western allies were all defeated, and now they were dropping bombs on Berlin. She wished the bombers would be stopped, shot down if necessary, but she wanted the Nazis to be defeated. The contradiction was enough to drive her mad.

The all-clear sounded and the dinner guests returned to their places. The hotel was untouched and so the insular world of Nazi festivities could continue, at least for a while. If there was damage to the homes and workplaces of any of the diners, they would find out soon enough.

The dinner eaten and the drop apparently successful, Frederica called an end to the evening. "Please thank the Reichsminister and his client for me for a lovely dinner," Dietrich said, taking her hand.

Frederica returned the warm clasp. "I shall be sure to mention that it was spent in part on a soldier of the Wehrmacht. That will please him, I'm sure," she replied diplomatically.

Katja leaned in for a casual kiss of departure, longing to stay inside the fragrant embrace. But she dutifully drew away and followed her husband to the Grünewald Strassenbahn.

The entire line had stopped during the air raid, allowing the passengers to seek cover, but by the time Katja and Dietrich reached the platform, the cars were running again. When they passed two buildings, a residence and an office building, where bombs had struck, Katja could see that firemen were already on the scene and ambulances were carrying away the dead and injured. The smoky air seeped into the Strassenbahn and people covered their noses with handkerchiefs. Some refused to look at the ruins; it was too sharp a reminder that they might be next.

"She's quite nice, your friend Frederica," Dietrich said, slurring his words slightly. Where did you meet her?"

"She was part of the film team, in Nuremberg. Don't you remember?"

"Oh, yes. You're right. I remember the supper now. They were a nice lot, clever, all of them. I like it that my wife has clever friends. Do you see the others too?"

"Not the cameramen. Most of them are on the front now, I think. Frau Riefenstahl is lord knows where, trying to make her movie."

"What about the one who took the picture? Rudi something? The one who sat in the middle?"

Katja hesitated. Should she lie? Was she going to have to lie about everything to him? "He's in Sachsenhausen."

"Good grief. What for?" He seemed genuinely shocked.

"Paragraph 175," Katja said as neutrally as possible.

"A *warmer*?! You know, I sort of suspected that. The fellow he brought with him, I bet he was too. They seemed very chummy. Of course, it's too bad when you find out someone you know is a pervert, but I'm glad the Nazis are cleaning that stuff up. If they can't cure it, they should just get rid of it."

Katja cringed. Another rift had opened between them. Dietrich's view was so far from hers, they had no common ground on which to even discuss it. She put it to the back of her mind, along with the question of how she was going to tell him she loved a woman.

When they were finally in the house in Grünewald in their own room, he had just enough clarity of mind to undress and hang up his uniform. His inebriation was not enough to discourage sex, though it did render the act brief, to Katja's relief. Then he lay on his side and took her in his arms.

"Liebchen, I'm sorry to tell you I'll be away longer this time. Many months, probably."

"Mmmm?"

"We're going farther eastward into Russia. The Führer's ready to attack Moscow, and that could end the war quickly. But it has to be a big effort, and they can't be sending soldiers home every couple of months."

She slid toward him to avoid sleeping on the wet spot.

"But when it's over, we'll go back to Nuremberg and buy the house near my parents that we've always talked about, I promise." His voice was blurred by drowsiness and in a minute he was asleep.

He hadn't seemed to notice that she never replied.

[illegible] I'll be away longer this time. Many months, probably."

Jamain.

[illegible]

[illegible]

Chapter Twenty-two

November 1941

Rudi Lamm was camp-hardened now. At roll call, he had learned how to stand with his eyes cast down, huddled under his camp jacket, and to call out his number smartly and mechanically right after the man before. He knew that when a specific skill was requested—carpentry, shoemaking, horticulture—he should say he had it, even if he didn't, because it usually meant a softer job. He had learned to stand two-thirds of the way down the line waiting for soup, since the first men got only broth, and the last men sometimes got short portions. He had learned to pack newspaper inside his jacket for added warmth at night but to remove it before roll call because it was forbidden.

But most of all, he had learned the value of sex. It must have been his soft gray eyes, his long girlish lashes, his curved lips, because with shorn head and thin wiry torso, certainly nothing else recommended him.

It was in the fourth week of his assignment to the clay pit, when the sadistic Kapo was replaced. The new man was almost as brutal, but had sidled up to Rudi and hinted he wanted some nice boy's mouth on him in the morning, and Rudi agreed immediately. Every day for the next five months Rudi had reported to the Kapo's quarters, a tiny room at the end of the prisoners' barrack. And every morning, after taking the Kapo's fat organ in his mouth, he earned himself an extra ration and a work assignment that would not kill him. After each grotesque act, he thought of Peter and the chasm of difference between the playful, loving sex they'd always had together and his whoring for survival. What else would he do to stay alive?

Word seemed to spread discreetly, of who serviced whom. And so, depending on the rotation of Kapos for his barracks or for the work details, Rudi alternated between being an ordinary brutalized prisoner during the lean months and a kept boy during the good ones. Each time he thought the starvation and labor and abuse would kill him, someone would discover him, and at the cost of nightly sexual debasement, sometimes brutal and sometimes not, he would gradually regain his strength. The irony never escaped him that the "crime" for which he was imprisoned was the only thing keeping him alive.

But his last protector had just been transferred to another camp, and now he stood shivering in the morning dampness, just another pink triangle. At the end of the numerical roll call, each block of men received an assignment. All the assigned detachments fast-marched off the parade ground, leaving some hundred men.

To his astonishment, the camp senior stepped aside and the camp commandant came to the fore. What did it mean? Without moving his head, he glanced sideways, trying to determine what made the remaining men different from those who had been assigned. He could make out no difference, except that none were Jews.

"Men," the commandant began, and Rudi was once again astonished. It was the first time they had been called that rather than "scum" or "assfuckers," so he felt a surge of hope.

"Look around you, men. You're all Germans, citizens of the Reich. You now have a chance to prove your loyalty to the Fatherland and to leave the camp. You can be rehabilitated in a special regiment, the SS Sonderregiment under the command of Sturmbannführer Dirlewanger. This is your opportunity to serve Germany rather than rot here as an enemy of the Volk."

At his signal, two prisoners carried a small table and chair to a spot just behind the commandant and one of the SS guards sat down with a large registry.

"If you sign here today, you can write one postcard to your family explaining your decision to serve in the military for Germany. Then you'll be released for training. Once you've signed, you can't change your mind."

Rudi wasn't sure. It could also be a trap. The camp was so overcrowded, the authorities were always rounding up men for "special" labor detachments that never returned. Rumors then circulated immediately that they had simply been killed, or worked to death in mines or other places invisible to the outside world. Would he be exchanging a slow death sentence for a quick one?

Most of the men stepped forward and signed up, but Rudi remained in place. After some half an hour of reshuffling of men, the volunteers were lined up and marched toward another yard for further instruction.

The Commandant addressed the forty or so men who remained. "No patriotic spirit, eh? Well, then you can work for the Reich in Flossenbürg. Let's see how you like cutting granite for the Führer's monuments."

❖

Standing at the edge of the granite quarry Rudi felt a rush of vertigo and took a step back. He had not expected anything so deep. One entire side descended at a 45-degree angle halfway to the bottom, where it broke off into a sheer vertical wall. Scattered within the pit were blocks of various sizes, and men scrabbled over them like vermin. Guards ringed the edges of the quarry, but there was no need for barbed wire, since it would have taken a man five minutes of hard climbing to get to the top of the pit, during which time he would have been shot ten times over.

Talking was not allowed, but men grunting over their labor caused a constant low buzz punctuated by the tapping of hammers on chisels and chisels on stone.

Rudi was assigned to a crew to load freshly cut blocks onto rollers and haul them with ropes up a single narrow ramp to the surface. He worked silently for two hours, trying to gauge which of the Kapos were the most dangerous. He needn't have troubled himself. His team had just loaded a new block onto the rollers, when an SS man snatched a cap from one of the prisoners. Laughing, he threw it high and it landed midway up the ramp.

"Prisoners are not allowed to remove their caps," the guard said, slamming his truncheon down across the prisoner's shoulders.

Recovering from the blow, the prisoner looked back and forth between the guard and his hat and began to shake. Walking up the ramp counted as an escape attempt, punishable by death. "I…I can't, sir," he whimpered.

"I told you to put on your cap," the guard repeated, striking him again, this time across the face. With a sob of resignation, the prisoner crept up the ramp, as slowly as he could, prolonging life with each second of delay. Then, reaching his hat, he stopped but didn't even bother to put it on his head. He just knelt down, crying, until the rifle shot struck him in the back and he toppled sideways.

Two other prisoners were assigned to drag away the body, and Rudi shut the image out of his mind. He threaded the heavy towing rope between the rollers and around the block and waited for the signal to begin hauling it to the top. Then he worked hammering for the next four hours until he could no longer hear anything but a ringing in his ears. His hands were raw and covered with abrasions from lifting the stone blocks, and he coughed constantly from the stone powder.

Lunch was soup, and half an hour later, he was on his knees hammering again, until he felt a hand sweep across his head, knocking off his cap.

He glanced up to see the same guard, grinning down at him. "Prisoners are not allowed to remove their caps," he said.

Rudi's jaw went slack. A death sentence had just been pronounced on him. He was going to die here, in this granite quarry, and no one would ever know. He didn't even have a god to pray to. It was simply the end.

He looked into the eyes of the guard and saw only sadism and derision, nothing else. He struggled to his feet, feeling both the thudding dread in his chest and the need to urinate. He took a step up the ramp toward his execution.

"Stop shitting around, Volker. Isn't one enough today?" A higher-ranking SS man confronted the tormentor. "Get the hell away from the prisoner and let him do his work," the SS man said. Then to Rudi, "Go get your cap. No one will shoot."

Rudi fetched it, scrambled back to his place, and knelt down to continue hammering blindly, aware only that he had soiled his prison pants.

At the end of the day, he approached the block senior. "If it's possible, could you inform the commandant that I want to join the Sonderregiment?"

Chapter Twenty-three

December 1941

The bright sunlight and the summer-like warmth of the day should have cheered Katja, but it didn't, for the first sight she saw when she stepped off the Strassenbahn was a truck carting away a Jewish family with three huge suitcases. Where were they being taken? The radio announcements said it was simply resettlement in the East, but rumors suggested it was to internment camps.

Katja shook off helplessness and despair, reminding herself that she carried good news. She entered the zoo just before closing time, then hurried immediately to the Lion House. She caught sight of Peter at the end of the corridor emerging from one of the lion cages. With a head toss of sudden cheerfulness, he shut the cage door behind him and motioned her into the storage room with him.

"I'm in the middle of feeding, but no one's around to check on me, so we can visit awhile. Here, sit down." He drew up one of the supply crates.

"I have something for you from Rudi." She handed him the one-line postcard from Sachsenhausen and leaned against him to read it again with him. "I'm being treated well and will be released soon to serve the Fatherland on the Eastern Front."

Peter laid the card against his heart. "Oh, Rudi. Finally some proof you're alive." He kissed Katja on her hair. "And thank God he wrote you instead of his father."

"He must have known the only way to reach you was through me. He doesn't know where you are, but he knows I'd try to reach you."

Peter reread the card and frowned. "What does he mean 'serve the Fatherland'? They're drafting him into the Wehrmacht? Is it a punitive regiment?"

"I asked Frederica, since the propaganda ministry is up on all those things, of course. She said it's a new SS regiment that started as a small group of poachers released to be trained as snipers and anti-partisan troops because they were so good with rifles. By the end of 1940 the SS realized they had a large source of untapped manpower and began to admit concentration-camp prisoners under the command of someone named Dirlewanger. That's all she knew about it."

Peter slumped against the wall, the postcard still in his hand. "At least he's out and has a chance. I hate hiding like this, like some maiden waiting to be rescued. It makes me crazy that I can't actually *do* anything to fight the Nazis."

Katja could think of nothing more to say. The darkening sky in the high window of the storage room drew her attention. "I'm sorry, I can't stay much longer. I have to get to the hospital for the night shift."

He took off his spectacles and rubbed his face, as if to bring life back into it. "That's all right. I've got only one more animal to feed. Come on, on the way out I'll show you how I do it."

He led her back into the corridor and pulled out a ring of keys. "This box up here controls both doors, this one right here, and the partition door to the outside cage.

"Look, the tiger's asleep. I won't have to bother with luring him outside. I'll just slip his bowl into the cage directly."

He turned the key in the slot and Katja heard the sound of gears.

"Are you sure it's—" A low, growling *rhuuuuu* rose quickly to the piercing *uiiiiiii* of the air-raid siren. The tiger sprang to his feet.

Peter spun around. "Damn! That's the second time we've been raided in the middle of feeding time," he shouted over the earsplitting whine. He reached up with one arm and gave the cage key a half turn. "Come on, the basement will do for a shelter. Let me run get a flashlight first. The fuse blew yesterday."

Peter rushed into the storage room and she waited, hoping for the usual three-minute time lag between siren and bombardment.

The shrieking of the siren prevented her from hearing the creak of the cage door behind her, and only when it clanged open against the wall did she turn around.

The Sumatran tiger stood panting, halfway into the corridor. He swung his massive head toward her, his jaw open, and his ribs swelled with each breath like the pulse of a vast, primordial will.

Katja stared, held captive by its empty eyes, and sensed its savagery, implacable and absolute. The tiger rumbled low in its throat and slowly dropped to a crouch, preparing to leap. Something flew past her screaming, and by the time she realized it was Peter waving his flashlight, the bewildered tiger had darted back into his cage. Peter threw himself against the cage door, holding it with his chest while he turned the key in the lockbox overhead, then collapsed panting.

At that moment, a bomb detonated somewhere near the zoo, its concussion deafening. Peter sprang to life again, seized her hand, and pulled her along the corridor through the door of the building. Off to the side of the entryway was a door that he yanked open, and they stumbled down the stairs as a third bomb hit, sending dust into the stairwell.

Peter pulled the door shut and they both dropped onto a bench. For several minutes, no one spoke and Peter directed the beam of light at the floor in front of them.

"Dear God. How could I have done that?" He laid his head in his hands. "You were almost killed, and it would have been my fault. I was so stupid."

Katja exhaled slowly through pursed lips. "I never saw anyone move so fast. You weren't afraid? I was paralyzed."

"I didn't think about it. I was just so furious."

"At what?

"At myself, at the war, at the whole thing. I mean tigers on one side and bombs on the other, and meanwhile, I just hide here, month after month, useless to Rudi and to you."

"Don't agonize over it. It's over, we're both safe now, and you have other things to worry about." She squeezed his hand. "There will be a time for courage, I'm sure. From all of us."

The all-clear sounded and Katja stood up, brushing dust off her clothes. "Listen, I have to go to work now. I'm covering the midnight shift and I have to take two Strassenbahns to get there. If the bombs have hit any of the tracks, I'll have to go by foot."

"Of course. I'll walk with you as far as the corner stop. It's the least I can do."

They strode together, arm in arm, as the fire trucks drove past them. Neither spoke, Katja out of relief and Peter out of shame.

She boarded the Strassenbahn, and although it was crowded as she expected, she did not encounter the sullen lethargy that usually followed a bombing raid. She heard something else, a buzzing, in the air, from all the people who were murmuring to each other. Had the bombs done catastrophic damage finally, and everyone wondered what to do?

She turned to the man standing right next to her, holding to the same pole. "Excuse me, sir. The bombs, did they destroy something big this time?"

"Oh, no, Fräulein. Just the usual damage. But the news came about an hour ago. The Japanese have attacked the Americans at Pearl Harbor."

America in the war? Katja thought. That changed everything.

Chapter Twenty-four

January 1942

Finally it was 18:00 hours. Katja finished marking the last patient's chart and retreated to the changing room. Wearily, she removed her cap and nursing smock. With the scarcity of soap, she tried to postpone washing it as long as possible, so it was a relief to find it had survived the day unstained by blood or urine. She hung the smock on the hook under her nameplate and had just slid one arm into the sleeve of her coat when the senior nurse confronted her.

Grete Rumoldt possessed every virtue of the master race. Tall, blond, the mother of three sons and a daughter, she kept a picture of the Führer on her desk, next to the one of her children. She stood as rigidly as a soldier and delivered work orders in such as way as to forestall reply. Katja grimaced; her arrival did not bode well.

"Sommer. Good that I've caught you. Heide Kram is sick and you've got to take over her shift. There's no one else."

"But I've just done ten hours and I have a sick father to take care of at home." She lied, though the ten hours' part was true. Nurse Rumoldt was not impressed.

"I don't want to hear any whining. Remember our soldiers are out there fighting for the Fatherland right now. They're cold, sleepless, and in danger, and ten hours moping around in a warm place like the Charité would be paradise for them. Report back to the nurses' station immediately." She left without waiting for a reply.

Sullen, Katja exchanged her coat for her calf-length smock and buttoned it up. Other nurses on the floor could have taken the shift, but Rumoldt had instantly disliked her the day she arrived. Katja wasn't sure why, though she supposed it was because she never once said "Heil Hitler," or spoke of the Fatherland, or complained about the Jews. She also seemed to take it personally that Katja, though dutifully married to a man in the Wehrmacht, was still childless, as if she was somehow derelict.

Katja reported as ordered to the nurses' station where Nurse Rumoldt stood recording the day's assignments. She looked up briefly, then slapped a clipboard into Katja's hand. "You'll do the rounds in wards 12, 13, and 14. Dr. von Eicken is in 12 right now with a patient and may need your help, so don't stand there. Go do your job."

Katja marched without protest to ward 12. As reported, Doctor Von Eicken was with a patient at the third bed, so she approached quietly and stood at his side, prepared to carry out any of his directives.

The patient was speaking. "You're sure it's not cancer?"

"Almost certain, Frau Möhringer. It has all the signs of a benign growth, the sort that we treat all the time." The burly, mustached doctor patted her hand. "We'll take care of that in no time and you can go home to your husband."

"My husband's at the front, Herr Doctor," she answered. He's a *Brigadeführer* and they can't spare him, so he comes home only once every two months."

"I'm sorry to hear that, but of course we all have to make our sacrifices for the war." He peered down at Katja through heavy glasses. "Nurse, please take a blood sample from Frau Möhringer so we'll know her blood type for the surgery tomorrow." He clasped the hand of the patient once more in both of his. "All will be well," he said, and left the ward.

Katja echoed the doctor's comfort. "Don't worry, now, Frau Möhringer. You're in the very best of hands. Professor von Eicken is an expert." She swabbed the woman's arm with alcohol and carefully inserted the syringe into the vein in the curve of her elbow.

"Oh, yes. I know. That's why I came to him in the first place. My husband checked into his record. What a surprise to learn that he had operated on the Führer's throat. Obviously, he must be the best in Germany, don't you think?"

Katja concealed her surprise. "I'm sure he must be." She drew the blood and slid the needle out of the vein, then pressed another wad of cotton against the perforation. "You just rest now and let Dr. von Eicken take care of you."

After noting the procedure on the patient's chart, Katja delivered the blood sample to the laboratory and returned to the ward to tend to the remaining five patients. She washed them, changed bandages, administered medication, whatever was scheduled on their charts, and reported back to the nurses' station.

As expected, Nurse Rumoldt was there when Katja handed back her clipboard. "Is it true that Doktor von Eicken operated on the Führer?"

Given the chance to show superior knowledge, Rumoldt nearly smiled and bypassed her usual criticism. "Yes, he did. Back in 1935."

Frau Klotzenberg, the oldest nurse in the wing, nodded. "It was for a lump. You know the fiery way the Führer speaks. It was just his way of reaching the people, but it ruined his vocal cords. Of course he needed to see the best specialist in Germany, but he didn't want to expose his throat to someone he didn't know." Frau Klotzenberg laughed an endearing cackle. "So he sent his adjutant to have his tonsils out." She cackled again. "Imagine that. Sending someone to test the doctor."

"Dr. von Eicken passed muster, of course," Nurse Rumoldt added. "That goes without saying. The next day he was called to the Führer, who was sure he had throat cancer."

"But obviously he didn't."

"Obviously," Frau Rumoldt parroted. "It was just a little polyp, the kind that singers get. Dr. von Eicken did the surgery right there in the Chancellery."

"But you left out the best part." The older nurse was smirking. "About the anesthetic."

"There's nothing to tell. They just gave the Führer too much and it took a long time to wear off."

"You bet it did," Klotzenberg said, snickering. "Twenty-four hours. And midway through that, the SS began to suspect an assassination attempt. But it was just the Führer, sleeping like a baby. You can just imagine the scene when he finally woke up, all those SS men wiping their brows."

Nurse Rumoldt did not appreciate their levity. "You should have more respect. It's no small thing when the Führer must go under an anesthetic. Of course he should have trusted us. A lot of loyal party members work here, even at the highest levels. They are at the very forefront of our new medicine, especially in the fields of Racial Research and Racial Biology. Real pioneers."

"Racial research," Katja said cautiously. "Still very theoretical though, isn't it?"

Nurse Rumoldt didn't like to sense the wind dropping from her sails, even if they were someone else's sails. "Well, if you insist on practical gains, our other doctors have developed an inoculation against malaria from experiments at Dachau, and very clever doctors are doing testing at Auschwitz. This hospital will be very important in the future of Germany, so there will be no more mockery."

Katja was silent. Did they experiment in all the concentration camps? Before Frau Rumoldt could add another anecdote about the Nazi doctors' medical miracles, a fourth nurse arrived at the station.

"Did you hear? Leni Riefenstahl, the actress, has been admitted to the hospital. She's downstairs, just one floor below."

"What happened? What's wrong with her?" Katja asked with a degree of concern that surprised even her.

"Something gastrointestinal. She collapsed while filming yesterday and they admitted her here. Dr. Sauerbruch is treating her."

Nurse Rumoldt glanced back at the work schedule. "Stop chattering, all of you, and finish your rounds."

Postponing any decision-making about Leni Riefenstahl or her status, Katja finished her extra shift. At two in the morning, she collected her coat and, grainy-eyed with fatigue, was about to leave. But something held her.

She descended one flight of stairs and went to the fourth floor nurses' station. The night nurse was tending to someone, but the patients' clipboards hung in a row behind the empty station. It took only a moment to find the chart marked Riefenstahl. There it was, on the end. Her attending physician was Sauerbruch, and she was in room 34.

The corridor was empty but for the janitor who was pushing his wide broom along the polished floor. She waited until he passed her, then hurried down the hall.

Room 34 was a single room, a luxury even in peacetime. Katja pushed open the door soundlessly and stood for a moment in the doorway, letting her eyes adapt to the darkness.

Leni Riefenstahl lay on the bed on her side in the fetal position. She looked small, pathetic. When the light from the corridor shone on her bed, she stirred.

"Nurse," she called out. "The pain's back. Can you give me some more morphine?"

Chagrined at being caught in her voyeurism, Katja approached the bed. "I'm sorry. I'm not the nurse on duty. But I'll tell her. What did the doctor say?"

Riefenstahl's expression wasn't visible in the dull light, but her hesitation revealed puzzlement. "If you're not the night nurse, what are you doing here?"

"I work on the floor above. Don't you remember me?"

Her voice registered impatience. "No, who are you? What do you want?"

"It's me. Katja Sommer. I'm sorry to show up in the middle of the night, but I just got off my shift."

"Ah, so this is where you ended up. I wondered," Riefenstahl said in a voice made tense by pain.

"Yes, I suppose filmmaking wasn't for me."

"Well, it's killing me. Can you get me more morphine?"

"I'll tell the night nurse as soon as I leave. I just wanted to stop by and…I don't know. Comfort you a little, I suppose. I'm sorry if I woke you."

"You didn't. The fire in my guts already did that."

"Did Dr. Sauerbruch tell you what it is?" Katja's eyes had adapted to the darkness and she could see the suffering in Riefenstahl's face. Her hair lay wet and limp around her head.

"He wasn't specific and said if the medication didn't bring me around I should take a couple of weeks' rest in the Alps. But that would play hell with the production schedule."

"Well, at least it will get you away from Berlin and the air raids."

"I don't care about the air raids. I have a job to do. I've managed so far through sheer brute will, but I don't know how much longer I can keep it up."

"You may have to stop driving yourself that way, at least for awhile, and let your body recover," Katja suggested, surprised at her own formulation. "In any case, see what Dr. Sauerbruch—"

"Hello?" the night nurse said quietly, her voice full of suspicion. "Are you supposed to be here?"

Riefenstahl spoke up. "It's all right. She's an old friend who stopped by after her shift." To Katja, "Thank you for your good wishes. I'll struggle through. I always have."

Katja touched her hand with a light tap and turned to leave, nodding at the nurse on duty. Once in the corridor, she felt the irony of the situation. The powerful Leni Riefenstahl, friend of Hitler, curled up like a colicky baby. "The Lord sendeth rain upon the just and the unjust," she muttered, and wondered how Rudi Lamm was doing on the Eastern Front.

Chapter Twenty-five

May 1942

Rudi Lamm kept to the rear of the group as his twenty-man unit clambered out of the troop truck and fast-marched into the Byelorussian village of Kliczów. He wasn't afraid of being shot. The local population had surrendered and been disarmed. But the others in his troop were far more ready to take out their anger on the local people than he was, empowering themselves by brutalizing a population even weaker than they.

The entire regiment had been recruited like himself, from the edges and dredges of society. Poachers, petty criminals, Russians and Ukrainians who hated Stalin more than Hitler. Then political prisoners, homosexuals, gypsies, all given the choice to fight for the Reich or turn to crap in a concentration camp. Where other troops might have felt loyalty to the Reich, his regiment was united only by cynicism and unfocused rage. When patients from the psychiatric hospitals joined the ranks, lunacy was added to the mix.

Desertions had been frequent until an iron hand kept them in place. But the regiment was effective in cleaning out partisan activity behind the lines, not because they were clever but because, uninhibited by a military pride or code of honor, they were ruthless.

The Scharführer had said partisans were active in the woods all around the village. This time they had ambushed four SS men and strung them up by their feet. Each one bore a sign on his chest that spelled out **месть**.

Revenge. An ancient, terrible word, as old as war. And revenge sowed and reaped only more revenge. Though the bodies had been found a kilometer away, the commander had decided that this, the closest village, would bear responsibility.

"You there!" The Scharführer called to him. "Move on up. Any man not doing his duty will be shot." The troop came to what had once been a garden in front of a house. Three men and a woman knelt, surrounded by the first soldiers that had arrived. A few dozen other locals stood in a group under German guard a few-dozen meters away "We've got them," someone said.

Them? Rudi wondered. "How do you know?"

One of the soldiers held up a rifle, an old hunting gun. "We found this on him. The others were with him. Russian scum." He kicked the nearest man.

"Nyet! Nyet!" the other man kept saying, along with a string of supplications.

Rudi translated. "He says he's the schoolmaster. The gun was to protect his wife. Someone was trying to rape her." He turned to his comrade, who was still holding the rifle. "That doesn't mean he had anything to do with the ambush. It's just an old hunting rifle." Rudi argued but already sensed he was too late. All guns had to be surrendered, and keeping one, even worse, threatening someone with it, was enough to seal his fate. Already one of the men was sloshing gasoline from a jerry can onto the wall of the house.

"Shut your face, and let a real man show you what we do to partisans." The brute of the group fired into the teacher's face, killing him instantly. The other two men scrambled to their feet and broke into a run. They had not gone more than two meters when they were shot in the back. Only the woman still lived.

She tried to throw herself over the body of her husband but two soldiers snatched her up by both arms. She thrashed wildly and managed to pull one arm free. Leaning back against the man who still held her, she kicked the other man squarely between the legs and he doubled over, clutching his groin.

"Filthy Russian whore." The soldier who held her struck her on the head and she dropped back down onto the ground. By now the house was ablaze and the soldier with the jerry can had run toward the altercation with the woman. Suddenly the injured man let go of his crotch and seized the can of fuel.

"Fucking whore. Teach you to attack a man like that," he said, and doused her with gasoline. "No clean death for you." He fumbled in his jacket pocket for a lighter.

Most of the men fell back a step, as if in doubt as to whether the Scharführer would stand for it, but he only watched and gave no order to stop.

The brute taunted the woman for a few moments, waving the flame of his cigarette lighter in front of her face. "So, little Russian whore. You're not so brave now, are you? Not so hot to break a man's balls. Too bad it had to end this way. It would have been more fun to fuck you."

He swept the lighter tip across her chest like a knife blade and her entire upper body burst into blue and yellow flames. She gave a single long scream. Without thinking, Rudi rushed toward her, snatched out his sidearm, and shot her through the head.

With open mouth and arms waving reflexively, she dropped like a marionette onto her back. Lying spread-eagle, she continued to burn, giving off a thick, greasy smoke. The crowd of villagers standing nearby broke apart and ran toward the woods, pursued by some of the guards. In the shock of what had just happened, Rudi had barely heard the click of a shutter.

An instant later, the brute turned his rifle toward Rudi. "I'll blow your ass off for that, you little prick."

"No, you won't, Müller." The Scharführer stepped between them, covering the lens of his camera. "Not now, anyhow. You'll set a bad example. We've got a village to clean out."

He waved an arm toward the others. "All right, you know how we do this thing: round up everyone in the square, set up the machine guns, and torch the houses. I don't want anything left moving."

As the troop dispersed to begin flushing civilians out of their houses, the Scharführer came alongside Rudi. "You're way out of line interfering with an execution. I could have you shot for that."

"Soldiers don't burn people to death," Rudi grumbled, but the Scharführer seized him by the shirt.

"Listen, you shitty little faggot. We have our orders to torch these villages and we're going to do it. So if you have any crap ideas about killing them gently, you can just forget about it. You get in my way, and you're a dead man."

CHAPTER TWENTY-SIX

February 2, 1943

For almost two years the Adlon drops continued, as Katja and Frederica had lunches at monthly intervals, sometimes in each other's company, sometimes inviting a friend or colleague so as not to draw attention to themselves as regulars. A few times, Peter joined them as escort, though the lack of formal clothing and correct papers always made him nervous. Always a Steinhäger bottle found its way into the trash and unknown hands collected its contents.

On this day, Katja enjoyed a cheerful lunch with one of the more easy-going nurses she had invited from the Charité. Since drinking a bottle of schnapps was beyond the capabilities of two women, they amended the Steinhäger exchange to a simple drop of a bottle concealed in Katja's purse. At the conclusion of the meal, Katja made the usual powder-room excuse. She rose from the table with purse in hand and made her way through the tables. The ladies' room was fortunately just beyond the door to the kitchen and the wide window through which trays of dirty dishes were slid. Everything seemed to go according to plan, as things had the last twenty times. She could do it in her sleep.

Something wasn't right. The two foreign workers who usually collected the dishes were not at their post. She peered as inconspicuously as possible through the slot into the kitchen. At the far end a cluster of kitchen workers blocked her view, but then the circle opened and she saw two men in dark suits shoving a man through the outside door. An arrest by the Gestapo.

She hurried on to the ladies' room. Inside the stall, she carefully extracted the four pages of text from the Steinhäger bottle and slid them inside her shirt against her skin. Then, breathing slowly to calm her panic, she left the bathroom and deposited the empty bottle in the trash.

❖

A week later, Katja unlocked her front door and entered her father's living room. She had reported the failed drop to Frederica immediately and, as with the loss of the kiosk, they could do nothing until Handel sent new instructions.

Sliding her shoulder bag off her shoulder onto the living-room floor, Katja let herself collapse onto the sofa. There on the corner table, she spotted the *Kriegspost* envelope from Dietrich. Letters were rare from him now since he was so deep into Russia, and while they were never very interesting, each one at least meant he was still alive. She removed her shoes and settled back, tearing open the letter. She saw immediately that it was different. His handwriting was erratic, as if he couldn't control his pencil, and the paper was water-stained. The message was ominous.

Dearest Katja,

I can tell you this now; it is no longer a secret. I am at Stalingrad. This letter will go out with the hospital plane. I just want you to know that I'm well. I wish I could say the same about my feet. These boots are fine for parade, but they're not up to snow and ice and minus-forty-degrees temperature. The Russians don't even wear them, but have some sort of thick felt things. The fighting is hard, from street to street, and truly, the Russians seem to be mad. They run at us, sometimes without rifles, and just pick one up from their fallen comrades. We're sure they attack for fear of being shot from behind by their own officers.

Whatever the reason, we keep killing them, but they keep coming back, like demons, inexhaustible.

But at night it stops. You can look up at the sky and the winter air is so clear that you can see millions of stars. It breaks my heart sometimes. They're so clean, so peaceful, it doesn't seem right they should be shining down on what's happening here. The Russians can see them over on their side too, and maybe they think the same thing. I wish it were all over. Pray for me, darling. That I come back from purgatory to the homeland and to you. I'll open my kitbag and give you a handful of stars.

Katja felt a pang of conscience. Though she had long ago ceased to want intimacy with him, at moments like this she loved him deeply for his innocence. Now he was in Russia, in snow, no doubt, fighting for his life. And all the while, his wife was helping his enemies defeat him. The coded notes she had recently carried told of the uprising in Warsaw and the collapse of the siege of Leningrad, both disastrous events for Germany.

The phone rang and Katja lurched for it. "Sommer," she said.

On the other end of the line, Frederica was brief. They doubted that the Gestapo would even be interested in tapping either of their phones, but the stakes were so high, they had to guard against it by keeping everything banal.

"The opera? That sounds lovely," Katja said, taking up a pencil and scribbling down the information. "Thursday in a week? That's fine. Do you have the tickets? Oh, good."

Katja understood that the SOE had provided another drop location. Apparently another dead drop, though she could not ask about it, of course.

"What opera, if I may ask? *Götterdämmerung*? Oh, that's wonderful. I like Wagner."

She hung up the phone thinking that someone in the opera management had a diabolical sense of humor.

❖

February 18, 1943

The night before the opera drop, Frederica spent long hours summarizing and coding the new pages of Joseph Goebbels' ramblings. The minister of propaganda exuded a constant flow of self-congratulation mixed with self-pity, like mucous seeping from an ulcer, but a portion of it was of vital interest to the Allies, and that was now in Frederica's pocket.

Katja had been able to read most of the summary before Frederica coded it, of the American bombing of the naval base in Wilhelmshaven, of the new conscription law for both men and women, and of the ominous loss of the airfield at Stalingrad.

And always it was a wrenching of both heart and mind. Every military failure was another blow to the Nazi state, yet it was her own country that was battered, her own people who were dying.

Most portentous of all was the news of the airfield lost to the Red Army. If Goering's Luftwaffe could not land with supplies for the battle-ravaged city, the Wehrmacht could not continue fighting. And it was winter. Katja tried to force away the thought of Dietrich in his marching boots.

Katja took Frederica's arm and they walked together up the stairs to the opera house on Unter den Linden. Setting aside her anxieties for a moment, Katja had to admire the splendor of the old building. Though it had been bombed and set ablaze in April of 1941, it had been so important to Berlin life that it was rebuilt within a year. In a world in tumult, the classical colonnade and Greek-Revival sculpted pediment acted as a sort of reassurance of cultural permanence, no matter what happened to the state.

But inside the ornate atrium, the war was real again. The women wore gowns, as always, but the majority of men streaming into the auditorium were in uniform. Intent upon the task at hand, Frederica seemed unaffected, by the elegance or by the danger, as the stream of people drew them up the carpeted stairs.

They halted at the cloakroom on the upper floor that held the loges and the seats where the officers sat. Frederica threaded her green silk scarf through a buttonhole of her treasonously laden winter coat, then surrendered it with an indifferent smile to the attendant. Was the cloakroom assistant Handel's agent? Or was it the person handing out wooden chips with numbers? Or neither one? Would some third person enter the cloakroom during the opera? Katja handed over her own coat, barely hearing the noise of the crowd for all the questions buzzing in her head.

Finally they were settled in their seats and Katja glanced toward the orchestra pit. She could not see her father from where they sat, but knew from experience that he was in the string section and waited for the conductor's arrival.

Finally the opera began, and the first ominous chords of Götterdämmerung sounded, the rich interweaving of leitmotivs that harkened back to a tragic-heroic history and at the same time foreshadowed the coming apocalypse.

Katja had grown up with Wagner. Grainy recordings had familiarized her in early childhood with the melodies. Though she knew the complex and slightly absurd tale, it was the music that washed over her, the oceanic ebb and flow that rose to stormy crescendos that allowed her to forget why they had come. But the powerful chords of the Death of Siegfried and the sight of him carried on the shoulders of his men brought a sharp reminder of Dietrich, and as her eyes filled, she wondered if he was still alive in Stalingrad.

The whole opera hit painfully close to home, for it was clear what had brought the downfall of Valhalla. Arrogance, greed, and a soul-killing will to power. During the final chords, as the great fortress of the gods thundered to collapse, she was numb with sorrow.

Frederica, apparently, was not. Even while the applause continued, she tugged on Katja's arm. "Come on, let's go. Either it's done or not. I can't bear to stay another minute."

Katja followed her up the aisle of the arena into the atrium and up the stairs against the flow of traffic. Dozens of people stood ahead of them, and the coat-check women were already handing over fur wraps and leather greatcoats.

Frederica dropped both of their chips into an attendant's hand, and Katja's coat appeared immediately on the counter. She pulled it toward her and slid her arms into the sleeves, anxious to be done.

But Frederica waited. The attendant disappeared again among the coat racks and it seemed an eternity before she returned. Without a coat. "I'm sorry, Fräulein. There's no coat on hook A26. There must be a mistake."

Katja felt panic rising and sensed Frederica stiffen next to her.

"That can't be," Frederica said calmly, though her darting eyes hinted at an urge to flee. Had the Gestapo confiscated it? Katja looked around for the hand that might fall at any moment on her shoulder.

In fact, a bulky man in a pinstriped suit strode toward them, Frederica's criminal coat draped over his arm. Katja tensed, ready to bolt. The buzz of the concert crowd faded behind the painful pounding of her heart. They were caught.

The man passed them and held out the coat to the attendant. "Excuse me, Fräulein," he said. "This is not my wife's coat. I'm sorry. I was distracted by the news from the front, and I picked up the wrong one."

Frederica reached for it before the attendant could react. "Actually, it's mine. Thank you for bringing it back." She drew it on quickly, and her barely perceptible nod of satisfaction told Katja that the package was gone from the pocket.

The gentleman identified the correct coat for his wife and then started away, mumbling, "Terrible, terrible news."

On an impulse, Katja caught up with him. "Excuse me, sir. The 'news from the front' you're talking about, what is it?"

"You haven't heard? Oh, I suppose not, if you were in the concert hall. My son just heard on the radio before coming to meet me here. Stalingrad has fallen."

❖

Fallen. That terrible ambiguous word that really meant killed. But surely an entire army would not be slaughtered before surrendering. Some men must have been taken prisoner. Some men, surely, had been carried out.

Each day she waited for another letter, saying Dietrich had come out in the last transport of wounded, or that his regiment had broken out before the others fell. But no letter came, and after two weeks, she learned to live with near-certainty. He was gone from her life, and she slowly absorbed the new reality as she worked, both for and against Germany.

The late-winter snow falling gave a yellowish tint to the evening light while Katja crossed the street to the familiar building. She stomped loose snow from her shoes and let herself in. The hall and stairs were still ice-cold, but when Frederica opened the apartment door, a fragrant warmth enveloped her.

"Come in." She slid her arm under Katja's and guided her to the sofa. "The Reichsminister is just about to talk."

The little *Volksradio* on the table by the sofa was tuned to the national broadcast. Katja listened to the announcer describing the packed Sportspalast while Frederica went to make some ersatz coffee. In a few moments she was back with two cups of a drink that, with enough sugar, reminded vaguely of real coffee.

Frederica sat down close to her and, as always, spoke in a voice lower in volume than the broadcast, so that Katja had to look at her to catch every word. They had fallen into the habit in the years they had talked about dangerous things, and now it was particularly soothing. "He's going to talk about Stalingrad, of course. He has to, and so do I. I want you to know I'm sorry, I'm so very sorry about Dietrich. He was a good, kind man, and he loved you. I liked him for that, that he loved you, and I respected your marriage."

Katja drew up her knees. "I think, at the end, you respected it more than I did. I found it harder and harder to be a wife. If he had come back, I would have told him it was over. It was a mistake from the beginning."

Frederica took her hand. "Why did you marry so suddenly anyhow? I remember you saying you were not in a hurry, but then one day you just did it."

Katja winced at the realization. "It was because of you."

"Me? I was the last person who would have wanted you to marry. I was half in love with you myself, even back then."

"I didn't know that. I only know that you were strangely close with Goebbels, and one day I saw him put his hands on you in a way that made me assume you were his newest lover. I had no claim on you anyhow. How could I possibly? The limping goat had won, and to spare myself humiliation, I ran away."

Frederica pressed Katja's palm against her own cheek. "Oh, my dear. That was the beginning of my assignment for the SOE, and it was critical that I become one of his favorites. That's what you saw, I suppose. But I loathe his touch. I feel soiled by him every time he lays a hand on me."

"So then you did…?" Katja could not bring herself to finish the question.

"Sleep with him? Would you care for me less if I did? Or wouldn't it be the same as all the times you slept with Dietrich?"

Katja grappled with both questions. "No, of course I wouldn't love you less, but it wouldn't be the same as Dietrich. Goebbels is a monster."

Frederica's silence was damning. "So you did sleep with him," Katja said quietly.

"Did you think I would have been able to sustain his interest for so many years without doing that? That he would have trusted me with his personal diaries if he had not thought I belonged to him?"

Another long silence, while Katja absorbed the sobering truth. "Does he still…?"

"No. Fortunately, at the moment, he has a new paramour and I'm just another passing fancy at the office. But he trusts me now, and that was always the important thing. That was my sacrifice, to allow that revolting little man to pollute me so I could help defeat him and his whole program."

Just then, massive applause crackled through the tiny radio speaker, and Frederica fell silent. The minister began.

I speak with holy seriousness, as the hour demands. The German Volk knows the gravity of the situation, but the heroic sacrifices of our soldiers in Stalingrad have not been in vain. The storm raging against our venerable continent from the steppes this winter overshadows all previous human and historical experience. The German army and its allies are the only defense.

"'Holy seriousness.' 'Heroic sacrifices.' 'Raging storms from the steppes.' He's really chewing up the scenery, isn't he?" Katja muttered.

"He'd better be. This will probably be the most important speech of his career. Germany has lost an entire army to an enemy that never attacked us. He's got to come up with a story that will make it all sound reasonable, even virtuous. Don't put it past him."

More applause hissed from the radio and Goebbels continued.

We underestimated the scale of the Soviet Union's war potential. This is a threat to the Reich and to the European continent that casts all previous dangers into the shadows. Two thousand years of Western civilization are in danger. If the Wehrmacht does not break the danger from the East, the Reich and then all of Europe will fall to Bolshevism. And the goal of Bolshevism is Jewish world revolution, an international, Bolshevist-concealed capitalist tyranny. This would mean the liquidation of our entire intelligentsia and the descent of our workers into slavery. The storm from the East that breaks against our battle lines threatens the existence of all of Europe. Behind the oncoming Soviet divisions we see the Jewish liquidation commandos, and behind them terror.

Katja sneered. "There you have it. Threat to civilization. Jewish world revolution against Europe, descent into slavery and terror. Listen to the audience cheering him on. They've swallowed the whole story."

"I told you he's good. A gram of truth and a kilo of lies. The revolution did bring chaos to Russia, and Stalin does seem to be indifferent to the starvation of even his own people. But the International Jewry stuff is where he's spinning pure fantasy. His darkest dreams."

Katja grimaced. "Do we have to listen to it? It's making me sick."

Frederica nodded woefully. "I'm sorry. He'll ask me about it tomorrow, and expect me to tell him where he was most eloquent. I have to prepare my answers."

The shrill voice in the radio buzzed on, and Katja stood up to separate herself from the noise. But even as she stared out the window into the falling snow, she could not block his words.

> *The tragic battle of Stalingrad is a symbol of heroic, manly resistance to the revolt of the steppes. The German nation is fighting for their holiest possessions: families, women and children, the beautiful and untouched countryside, their cities and villages, their two-thousand-year-old culture. Terrorist Jewry had 200 million people to serve it in Russia. Women and children in armaments factories and in the war itself. We have to respond with similar measures and use all our resources. Total war is the demand of the hour. The German people are shedding their precious national blood in this battle, but the future of Europe hangs on our success in the East.*

A roar of agreement rose from the audience in the Sportspalast. She could hear the beginning of chanting.

Katja winced. "Listen to them. They're in a frenzy. Are Germans so easily driven mad?"

"Maybe. But in this case, he's also got a select audience. It's all staged. You'll see."

> *German comrades. In front of me are rows of wounded German soldiers from the Eastern Front, who've lost legs and arms, or their sight. Some wear the Knight's Cross. Behind them are workers from the tank factories. Soldiers, doctors, scientists, artists, engineers and architects, teach-*

ers, office workers, people from every area of our intellectual life. I see thousands of German women. The youth is here, as are the aged. Every class, age, and occupation. Before me is gathered the German population, from the homeland and the front. Here is the entire nation.

The mass of people packing the hall roared its approval. Then his questions began.

Do you believe in the final victory of the German people?

The crowd sent back a hurricane of affirmation and wordless cheering.

Katja still stood before the window, her arms across her chest. "Lies. It's all lies. And Dietrich died for them."

Frederica joined her. "Hans Gottschalk died for them too. I just heard. On the *Bismarck*." She stared off into the distance. "And millions of British and French and Russian soldiers did too." She slid her arms slowly around Katja's waist.

Will you follow the Führer, accept the burdens, and work twelve hours a day?

Katja leaned back into the embrace. "Please don't leave me. You're all I have that's untainted by this."

Frederica brushed her lips over short brown hair. "We're all tainted, my darling. But, no, I'll never leave you, I promise."

Katja turned around in Frederica's arms and laid her head on her shoulder. As the warmth between them grew to arousal, the shouting on the radio grew more intense. Frederica covered Katja's mouth with hers, insistent, more urgent than party melodrama. The minister's exhortations, so avidly followed by the Nazi neighbors and millions of war-weary Germans, faded away. Katja could think only of Frederica's hands, holding her tight, of her breasts that pressed against her own.

She opened to the sudden kiss and gave it back, luxuriously and long, wordless release of the yearning she'd harbored so many years. She stepped back, wet-lipped and panting, gazing in joy, disbelief, and gratitude into gray-green eyes. "Frederica..." was all she could utter. No other word was as rich. Frederica drew her toward the dark bedroom.

Do you take a holy oath to the front line that the homeland stands behind them and approve the severest measures against those who harm the war effort?

The shrill voice called after them from the other room, high-pitched and tinny.

Frederica drew off Katja's sweater and then her own. "I've waited so long, so long," she whispered, pressing ardent lips on her brows, her eyes, her cheek and ear. "A thousand times I've imagined leading you here to my bed, pressing you down just like this, feeling the shape of your body that I've always only seen."

Wordlessly, Katja pulled her close and held her motionless, feeling each exhalation warm against her throat.

Is your faith in the Führer absolute?

The radio voice buzzed on, like a rodent gnawing behind a wall, while Katja marveled at the thrill of Frederica's body, not a weight on her but another part of herself. "How can you still want me after all these years?"

Frederica slid her knee between Katja's willing thighs. "I've wanted you since I saw you filming that day in Nuremberg. The entire stadium was silent, watching that monster march across the field, but I saw only you, up on your platform. I had lewd thoughts of you even then."

"I've thought about you too since Nuremberg." Katja squirmed deliciously, feeling the sudden moisture of her arousal. "I tried to imagine you when my husband touched me, but he was so clumsy and I knew you'd never be." She slid her tongue quickly along Frederica's open lips. "And it never, ever, felt like this," she breathed.

I ask you, do you want total war? A war more radical than anything we can yet imagine?

The radio in the other room broadcast a tumult of "Heil!" and "Führer command!" over and over again, but they were like bursts of rain on the window.

Frederica bit softly. "I've had you so many times in my imagination. I know how you feel and taste. I've learned you, centimeter by centimeter." With each word Frederica slid downward to brush her lips over Katja's throat and chest, and the softness of each breast, as delicately as if she kissed a bird. Then, reaching the tip, she traced a circle around it with her tongue.

A shock went through Katja and she moaned and squeezed tangles of Frederica's hair, inhaling the earthy fragrance. "Oh," she murmured back, "so this is what ecstasy is like."

"No, this isn't ecstasy, my love. Not yet. I'll teach you ecstasy." Frederica's hand slipped down along her belly and over her pubis, her fingers meeting the slick groove at the center. She stroked gently, patiently, letting the warm flesh swell to receive her. When she felt the tiny hood grow rigid under her fingertips, she slid them inside.

"Witch," Katja breathed into Frederica's hair.

Frederica chuckled softly. "Witch? Oh, yes. And here's the cauldron," she teased, beginning her gentle thrusts. Unhurried, she penetrated and withdrew, and penetrated again, with soft bites on Katja's breasts and throat. Skillfully, tauntingly, she turned the coil of desire ever tighter and brighter.

A command reverberated from the distant radio like the buzzing of a fly.

Now, Volk, rise up, and storm break loose!

Katja's soft moans dissolved to breathlessness, until the burst of incandescence and her cry of consummation.

In living rooms all over Germany, people prepared to submit to Total War. Only in Frederica Brandt's tiny apartment in the Richterstrasse was it a night of liberation.

PART THREE

JANUARY 1944

BERLIN, GERMANY

Chapter Twenty-seven

When the bomb struck, Katja was thrown to the floor, along with the patient she was guiding. The windowpane shattered at the end of the corridor, sending a spray of glass shards several meters into the hospital.

"Are you all right?" she asked the patient. Though he was ambulatory, he was blind and recovering from concussion and deep cuts to the scalp.

"Crap." He pressed his hands to his bandaged forehead. "Dizzy, head hurts." He slid sideways and leaned against the corridor wall.

"Stay down," she said, scrambling toward him to examine his bandages. "No sign of bleeding. Just stay quiet until the raid is over and we'll get you back in bed."

"Shit, shit, shit. Head hurts so bad." He moaned.

"What did they hit?" someone asked.

Peering outside from the corner of a shattered window, one of the orderlies said, "It looks like the lecture hall, but there's so much smoke, I can't tell." He crept farther back along the corridor away from the broken glass and leaned against the wall with the others.

"Now the bastards are bombing the wounded," someone said.

It *was* an outrage. The roofs of all the buildings were painted with huge white crosses, identifying them as a hospital. They had no air-raid shelters, since it would have been impossible to evacuate the sick and the wounded into any one safe place.

"God damn them all," the patient snarled. "The filthy Brits and the filthy Ruskies and the filthy Nazis." Katja and the other nurses recoiled from the treasonous talk.

"It's the RAF," one of the other nurses said, attempting to divert the anger toward the appropriate object. "It's always the RAF. The *Amis* only come at night, and the Ruskies can't fly this far yet."

"Shit on all of them," the patient muttered, still holding his face. "I don't care any more. The bastards on the other side shot me and I came home and got patched up, and the bastards over here sent me back where the bastards over there shot me again. The bastards over here fixed *that* and sent me back a third time, so the bastards over there blinded me. Now I don't give a damn."

"Be careful, soldier," one of the orderlies said. "People can hear you. This is total war, and it's a crime now to talk like that."

"Shit bags. They're all shit bags, the Nazis too, and the shittiest shit bag is the ugly little dwarf who got everyone to agree to this shit bag of a 'total war.'"

"Shhhh." Katja tried to silence him. "It's the injury talking, not you. I know you're a good soldier, a good German. Just be quiet and let us take care of you."

He wrenched his arm out of her grasp. "Oh, yeah, take care of me. Like this Nazi hospital took care of my cousin Manfred? So he was slow, so he couldn't learn. He was a sweet kid and never hurt no one. But you know what they did? *Gnadentod*, they called it. A mercy death. A goddam *murder*, it was. What a shitty thing to do to a kid who trusted everyone."

"Please, you've got to be quiet. You can't say these things." Katja was the only one talking. The other nurses and patients crouching on the floor were speechless.

"You think I'm wrong?" He moved his bandaged head back and forth as if addressing a wide audience. "I recognize your voice. I heard you say you lost a husband last year. That doesn't make you mad? What did he die for? For crap. For a big shit-stinking lie."

"He died at Stalingrad fighting for Germany," she said softly.

"For Germany? What was Germany doing in Stalingrad? Russia never attacked us. It was a battle we didn't have to fight. You know I'm right. I can tell it in your voice."

"There's nothing in my voice but exhaustion, and that's what you're feeling too. Because it's taking so much longer than we all thought. You're discouraged. We're all discouraged."

The noise of the raid tapered off and finally the all-clear sounded. "There's no place for people like you in this hospital." Katja glanced over her shoulder at Nurse Rumoldt, at the full height of her patriotism. "Wounded or not, you're talking like a traitor."

"Let him go back to his bed," Katja said. "Tomorrow he won't even remember saying it."

"And you, you're just as bad, humoring him." The nurse looked contemptuously down at Katja, who still squatted next to the patient. "This is total war. You know the laws. You're not going to undermine the morale of the nation when those swine are bombarding all of us. It's a capital crime."

"He's got a brain injury. He's out of his head and doesn't know what he's saying."

"But he's still saying it, and other wounded men can hear him. And you, you're worse than him. I heard you agreeing with him. 'Discouraged,' eh? That's treason, plain and simple." She stamped away back to the nurses' station farther down the corridor.

"Don't mind her," another nurse said. "The air raids are just making her edgy and she gets that way sometimes. Nothing will come of it."

"They're making us *all* edgy. Here, help me get him back into his room."

An orderly stepped in, grasped the patient under his arms, and hauled him to his feet.

"I'm all right. I can walk by myself," the patient grumbled. "Someone just guide me, okay? The one with the nice voice."

"I guess that's me," Katja said, leading him by the arm back into his room. "You're lucky. No broken window here. Come on, you'd better get back into bed and learn to keep your mouth shut."

"I don't care any more. My parents were killed by bombs. My brother fell in Russia. I was a farmer, but how am I going to farm blind? What woman's going to marry me? I'm finished, and I don't give a shit about their 'total war' against Bolshevism."

"Finished is right. Undermining the war effort is a crime against Germany."

Katja glanced toward the door from where the accusation had just come. Two nondescript men in dark suits. The taller one came forward and took hold of the patient's arm. "Put your pants on, traitor. You're going to continue your 'treatment' with us."

"You can't do that. He's my patient. He's got a right to stay here."

"He's got no rights at all. And neither do you. You're under arrest."

❖

February 1944

The arrest, perfunctory hearing by the SS, incarceration in Moabit prison, then a day in a boxcar all happened so fast, Katja felt she had fallen from a cliff. Did her father know her whereabouts? Did Frederica? Where was she, in fact?

The boxcar door slid open and she looked out toward rows and rows of huts, surrounded by barbed-wired fencing and surmounted by guard towers. A concentration camp. Directly below the rail embankment was a stream, with a thin lace of ice along its edges from the winter cold. She stood, bewildered, in the prison clothing issued to her at Moabit.

"Alles raus! Schnell!" Guards came toward them with dogs, and the women clambered out of the boxcar onto the ground. Katja could see how long the train was now, some twelve cars, all loaded with women. The guards tried to line them up but, mad with thirst, the majority simply scrambled down the embankment toward the stream. The guards let them drink and then herded them back into a column and marched them forward.

Cramped from sitting in one spot for so long, but anxious to be indoors once again, Katja let herself be pulled along toward the camp entrance. Her feet were cold, but she was better off than most of the arriving prisoners. Some of them staggered and fell, obviously having been in the freight cars far longer than she had.

The sign over the entrance said RAVENSBRÜCK.

Just beyond the entrance, the column divided into two lines, both filing through a small building with a counter. Upon reaching the counter, each prisoner had to surrender her coat and any jewelry. As Katja edged closer, she could see some of the women crying as they gave up their wedding rings. Katja had no valuable jewelry, and she already wore prison clothing, but when she had to surrender the jacket the bitter afternoon air struck her like an ice bath. She hugged her arms to her chest as she passed on to the one of the four barbers. More women began weeping as they lost their hair, but Katja endured the scissors stoically. Within a few moments, her hair was shorn, and the exposure of her scalp to the cold air made her shiver.

But she saw immediately that it would get worse, as they were again prodded into columns and into a courtyard where they were stripped of the rest of their clothes. A guard counted them off into groups of fifty and sent them into a shower room where cold water that smelled of disinfectant sluiced over them.

The shower room served as the actual entry into the camp, for some forty meters away from the exit, women were handing out prison clothing—underwear, a dress, and a coat—to the naked arrivals. The dress and coat were a set, and each set bore a number on the left shoulder. Katja drew hers on as quickly as possible, noting that her number was 112,013. Laid out on the ground were hundreds of pairs of wooden shoes, and she slid her bare feet into the ones closest to her size.

The line wound past a final table where each prisoner received a triangle of fabric designating the category of "crime" in each case. Everyone around her had a red triangle, so evidently the transport that brought them consisted largely of political prisoners

Exhausted and trembling with cold, she was finally assigned to a barrack along with a dozen or so others. The new arrivals clustered at one end of the block, while the block senior walked along the center aisle of the barrack and read the names already posted on the sides. Wherever there was space, she assigned a new prisoner.

The "beds" consisted of three levels of wooden platforms with thin straw mattresses. Judging by their width, she guessed they had been designed for two prisoners to sleep side by side, but the row of numbers tacked to the posts at the head of each one suggested they contained more.

"You." The block senior pointed with her baton toward Katja. "You take this one."

Katja obeyed, noting that it was at least a middle platform. She climbed up onto it and asked. "Do I get a blanket?"

"No more blankets," the block senior said indifferently. "Everyone shares," she added ominously. Katja could not imagine anyone willingly relinquishing half a blanket in a place like this. Would she be able to sleep uncovered in the ice-cold barracks?

The earsplitting sound of a buzzer broke her brief reverie. "Roll call is over," the block senior said. "Stand by your bunk when the others return, otherwise you'll sleep on the floor."

Katja hurried to obey, amazed and ashamed at how quickly she had learned subservience. But the deprivations of the boxcars—no blankets, no food or water, and a bucket for bodily needs—had shown her how bad things could become. She would *not* relinquish a space on one of the bunks.

In just a few minutes, the block was filled with women, dirty from work, faces drawn from exhaustion. They lined up shoulder to shoulder in front of their respective bunks, and Katja found herself standing next to the women with whom she would soon sleep. She eyed them sideways as the block senior announced the additions. Talking was forbidden as the evening soup and bread slice were distributed, but the moment the meal was finished and the block senior was gone, eighty women began to talk at once.

The woman to Katja's right looked at her venomously. "Where's your blanket?"

"I wasn't issued one. They said they don't have any more."

"Well, shit. You're not getting any of mine."

"You don't *have* a blanket," the woman on her left said. " We're all sleeping under mine, so you can just move your ass over a little." She turned to Katja and held out her hand, "Cecily Lefort. This here is Violette Szabo and Denise Bloch, and Miss Generosity over there is Bertha something or other."

Katja nodded at each name, then replied, "Katja Sommer." She looked down at her empty bowl and added. "Is this all you get for supper here?"

"It's all you get at all. Some filthy hot water in the morning, but that's it until after the fourth roll call."

Cecily climbed up onto the middle of three bunks and took her place at the far left. Violette and Bertha clambered in after her, and Katja pressed herself into the space remaining on the far right. Denise slept in the middle row of the platform across the way.

"How do they expect us to work if they starve us to death?" Katja asked. "Even slaves have to eat."

Cecily rose up on her elbow and spoke across the two bodies between them. "Because we're lower than slaves. We're disposable labor. The camp hires us out to factories and businesses for profit. Fortunately for them, there's lots of us, and more coming every day. So, they work us to death and replace the dead with fresh workers. It's a perfect wartime business model."

"Tell her about the *Jugendlager* and the crematorium," Violette said.

"The Jugendlager is where they take you to die," Cicely explained. "They say it's a recovery camp, but no one ever recovers. Their dresses come back the next day for reissue with new numbers."

"Thus the crematorium," Violette added coldly.

"They never reuse the numbers?" Katja asked.

"No. It's their way of keeping a record of the arrivals and 'departures,'" Denise said from the other side of the aisle. "They just keep adding higher numbers. Low numbers show you've been here for a while. For whatever reason."

There was a certain logic, Katja agreed, then noticed that Cecily's dress number was 111,222, while Violette and Denise had higher but almost identical numbers ending with 98 and 99. The two must have arrived later, but together.

Just then the lights went off and the block senior's voice called out. "No more talking! If I hear anyone making noise, they'll sleep outside."

Katja stared bleakly into the darkness. She tried to comfort herself with the knowledge that at least Frederica was safe, but the physical stress of where she lay was too great. She began to shiver and tried to huddle close under the blanket that was now covering four women, but Bertha shoved her away.

❖

February 1944

At four in the morning the sky was still dark, but the *Lagerstrasse* that ran down the center of the camp was lit by fiercely bright lights atop high poles. The women lined up ten by ten to make up units of one hundred. Katja had no way to gauge the total number in the roll call, but had the impression it was several thousand. For the briefest moment, she had a memory of uniformed men standing in similar blocks on a wide field, patriotic, waiting for command.

The thin and rather oily prison coat Katja had been issued was wholly inadequate for the winter air, and when the second roll call to assignments began she was shivering violently. Finally, as dawn broke, she heard her number follow those of her barrack-mates for the wood-collection detail.

The gates of the camp swung open and they began the half-kilometer march to the woods. Katja went with a forward detachment of twenty women to cut the wood while the second team of six came after them pushing a cart along rails. One Kapo and one female SS guard oversaw the work, and although talking was not allowed, amidst the sound of sawing and cutting, Katja noticed that the women exchanged quiet remarks.

The Kapo seemed intent on proving to the SS woman that she had control over the other prisoners, and she prodded and shouted at them as they worked, though it did not change the pace of collection in any way. When the cart arrived, Katja began to drop bundles of the cut wood into it, keeping her eyes lowered to avoid attracting attention. "How are you doing?" a voice next to her whispered.

"Oh, Cecily, it's you." She glanced toward the Kapo, who seemed indifferent. "I'm all right."

"Save your strength," Cecily murmured. "We'll be doing this for twelve hours, and you don't want to collapse and be sent to the medical barracks. You don't want to be anywhere near the doctors."

"Why?" Katja asked under her breath, hefting another bundle of kindling into the cart.

Cecily glanced around and saw that the Kapo was out of earshot. "Experiments. Two women from our barracks went in with small saw wounds on their hands, and the doctors sewed something inside to start an infection so they could try out some new medicines."

Nurse Rumoldt's boast about the medical testing by Charité doctors shot through her mind. "So what happened? Did the wounds heal?"

"No." Cecily changed the subject. "Why were you arrested?"

"Undermining the war effort. I listened to a patient raving about losing on the Eastern Front. I worked at the Charité as a nurse."

"Oh, good. You'll be helpful in the barracks so we don't have to go to the doctors."

Katja couldn't imagine how she could be. Without medicines or soap or bandages, she was the same as every other prisoner. All she could do was name the things they were sick and dying from. She knelt to tie up a bundle where it was harder to be overheard. "What about you? I hear your English accent."

"I'm Anglo-French, actually. I was caught in France, and Denise and Violette a few weeks later. For sabotage."

"All of you sent over from England? How brave you are. Every little bit helps."

Cecily shrugged laconically. "Only until you're arrested. But we all managed a few jobs before they caught us."

"Did they try to coerce you to tell more?"

"They already knew about the SOE. They tortured us in the beginning for more names, but we all kept strong, and finally they left us alone. I guess it was enough that they had our radios and our transmission codes."

SOE? Frederica's organization. Katja was stunned. Then she remembered the names. These were the agents Frederica had talked about. She longed to confide in them that the woman she loved was one of their own. They might even know her by her code name, Caesar. But it seemed a betrayal of Frederica, a needless and highly dangerous one. Many ears were listening, of people who would gladly provide information to the camp commandant for as little as a full meal or a blanket. And if it were known that she had SOE connections, she would certainly be tortured. She was not at all sure she could "keep strong."

The Kapo began to stroll toward them and so they fell silent and set to hacking their tree branches into kindling.

Chapter Twenty-eight

The air raids over Berlin intensified as the British Mosquitoes gradually gave way to the heavier bombers of Britain and the United States. But for all that, Peter ceased to take shelter under the Lion House, partly out of sympathy for the big cats, terrified by the tumult. In the midst of the hellish cacophony, he stayed with them, in front of their cages, trying to soothe them. But he also hated cowering in the cellar. It seemed just an exaggeration of the abject hiding he did every day, and it sickened him.

The bombers usually came in the evening, just before sunset, using the last of the daylight to spot targets. But one day they came an hour early. Peter ran to comfort his cats.

"It's all right, Sultan," he said to the male Sumatran. "I know how it feels to be caged and helpless while they're doing this. But this is what happens when men become savage beasts. They don't just kill one another, face to face. They destroy each other's cities."

There was a deafening crash as a bomb hit close by. Peter hit the floor and covered his head. A second explosion sounded, slightly less loud, perhaps in the next street. He stayed on the floor through the rest of the raid, hearing other detonations farther away and finally nothing. Then the all-clear sounded.

The Lion House was unharmed and the cages intact, and when he ventured outside, he saw immediately the cause of the ear-splitting noise. The zoo canteen had been struck.

The commercial building across the street was burning as well, and fire trucks and ambulances were just pulling up there. The empty canteen was for the moment ignored, so he jogged toward the twisted steel and stone wondering if he could retrieve any food.

The bomb had struck one side of the building, reducing it to rubble, while on the other side, which still stood, a gas line had been broken and a fire raged, fueled by the cooking gas and shattered wooden tables. He could see the copper pipe jutting from the side of a pit, with a long blue flame projecting from the end of it.

He stepped carefully among the rubble, looking for anything to carry away, then felt something soft under his foot. He recoiled when he saw the arm of a half-naked woman. It was one of the cooks, the one who often gave him food. He couldn't remember her name. The angle of her head suggested a broken neck; in any case, it was clear she was dead. But what was she doing bare-breasted in the canteen?

Peter searched farther among the rubble and found the answer. A Wehrmacht soldier lay crumpled, his skull crushed. It looked like one of the soldiers from the nearby flak tower had sneaked off for a quick one with his girlfriend. The impact had thrown him sideways, where a section of ceiling had fallen on him. The concrete must have crushed him immediately, before he could even button up his trousers.

Peter made a sudden decision. It took all his strength to lift the block of concrete, but he finally managed to free the body. Quickly, he yanked off the boots, then stripped the tunic, regulation shirt, and trousers from the dead man. At the last moment he recalled the metal identity tag and snatched it from the man's neck. Then he dragged the cadaver toward the flaming copper pipe and tipped it facedown into the pit where the fire still crackled.

He gathered up tunic and cap along with the other clothes, and with his arms full, he fled the rubble, just as the emergency service arrived from the other direction.

Peter was confident that after the heavy bombing, the police would not try to identify the charred flesh of the man in the burning rubble. Most likely, he would join the hundreds of bodies laid out in various city gymnasiums waiting to be identified. The soldier would be listed as missing from duty from his regiment, but nothing would connect him with the naked cadaver or with Peter, the all-but-invisible zoo caretaker.

He hurried back to his storeroom and locked the door. Brushing off the dust and ash, he rifled through the pockets of the tunic and found the soldier's *Soldbuch.* The first page held the dead man's full name, Gearhardt Kramer, and his rank, Lieutenant. Across from it was a thumbnail photo of Lt. Kramer in his new uniform looking vaguely, very vaguely, like Peter. Already a plan was forming in Peter's mind.

The number of his dog tag was listed, as well as his company and battalion numbers, his blood type, gas-mask size, service number, date and place of birth. His religion was Catholic, his civilian occupation had been accountant, and the detailed physical description, along with distinguishing marks, matched the photo.

Several pages down were his unit information and his list of promotions, his reporting station, company and unit number, training locations, and a list of the clothing, equipment, and arms issued to him.

Peter was amazed at the detail. Lt. Kramer's marital status was single, his father was listed as a civil servant, his parents' address was Karlsruhe.

The soldier's medical record was brief. Other than the required inoculations, he had made a single visit to a military medical facility, for an accidental fall, and to the army dentist for removal of an abscessed molar. He had a few decorations, Sharpshooter 2nd class, a silver medal for four years' service, outstanding-service medal in a flak battery, and a close-combat medal, bronze.

The last pages held his record of leaves and furloughs, and indicated an ever-decreasing frequency of visits home. Perhaps no fiancée waited for him, which might also explain the fatal sexual adventure in the zoo. The details gave Peter a feeling of familiarity with Lieutenant Kramer. Would he have found him attractive if they'd met in a bar?

Peter closed the Soldbuch and turned his attention to the uniform itself. Having it opened up new opportunities.

The tunic was gritty with ash, but unstained. The pants, however, were torn and bloodstained. In the following days, Peter brushed the tunic meticulously and polished every button. He washed the pants carefully in cold water and a dilute solution of the cleaning agent he used in the animal cages. It caused the stain to mute and lighten, so it was less visible to the casual eye. After drying them, he pressed them between two boards and slept over them on his mattress.

The uniform was slightly large on him, but years of sewing theatrical costumes had made him an expert tailor. He ventured into the city briefly and purchased sewing needles, scissors, and thread, none of which were rationed, and set about making the repairs and alterations.

A few days later he put on the tunic and pants and ventured out, striding purposefully through the streets, though keeping far away from the zoo flak tower where the lieutenant would by now be missed. With so many soldiers in the city, almost no one looked at him.

At first he simply enjoyed the freedom of walking down a street and seeing respect in people's eyes.

But one afternoon he saw two soldiers in the next street dragging a man out of a building. A Jew, apparently, who had managed to hide. They slapped him a few times, then forced him into the back of a truck.

Peter backed away, to avoid being called upon to assist, and hurried off in the opposite direction, his heart pounding with impotent rage. He was dressed like the soldiers, but as a Mishling, he was one of the wretched they terrorized. No, he muttered, almost stopping. He would no longer be terrorized. He would stand up to them, even if it cost him his life.

In the safety of his storeroom, he brooded on what he could do. He had no knowledge of how to interfere with communication or block deportations, but he did have access to flammable solvents. And he knew how to start a fire.

The hydrogen peroxide he had been issued for diluting and cleaning was an excellent fuel and, undiluted, it burned explosively.

The cool, quick fire would do to ignite other materials, so he searched for targets that contained them.

A week later he decided on the AEG Turbine factory in Moabit. He finished his work early and used the afternoon to survey the factory. The machines were too big for him to tackle, but he could at least disrupt the administration and thus slow down production.

He returned to the shabby industrial suburb the next day with his tools in a suitcase and waited for the air raid to provide cover. When the air raid alarm sounded, he noted that the factory workers stayed at their stations. Only the German staff were permitted to take shelter in the basement. When they had vacated what seemed to be the command center, he broke a window and threw in three wine bottles filled with hydrogen peroxide. They shattered upon hitting the floor, sending the liquid out in a wide pool. He tossed in bundles of rags to soak it up and hold the flame, then lobbed in a burning match. The entire width of the floor gave off a bright explosion with a crackling "wooof" lost in the thunder of the bombardment. Then he fled.

The next day's newspaper listed the neighborhoods that sustained the most damage but didn't mention the fire at the AEG factory. Compared to the air raids, he was only an annoyance.

He had to expand his explosive capacity. The hydrogen peroxide caused a sudden bright flame but would not sustain a fire and could only ignite other materials. Then it occurred to him that Berlin was already loaded with explosives, in the munitions factory in Spandau.

As soon as he was able, he passed by the factory and scrutinized it. To his dismay, the factory was well guarded and, by all evidence, impenetrable. In an air raid, it would simply go into lockdown. But he noted trucks moving in and out all day. The arriving trucks carried the raw materials, and the out-going, presumably, the munitions themselves. With good timing and a little luck, he could blow up a truck. Or two. He merely needed to devise a slow-burning fuse that would allow him the time to escape.

It took weeks to prepare the device, since he had to contact his black-market friends to ask for black powder and fuse material, then wait until they could collect it. It cost him all the cash he could muster. But when everything was ready, he returned to the Spandau site with a canister full of thick cotton wicks soaked in hydrogen peroxide and two long coils of fuse. The benefit of the long fuse was also its drawback, for the two minutes it would take to burn would allow him to escape but would leave the fuse exposed. Anyone seeing it could simply snatch it away from the wicks, and the device wouldn't explode. He depended on the British bombers not only being on time, but also laying down heavy enough fire that no one would want to venture out. He found an inconspicuous spot some distance from the factory and waited.

When the bombers struck and the sirens cleared the streets, he rushed toward the loading dock where two trucks were parked. He unscrewed the caps from both their fuel reservoirs and threaded in the wicks, attaching the outer ends to the meter-long fuses. He ignited them and ran for his life.

He had made it across the street when the gas tanks in the trucks detonated. A second after, one of the trucks exploded in a fireball and the heat scorched his face. Hoping the explosion would be attributed to the bombardment, he turned and marched purposefully toward the nearest air-raid shelter, joining the police who guided people to safety.

Upon emerging at the all-clear, he was pleased to see smoke still coming from the direction of the factory. It seemed unlikely he had prevented the production of a single shipment of arms, but at least he'd finally struck a blow. He was a resistance fighter now, not a cowering victim.

Over the next months, he repeated his little acts of sabotage, at the munitions factory in Kreuzberg, and at a military supply depot.

Peter was no fool. Reducing the ammunition supply from one factory, or the army supplies from one warehouse would have no effect on the war. But each act of arson was a blow struck for Rudi and for Katja against the Reich that had taken them away from him. He had been terrorized for far too long. Now he was the terrorist.

❖

March 1944

It was Katja's turn to sleep as one of the two on the inside. She had grown used to the odor of sweat and unwashed hair and rank clothing, her own and that of the others. But she had not grown used to the ravening hunger and had begun scraping moss off the trees for food. She couldn't eat much, for it was hard to digest, but she brought back bits of it in her jacket cuff and chewed it before going to bed. Along with the exhaustion, the sensation of having something in her stomach helped her fall asleep.

Unfortunately, she wakened often, from the crowding and prodding of her bedmates or from the sounds of coughing or quarreling from the other bunks. Everyone was sore and sick and struggling for the slightest comfort, and a sudden dispute over a blanket could elicit a storm of complaints from all the others trying to sleep.

Tonight she lay between Violette and Bertha. Bertha, a German who had been arrested for black-market trading and whose red "political" triangle made no sense at all, had never forgiven Katja for reducing her portion of the bunk from one-third to one-fourth. She had never joined the camaraderie of the others, and Katja suspected her of being an informant to the Kapo. She could find no other reason for Bertha's sudden removal from the wood-cutting detail and transfer into a far better job. *Bekleidung*, the assignment of maintaining prison clothing, was one of the most desired in the camp. The work was in a heated cottage, and all one had to do all day was repair rips and sew on strips of cloth with new numbers as the clothing of the dead was recycled for the new arrivals.

Katja turned her back to Bertha and rested her forehead on Violette's back without waking her. She thought briefly of Rudi Lamm and wondered if he had slept in the same way at Sachsenhausen. Where was he sleeping now? In a tent, or on the frozen ground somewhere in the East?

With a stab of longing, she thought of Frederica, carrying out her mission with the same courage as Cecily and Denise and Violette had carried out theirs. The comparison sent a shudder of fear through her. No, Katja resolved. She would never breathe a word about her. The thought that Frederica was still free and still Caesar sustained her.

She wondered briefly how her father reacted after receiving the single postcard she was allowed to send telling him her whereabouts. Was he ashamed, or angry, or afraid? He had refused to be "political" but now politics had come to him.

"Not-political" made her think suddenly of Leni Riefenstahl, lying on her own bed of pain, begging for morphine. Did she know about places like Ravensbrück, where women, beaten and starved, slept four to a bed? Did she know about the medical experiments, or the Jugendlager and the crematorium?

No, she couldn't. She knew only about the glory, and the perfect photos, and the magnificent spectacle of a field of 150,000 uniformed men.

Katja fell asleep to images of blankets and flags and of wandering through a vast phalanx of men standing at attention, searching for Dietrich's face. She could not find him and became ever more fearful as the men began to menace her and she finally fled.

Chapter Twenty-nine

March 1944

Like a wounded soldier who continues battling because he can't retreat, Frederica carried on. Only the knowledge that she had a plan kept her sane, though it involved Leni Riefenstahl, and for the time being, Frederica couldn't find her. Work on her film had been suspended for a time, and no one knew where Riefenstahl had gone to take a rest, or if they did, they had been instructed not to reveal it. So Frederica waited, tense and determined, and continued to transcribe the revealing diary entries.

But smuggling them out was now a problem. With Katja, a biweekly concert at the opera house had never drawn attention, for what was more natural than a daughter seeing her father in performance? But now Frederica was alone, and a single young woman always drew attention. She had male acquaintances but feared to ask them, afraid of giving the impression of romantic interest. Moreover, she would have made them suspicious, for she had no control over what seat she could purchase, and it was invariably nowhere near the critical cloakroom.

At last, with four weeks of coded transcriptions of military discussions accumulating, she decided to risk making the drop alone.

The Staatsoper had been closed since the previous August as part of the Total War program, but the Nazi leaders still permitted themselves a schedule of symphony concerts where they could wear their pretty uniforms. And so it was on a Thursday evening that Frederica was to listen to a Bruckner symphony from a seat on the other side of the hall from the cloakroom drop.

The concert was scheduled well after dark, during the usual lull between the late-afternoon bombing of the RAF and the late-night bombing of the USAF. Pressed within the dense crowd of concertgoers, Frederica felt reasonably safe, even though the notes formed a dangerous bulk in her coat pocket.

She shuffled along in the mass of people moving up the stairs to the first tier and suddenly felt a small hand on her shoulder. The tinkle of bracelets told her it was a woman.

"Frau Goebbels?" Frederica held her breath.

Magda Goebbels smiled warmly. "Are you alone?" the perfectly coiffed first lady of the Third Reich asked. "Come sit with us in our box. We've got two seats that are always empty." The leering face of her husband standing behind her showed that he approved the idea, perhaps even suggested it.

"I…uh…" Frederica stammered. Thoughts raced through her mind of lies she could tell to escape them. The dignitary boxes used a different cloakroom, and even if they didn't notice her coat pocket swollen with notes, she would have had to surrender her coat at the wrong spot.

"Thank you so much, but I have a very good seat," she said with what she hoped sounded like gratitude.

Magda insisted. "Don't be silly. We have one of the best spots in the theater, right next to the Führer's box. It's been ages since I've seen you, and this way we can chat."

"Very kind of you Frau Reichsminister," a male voice suddenly said. "But Fräulein Brandt is in my company this evening, and we have our own special place. You understand, I hope. We have so little time together. Thank you again and good evening."

Frederica struggled to conceal her astonishment as, with a barely audible tapping of heels, Peter Arnhelm, in the uniform of a lieutenant, executed a sharp military bow and led her into the crowd.

Questions crowded in her mind like clowns in a doorway, and none of them could make their way out to her mouth. There was no way to talk in the crowd anyhow.

She surrendered her treasonous coat at the correct cloakroom and joined the new lieutenant waiting near the wall. "I have only a single ticket. If we want to sit together, we'll have to go up to the highest balcony."

"That's fine. That's where I've got a seat anyhow."

In just a few moments they were seated, and as the house lights darkened and the orchestra began to tune, she leaned forward to whisper, "Wherever did you get that uniform?"

"Becoming, don't you think? Its previous owner was killed in an air raid," he whispered back. Then the conductor stepped up to the podium and the concert started, preventing further conversation.

❖

When both concert and information drop were done and they were on the street, she could finally talk to him. "How did you know where I was? What made you do this insane thing?"

"It's not insane. I told you I couldn't stand to stay locked up any more in the zoo, that I had to do something. With this uniform, I've been able to strike a few small blows, setting things on fire or blowing them up. But best of all…" He tapped the black leather holster that hung from his belt. "With this, I'm not a victim any longer."

"But why did you come here tonight? How did you know?"

"Your neighbor said you'd gone to the opera, that you usually go the last Thursday of the month. By the way, you look lovely."

"What?" Frederica was shocked. "My neighbor knows when I go to concerts?" The thought made her sick to her stomach. "But why were you looking for me in the first place?"

"To tell you I found Leni Riefenstahl."

"Oh, thank God!" She embraced him. "Why didn't you tell me sooner! Where is she? How did you find out?"

"She's in Kitzbühl with her mother. She's due back in her Berlin apartment in a couple of weeks. I contacted an old friend of Rudi, who in turn contacted Sepp Allgeier, one of her cameramen friends. Allgeier must not have known her whereabouts was a secret and so told this guy as soon as he asked."

Frederica took his arm and leaned sideways against him. "Peter, you're amazing. If things get really bad, I hope we're together."

"You mean *this* isn't really bad?" He chortled. "But don't worry, no matter what, I plan to be there with you."

Chapter Thirty

April 1944

Karl Sommer laid down his violin bow with a limp hand. In front of him, the conductor gathered his sheet music and stepped down from the podium, signaling that the orchestra rehearsal was over. The musicians packed their respective instruments into their cases, and made small talk among themselves, inquiries about family, speculations as to which Strassenbahn was still running, complaints about the scarcity of soap. Karl sat motionless for a long while, his violin resting on his knees.

"Better hurry up, Sommer," the oboist remarked. "You've got a long way to Grünewald, and I'm sure you want to get there before the RAF pays its evening visit. Their aim is getting better too. Did you hear? Last night they took out two more beer halls. At this rate, there won't be any places for Goebbels to give his speeches."

Karl nodded faintly, laid his violin and bow mechanically in his case, and covered it with an old velvet cloth. Lethargically, he took his music from the stand and laid it on top. He stared at it for a moment, then snapped the case shut and shuffled along behind the other orchestra members.

Oblivious to the people hurrying past him, he barely changed pace as he made his way along Unter den Linden. When he reached the Strassenbahn stop, he saw the vehicle traveling away from him in the far distance. He had missed it by several minutes. Slight disappointment percolated through his indifference; it would be another half an hour before the next one, and even that was unreliable.

Without a conscious decision, he simply kept walking, in a stupor. He wasn't in a hurry. He had no one to go home to now in the Brahmsstrasse, no one who would care if he arrived late at night. He walked for nearly a kilometer, more or less southwest, toward Grünewald. Finally, his feet began to hurt and he realized he was thirsty. He had been too depressed to eat that day and still had no appetite, but walking did make his mouth dry. Another two hundred meters and he found a Gasthof that still had beer.

He drank one, then another, and a third, then gathered up his coat and case and shuffled on. His feet still hurt, but he was fuzzy-minded enough to no longer care. He passed a street where bombs had taken out a building and found it laborious to walk along the fine rubble that pressed through the worn soles of his shoes. He also needed to urinate.

A year before, he would never have considered relieving himself in the street, not even under concealment. He was just too civilized. But he glanced around at the rubble that stretched half a block and felt the constraints of civilization fall away. He forced himself to march a while longer, to where the buildings still stood, and turned into an alley. Glancing around one more time, he set down his violin case and undid his trousers.

While he relieved himself, he looked across the street at what was once a building, the ruined concrete edifice a metaphor for the ruined structures of his life. How did all this happen, he asked himself. How did he lose so much in just a few years' time? First the Nazi government had taken his beloved Kroll Opera. Then he'd lost a wife to cancer, a son-in-law to Stalingrad, and finally his daughter to Himmler's concentration camps. Now he was about to lose his homeland too. Why was he still playing concerts? For pampered Nazis, to take their minds off the bombing raids they had called down upon themselves?

As if in response to his seditious thoughts, an air-raid alarm sounded. More or less on schedule. He zipped his trousers and stepped out of the alley to scan the street for signs of people filing into a shelter. He saw one far behind him in the direction he'd just come, but he didn't want to retrace his steps on his throbbing feet.

And so, for the first time, he ignored the piercing sirens and simply plodded forward toward Grünewald. When the bombers rose from the horizon in geese-like squadrons, then broke formation to avoid the flak guns, he stopped under a portico and watched them with intense interest. It was deafening—the roar of the aircraft, the thunder of the detonating bombs, and the constant high pitch of the flak cannons. The main ones seemed to come from Berlin proper, probably the zoo tower.

Only once did the flak actually strike the fuselage of one of the bombers, so that the aircraft spiraled downward at a steep angle. It blew up half a city block upon impact, as lethal in its dying as in its bombing.

The colors mesmerized him. A backdrop of bright red and iridescent orange going toward pink, with closer objects silhouetted black against it.

Curiously, in the midst of the thunderous blasts, he could still hear music in his head, as if his mind detached itself from the hell around him. Out of nowhere rose the melody from a Schubert Lied, *To Music*. He hummed it to himself: *Oh lovely Art, in how many grey hours, When life's fierce orbit ensnared me.* Bombs dropped at both ends of the street, suddenly heating the air and filling it with smoke. His ears ringing, he backed farther into the portico, choking on the hot gas. But the tune would not stop, for a lifetime of familiarity drove it through his hearing memory. *Have you kindled my heart to love*?

A bomb detonated in the building behind him. *Carried me away into a better world!* The last words of the song ripped through his memory before a block of exploding brick wall smashed into his head and he collapsed. Fire ate through the wooden support of the portico until it dropped on him, the flames consuming first the violin and then the musician.

❖

Ninety kilometers north of Berlin, Ravensbrück was untouched by bombs and continued its industries. News of her father's death struck Katja hard, but the friendship that had developed with the Anglo-French women, especially Cecily, sustained her. The four of them shared everything, and on the day Katja received the news, the others stayed close to her and tried to lighten her workload.

They had welcomed Bertha at first, but when it became clear that the *Blockova* favored her and she wouldn't share her benefits, they excluded her. Her retention of almost normal weight, while the others grew gaunt, suggested she had other ways of obtaining food, perhaps during her work in Bekleidung.

The entire block made it through the icy rains of April with no fatalities from the cold. But Violette, especially, was becoming emaciated, so Cecily and Denise took turns helping her with the saw. The Kapo didn't care, as long as they cut and gathered the requisite amount of wood and no blame came to her. After the half-hour break for their scrap of bread, a single slice divided by four, they returned to cutting and had fallen into the normal rhythm.

The Kapo suddenly sprang to attention, and the women stopped cutting. A Kapo and an SS officer marched along the track toward the work party. The officer spoke briefly with the SS man in charge of the detail, who then called out, "Violette Szabo, Denise Bloch, step forward."

The two women glanced at each other, ashen, then crept toward the SS man.

"Come with me," the officer ordered, and did an about-face. He strode back the way he had come, and the women fell into place behind him. Denise Bloch looked back, anguished, over her shoulder and gave a small wave of good-bye.

"Back to work," the Kapo snarled. Stunned, Cecily and Katja gathered up their cuttings.

"What does that mean?" Katja choked out.

"I don't know," Cecily whispered back, but the Kapo's truncheon came down on her shoulder.

"No talking."

❖

After the last roll call, the whole barracks was subdued, as it was whenever someone collapsed on work detail or was sent to the Jugendlager. The separation of the two Anglo-French women was ominous, and no one knew what to make of it. But that night on her side of the bunk Bertha said softly, "I know."

"What do you know?" Katja asked, angry at her smugness.

Bertha paused dramatically. "Their dresses came into Bekleidung this afternoon for renumbering," she announced, not bothering to name the two women. "In case you want to know. They're dead." She paused again, savoring the effect she was having. "Forget about them." She pulled the blanket, of which she now possessed a third, over her shoulder and turned on her side. "They're smoke."

Katja bent to her work for the hundredth time, and though she had been interned for three months, it seemed now that normal life had stopped years ago. She functioned at the level of animal survival. She ate and rested when she was able, communicated little, usually only with Cecily, and sorrowed, fearing that Frederica had forgotten her. Frederica couldn't afford to attempt communication, but surely in three months, she could have given some sign.

Another prisoner had been added to her bunk and to her single blanket, bringing the number back to four. Katja focused her attention on Cecily, sleeping next to her and helping her conceal her fragility. The camp was bursting now, with more arrivals than vacant space, and the SS combed through the barracks regularly looking for those no longer able to work. The feeble and infirm were promised recovery in the Jugendlager, but everyone knew the terrible truth.

Now it was June, and the midday sun soothed even Katja's depleted body. The twelve-hour labor was still killing the prisoners slowly, but both the Kapo and the SS guard seemed placated by the spring warmth and left off tormenting them.

At day's end, the women put their shoulders to the heavily laden cart and shoved it over the rusty track toward the camp. They unloaded the cuttings into the wood yard and were ordered to take up formation for the final roll call.

Cecily still collapsed over the last pile of kindling. "I can't," she muttered. "I've got nothing left."

"You have to," Katja insisted. "Come on, march next to me. I'll hold you up. You can sleep as soon as the roll call is over." She draped Cecily's limp arm over her shoulder and took the first step, pulling her along.

Throughout roll call, Katja held Cecily upright, calling out both her own number and Cecily's to avoid delay, and soon they were back in their barracks. Cecily could no longer sit up without help, but Katja saw to it that she got her ration of soup and bread, and added half her own to Cecily's bowl.

Katja helped the exhausted woman up onto their platform and watched her until she slipped into unconsciousness. Only then did she allow herself to fall asleep.

The disruption next to her awakened her, and she wrenched herself out of her own stupor. Two Kapos had dragged Cecily off the platform and were carrying her on a stretcher toward the door. Panicked, Katja clambered down from her place and staggered after them.

"Don't take her. She's still strong. She can work!" she begged, but the absurdity of the claim was obvious. Cecily couldn't even raise her head. She signaled "come here" and Katja leaned close to her face.

Cecily's whisper was barely audible, but Katja understood. "Stay alive for me. You must…tell what happened. Promise."

"I promise. I swear," Katja said through tears. "I promise," she mumbled again as the Kapos carried the stretcher through the door into the darkness.

The roll-call block of one hundred was reconstituted the next morning, Katja noted with numb bitterness. A new woman stood next to her, though it was not yet clear what language she spoke. In recent weeks, the nationalities of the inmates were increasingly mixed as barracks were filled to bursting with new arrivals. Katja no longer cared. About anything.

At the end of the second roll call, as the wood-collection detail was assigned, she didn't hear her name. What did that mean? Where was she being assigned? Then, as the work columns began to march toward the camp exit, she heard, "Sommer, report to the commandant."

Had the Gestapo found out about the spying? Or was it simply her turn to be taken to the Jugendlager? She was too exhausted to be more than faintly alarmed and followed the SS *Aufseherin* to the commandant's office.

SS Hauptsturmführer Fritz Suhren grimaced in obvious annoyance as Katja was led in, and she dropped her eyes anxiously. Being the cause of annoyance could be fatal. The commandant cleared his throat. "Well, well, Fräulein Sommer," forcing her to look up at him. His square Aryan face and blond hair reminded her briefly of Eric Prietschke, though the scowl was more severe.

"Obviously you have a friend in a very high place. We have received a communication from the Führer himself requiring your release."

Katja stared in disbelief. Had she misheard? But no. The commandant opened a register and made a note in a column next to what appeared to be her name. Then he handed her a folded document. "Your release papers. You'll need them at the gate. The Aufseherin will provide you with regular clothing and accompany you to your barracks to change. You are to leave Ravensbrück without delay. That will be all."

"Yes, sir," Katja stammered, and as the commandant turned away in disinterest, she timidly backed out of the office. The Aufseherin met her outside. She already held a woolen dress bundled under her arm and thrust it against Katja's chest as they walked.

Once in her own barrack, she changed clothing, noting the way the wool dress hung on her. It smelled a little of its previous owner, whoever she was. A new arrival, perhaps, who would be assigned to replace her on the wood detail. An exchange of souls in purgatory.

She left her prison rags on her bunk and followed the Aufseherin back out into the Lagerstrasse, still clutching the release documents. Bertha was approaching, presumably to collect the discarded clothing for renumbering. But she already carried a dress. As she came near, Bertha held up the dress to display its number and Katja halted as if struck. It was 111,202. Cecily's number.

Bertha smirked. Cecily Lefort had already been gassed.

The Aufseherin propelled Katja forward, and with the image of Bertha's gloating face imprinted on her mind, she stumbled toward the main portal.

An SS man stepped out, his Mauser on a strap across his chest, and she mechanically held out her papers. He thumbed through them, then signaled for the gate to open.

While the gate slowly rolled toward the side, Katja glanced back at the Aufseherin returning to the camp. The rows of barracks were quiet now. The work details had marched out and only a few women remained to clean the grounds. In the distance she could see the chimney of the crematorium. A thick, sooty column of smoke rose silently into the springtime sky.

Chapter Thirty-one

Frederica had arrived before dawn and waited, staring at the high concrete walls that flanked the entrance to Ravensbrück. Between the walls was the gate, made of steel panels as high as she stood, with a row of openings at the top. In the predawn stillness, she heard the muffled sounds of a mass of people calling out numbers and assumed it was the roll call. It terrified her to stand before the entrance to the camp and know what went on inside. In the dull gray light, it seemed a vast, alien predator with a wide metallic mouth that threatened to swallow her the moment it opened. Only the knowledge that orders of Adolf Hitler protected her allowed her to stand so close.

The waiting was excruciating. She'd handed over the Führer order to the guard upon arriving, assuming that a telephone call from headquarters had preceded her. But she had no way of knowing. She was realistic enough to appreciate the distance between Riefenstahl's vague promise, "He said he'd order it for Thursday morning," and the realities of favors granted when they had no strategic value.

And so she waited. Waited while the external work teams marched out and climbed into trucks for their respective fields or factories. She scanned the passing faces and none was Katja, though the women's heads were covered by headscarves and she couldn't be sure. What if she had missed her? What if an angry commandant was countermanding the Führer order at that very moment?

At eight fifteen the gate slid open again, its wheels rattling over the uneven ground, and this time it stopped after a meter's width.

Silence followed and Frederica stood white-knuckled for what seemed an eternity.

Then a small, bent woman crept forward, clutching herself, as if her own arms could hold her up. She half stumbled past the wall of iron, her kerchief-covered head lowered, and even as the gate clanged shut behind her again, she stared at the ground.

Frederica approached gently, as before an injured bird. "Katja? Is that you?"

The creature glanced up, desolation in her expression, and burst into tears.

"I was so afraid you wouldn't come. That something had gone wrong." Frederica rushed toward her and embraced her tightly, pulling off the hideous kerchief and exposing ragged short hair. "Oh, my God, what have they done to you? Oh, the bastards."

Katja stood passive and shaking in Frederica's arms and rested her head on the soft shoulder. Frederica held her for several moments, then drew back. "Come, darling, get in the car so we can get out of here. Everything's going to be all right now. I promise."

Katja nodded obediently, still not speaking and, dreading the silence, Frederica chattered on. "Here, let me help you. It's Leni Riefenstahl's car, in case you're wondering. I'll tell you all about it later." She opened the door and gently pressed Katja into the passenger side. Taking a blanket from the backseat, she folded it into a pillow, tucked it behind Katja, then closed the door. Returning to the driver's side, she started the motor and pulled away from the camp.

Still numb, Katja stared straight ahead through dull eyes and Frederica stopped talking. They had to stop several times at checkpoints, but Frederica presented all the necessary passes for the journey and they continued. After nearly twenty minutes, Frederica asked, "Are you hungry? I brought some sandwiches."

Katja shook her head.

Five more minutes passed and Frederica could stand it no longer. "Please, talk to me, Katja. Tell me you recognize me. Tell me what you need."

Katja released a long breath and squeezed her eyes shut for a moment, then spoke in a monotone. "There was someone inside, a friend, who took care of me. Every day. Kept me going, waiting. This morning, the Kapos took her to the gas chambers. They were cremating her as I walked through the gates."

"Dear God," Frederica whispered, and took Katja's hand. "Listen, I want you to tell me everything…later, when you're stronger. Don't think about it now. Try to empty your mind and rest. Here, move the blanket around and lean against my shoulder. Sleep if you can, darling. You're safe now. You're free."

Katja did as she was told, resting her head against the welcoming shoulder, and grew drowsy. "Free," she murmured. "Not yet. Just in a bigger prison."

❖

To Frederica's relief, Katja had slept most of the way back to Berlin, exhaustion and the warmth of the car interior finally overcoming her trauma. When she awoke, as they turned the corner into the Richterstrasse, she was less morose.

Frederica helped her up the steps into the apartment, and while warm water ran in the tub, she undressed her gently. She suppressed a gasp as she saw the signs of battering and starvation. "Look what those bastards did to you." She ran a hand gently down Katja's upper arm. "My poor darling. You've got sores on your hands and feet too. I'll put some iodine on them after your bath." She helped Katja into the warm bathtub and sat on the floor next to her.

"Shall I shampoo your hair? All I have is bar soap, but it's better than nothing."

Katja nodded consent.

"When did they cut your hair?" Frederica knelt beside her on a towel and rubbed the block of soap over the matted hair until a thin film of foam emerged. Then she threaded her fingers into the hair and began to squeeze the soap through it.

Katja closed her eyes. "They didn't just cut it. They shaved all our heads the day we arrived. But after that, they left us alone and it grew back." She leaned her head back into Frederica's hands. "Tell me about Leni Riefenstahl. How did you convince her to help me?"

Frederica spread the lather downward to wash the lines of soot from around Katja's neck, wiping gently around the protruding bones of her shoulders and back.

"It wasn't easy. When I found out what happened to you, I tried to track her down. She had just gotten out of the hospital and had gone off for some kind of cure, but no one would tell me where. After more than a month, Peter found out she was in Kitzbühl with her mother, but I had to wait another month until she was back in Berlin. Then I went to her house and stood in her living room until she listened. I convinced her that German victory was looking more uncertain every day and she had to decide whether to act like a Nazi or a human being. If anyone deserved her help it was you, and that she owed it to you."

"That was audacious. I said the same about Rudi, but she claimed she had no influence."

"At first she said more or less the same thing, but I insisted that she was one of the few people that Hitler trusted. She could use that friendship at least once to rescue someone, and if it couldn't be you—a faithful secretary and loyal German who'd lost a husband at Stalingrad—then she should be ashamed."

"You actually told Leni Riefenstahl to be ashamed? That took nerve."

"Yes, I even shocked myself." Frederica poured warm water through Katja's hair and lathered it again for a second wash. "And since the war-widow remark seemed to impress her, I mentioned your other virtues, such as the fact that you had at one time worked for Dr. Carl von Eicken, Hitler's throat physician."

"For five minutes, maybe. I handed him his clipboard."

"She didn't know that. Then, for good measure, I added what I'd heard from the nurses, that you hadn't really said anything seditious, but only comforted a soldier with a head wound who was raving. Anyhow, cumulatively, it worked. I convinced her and she was able to persuade Hitler, on this one occasion, to intervene. It took her a few weeks to get an audience with him, but she got him to order the release and the travel permits that would allow me to drive there to get you in her car. However, there are two conditions."

"Oh, hell," Katja moaned, closing her eyes. What?"

"One, that you return to the Charité and resume your work as if nothing had ever happened."

"I suppose I'd do that anyhow. I need to work."

"And that you never talk with anyone about your time at Ravensbrück."

Katja grimaced. "What? What sort of a devil's pact is that? What goes on there is hideous. The world has to know about it."

"The world *will*. All in good time. You can't accuse the Nazis of anything now. They'd clap you back into Ravensbrück in a minute. You can tell me, though, and I'll get the information out to Handel and the SOE, if it concerns them."

"It does. I haven't even told you the worst yet. Aside from the hunger and brutality that everyone already knows about, the camps are for killing."

"I think people are beginning to grasp that. Stories filter back from the East."

"Not only in the East. In the German camps too. Anyone who comes in is automatically under a death sentence. Death takes place deliberately and randomly, and in a dozen different ways. At Ravensbrück they killed three women from the SOE."

Frederica's hands fell still. "What? How do you know?"

"I met them. They told me their names. Do you know Denise Bloch, Violette Szabo, and Cecily Lefort? The SOE parachuted them into France, but after only a couple of months, they were all captured."

"Dear God, yes, I know the names. I even met Cecily a few years ago. We trained together in 1938. You saw them at Ravensbrück?"

"I was on a work crew with them when Violette and Denise were taken away and executed—and cremated right after. That's the way they do it. I saw their prison dresses come back from the crematorium. Cecily held out longer. Maybe they wanted more information from her, but they let her die of starvation and exposure. She was still alive when they carried her out of my barracks, just a few hours before I was called to the commandant and released. She made me promise to get the news out to the world, and I swore I would. Then they killed her too. They were burning her just as they released me, as if it were some kind of grotesque exchange, her life for mine."

Frederica was somber. "No, darling, you can't think of it that way. You were both victims, but they succeeded in murdering only one of you." She chewed her lip for a moment in silence. "Handel has to know, of course."

"Yes, of course." Katja stood up on uncertain legs and Frederica enveloped her in a towel.

"Come to bed now. Our first concern is getting you back to health."

Katja followed obediently and let herself be dried and tucked in bed. "I feel so guilty, wanting to just fall asleep by your side and stay that way for weeks. But I know we've got work to do."

Frederica slid in beside her. "We'll start doing it tomorrow. First get a good night's sleep."

"So how's Peter? Is he still all right?" Katja was becoming drowsy again.

"He's doing wonderfully. Wait till you hear—"

"Frau Riefenstahl. I need to contact her, to thank her."

Frederica caressed her cheek. "No. She specifically said she didn't want to hear from you and only wanted her car returned. She's back to working on her film. Amazing, isn't it? Total War and they still want to make movies."

Beginning to doze, Katja could hardly form a sentence. "So much to do. Want to work, have to stop them."

"We will. Now it's certain."

"Why now? What's changed?" She was mumbling now, half-unconscious.

"Of course. Nobody told you at the camp, so you don't know the good news. Yesterday, the Allies landed at Normandy."

PART FOUR

APRIL 18, 1945

BERLIN, GERMANY

Chapter Thirty-two

In one of the offices that had survived the partial bombing of the propaganda ministry in March, Frederica sat at her desk brooding on the deaths of the SOE agents. Cruel irony that they'd been captured while she, in the heart of the enemy country, had survived so many years. But it was perhaps precisely because of her location that she had become immune to suspicion. It had cost her a lot, but now she was part of the machinery of the Nazi government. She worked at the very right hand of the second most-powerful man in the Reich, and she read his every notation.

But it had become harder to keep up the charade. The horrors and deprivations at Ravensbrück had etched a sort of solemnity into Katja's face that she retained even now, nearly a year after her liberation. Seeing her day after day, Frederica felt protective and vengeful in equal measure. And what had become of Rudi, who had perhaps suffered even more?

She forced her mind back to her typing. Yet another diary entry full of strategically vital information that she tried to memorize as she transcribed it. As soon as she got home, she would summarize whatever she was able to retain, then code it. She was getting quite good at it now.

"What do you think?" a voice said, startling her so that she jumped.

The Reichsminister had caught her off guard.

"As always, it's…uh, precise, intelligent." She warmed to the lie. "I mean, given the magnitude of the issues you address. Yes, very dignified." She exhaled slowly and, she hoped, discreetly.

Goebbels smiled at the compliment then cleared his throat for an announcement. "Frederica, circumstances require that I relocate to the Reich Chancellery, and I want you to come with me. My work is more important than ever now and I need you by my side. Not to mention that I like having that pretty face around."

"Herr Reichsminister, I…I…" Frederica stammered. "But the chancellery has been badly shelled. I understood the offices have closed."

"They have, but the government is functioning from below ground. Everything is being controlled now from that center. Everything. I need you there and the Führer needs you. Please take the afternoon to pack a few things."

Frederica was speechless. Pack? That meant she wouldn't be able to leave. She focused on the thought of being imprisoned with Goebbels and so was slow to grasp what the announcement implied. But then realization struck: the rumors were true. There was a bunker under the chancellery. And the Führer was directing the war from inside it.

Did the Allies know that?

"Are you sure I can't assist you from here? I mean the telephones are still working. I can carry on—"

"No, no. We will need you right at hand. There will be communiqués, any number of secretarial tasks, and I can't do without you." Obviously, it was a command, not a request.

"Come, come." He was losing patience. "I've got a car ready that will take you to your apartment and wait outside while you pack. Gather up some clothes for a few days, your toiletries, the things that women carry with them. You should leave right now so you can report to the chancellery before the evening air raids."

"Herr Goebbels, I…" He was already walking out of the room.

She sat, paralyzed for a moment. How could she notify Katja? She'd have to leave a note in the apartment. They were supposed to drop a new message the next day, but she'd have no time to code it now. She was about to be cut off from Handel. Would he assume she had been captured? She sagged in resignation. In a way, she had.

❖

Burly Dr. Carl von Eicken, head of Berlin University's otolaryngology department, hurried along the corridor past Katja, obviously no longer recognizing her from the year before. She stifled a smile. He'd never know that his name had saved her from death in a concentration camp.

Three weeks after her rescue from Ravensbrück, she had regained enough strength to resume work at the Charité. Most of her colleagues knew what had happened to her, but remained silent about it, out of embarrassment, either for her or for themselves. Only the white-haired Klara Klotzenburg had crossed the line of propriety and actually addressed the matter.

"I'm so glad to see you back," she said under her breath as they walked along the corridor together. "Thank God for that. I hear they shave people's heads, but on you, the short hair looks good. Rather stylish."

"Concentration-camp chic, heh?" Katja had quipped, and they shared a moment of levity before dropping the subject for good.

But Ravensbrück was seldom on her mind now. Least of all while she worked with the incoming wounded soldiers in a new section of the hospital. Here, everyone was busy treating battlefront trauma and no Nazi nurses monitored her behavior.

She hurried down the steps of the hospital toward the train station and joined the orderlies and nurses unloading the last hospital train. They were shabby affairs now, though she remembered the first one she'd met, an impressive and efficient *Lazarettzug*. It had been sixteen cars long, the first ten of which were "ward" cars with beds for soldiers. Following them were a pharmacy, operating room, and the oven car for cooking and for burning septic bandages and materials. Somewhere at the end were the cars for supplies, staff sleeping quarters, and administration. She had been impressed at how well the whole procedure worked, the unloading of wounded according to degree of urgency, the level of cleanliness and care. The wounded were dispersed into the hospital as their injuries demanded, some to operating theaters for surgery or amputation. Others, with massive infections, were taken to wards for treatment with sulfa and other drugs. And always, one or two went to the morgue.

Katja had learned how to inject morphine for the massively injured so they could endure being carried, to bandage limbs close to the body, to cushion bandaged heads, and in general to afford comfort as orderlies lifted the litters from the cars and bore them into the waiting ambulance busses.

Now the entire German army was in full retreat and the trains no longer had to come long distances. They were fewer now, many of them damaged, and all manner of rolling stock had been adapted to carry wounded. And morphine had become scarce.

Katja leaned over a soldier who clutched her hand like a vise. A bandage covered his head and one of his eyes, and most of his left leg was missing. "It's all right, soldier. You're safe now. We'll patch you up," she lied.

"Please, Fräulein. Don't leave me." The soldier looked up at her through his one good eye. "My left leg feels really strange, like bugs are eating at it. Can you look at it?"

All she could do was repeat the usual reassurances. Too many other soldiers needed her too. "The doctors will look at you as soon as possible. Don't worry. You'll be fine. The ambulance will take you right to the hospital." Gently, she withdrew her fingers from his grip. His hand clutched the air as she backed away.

Katja made her way slowly to the end of the ward car, checking bandages, giving morphine only to the most desperate cases, then halted, not certain what she was seeing.

The soldier looked back at her, equally uncertain.

It can't be, she thought. Fatigue and wishful thinking were giving her hallucinations. She turned away.

"Katja? Is that you?"

She spun around. "Rudi! It *is* you. I was afraid to believe it!" Unable to embrace him for the splint and bandage that held his elbow aloft, she kissed him on the cheek.

"The last we heard you were sent to a penal regiment in the East. We were sure it was just another kind of death sentence."

"It was supposed to be," he said weakly. She leaned closer to hear him. His once-beautiful eyes were sunken now and ringed by a sooty gray skin. His voice was hoarse. "I guess my number wasn't up yet." An orderly stood by her now, unfastening the bunk and preparing to carry it as a stretcher.

Rudi looked up anxiously at Katja. "Peter. Is he all right?"

Katja clasped his hand. "Peter's fine. You'll be proud of him. He's been working very hard for the cause. I'll go tell him where you are when I get off work."

Rudi fell back against his pillow. "Oh, thank God!" he whispered, then seemed to fade back into sleep.

"Nurse, please give me a hand here," a doctor called to Katja from the other end of the car.

"I'll find you later in the hospital, I promise." She kissed him again and hurried to the next patient.

Peter slid the pan of horsemeat and flour through the slot of the tiger cage. The big male rumbled menacingly at him, then bolted down the mixture with one or two snaps of the jaw. Still ravenous, he lunged at the cage door.

Regretfully, Peter stepped back and moved on to the tigress in the next cage. All the big cats had been on half rations for weeks and their hip and shoulder bones were visible under their sagging flesh. The zookeeper had been forced to add ever more grain to the diminishing supply of horsemeat, and even that was not enough to keep them from slowly starving.

He scraped the last scrap of fat onto the pan for the ocelot just as the door at the end of the corridor opened. Riedel, his face drained of color, held a rifle in one hand and a cartridge belt in the other.

"What's wrong?" Peter asked, though he sensed the answer. It made him sick.

"There's no more food, and none coming. Nothing."

"But we can't let them just starve to death," Peter said, knowing full well the absurdity of the remark. Of course they wouldn't let them starve. His eyes locked onto the rifle. "You're going to shoot them."

"No. You are. I've done a dozen other animals this morning and can't stand it any longer. You've got to shoot these." Riedel pressed a Mauser into Peter's hand. "It's that or let them starve or be bombed, and I know you're not that cruel." He draped a cartridge belt over Peter's shoulders. "God help us all," he said, and walked away.

Peter stood in the doorway, dumbfounded, holding the terrible objects. He couldn't do it. He just couldn't. He felt as if he would vomit.

With the rifle in hand, he left the Lion House and wandered toward the other animal houses. Some of the animals had been transferred the year before to zoos in the South where there was less bombing. Why hadn't all of them been saved? Why had the zoo stayed open so long? Too late now to ask.

He arrived at the hippo pen. The huge beast lay on her right side, her left legs protruding horizontally from a torso that had already begun to swell. Her calf lay next to her, its strange square mouth wide open, as if calling out at the last moment.

The Gorilla House was not so gory. The chimpanzees and smaller monkeys had been relocated in time, and only the mountain gorilla lay curled in a ball in the corner of his cage. A circle of blood formed a halo around his head.

Peter wandered around the zoo as if in a trance, seeing the cadavers of the animals. Curiously, the birds had been spared, whether out of a sense that they might feed on insects or simply a reluctance to kill such delicate, harmless things.

But all the large mammals were dead, and flies already buzzed around them.

As if in a trance, Peter returned to the Lion House and loaded the first five cartridges into the magazine. He began at the ocelot cage, sliding the barrel through the bars. One clean shot did the job, but the sound was deafening, and the kickback onto his shoulder surprised him. He braced himself better and shot the lynx and the cheetah. His ears rang from the concussion.

He'd never been religious, but recalled a psalm he'd learned as a boy. "Yea, though I walk through the valley of the shadow of death, I shall fear no evil, for thou art with me." He realized bitterly that he sensed *no one* with him. No one comforted him and nothing guided his hand but the bitter exigencies of war. And *he* was the shadow of death.

The leopard and the panther went down quickly, but he was beginning to lose his nerve. His jaw started to tremble, as well as his hand, as he loaded the clip with the next five rounds.

Unsettled by the gunshots the bigger cats roared and arched their backs. Peter, standing in front of the cubs, broke into tears, then shot them, one after the other. They tipped over with a sort of growled whimper, their little paws twitching in muscular reflex. The lioness leapt toward him but he felled her in mid-leap. His shoulder hurt from the rifle's recoil, for he held it too tight. His chest hurt more.

The male lion simply stood panting before the bars as if he had decided to die with dignity, but Peter's trembling made it hard to aim and the shot was a little off. The beast swung his heavy head, as if to rid itself of a ferocious headache, then dropped to the floor. His rib cage sank with his final exhalation.

At the tigress's cage, Peter braced himself against the bars to keep from trembling. The great beast paced rapidly back and forth across the narrow cage as if to foil his aim. He let her pace three or four times and on her last turn, in the instant she faced him, he fired. She spat at him, swiping the air with a wide, striped paw, then collapsed.

In the last cage Sultan, the magnificent male Sumatran tiger, roared, seeming to sense that all around him was death.

Weeping, Peter slid the rifle barrel between the bars and took aim. "Sultan, I'm sorry, forgive me, please." He pulled the trigger.

Click.

Peter sobbed out loud. The clip was empty. He had to reload, while Sultan retreated to the back of the cage. Both hands were shaking as he slipped the final clip into the magazine. His face swollen with tears and mucous, he fired into the tiger's head. Once, twice, a third time, and each recoil against his shoulder was like a reproach, the pain almost a comfort.

When Sultan lay still, Peter dropped the rifle and climbed up into the cage. He knelt beside the beast, stroking its still-warm carcass, then laid his head against the tiger's skull, sobbing uncontrollably. He wept for the tiger, but also for Rudi and the Jews and all the others in the camps, and he wept for Germany.

Finally all the sorrow drained from him and only hopelessness was left. He stood up, crept back to the storage room, leaving all the cage doors hanging open, and dropped onto his mattress. He lay awhile in a stupor, wondering if he had the courage to shoot himself.

"Peter?"

"Who's there?" His voice was still tight from crying. Katja stepped cautiously into the storage room and stood over him. He held out his arm toward the cages of dead cats. "Look what we've done," he said mournfully.

Katja had walked along the corridor, and she knew. She sat down next to him and tenderly took off his blood-splattered glasses. He wept again and she held him for a few moments, then wiped the lenses clean with a handkerchief before putting them back on his face.

"Look, you have to get past this, and you can't stay here anyhow. Maybe you should stay with me. By now, the Gestapo all have better things to do than hunt down a half Jew."

"What's the point? They've destroyed everything." He did not specify who "they" were, but she understood. "I might just as well stay here and go down with the next bombing raid. I don't care any longer. I really don't."

"You have to care. Someone needs you."

"What are you talking about?" Peter grumbled, wiping his sleeve across his dripping nose.

Katja smiled weakly. "Rudi's made it back to Berlin. He's wounded, but alive, at the Charité."

"Rudi alive?" Peter slumped against the wall, tossing back his head and inhaling deep gulps of air. The joy of the news couldn't cancel the horror of the morning, and so both emotions tore at him at the same time, like two waves crashing from different directions.

"Oh, Katja," he said finally, embracing her again. She held him for a moment, then stood up out of his grip. "Look, we don't have time for this. If you want to see him, you've got to go now. You'll have to search through the wards, but start by asking for the ambulatory wounded from today's transport. That should narrow it down. Then, with a little luck, you can make yourself useful there. They're desperate for help, so just put on an orderly's jacket and go to work. No one's going to ask for identity papers in the middle of that chaos."

He drew a handkerchief from the pocket of his overalls and blew his nose. "Yes, yes. I can do that. I'll leave right now. And I won't come back. Just let me collect a few things." He took a knapsack from a corner and crammed in a shirt, some underwear, and the remnants of some dried sausage. "What do you think I should do with this?" He lifted the mattress where he slept on the floor, revealing the Wehrmacht uniform. "This helped me do a little damage this year. Do you think there's any point in taking it?"

"I don't think so. The Russians are almost here and it's not a good time to be a Wehrmacht soldier."

Peter nodded agreement. "Good-bye, Lieutenant Kramer," he murmured over the familiar tunic. He felt as if he were abandoning an old friend as he tucked the Soldbuch back into the pocket and let the mattress drop into place. "I'm taking the pistol, though," he said, getting to his feet and dropping the holster into his rucksack. "Let's go."

"Unfortunately, the Strassenbahn tracks are all torn up, but goods trucks are taking passengers along the main avenues. It's how I got here. You can try to wave one down and still get to the Charité tonight, or you can come to Frederica's place with me."

"Don't worry about me. I have a delivery bicycle, a big one, with a platform on the back for freight. It can carry a passenger too. I'll take you to the Richterstrasse and then I'll go on to the Charité."

Together they abandoned the storage room and marched along the corridor of carnage. Katja glanced once at the dead lion cubs, then looked away. It was unbearable.

❖

With the streetlights cut to protect from night bombing, Frederica's apartment building was dark, as were all the other buildings on the street. The lack of foot traffic at that late hour also added to the general gloom. Katja dismounted from Peter's freight bike and gave him a quick hug. "Lock this bike up well. It's going to be the only reliable transportation for a long while, I think. I'll look for Rudi when I get to work in the morning, so I expect to see you then."

It was already eleven when she arrived at the door. Hopefully she could get a few hours' sleep in Frederica's arms with no air raids to disturb them.

Alarmingly, the apartment was dark. Katja called out when she entered, but had no answer. She clicked on one of the lamps and went to the bedroom. The apartment was empty. Panicking, she rushed back to the living room. Had Frederica been arrested? Mercifully, she found a note on the dining table.

> *No time for details. Driver waiting downstairs for me to pack change of clothes. I'm ordered to go with JG to command center in Führerbunker in the chancellery. Don't know when I can get out again. I love you.*

Führerbunker? What was that? It took a moment for Katja to grasp the several facts contained in the word. Adolf Hitler was in Berlin, in a bunker near, or more likely under, the chancellery. He would direct the final battles from there, alongside his chosen men. That, of course, included Joseph Goebbels and some of his staff.

Katja was appalled. Being forced to stand by the Führer at that late date was worse than being sent to a concentration camp. The camps were being liberated by the advancing armies, but those same armies would soon destroy Adolf Hitler, along with those defending him.

She dropped her head on the table. The inevitable had happened. They had carried on, week after week, and had never talked about what to do when the apocalypse struck Berlin. Now Frederica was trapped. All Katja could do was remain where Frederica could find her if she could ever escape.

She curled up on the bed with Frederica's pillow but sleep would not come.

Chapter Thirty-three

April 19, 1945

In the chancellery garden, Frederica halted before the concrete entrance to the bunker as the security detail checked her papers. Then she descended timidly, sweeping her eyes over the unpainted cinderblock walls and ceiling of the bunker. She fought back claustrophobia.

"Follow me, please, Fräulein," the SS man said. "I'll show you your quarters in the forward bunker." At the foot of the long flight of steps he swung open a heavy steel door and motioned her to go ahead of him. As soon as it closed, she became aware of a dull humming. "Ventilation," he said. "You'll get used to it."

They passed a guard station where an SS man sat with a typewriter. Two others loitered nearby, idle and apparently off duty. A second door opened to a corridor with a row of tables. Some dozen chairs were arranged along the opposite wall, as if for a party. "The dining room," her guide said. "We have two meals a day. Cold breakfast between seven and nine, and supper at six. After that, you have to go ask the cook for something. That's the pantry." He pointed with his thumb toward a door on the left.

"What's in there?" Frederica asked, pointing to the door next to the pantry.

"Toilets and bathroom." He walked ahead of her past another barricade to a second corridor and knocked on a door to his right.

When no one answered, he opened it and ushered her in. "This is the secretaries' quarters. It looks like that bunk over there is still free." He pointed to the upper bunk on the left side of the room where folded linen lay on top of a bare mattress.

"I'm sure the Reichsminister will call on you at the appropriate time. Otherwise, supper will be served…" He looked at his watch. "In about half an hour." With that, he let himself out of the room, leaving her standing with her suitcase.

She turned in a circle, studying the gray concrete walls devoid of wardrobe or visible storage space. Suitcases were stowed beneath the two bunk-bed sets, and she guessed that they served as lockers. She slid hers underneath the lower bunk on her side and sat on the single chair in the room with a curious mixture of dread and fascination. The dread was stronger because she was well and truly trapped underground with the men she feared the most. Worse, when the enemies of the Third Reich descended on this stronghold—which they certainly would do—she would be in among the hopeless defenders. Unless something miraculous happened, she would die here, unaccounted for.

For all that, she was intrigued. She had worked for years to reach the heart of the Nazi government in order to expose it but had never imagined she would come so far. Adolf Hitler himself was close by, somewhere in the lower bunker behind one of the steel doors. Would she ever meet him?

The door suddenly opened and a girlish face showed surprise and then welcome. "Uh, hullo."

Frederica stood up and offered her hand. "Frederica Brandt. I work for Dr. Goebbels."

"Ah, yes. Of course. I'm Traudl Junge, the Führer's secretary. One of them. Pleased to meet you." Just then two other women came in behind her, and she continued the introductions. "This is Christa Schroeder, another secretary, and Erna Flegel, his nurse. Well, our nurse too, when we need one." She giggled softly.

Frederica shook hands with all three. "Have you been down here a long time?"

Traudl shrugged. "A few days. It's not so bad when you're busy. But when you're just sitting around waiting for orders, you can get a little stir-crazy."

"I don't mind it," the one called Christa said. "It's a small sacrifice to make for the Führer, when you think of what the soldiers are enduring. And it's not like you're a prisoner. If you want to go upstairs for a smoke, you can usually find an SS man to take you up."

"You go up to smoke?" Frederica wondered if that might provide an escape route.

"You can smoke in this bunker, but not in the lower one. The Führer *hates* smoking. But it's an excuse to get out of the hole for a few minutes." Christa glanced at herself in the mirror, and with a brief "tsk" she set about rearranging her hair. "Oh, look. It's almost time to eat. The coffee is ersatz, but the wine is real. I tell you, they feed us so well here, we're all going to get fat."

The supper was served buffet style, and Christa was right, the food was better, and in larger servings, than she had eaten in months. They had potatoes, of course, but also a large quantity of pork. And a few surprises.

"Tomatoes? Wherever did they get tomatoes?" Frederica asked.

"The chancellery has a greenhouse. I'm sure the glass is all shattered by now, but it's spring anyhow, and these grew all winter. At least that's what they told me," Erna Flegel said. "Important to have vitamin C when you're living down here," she added.

"To go with the champagne." Christa chortled. "One needs to keep in good cheer, don't you think?" Observing the quantity of champagne on the table, Frederica wondered if it was in fact the main source of everyone's bravado.

Joseph Goebbels appeared suddenly behind her. "Ah, Fräulein Brandt. I'm so glad the others have taken you under their wing. But when you're finished, would you report to me, please? I have something to dictate. An address I hope to convince the Führer to deliver on the radio."

"Yes, certainly, Herr Reichsminister." Absurd that he spoke so formally, after all he had done to her, but of course it kept up appearances.

Goebbels moved on through the dining hall, acknowledging some, shaking hands with others, and Frederica returned to her supper. It seemed otherworldly to be eating, drinking, bantering, as if at a sort of underground picnic, while just over their heads, all of Berlin was being blasted to pieces.

At the end of the meal, she reported to the reception room Dr. Goebbels had pointed out and where he was already reading through some reports. She sat down before a small table with a typewriter, rolled in a clean sheet of paper, and waited.

He turned his chair around to face her and crossed his legs, drawing attention to his well-polished boots. He tilted his head and smiled, obviously wishing to engage her. "I think it's critical at this late date for the Führer to make his voice heard to his people. It would do wonders to raise morale, don't you agree, Frederica?" It had been a long while since they had "socialized" and he had called her by her first name.

"Uh, yes. Yes, it definitely would." Frederica saw no benefit in disagreement, though how he could possibly imagine that the situation could be saved was beyond ridiculous.

The minister gazed ceilingward for a few moments, then began dictating. "Men and women of Germany, in this our bloodiest, but also our finest hour…" He stopped and tilted his head again, a new quirk. "That's good, don't you think? I mean 'finest hour.' A little Churchillian, but I can steal a bit from the old man."

The question was apparently rhetorical because he continued dictating. The speech was not long and he spoke slowly enough for her to type it correctly the first time. She could correct her few typos by pencil. She pulled out the sheet and handed it to him.

As he was reading, someone knocked and then opened the door. An SS man announced, "Herr Reichsminister, your family is here."

Goebbels sprang to his feet. "That will be all for now, Fräulein Brandt," he said, laying the address to one side of the table. He exited the room but left the door open so, peering through the doorway, Frederica witnessed the arrival of the Goebbels family.

Magda Goebbels was an attractive woman, or at least had been. Now she looked under a terrible strain. Immediately behind her came her six children, the adopted darlings of the Nazi party, all in their best dress. Frederica had visited them twice at their summer home and so knew all their names: Helga, Hilde, Helmut, Holde, Hedda, Heidrun. She had also seen them occasionally at state events where they played the role of perfect Aryan family, both for the minister and for Hitler himself.

After some discussion, Magda and the children moved into a room just across the corridor from the secretarial bunkroom. In the grim atmosphere of the bunker, it would be nice to be close to a family of bright children. Their chatter reminded Frederica of peacetime and normalcy. Then she remembered what they all were doing there, hiding in a hole until the Russians came to kill them.

❖

April 20, 1945

It was an act of desperation, for Katja couldn't bear to do nothing. After the end of her hospital work shift, she flagged down one transport truck after another until she reached the chancellery. It was surrounded front and back by *SS Leibwache* guards, as she knew it would be. She approached one of them and simply asked if she could pass a message to a staff member of Dr. Goebbels. The guard barely deigned to look at her. "You have no business here, Fräulein. You can pass a message through the ministry." She backed away.

As an alternative, she circled around to the rear of the chancellery, approaching through its gardens. She was stopped immediately and forcefully. Two Leibwache guards held her roughly by the upper arms while a third pointed his rifle at her. "I am ordered to shoot anyone who steps foot onto these grounds without authorization," he threatened her.

She explained that she only wanted to send a simple message into the bunker. The guard was irate, obviously because people weren't supposed to know there *was* a bunker.

Then she realized how close she had in fact come to the bunker entrance. Just behind the guards interrogating her she could see two concrete structures, one square with a door and the other a silo with what appeared to be a ventilator at the top. No wonder the guards were angry.

"Should we arrest her, Sturmbannführer?" one of the guards asked.

"Yes, take her to the Prinz-Albrecht-Strasse. We'll see what the Gestapo think of her," the officer replied, but just then, the door at the center of the concrete block opened and three women stepped out.

Katja called to them. "Ladies! Friends! Please help me! I have to contact Dr. Goebbels' secretary. Do you know her?"

While two of the women lit cigarettes—the apparent reason for their emergence—the third strolled toward the SS guards and their prisoner. Someone's secretary, apparently. She had a rather bland, pleasantly girlish face and obviously blond-tinted hair.

"Please, Fräulein," Katja begged her. "I just need to send a very small note to my…sister. Frederica Brandt. She works for Dr. Goebbels. It's just a scrap of paper. You can read it, of course, and show it to Dr. Goebbels. It's about her fiancé."

The woman lit her cigarette expertly with a Zippo lighter, faintly interested in the stranger's supplication.

"Sure, why not?" She held out her hand, and Katja deposited a small piece of blue note paper, folded in quarters, into her palm. "Thank you, Fräulein. I'm very grateful," Katja said, still in the grip of the two guards. The secretary's acceptance of the note apparently overruled the irate Sturmbannführer's command. As if he had intended it all along, he ordered his men to escort her to the far end of the chancellery grounds.

Katja put up no resistance as the guards fast-walked her to the periphery of the gardens and let her go. She hurried away, wondering if the brief message would be her last words to her lover.

❖

Frederica had dozed off again. With nothing to signal day and night, and the continuous lighting of the corridor, she had lost all sense of time. She was lethargic, and when she tried to read, she simply fell asleep. But a noise outside her room awakened her and, hungry for diversion, she went to the door.

An SS man was just leading a handsome and obviously quite docile German shepherd on a leash. "Come on up, Fräulein," he said. "There's to be a ceremony, and it's time for Blondi's walk anyhow."

"What's the occasion?" Frederica asked.

"The Führer's birthday. He's meeting a contingent of the *Volkssturm*. I'm sure he'll like having an audience."

She could see the other secretaries farther ahead and followed the line of people filing up the staircases, glad to have a reason to surface. She hoped they'd timed the ceremony to avoid the daily air raids. Or had the shelling from the Russians begun yet?

The day was cold and overcast but at least the air was fresh, if you didn't count the odor of ash and gunpowder that had been in the air now for a week. Frederica kept to the rear, close to the SS man and Blondi, occasionally stroking the well-groomed canine coat.

She watched as some two-dozen Volkssturm fighters filed into the inner garden of the chancellery, old men interspersed with young boys. She was shocked at the age of the one and the youth of the other. They wore a motley collection of "uniforms": gray camouflage, a Hitlerjugend kit, a postman's outfit, old S.A. shirts tucked into mismatched pants. Several of the older men simply wore suits and overcoats with an armband that read *Deutscher Volkssturm Wehrmacht*.

Then the bunker door opened again, and Hitler himself came out. He wore his high peaked uniform cap and appeared Führer-like, but his overcoat collar was drawn up around his neck, concealing most of his face. It was the first time she had seen him up close, and she was appalled at how pathetic he looked. As he passed her, she saw that he held his left arm tucked back behind him against his coat, but he could do nothing to conceal the extreme trembling of his left hand. This was the leader of Greater Germany?

He paced with deliberation down the front line of Hitlerjugend, shaking each hand, pinning medals onto narrow boyish chests, occasionally patting a cheek or giving a paternal tap on the shoulder.

When he got to the end of the line, Frederica blinked in disbelief. The man Hitler shook hands with was Marti Kraus, Leni Riefenstahl's elderly cameraman for the documentary that seemed to have started it all. God, how he had aged in eleven years.

Frederica was startled a second time when he laid his arm around the boy next to him. The young fighter that Hitler had just pinned a hero's medal on was Marti's son, Johannes Kraus. Johannes, who'd been a child at the film crew's last supper in Nuremberg, was now a decorated soldier.

Artillery fire sounded in the distance, then the detonation of a shell a few hundred meters away, so the organizers deemed the ceremony at an end. The Führer turned with trembling hand back to his bunker while his newly decorated home guard marched off to defend what was left of the Fatherland.

Feeling suddenly old, Frederica followed Blondi and the other secretaries back down into the bunker. In the corridor dining room she sat down with the others to a tiny piece of cake to celebrate the Führer's birthday. Someone had just handed her a cup of ersatz coffee when a woman approached the table—pretty in a bland sort of way, with artificially blond hair.

"Are you Frederica Brandt?" the woman asked.

Frederica nodded, and the woman dropped a note on the table in front of her. "It says 'Rudi is alive—at the Charité. I love you.' I hope it's not code for something seditious, because I don't want to get into trouble."

Frederica felt tears welling up and choked them back. "Thank you so much. This is very good news."

The stranger walked away, and Frederica turned to Traudl, who sat next to her. "Who's that? Somebody's secretary? Why haven't I met her before?"

"That's not a secretary. That's Eva Braun."

❖

April 25, 1945
Blankenfelde, Germany

By the time Lieutenant Yevgeny Khaldei reached Germany, he was used to the squalor and ignominy of war. As an ambitious young TASS photographer, he had captured its horrors up close and far away.

For over fourteen hundred days of the war with Germany, he had photographed the most somber images, conveying the bleakest of moods, of ghettos, concentration camps, cadaver-strewn streets, bombed-out camps with refugees dragging carts full of rags. But now, as the Red Army entered Berlin, he had something new to capture, something he was thematically not prepared for. Victory.

An old image shot through his memory of sitting at a table in a Berlin bar, and then at an apartment admiring the photos of two new German friends. What were their names? Rudi something. Now, of course, they were his enemies. Would they be fighting in defense of Berlin? He brushed the thought from his mind; he had more important things to think about.

"General Ivanov, how long do you suppose it will take? I mean under optimum conditions."

The general took a deep breath, expanding the chest of his field tunic, which, though no longer clean, was heavy with medals. Three distinguished-service medals were pinned across his left pectoral and another hung from the left pocket. Three silver soviet stars decorated his right side, and a Stalingrad medal hung from the pocket lid. He took off his dress cap—flatter and less clownish than that of his German counterpart—and ran a meaty hand through his gray-black hair. "Hard to say. We'll be fighting in the city streets in just a few days. A week at the outside. But how long it will take to make them surrender is another question. It could go back and forth for a long while."

Lieutenant Khaldei pressed for more precision. "So, minimum five days, you think? Before we reach the center?"

"Yes, I think they'll hold out at least that long."

"Good, then there's time. Major, can I get on the night transport back to Moscow?"

"I suppose so. Your credentials give you that right. Why? You have a sudden craving for borscht?"

"No. Not at all. For spectacle."

❖

April 30, 1945

Lieutenant Khaldei sat behind the pilot clutching his precious cargo. It had taken him four days to get it, and at that moment, he would have faced down a hand grenade rather than give it up. Astonishing that, in the middle of a war, Moscow could spare no large Soviet flag. And it was breathtaking to think he had actually had to argue with party bigwigs before they would surrender two good red tablecloths. Thank God for relatives in the garment trade, for it was his uncle who had known how to cut out a hammer and sickle in the right proportions, then had spent the night attaching one to each side. Now the entire bundle was as heavy as a dead horse, but safely at his side.

Chapter Thirty-four

April 26, 1945

The Charité hospital was nearly in ruins. Bombs had destroyed the dermatological and eye clinics and severely damaged many of the buildings housing patient wards. All surgical operations had been moved to cellars and newly constructed bunkers. Beds were distributed through every undamaged part of every remaining building, wherever possible according to the nature of the wound or ailment. But the staff was overwhelmed, and the shortage of medication, antiseptics, and morphine rendered much of the hospital service merely palliative, and scarcely even that. As an ambulatory patient, Rudi had been moved to a low-maintenance sector, and Katja was at first not able to find him. Only after she recalled the name of his regiment was she able to locate his patient number and subsequently the ward into which he was placed.

But the chaos obviously enabled Peter to integrate himself somewhat invisibly as an orderly and thereby stay close to Rudi. While he helped feed or carry patients, or tend to the basic physical needs of bed-stricken men, no one asked him who he was. So far.

When Katja came in, Rudi was sitting up in bed. She passed Peter, who was mopping the floor nearby, and embraced Rudi, careful not to touch his injured shoulder. "I'm so glad to see you up. Can you walk?"

"A little. With help," he murmured. He didn't say any more but his eyes darted back and forth, as if he watched some event invisible to everyone else.

"What are you doing here?" a woman's voice behind her asked. Katja turned to see Nurse Rumoldt confronting Peter as he mopped. "You're not on the staff. Why aren't you in uniform? Filthy coward, do you think you can hide here? She waved over the SS guard who stood at the end of the corridor. "I do not recognize this man. Would you please ask to see his identification?"

The SS man held out his hand. "Papers, if you please," he said.

"Well…I…don't have them at the moment…"

"Of course he doesn't have them at the moment. Can't you see he is on duty? Please allow my orderlies to do their work."

Katja stifled her surprise at the unexpected intervention. "Thank you, Dr. von Eicken," she said calmly. "In fact, I need the orderly here to help this patient to the lavatory."

Von Eicken nodded agreement. "Yes, carry on, both of you. Nurse Rumoldt, perhaps you can accompany me to the pharmacy to see if we have any antiseptic soap left." Glancing once over his shoulder, the doctor led the thwarted nurse down the corridor away from the suspect.

"That was a warning, Peter," Katja said. "And she's a shark. It's only a matter of time before she comes at you again. I think you both should come with me to the house at Grünewald. No one knows what's going to happen when the Russians overrun Berlin, but I'd feel better if you both were out there with me. At least we'll have a little food and a few places to hide."

"What about Frederica," Peter asked. "Will she come too?"

"No, she can't. She's with Adolf Hitler."

❖

April 27, 1945

Erich Prietschke hunkered in a doorway scanning the street before he emerged. In the kilometer-by-kilometer retreat since

Stettin, the 11th armored grenadier division Nordland had been decimated. Now, in the suburbs of Berlin, the artillery fire that had destroyed his unit had given way to small-arms fire, and he had to watch his every step.

The street was a jumble of wrecked vehicles, twisted Strassenbahn rails, open sewer pipes, and smoking bomb craters. It provided just enough cover for him to make his way along the avenue. He saw a Volksstürmer crouched and waiting with a *Panzerfaust* on his shoulder. Farther along, a team of Hitlerjugend squatted in a shell hole manning a machine gun on a tripod. They rattled off a round at intervals, more out of nerves than the likelihood of hitting an enemy target.

Erich himself was at loose ends, for no one was left in his unit to mount an offensive and he was reduced to fighting alone. He stood now, one brave soldier defending the capital and last stronghold of the Reich, and felt the power of the oath he had sworn to Adolf Hitler to fight until the last cartridge.

But already he was seeing signs of cowardice among his own people, and it enraged him. The Hitlerjugend were brave, but too many of the Volksstürmer lacked the moral stamina to stay at their posts until the end. Nothing infuriated him more than seeing them break and run.

At that moment, two figures, an elderly man and a boy, sprinted toward him, away from the advancing Russians. They both wore Volkssturm armbands. Cowards, surrendering the homeland, he thought. He'd put a stop to that. "Halt!" he called out, and marched toward them. Both were covered with the soot that rose from the street at every new explosion. "Get back to the front, you swine!" he barked, holding his luger at arm's length toward them.

The older Volksstürmer stopped in front of him and peered at him for a moment through bloodshot eyes.

"Erich Prietschke? Is that you?"

"What? Who the hell are you?"

"It's Marti Kraus. Remember me? Leni's cameraman. This is Johannes, my son. You met him back then too? He was a baby then."

"I don't care who the hell you are. A million men have died for Germany, and you think you're special because you made a film? Get back to the front."

"Erich, be reasonable. Why should three more of us die for this insanity? My son, especially, deserves to live." He stepped past Erich but Johannes didn't move.

Prietschke grabbed Kraus by the upper arm. "Don't make me shoot you. You took a sacred oath. We all did, to Germany and the Führer. Running away undermines what the rest of us are doing. It's spineless and it's treason."

"He's right, Vati. I'm not a coward!" Johannes did an about-face and dashed back toward the advancing soldiers that skittered along the far end of the street. He held his rifle out in front of him, as if it alone could shield him. He had not run more than a hundred meters when two figures emerged and stood shoulder to shoulder. With automatic weapons, they raked the street from side to side, before disappearing again. Johannes fell without firing his rifle.

"You stinking bastard!" His father spun toward Prietschke. "You and your filthy oath!"

"Coward! Traitor!" Erich Prietschke fired his luger point-blank at the cameraman. He had no time to reflect on what he had just done; the Russians with the automatic weapons were advancing again and he had to take cover. But at least he had Russians to shoot at now.

❖

April 29, 1945

Frederica sat on her bunk watching the other women play cards, hoping to be called out for dictation or to type a communiqué. The radio speech that Dr. Goebbels had so carefully prepared for the Führer to deliver to his people lay unread on Hitler's desk, and Goebbels had not called on her again. She felt suffocated.

How could she escape? Could she feign sickness? Go up to the surface for a smoke with one of the other women and run for it through the line of guards? Impossible. She was trapped with the monster and she would die with him. If only she could contact Katja.

After tapping on the door an SS guard opened it a crack. "It's time. Would the ladies be so kind…" He held the door open and signaled with his arm that they should go down the corridor to the lower bunker.

It was the first time she had been invited to the Führerbunker, but she saw that it was laid out just like the upper one. Very likely the walls were thicker, but the same central corridor led them past doors to the left and to the right. Only the carpet was nicer, and paintings hung on the walls. She had no time to study them, but was certain they were all original.

They stopped at the end of the corridor where a table had been set up with bottles of champagne and trays of small cakes. Through an open doorway to a sort of sitting room, she could see two figures with their backs toward the door, and it took her a moment to realize it was Hitler and Eva Braun. In front of them, facing the doorway, someone was speaking to them while Joseph Goebbels and Martin Bormann, Hitler's right-hand man, stood behind him. When Eva Braun said, "I do," with a nervous giggle, Frederica knew she was witnessing a wedding.

A few minutes later the new couple emerged to polite applause and walked slowly along the row of well-wishers to shake hands. Frederica was once again appalled. The Führer of Germany was stooped and haggard, his eyes bloodshot and dead. He smiled mechanically at each greeting. When he reached Frederica, she shook his hand, found it soft, his grip limp. He held his left hand behind his back, but the trembling had grown worse and showed in the jerking of his shoulder.

"Warmest wishes." She spoke the usual formula, though it seemed as grotesque as the ceremony itself. "Thank you, my dear," Adolf Hitler replied and moved on to the next secretary. All that Frederica noted was that the brief ruler of Europe had brown teeth and foul breath.

The new bridegroom then invited the three secretaries, nurse, doctor, Herr and Frau Goebbels, Bormann, and several adjutants to champagne and cake, and all drank a stiff, hurried toast. The cake, Frederica had to admit, was rather good, only the second piece she'd had in years.

Eva came around for a little cheek-kiss from each of the guests and fluttered in the imitation of a happy new bride. Frederica overheard her whisper to Traudl, "Actually, I'd hoped for a bigger ceremony, but considering the circumstances…"

The reception was short, and then the new couple withdrew for the rest of the night. Frederica checked her watch. It was four o'clock in the morning. The newlyweds looked worn down, and Frederica rather doubted they would carry out the nuptial rite. She shook the grotesque image of their coupling from her mind and returned to the upper bunker with the other secretaries.

As she stood at the door of her room, Joseph Goebbels approached her. With unusual informality, even warmth, he asked if she would carry out one more assignment the following morning.

The Führer would dictate his final testament to Traudl Junge, he explained, but he himself wished to simply make a final statement, and would she type it for him? She agreed and then, emotionally drained, took to her bunk.

Morning came within hours and breakfast consisted simply of coffee and rolls. The larder was running short. Goebbels appeared and led her once again to a room in the lower bunker where a typewriter was already set up.

"My last declaration will be short, a simple explanation of why I have remained here with my family. Please, begin typing as I speak." He cleared his throat.

> *The Führer has ordered me, in the event of the defeat of the capital, to leave Berlin and to lead a new government appointed by him. For the first time in my life I must categorically refuse to obey an order of the Führer. My wife and children join me in this refusal. Otherwise, for the rest of my life, I would consider myself a dishonored deserter and cowardly turncoat, who would lose not only his self-respect but the respect of his people—a respect*

which is the prerequisite for any further service in the building of the future of the German nation and the German Reich.

She typed the brief statement in duplicate and presented it to the Reichsminister. He read it, distracted, and handed it back to her. "Please keep it in your possession. I expect you'll be asked to present it at some future time."

"Yes sir," she said, and folded both original and copy carefully into thirds and slid them into her skirt pocket.

The door to the adjoining room opened and Traudl Junge emerged with her own typescript and passed her in the corridor. Hitler stopped before Frederica and took her hand again. "Fräulein Brandt. You still have time to leave Berlin and I give you permission. A small contingent of people will break out soon, and you should go with them."

For all his momentary generosity, Frederica knew she looked into the face of depravity. Not of the sadist or the brute, for she doubted he had ever laid a cruel hand on any creature. No, it was not as interesting as that. It was simply the face of a bland, petty, simple-minded man who had sensed the smoldering resentment of a defeated people and fanned it year by year. He'd taken anger and made of it a hunger that grew until it became vast and predatory. Then he had unleashed it upon the world.

Yet she smiled gratefully, her hand in his. She expected it to be cold, the bloodless claw of death, but it was warm, fevered, and trembling. Then after a soft squeeze of her fingers, he let go and shuffled back to his sitting room.

Relieved at the sudden change in her fate, Frederica turned to Goebbels, who stood nearby. "Is it all right? Can I leave?"

"Yes, of course, you're not a prisoner. But I would beg you to stay a few more hours. I require one last, very important thing. If you don't mind."

Frederica nodded reluctant agreement, knowing she had no choice. Generals brushed past them to confer with the Führer, and so Frederica returned to the upper bunker to await instructions.

Half an hour later, the same generals strode past her again, their expressions grim. She did not need to know the content of the last military briefing. It was written on all their faces. The Reich was in its death throes.

For lack of other occupation, she sat with Traudl and the Goebbels children, amazed at how well-behaved they were. Perhaps they had absorbed the fatalism that now pervaded the bunker and hoped, the way children do, that good behavior would keep them from harm. Traudl had just dealt cards when they heard the gunshot.

"Bull's-eye!" Helmut Goebbels piped out with boyish delight. But a gunshot in the lower bunker could mean only one thing. Magda Goebbels stood up and rushed the children into their room and closed the door. Frederica sat frozen in place.

In a few minutes, SS men came along the corridor carrying two bodies on stretchers. Though both were covered, the head of the larger corpse had a bright red stain seeping onto the cloth. Frederica grasped now why Goebbels had asked her to stay longer. He wanted someone to record the macabre events. She wondered for a moment what the soldiers would do with the two bodies.

She'd lost all sense of time again, and though she returned, spent, to her room, she slept in fitful segments, fully dressed. At one point she was awakened by the voice of Goebbels quarreling with his wife. "No, I'll do it! That's final," Magda said, her voice high and shrill. Frederica shuddered.

The children's room was just across from the secretaries' quarters, and Frederica needed only to stand in the doorway to see the grim drama begin. Magda entered the children's room solemnly. Goebbels himself glanced once at Frederica and then began pacing the length of the corridor. He'd made ten lengths, back and forth, when Magda came out, her face frozen. Husband and wife looked at each other briefly, then Goebbels did an about-face and marched toward the steps leading up to the entrance. Magda followed him in large hurried strides, as if late for an engagement.

Frederica followed. As she passed the telephonist at the guard station, she asked him, "What day is this?" and he answered, "May Day. The first."

Two SS men already stood by, jerricans at their side. Without ceremony or embrace, Joseph and Magda Goebbels stood across from each other, stone-faced. The Reichsminister compressed his lips as he pointed his pistol at his wife's head and fired. Though she dropped immediately at his feet, Goebbels did not look down before firing into his own head and falling over her.

The soldiers separated them and laid them roughly parallel, then poured gasoline over the bodies. Frederica watched, riveted, as they dropped a match onto the bodies, which lit with a soft "whoof." A blue flame engulfed them, first consuming their hair, then blackening their faces, then Frederica turned away. But there, just to the side of where she stood, was another shell pit, and in it lay two other charred bodies. She guessed who they were.

Shells were landing at the far end of the chancellery garden, and Frederica started toward the bunker. But in mid-step, she weighed the two horrors: being trapped underground when the Russians arrived or running the gauntlet between their shells. The choice was clear. She strode purposefully across the smoking, blasted ground of the chancellery garden and no one stopped her. None of the SS guard seemed to care any longer and, in fact, they had no one left to guard.

It was night but the city under fire was neither light nor dark, just a sooty gray that brightened with each explosion, then returned to purgatorial murkiness. She stumbled over rocks and bricks and shell holes, struggling toward the Wilhelmstrasse. At the southern end, she could make out a tank, presumably Soviet, but she ducked around crushed vehicles and presented too small a target for its shells.

She headed directly north to the River Spree where the Wilhelmstrasse became the Luisenstrasse. Before the bombing, it would have been a pleasant fifteen-minute ride on the Strassenbahn from the propaganda ministry to the Charité, but now she would have to cover the entire distance dodging fire and more or less in a crouch. She saw a dead Wehrmacht soldier in the middle of the street and snatched up his helmet without stopping. It was too large and sat low on her head, but it might save her from shrapnel or falling bricks from walls exploding all around her.

She crouched, waited for an opportunity, then dashed to the next semblance of cover. In fifteen minutes, she was sore and exhausted, her knees and palms scraped raw, and she had only reached the Behrenstrasse. She saw open fire between tanks and Volkssturm men on the Unter den Linden and had to wait until the Soviet tanks rolled past her toward the Brandenburg Gate. Then she crossed the wide avenue and in a few minutes she could see the bridge over the Spree. Still intact, though it seethed with Volkssturm and Hitlerjugend rushing south to face the Soviet tanks.

Frederica huddled out of sight as some dozen fighters came past, men in civilian overcoats and children in Hitlerjugend uniforms. Running to their deaths, not knowing that their Führer had already abandoned them. Then she continued her headlong dash toward the bridge and, though she heard the constant popping of small-arms fire, made it across with only bleeding knees.

Finally, at the break of dawn, she was in the Luisenstrasse and the vast expanse of the Charité grounds lay in front of her. She was stunned. In the week of her confinement in the bunker, the hospital had been heavily damaged. Almost every building she could see was blasted, and she was certain that patients and staff had been evacuated to the basements and lower floors.

She began her search in the trauma ward, which had been on the ground floor, but it too had been evacuated. She moved down to the basement and found herself in a sea of wounded. Beds were crammed together in twos, with the narrowest space between the rows for attending staff, and in the corridors, they were head to foot, in an unbroken line. At the center of the ward, patients simply lay on the floor on blankets. She stopped an orderly.

"Please, how can I find one of your nurses? She was among the ones meeting the troop trains."

"No idea, Fräulein. They've assigned people anywhere they can grab them. Not that we can do any good now. The Russians came and took what was left of our medicines." He rushed on past her. Russians already in the hospital? She was afraid of that.

She went from building to building, cellar to cellar, and it was always the same. The wounded were everywhere, calling for help, with staff rushing among the beds to bring water, bedpans, bandages. But Katja was nowhere among them.

Then she saw a familiar face, one she had seen in the newspaper. "Dr. von Eicken!" She ran toward him. "Forgive me, but I'm desperate to find a nurse, Katja Sommer."

"Fräulein, we are all desperate here. Can't you see? I'm sorry I can't help you, but you might take some water to the patients while you look." He hurried away and Frederica was chagrined. He was right. She could at least carry a pitcher with her from ward to ward.

She fetched one from what appeared to be a nurses' station and filled it, then went along the aisles between the beds, trying to catch a glimpse of every nurse she passed. And each time someone called out to her, she went to help. She passed most of the night alternating between searching and helping patients. It became a mechanical sort of work, and for brief moments, she almost forgot that she had any purpose other than to bring water.

"Frederica?" someone called. She spun around. Water sloshed over the rim of the pitcher onto the floor.

"Rudi? Oh, my God, I thought I'd never find you. I've been looking for Katja for hours." Frederica rushed toward him and kissed him on both cheeks.

He offered a wan smile as she sat on the edge of the bed and took his hand.

"It's been so long. I wouldn't have recognized you if Katja hadn't told me you were here. You must have been through hell."

"Don't want to talk about that," he mumbled, and Frederica had no time to press further. "Listen, we've got to round up Katja and Peter and try to break out of here. Can you walk?"

He nodded. "Slowly. Arm hurts."

"Frederica!" This time it was Peter, still with a mop. He propped it against the foot of the bed and embraced her. "You escaped. Thank God."

"Listen, Hitler's dead, and so is Goebbels. I'm not sure who's in charge now. But the Russians are still coming in waves so we have to get out of Berlin. All four of us. Do you know how to find Katja?"

"She was with the surgeons in the bunker this morning but could be anywhere now. You'll have to wait here. She'll come back sooner or later to check on Rudi. He's in bad shape."

Frederica focused again on Rudi and saw that he was almost in a state of stupor. He could talk, but didn't want to. She looked questioningly at Peter, but he only shrugged and changed the subject.

"Frederica, dear. You look terrible. Why don't you rest? Lie down here under the bed on a blanket where you won't get stepped on. We'll watch over you until Katja comes back."

"Rest, yes. A good idea. I'm so tired." She let herself drop to the floor onto the blanket Peter offered her. Lying on her side, she drew up her badly scraped knees and laid her head on her forearms. Outside the hospital walls, Berlin was being destroyed, but in the dizzying fatigue that overcame her, Frederica felt safe among friends and fell asleep within minutes.

Chapter Thirty-five

God damn it! The flag's gone," Major Tcheletchev swore. "Marshall Zhukov ordered a flag on the Reichstag building before May Day and we gave him one, but here it is two days later and the Nazis have gotten up to the roof and removed it. This time we're going to kick the shit out of them. Bring up the mortars."

At the major's signal, two mortar teams rushed forward with their 82 mm cannons on tripods. They set up in moments, and with a single barrage, the two mortars succeeded in punching through the bricked-up doorway. Seasoned fighters poured into the building through the opening. Once inside, they split into teams, some confronting the Germans who emerged from the cellar and others climbing to the upper floors. In less than an hour, they managed to seize the building completely. Outside, Lieutenant Yevgeny Khaldei stood by, one hand supporting a massive red flag wrapped around a pole and the other holding his Leica camera.

When the last Germans emerged from the building under a white flag, Yevgeny called to a knot of nearby soldiers. "Who's going up on the roof with me? Alyosha Kolvalyov, what about you? You want to be a hero today?"

"Sure, if I don't get my head blown off."

"Ismailov, what about you?"

"To get my picture taken? Why not? Yuri'll come too." A third soldier nodded.

The four of them scuttled up the steps into the now-pacified parliament building and made their way up onto the roof. Broken slate and a layer of grit made poor footing, and they had to scrabble part of the way on their knees. But finally they reached the highest part of the Reichstag roof and looked down onto the street. Below them, their fellow soldiers looked like ants, and their tanks like so many toys.

Alyosha Kolvalyov pointed toward an ornamental column. "How about there?"

Lieutenant Khaldei positioned himself on a ledge just over the heads of the other men. "Can you climb up on the column?"

"More drama, eh?" Kolvalyov scrambled onto the rounded top of the column and dropped to his knees to keep his balance. Ismailov held one leg, as Kolvalyov unfurled the flag and let the wind catch it. It fluttered handsomely in the soot-filled breeze.

"Great shot!" Khaldei hefted his Leica in front of him and began shooting. Again and again he snapped, from various angles and perspectives. The third man stood back watching his two comrades and called up to him. "You think people are going to give a shit that we put a flag on an empty building?"

Yevgeny Khaldei snapped another frame. "Yeah, I think they will. Besides, I owe some friends a flag picture, and now, mine's better than theirs."

Frederica awoke to the sound of shouting. She pulled herself up between two beds and realized she was hearing Russian. She ran to the corridor and saw them, Soviet soldiers streaming in from the stairwell. "Doctor come!" they were shouting, and dragging with them doctors, nurses, orderlies, anyone in hospital uniform. Were they being pressed into service to tend the Russian wounded or would they be executed? Then, to her horror, she saw a Russian soldier emerging from the lower staircase dragging Katja by the arm.

Peter was already lurching toward them and he waved to the Russian. "You, come here. Medicine." He mimed using a hypodermic. "Here in the closet." He swung open a door to a broom closet, but it contained a shelf holding a row of bottles of disinfectant. The soldier came forward to investigate. Katja wrenched loose from his grip but the soldier, having caught sight of the cache of chlorine bottles, no longer cared. "Is good?" Peter asked, as if he had been trying to help him all along.

"Is good," the soldier replied, loading his arms and lumbering away with the last four bottles of disinfectant.

Katja and Peter ran to Rudi's bed where Frederica was helping him to his feet. "We've got to get out," she said. "We'll go west to the Allied lines, where they can send a message to the SOE. Handel can identify us."

"Do we know where the British are?" Katja asked.

"Somewhere north. The Americans are closer." Frederica gathered up Rudi's blanket and began folding it.

"The radio said they stopped at the Elbe," Peter said. "That's quite a distance. If you two can walk that far, I can carry Rudi on my freight bike. I suggest we go ahead and wait for you in Potsdam. I used to live there and know some of the shopkeepers. I can probably negotiate some food and a place for Rudi to lie down for a night, maybe some civilian clothes too."

"Good idea," Katja said. "In the meantime I'll pass back by my father's house and pick up some warm clothing and a few valuables. Here, take this." She handed Peter the folded blanket. "In case you have to sleep in the open. And this too."

She pulled an unopened package of French cigarettes from her apron pocket. "From my father's supply. I've been giving them to the patients in place of painkillers. But these are for you and Rudi to exchange for food."

"Where should we meet you in Potsdam?" Peter asked.

"At the railroad station. Last I heard, it was still in one piece. If you have to leave, put up a notice there. Otherwise, we'll look for you there in two days."

"Fine." Peter reached for Rudi's service jacket to help him dress.

"No, not the jacket," Frederica said. I think he'll do better as a civilian, even in pajamas. If he's in uniform, both sides will be after him, not to mention the snipers. The sicker he looks the better."

"All right. Pajamas and blanket it is." Peter knelt to put Rudi's hospital slippers on him, and Rudi took faltering steps away from his sick bed. The others followed, making their way among the beds and pallets of the helpless.

Katja felt a pang of regret for leaving the wounded soldiers behind. Some of them had happily enlisted, others had been forced, but all had fought for Hitler. She had to make her own choice now, between aiding them until the very end or leaving them to the fate their leader had brought them to. It seemed to her that three months in a concentration camp had given her the right to flee.

Though Soviets still streamed into the hospital in search of medicines or booty, enough civilians were running about, agitated and frightened, that the four of them were able to reach the street unmolested. Together they made up an odd and rather pathetic little group. Three civilians, wheeling a patient in a blanket on a freight bicycle, along the Luisenstrasse. Russian military vehicles swung around them and foot soldiers ignored them.

As they crossed the River Spree where Frederica had come a day before, they could see down the length of the Wilhelmstrasse. It was filled with advancing Red Army troops but their guns were silent.

"I don't want to march past those troops, even if they know by now that Hitler's dead," Peter said. "Turn right, toward the Reichstag."

They passed German civilians, the very elderly, who seemed to have just emerged from their cellars. More Russian soldiers drove past them in a jeep, laughing.

They wove in and out of burnt-out vehicles, blasted buildings, piles of rubble. On all sides of them lay dead men and the bloated carcasses of horses. It was important to keep moving. While Peter pedaled over broken brick and gravel, Rudi rode bumping up and down on the rear platform of the bicycle. In his bandages, which covered his upper chest, right arm, and left knee, and the obviousness of his suffering, he gave them credence as non-combatants.

Suddenly Peter stopped pedaling. "Ohmygod, look. Up there."

He pointed with his chin toward the Reichstag building. Black with soot, it held a single spot of color, a bright-red Soviet flag. "Look, you can see the men on the roof holding onto it. Another one's off to the side taking pictures."

Rudi looked up through bloodshot eyes. "Great flag picture. Better than ours."

"So it's over now, I guess," Katja murmured. "Finally, peace."

"I wouldn't count on it," Rudi said, hoarsely. "I know what we did to the Russians. We've got it coming back to us." He fell silent again, his expression grim.

Katja's mind was elsewhere. "Listen, Peter. The shortest route to Potsdam is southwest along the Potsdamer Chausée. It runs parallel to the railroad line. It'll also be safer since there's bound to be lots of other refugees to give you cover. In the meantime, Frederica and I will follow the Kurfürstendam west to Grünewald."

"All right then," Peter said. "Try not to take too long. We really don't want to meet the Allies without you to plead our case."

Peter's bicycle wobbled off due south, while Katja and Frederica joined the ragtag groups heading westward. Reluctant to talk around strangers, Katja fell to brooding. Could they make it unscathed to the American lines? So many disasters were still possible: Russian rape, SS-style execution, banditry on the road. Even if they reached American lines, would anyone bother to contact the SOE? And if they did, how much would her service count? Not to mention Rudi, still debilitated and technically a POW, no, technically a criminal, for homosexuality remained illegal, war or no war. And Peter? Would the Allies even remotely care about a half-Jewish homosexual and part-time terrorist? Frederica's arm around her shoulder reminded her to take one step at a time.

❖

Katja's family house on the Brahmsstrasse in Grünewald was mercifully intact, and entering it after wandering the bomb-blasted streets of downtown Berlin was surreal.

They dropped onto the soft furniture in the living room and Frederica gave out a long sigh. "Okay, I know we can't stay here when we're just hours ahead of the Russians so, before I fall asleep here, tell me the plan."

"Plan," Katja repeated. "You know, I wanted more than anything to make a hot meal for us both, crawl into bed, then spend a loving night with you for the first time in weeks. But I guess that would be insane." She turned sideways and tugged on Frederica's jacket.

"To start, you have to get out of those pretty secretary clothes. We've been lucky so far, but eventually you'll attract the attention of sex-starved soldiers. You can put on an old coat of my mother. The only way we'll be safe is to dress like old women, with dirty faces."

"Do you think we'll fool anyone?"

"Not up close. But among the thousands of refugees heading west, we'll look just like all the other old people. Now come down to the cellar with me and help me choose food to pack." Katja drew a battered suitcase from the bottom of a cabinet and dragged it down the stairs.

The cellar smelled of mold, but Katja was pleased to note the supply of the food her father had kept "for emergencies": dried *Landjäger* sausage and Emmentaler cheese. Even a case of beer, which she'd forgotten about.

"The beer's going to be too heavy to carry, but we can take a couple of these for our first night." She held up two of the spring-stoppered bottles and laid them side-by-side in the suitcase. "There's even a jar of my mother's pickled red cabbage." She laid it reverently among the sausages and cheeses.

They dragged the suitcase back up to the living room and stood panting over their three-day survival rations. Katja looked around the living room, at all the familiar objects she had grown up with. "There are a hundred things I wish I could take along, but it's impossible—though I suppose it's no different from losing it all to bombs."

She thought for a moment. "For sure, I don't want to leave my mother's jewelry. It's just a few pieces, but they're all I have of her. While I get them, why don't you wrap the bottles in towels and pack what we've collected. I'll be right down with blankets and a coat. Maybe I can also find some wheels so we don't have to carry everything."

Once upstairs, Katja rummaged quickly through the family chest, caressing the items she had kept from both her mother and father. Her mother's soft night shawl, a pair of formal kid gloves, a string of pearls, an embroidered vest, her wedding ring. There was her father's watch and his opera "treasures": an autographed photo of the great Lauritz Melchior; the string part to the opera *Tosca*, signed by Toscanini; black velvet gauntlets worn by Mephistopheles in *Faust*; the flashy dagger from *Macbeth*. Would Frederica find the cache of souvenirs amusing?

She froze suddenly at the sound of the front door opening. Had the Russians reached Grünewald? She'd heard stories about what the Russians did to women. She stood up clutching the prop dagger. It wasn't sharp, but with enough force…

Silently, she crept to the top of the stairs and looked down into the living room. She saw no Russians, to her relief. Just a single man in an SS uniform. She was about to go down and investigate, but something made her stop.

Frederica's voice was loud with surprise and annoyance. "What are you doing here? How did you know—"

"I saw you in front of the Reichstag building and kept following you. You're not seriously thinking of fleeing west to the Americans, are you? That would be stupid."

Katja recognized the voice of Erich Prietschke. A flush of anger went through her, but she remained on the stairs, out of sight.

Frederica sounded calm. "Nice uniform, Erich. I see you've been promoted. I'm not that good at reading SS ranks, but it looks like you made Obersturmführer."

"Hauptsturmführer, in fact. Not that it makes much difference now."

"No, it doesn't make any difference. So go home and take off your tunic and your military trinkets. Hitler's dead. Goebbels too. The SS is finished."

Erich's tone became more ominous. "I know. The German nation is lost and it's people like you who are responsible." He stepped toward her out of Katja's line of sight.

"What *are* you talking about?" Frederica was obviously fed up.

"You know what I'm talking about. You were whoring around with Goebbels, but you never were a National Socialist, were you? You never joined the party. Why? You didn't approve of our program for a glorious race, for German superiority?"

Katja took another step down the stairs, uncertain. What could she do to get him out of the house?

Frederica was not intimidated. "Erich, what the Nazis wanted was absurd. An Aryan race? What nonsense. Do you remember what they all looked like? Hitler, Goebbels, Himmler, not to mention Goering, all tarted up and drugged? That's who you followed."

"You're wrong. A few corrupt men, a bad strategy, traitors in the leadership—none of that changes the beauty of the idea. We *are* a master race, at least some of us. The ones who have the animal courage to take what's ours."

"What's that supposed to mean?" Frederica's voice grew more tentative.

"We'd have made a great couple, once. But you dumped me for the Reichsminister. Why? Because he could buy you nice things, take you to his country house? Well, he's dead now, and I'm alive, so you and I, we're going to have one last dance."

There was a pause. "Where's your girlfriend. I saw you two come back here." He called out in a singsong voice, "I know you're here, Katja. You want to come out and see a real German man stake his claim?"

He seemed unconcerned that no one responded.

"If she comes out while we're at it, she'll get a little surprise, won't she?"

Katja heard the sound of the metal buckle on his uniform belt and a moment of silence while he presumably unbuttoned his trousers.

"Oh, look, a nice hard one. Just for you. It would have been nicer at your house, but this place will do too. I'll try to make it worthwhile."

Horrified, Katja advanced farther down the staircase. She could see Frederica, holding out her hand to stop him.

"Erich, get ahold of yourself. This isn't you. You're an honest soldier, not a rapist."

He stepped up to her and slapped her across the face. "Shut up. I'm claiming what's mine and you're going to take it." He shoved her, causing her to topple back onto the sofa, and let himself fall on top of her. "Don't fight me, you little bitch, or I swear I'll shoot you and then put it in you."

Frederica struggled, but he pinned her down while he yanked up her skirt and pressed himself between her legs.

It took all of Katja's will to not rush in and try to separate them. He was big, and he still had a pistol, although at the moment it lay in its holster on the floor right next to him. She couldn't possibly get to it in time.

She forced herself to wait, and wait. Then, when his grunting told her his entire focus was on gratifying the fire between his legs, she moved.

The carpet muted her step while she raced across the living-room floor, but he must have heard her inhale as she raised her arms for the strike. He turned his head, his initial smirk changing to astonishment as he saw the knife and tried to lift himself up.

"Uhh!" Katja grunted as she slammed the dagger with two hands into his back. His shift of position caused the blade to enter at an angle and the fabric of his tunic slowed penetration, but the shock caused him to collapse back onto his elbows. Without thinking, she withdrew the blade and struck again with all her strength. This time the blade pierced more deeply and he jerked in rage, falling sideways off Frederica. He crouched on the floor and his wheezing told her she had collapsed one of his lungs.

"Fucking cowards…" he rasped through clenched teeth, clawing himself up to his knees but held prisoner by his own trousers that were twisted around his legs. "I'll…kill…you…" He reached out to seize Katja by the leg.

"Real German man?" The memory of concentration camp guards flashed through Katja's mind. She plunged the dagger again, this time between his neck and shoulder, and heard the squishing sound as it slid down to a satisfying depth. "This is for Cecily," she snarled, lifting the weapon and bringing down again in the same place, "and for Violette and Denise." She drew back for a final thrust but felt Frederica's hand on her arm. Somehow she had gotten to her feet and pulled down her skirt.

"Leave him. He's done for," Frederica said, snatching Erich's holster before he could reach it.

Katja stood panting and dazed for a moment, watching him slip to the floor, when she heard the sound of motor vehicles in front of the house.

"Russians. Let's get out of here." Frederica tugged on her arm and pulled her along to the rear of the house. They were at the back door just as they heard the front door open and the sound of Russian voices.

In less than a minute they passed through the garden and had made it into the underbrush of the neighboring woods when gunshots rang out. "I guess they finished him," Frederica said.

They were among trees now and still running, stumbling, not pausing to look back until they both were exhausted. They stopped to catch their breath and listened. No snapping of wood, nothing but the distant sounds of military vehicles, the occasional faint rattatat rattatat of soldiers celebrating victory by firing into the air. Katja focused now on Frederica.

"Are you all right, darling? Did he hurt you? I'm sorry I let him go so far. I had to surprise him."

Frederica leaned forward, elbows on her knees. "I'm all right. Thank you for rescuing me, but my God, I've never seen you that... savage. The fool was going on about animal courage, but I'm sure he never expected to meet it in you."

"I didn't mean to kill him. I saw him hurting you and I just wanted to stop him. And he said he was a Hauptsturmführer, like the commandant of Ravensbrück. I suppose I lost my head. I don't know."

Frederica took Katja's hand. "Whatever it was, thank you. And by the way, how did you come up with a knife while you were upstairs?"

"It was a dagger, actually. An opera prop from *Macbeth.* One of my father's souvenirs. A horrible thing to use on somebody." She shuddered.

"Well, now we have something better." Frederica held up Erich's heavy holster. "I'd rather we'd gotten away with all the food we packed, but now that Germany's collapsed, nothing else is going to protect us." She shaded her eyes as she surveyed the newly verdant fields and woods between the clusters of houses. "By the way, do you know where we are?"

"Yes, I know the Grünewald area very well. If we keep going west, we'll eventually come to the Havel River. Then we follow that south to Wannsee. From there it's only a few hours to Potsdam."

"Let's get started then." Frederica linked her arm in Katja's and they trudged along, keeping a steady pace toward the west.

The sun was on the horizon when they reached a body of water where refugees plodded southward along the shore, silhouetted like dreary phantoms. "Is this the Havel?" Frederica asked.

Katja pulled her close, comfortingly. "Sorry, no. It's only the Grünewaldsee, but we'll follow the shoreline with the others as long as our feet hold out, then look for a place to sleep. I'm just wondering why there aren't more Russians here."

"I'm sure there will be shortly. All the battle reports I heard in the bunker said Berlin was surrounded on all sides, though probably more thinly on the western side. So they must be out there somewhere."

They kept a steady pace and Katja tried not to think about the supplies they'd had to leave behind, but as darkness fell, they began passing groups that had set up little campsites, some with children and elderly.

"Do you think we should stop?" Frederica asked. "Someone might share their space and a little food with us." They wandered near a family that had built a bonfire and were heating something in a pot. But one of the men from the circle stood up and confronted them.

"There's nothing for you here. Sorry, but we don't even have enough food for us. Move on." He tilted his head in the direction he thought they should go.

They backed off and drifted away from the campsites. "So much for the solidarity of the Volk," Katja grumbled.

They plodded on for two more hours, pushing themselves to their limit, trying to cover ground. Then, as they feared, it began to rain, lightly at first, then insistently. At the same time, a dark structure loomed up before them.

"The *Jagdschloss*," Katja exclaimed. "I forgot about that. The old royal hunting lodge they turned into a museum. It might just save us tonight."

"You're thinking of breaking in? If not, let's *do* think about it."

"Not into the main building. I'm sure it's locked and guarded. But a big place like that has to have maintenance quarters, and they can't be guarding every room and corner."

As if to encourage them further, the sky gave off a clap of thunder. Another five minutes of hiking with soaked feet brought them to the perimeter of the building complex. Light shone in some of the top-floor windows of the central building, but no vehicles were parked outside the complex, and all the surrounding low buildings were dark, their windows barred. All they could hear was the splattering of rain and the sound of water gurgling through a nearby waterspout and plashing onto stone.

They made their way around the rough stone walls past an entry tunnel wide enough for a car, then along a range to the south, tugging on each set of bars. Nothing seemed penetrable until, on the southeast side, they came upon a framework that was damaged and loose. Frederica took hold of the bars and, at the next thunderclap, wrenched the entire iron grid out of the window emplacement. Using the handle of the Luger, she shattered the window and pried out the shards of glass. In just a few moments, both of them were inside.

They stood for a moment in the darkness, water dripping from their hair and clothing. Slowly their eyes adapted and they could make out vague shapes. They stepped to the other side of the room and peered through the windows looking toward the inner court.

It was wide, partly paved and partly covered in lawn. The hunting lodge itself was a three-story building around a central tower with a cupola. The façade was whitewashed, the surfaces between the windows dotted with antlers. Two *Kübelwagen* stood parked in front.

"Military vehicles," Katja whispered. "German. They haven't evacuated yet."

"Where would they evacuate to? There's no place left to go. But look," Frederica said. "Here are lanterns. Just what we need. This must be a gatehouse or watchman's quarters. Matches would be nice too, of course."

Katja groped her way around the room, stumbling over various crates, stools, buckets. Then at the corner she felt a cabinet and opened it. She could see nothing but a wall of darkness so she ran her hand gingerly down the surface. "Ah, drawers. Too bad we don't have a lantern to see into the drawers," she quipped.

"I've got something," Frederica whispered from the other side of the room. She held up a box, shook it, and was satisfied with the sound. "Matches." She struck one and held it to the wick of one of the lanterns. It caught and she adjusted the wick, then held up the lantern.

"Looks like a carpenter's shop. Would be nice if we could find a safe place to sleep."

Shielding their lantern so it projected light only in a dull circle onto the floor, they pushed the door at the end of the room. It opened to a stairwell leading downward. "Let's try the basement," Katja suggested. "At least we won't have to shield the light."

The first room held nailed crates with numbers on them. At the far end of the room was another door. Frederica tried it and it opened. "Well, this looks more promising."

Large rectangles of what were obviously paintings were wrapped in canvas and sheltered against the walls by sandbags. Crates down the center of the room, also packed on both sides by a wall of sandbags, seemed to contain more of the same. Katja moved quickly beyond them to four statues wrapped in heavy padded material. Painted halos that protruded from the top of each bundle revealed they were wooden saints.

"Exactly what we need," she announced.

"We need saints?"

"No, something to sleep on." Setting down the lantern, she began to undo the knots that held the bundles together. In a few minutes, they had unwrapped and laid out four thick packing quilts at the feet of the wooden effigies. As an afterthought, she rolled up one of them as a long pillow and patted it with satisfaction.

"Soft *and* dry. Now we can take off all this wet clothing. God, what a relief. Even this leather holster is soggy."

By the lantern light, they rid themselves of their drenched clothing, wrung each article out as well as possible, and draped it over the statues. Only their shoes and the holstered gun stayed close by. They were shivering by then, so they lay down, warming themselves against each other back to front.

"This is the first time we've been together in weeks," Katja said. "It was so awful coming home night after night and having to sleep in your bed without you."

"Yes, while I was away on vacation with Adolf Hitler," Frederica murmured into her ear.

"Don't joke about that. I was terrified the Russians would kill you along with him."

"Let's not talk about Hitler. Let's just enjoy being here together, so close to rescue. We only have to get to the Allies and Handel will take care of the rest." She kissed slowly down the center of Katja's back, warming the cool, damp flesh with her mouth.

Katja squirmed playfully and tried to press closer. "You have an awful lot of confidence in this Handel. Do you think he cares about us now, or are we just pawns in the game of espionage? Dispensable, now that the war is won and you don't need your code name any more."

"I hope he cares. All this time I've imagined him as a father figure, wise and protective. The family I didn't have, I suppose."

"Well, we need him to get us out of Germany, but I'm your family now, and I'll mother you if ever you need me to."

Frederica nuzzled against the back of her neck. "I'm not sure I'd know how to act around a mother. I don't feel like I've ever really had one."

"It makes me so sad to hear that."

"No need to be. My father filled in pretty well and got me through nearly to adulthood before he died."

"What a horror. How old were you then?"

"Eighteen, so I wasn't a child any more. It *was* frightening at first, to know I was alone and, if I fell, no one would catch me. But then Rudi arrived and I had a sort of brother."

"You must be terribly bitter toward your mother."

"No. Not any more. I've carried around my anger so long it's grown stale. Besides, I sort of understand her now. I mean about not wanting to be tied down to a boring husband and a child when you can be on the barricades, saving the world. In a way I'm a little like her. I wouldn't have taken the risks I did at the propaganda ministry, flirting with Goebbels, flirting with death, actually, if I'd had a family. But that's over now. Now there's you."

Katja turned in Frederica's arms and exhaled luxuriously against warm breasts. "When I'm in your arms, I can almost forget that the world is half in ruin. I can't believe I lived so many years without you. Without this." She drew herself up and pressed her lips to Frederica's mouth the way she had so often in the last year, and every time it was a coming home. This time too, it began as gratitude, then grew to hunger.

Frederica's insistent hands explored the long-familiar places, and Katja responded with animal pleasure. "Hail, Caesar," she breathed, and opened her legs to the delicious invasion. The exquisite tension began like flickering lights, fireflies igniting and then disappearing, but the adept hand teased them back again and again in brief tormenting flashes. Each one was longer and brighter and more electric, until they combined in a bright pulsation and the dazzling eruption of climax.

Katja panted, spent, as the afterglow spread to every muscle, but she resisted drowsing. Next to her, she felt Frederica's ardor, and she turned on her side to caress the already moist thighs. "I want us to fall asleep this way every night," she murmured into Frederica's throat, and slid her own fingers into the welcoming place. She gave back the delicious torment, drawing forth the hot filament, then halting, then fanning it again until Frederica moaned surrender. It seemed a sort of victory—of their love over the Führerbunker, over the war, over the madness that still blustered above their heads.

Chapter Thirty-six

The yanking open of the basement door awakened them, and they bolted upright. The two soldiers were obviously surprised as well and halted in astonishment. Katja pulled the quilted mat up to her shoulders and muttered softly, "Shit. The Russians have arrived."

Seeing that they were naked, one of them, an Asiatic with a wide, flat face, broke into a grin and pulled the cellar door closed behind him. He remarked something to his comrade, and his predatory leer made it clear what he was proposing. The second man leaned his rifle against the wall and knelt down in front of them. Chuckling softly, he took hold of the mat and tugged it slowly toward him, leaving them naked and cowering.

The Asian also laid down his rifle and advanced slowly, undoing his trousers as he neared.

Katja waited until they were both kneeling on the mat, close enough for her to smell rancid sweat and tobacco.

"Nyet!" she said, pulling the Luger out from under the mat and pointing it at the first soldier's eye. Bewilderment crossed both men's faces.

"Quick, get the rifles," Katja ordered unnecessarily, for Frederica was already on her feet and reaching for them. She slid one of them out of reach behind the cellar door and aimed the other one at the two Russian heads.

With guns pointed at them from two directions, the men remained immobile on the floor. Katja slipped to the side and rose.

She pressed her foot on the backs of both soldiers, forcing them to lie flat. Then, with the ropes that had held the packing quilts around the statues, she tied their hands and feet. One of the soldiers struggled and tried to get to his feet, but Frederica pressed the tip of the bayonet of the man's own rifle into his back, and he settled down.

As a last precaution, Katja stuffed a corner of the packing quilts into each man's mouth. She stood up, panting from the exertion, then hurried to dress. "I wonder how they're going to explain this to their buddies. Being tied up by two naked women."

"They can shoot them, for all I care. I'm so tired of men trying to rape me," Frederica said, throwing on her own still-wet clothes. "Now let's get the hell out of here."

In damp, chafing shoes, they scurried back to the carpenter's workshop and clambered through their original entry window, onto the ground outside the Jägerschloss compound.

They ran, simply to be out of range when the alarm was sounded. Finally, winded, they slowed to a walking pace, trusting that the Soviet officer would see no value in tracking down two women.

"I'm trying to remember what the nearest village is before Potsdam," Katja mused, shading her eyes against the early morning sun. "Any place where we can try to buy or beg food. I can't go much longer without eating."

"Well, we pass Schwanenwerder, don't we?" Frederica asked. "How do you feel about stealing from the dead?"

"What dead do you have in mind? I'm not keen on exhumations."

"Joseph and Magda Goebbels. They have a villa on the Schwanenwerder, right on the waterfront." She tossed her head southward, as if she could already see it beyond the trees.

"And you're sure they're dead."

"Quite."

They were in a meadow now, resting, and Katja took off her shoes to relieve her blistered feet. "Then I'd have no problem at all stealing from them. I spent three months in a concentration camp because of his filthy Total-War laws, and he owes me a lot more than food. But how do we know the Russians aren't there?"

Frederica glanced back in the direction they'd come. "It's possible, but they seem to always be a little bit behind us. Besides, they won't send a detachment there for military reasons. They couldn't possibly know which summer house belongs to Joseph Goebbels."

"But you do."

"Yes, I was there for a couple of meetings right after the propaganda ministry was bombed. I doubt the SS will be guarding it. They're all breaking their necks to go west to surrender to the Allies, so the most we'll run into will be squatters and thieves. Like us."

❖

The house, with its large bay windows, was eerily quiet as they approached. Birds chirped and mosquitos buzzed around the garden as if unaware of the war and Germany's reversal of fortune.

"It looks empty." Frederica knocked on the door. No one answered. She knocked again, more aggressively, then tried the door. Locked. "All right, then," she muttered as she stepped off the front porch and explored along the flank of the house.

As expected, the windows were all locked. She swung around to the rear of the house where a large bay window with side panels faced the water. She nodded once, as if agreeing with herself, then picked up a rock and tapped it against the glass. A crack appeared and she tapped along it until it reached to the top. A press of the hand, covered with her coat sleeve, broke open the window with a soft tinkling of glass.

"Very nice," Katja said. "Do a lot of burglary?"

"Oh, yes. This is my second since yesterday. I'm apparently quite good at it."

They pried out the remaining glass shards and climbed inside, into a well-appointed sitting room. A brown-and-cream carpet complemented a beige overstuffed sofa flanked by spare mahogany tables and spherical table lamps. "All modern. Who would have thought?" Katja observed.

"I wonder if there's still food." Frederica wandered toward the kitchen. "They have a real refrigerator, you know. Come take a look." She patted the top of a waist-high, white metal container. "You know, according to Goebbels, the plan was to make 'People's refrigerators' for everyone, but the war got in the way, so only the big Nazis got them." Katja stood in the doorway, skeptical of the new gadget. "Nice, but you'd only need it in the summer, wouldn't you? The windowsill does fine for most of the year."

Frederica opened the refrigerator door and winced. "Rotten vegetables. I guess they left in a hurry." She closed it again and checked the cupboards. "Oatmeal for the children, good, we can take that. Dried prunes, good. Marmalade even." She turned it in her hand. "Sour cherry, my favorite. Should we eat some now?"

Katja answered from the other side of the kitchen. "No. I found something much better for breakfast. Pâté de foie gras, caviar, and biscuits." She opened the adjacent cabinet. "You're not going to believe this. Real coffee. And here's the coffeepot." She held up something shiny, with a long spout.

"Ohmygod. Let's make some. Is the gas turned on in the stove?" Frederica tried the burner. "Yes. Oh, I'm in heaven."

While the water seethed and then boiled, they ground a portion of the coffee in a hand grinder and poured it into the sock attached to the coffeepot. The rich, frothy brew gave off an almost-forgotten fragrance.

They found two demitasses, poured the coffee over a cube of sugar in each, and sipped with something close to reverence. "I really love that this is all stolen from the second biggest monster in Germany. It's only a pity we can't share it with Rudi and Peter."

"Well, we can. There's lots more to pack up here, and we haven't even checked the cellar yet." Katja scooped out another spoonful of pâté and laid it in a lump the size of her thumb on her biscuit.

Frederica finished her coffee. "You unload as much as you can from the cupboards and I'll go upstairs to look for something to carry it in." Invigorated by the coffee, she mounted the steps two at a time, but halted at the top of the stairs. The door in front of her was open to one of the children's rooms, and she felt a twinge of sorrow that six small children had to die for the fanaticism of their parents. Then she recalled that hundreds of thousands, perhaps millions of other children had died for it as well, most in not nearly so peaceful a way.

In the second children's room she found what she was looking for and took it up under her arm. A wagon, painted wood with a long handle and rubber wheels. She couldn't have imagined anything better. "Thank you, Helmut," she whispered to the dead child, and descended the stairs in a dance.

"I've got our transport," she announced. Now let's see what we find in the cellar to fill it up with. There's got to be a few bottles of *something*." She unhooked a canvas bag from the back of the cellar door.

They descended the steps in a crouch. "Not much of a cellar," Frederica remarked, touching the low ceiling.

"Probably too close to the waterline to dig any deeper. But obviously it was just fine as a wine cellar." She stood, admiring the shelves of wines and champagnes, more than they could ever carry away.

"I knew Goebbels and his wife had taste," Frederica said. "How nice of them to share."

"You know, Reichsmarks won't be worth the paper they're printed on now, so I suggest we take two or three of the champagnes, to barter with." Katja blew the dust off some of the bottles. "Ah, Veuf Clicquot and Dom Pérignon. These will do nicely. You finding anything else worth pilfering?" she asked over her shoulder.

"Lots more tins of foie gras, and another jar of marmalade. For the children, I suppose." Katja shook her head, remembering Ravensbrück. "Thousands of us slowly starving to death, and those bastards were eating *this*." She loaded her canvas sack and they trudged back upstairs to the living room.

She halted suddenly and heard her own sudden intake of breath.

A man with a pistol stood in the center of the room. In his brown shirt and riding britches, he looked like an SA man of the early thirties before the outfit became unfashionable. "Who are you and what are you doing here?"

Frederica strode past her to confront the SA man. "Oh, hello. You must be the block leader. I'm glad someone's keeping an eye on things. I'm Frederica Brandt, Dr. Goebbels' secretary. Don't you remember me? I was here once when you stopped by."

The man narrowed his eyes, as if trying to remember. "Let me see your papers."

She held up her identification in front of his face. "Listen, Herr…excuse me. I've forgotten your name."

"Müller," he muttered, not at all placated.

"Yes, Herr *Blockleiter* Müller. I've just come from the Führerbunker under the chancellery and I have some very bad news for you. Herr and Frau Goebbels are dead. Suicide. Their children too." She dropped her voice. "Homicide. Oh, the even worse news is that the Führer shot himself too. Two days ago. Obviously there has not yet been a general announcement, but I can assure you, there will be."

The block leader's eyes oscillated back and forth between them, uncertainty obviously paralyzing him. Finally he waved the pistol at them, trying to aim it at both of them at once. "You are under arrest until I get further orders."

"I don't think so, Herr Blockleiter," Katja said, pointing Erich Prietschke's Luger at him. "You see, we have a gun too. From an SS man. But we don't want to use it. Because there's no point, you see. The war really *is* over, and you won't be *getting* any further orders. All the big shots are dead. Or captured. Or fleeing westward hoping like hell to surrender to the Allies. I'm telling the truth, but even if I weren't, you already know that the Russians are swarming across Germany and will be here shortly. Probably today, and when they take a look at that stupid SA uniform, they're going to blow your head off. You can pretend it's not true and be a good Nazi, or you can protect yourself and your family by throwing it away and collecting food for the next few months. The peace is going to be very, very hard."

Müller said nothing, but his hand dropped to his side and he backed toward the door, where he turned away. Frederica called after him. "No need to hurry off. There's expensive champagne in the cellar. You might want to claim some of it before the Russians get it."

He left without closing the door.

Katja frowned. "I'm sure he's coming back with reinforcements, so let's load up and get out of here. Is there anything else worth taking?"

"How about tobacco? Also good for barter." Frederica opened the door to what appeared to be an office. A quick perusal uncovered only a few packs of cigarettes in the desk drawer. They would do.

"Look here," Katja said, opening a wardrobe door. "There are some of Magda's sweaters. It makes my skin crawl to wear their clothes, but it's better than freezing. Here, swallow your pride." She tossed one of the thick cable-knit sweaters over her shoulder and put another one on.

Frederica grimaced but yanked off her still-damp shirt and drew the thick pullover over her head. "You're right. It's warm and feels very expensive."

They loaded the wagon with their canvas bag full of champagne, foie gras tins, and the miscellany they had found in the cupboards. Frederica tossed in the cigarette packs on top.

It was still early in the day when they left the house that Joseph Goebbels built. With a certain cheerful maliciousness, they left the front door wide open.

Chapter Thirty-seven

They finally arrived at Potsdam at dusk but found little to be cheerful for. Palaces filled the centuries-old residential city of Prussian kings and emperors, almost all damaged and their royal parks pitted with craters.

They migrated toward the main station as they had agreed, though when they came within sight of where it should have been, they saw only rubble. Apparently some of the railroad lines still functioned and a few trains came through, but the principal building had been bombed. Women and old men gathered around the ruins dragging their life's possessions. Hundreds camped out waiting for a train, any train, to take them westward.

"We're not going to find them here tonight," Frederica said, "but look, there's a message board over there." She pointed toward a portion of wall where a dozen people clustered trying to make out messages. They hovered at the periphery of the group, but the darkness hindered reading without lantern or matches.

"Are you looking for someone in particular?" a man's voice asked. In the dusk, the figure in an SS uniform was ominous.

Katja stiffened. "No, we're just looking to see if we know anyone."

"I saw you come into town. Are you looking for your husbands? Brothers?"

"Why do you ask?"

"Because we caught some deserters today. In civilian clothes, of course, on a bicycle, but one was wounded. All the evidence we needed. We strung them up."

Katja felt suddenly sick, but Frederica replied calmly, "No, we're not looking for anyone. Where did you hang them?"

"In front of the old town hall. Should be a lesson to others." He strolled away, as if he had just announced the next day's weather. They waited until the SS man was out of sight, then rushed, as fast as their blistered feet and the clattering children's wagon would let them, to the town hall.

"Dear God," Katja murmured as the scene came within view. A crossbeam nailed over two upright stanchions served as a grotesque impromptu gallows. Two bodies dangled on it, swaying slightly with each gust of wind. Katja slowed her pace, trying to delay the appalling verdict. The faces were bloated and not clearly identifiable, so they had to move closer, but revulsion fought with the need to know.

When they finally stood directly beneath the pitiful victims, Katja breathed relief. It wasn't them.

They stood awhile beneath the gibbet. "So, what now?" Frederica asked, though the answer was apparent.

"Back to the station. It's the only place they'll know to look for us."

Katja felt a tug on her coat and looked down. A girl of about five looked up at her, then glanced back at the wagon Katja held. "Do you have bread, Fräulein?" she asked in a tiny child's voice.

"No, darling. No bread. I'm sorry."

Frederica called the child over. "I'll give her the marmalade. It'll bring her a little happiness." She knelt down and rummaged through the canvas bag, finally pulling out a small glass jar. She placed it into the little hands and asked, "Did you see men on a bicycle yesterday, a big green funny bicycle? One man riding working the pedals and a sick man riding on the back?"

The little girl nodded yes but couldn't take her eyes from the canvas bag that obviously held more treasures.

"Yes? You *did* see them? Where?" Frederica suddenly brightened. But the question seemed to puzzle the child. In a ruined city, with few streets remaining, "where" had little meaning.

"Look, sweetheart. If you help us find those men with the bicycle, we'll give you some oatmeal. Your mommy can cook it, to go with the jam." The child nodded again without speaking, then ran off.

"I don't think we should get our hopes up. Lots of people are fleeing on bicycles, and she was probably agreeing with you just because you had food."

"I'm sure you're right. Let's go back to the station and see if anyone's willing to share their campfire."

Campfires, as it turned out, were rare, and no one was willing to share with newcomers unless they brought their own firewood. Defeated, Frederica and Katja dropped onto the ground beneath the message wall. Katja ached in every muscle and bone, but leaning back against the wall, she managed to doze fitfully until a soft tug on her sleeve awakened her. She opened her eyes to see the little girl.

"Oh, hello," was all she could think to say.

An elderly man stood over the child, his hands thrust deep in his coat pockets. Without kneeling, he said, "Thank you for giving my granddaughter the jam."

"She's quite welcome. It belonged to someone who doesn't need it any longer."

"I understand you're looking for a man with a green bicycle?"

Frederica was awake now too. "Yes, two men, in fact, one of them was bandaged and the other blond with glasses and a scar on his chin. Have you seen them, perhaps?"

"You are Frederica?" the old man asked.

"Yes, how did you—"

"Come with me then." The old man made no effort to help them to their feet, and when they caught up with him, they saw why. Just above his shoe, the ankle of a wooden foot was visible, supported by metal braces on both sides that allowed mobility but no cushioning. He could walk, but only with effort and a limp.

Once they were well away from the people at the message wall, he spoke. "They're safe. In my barn. The deputy *Gauleiter* is hunting down deserters, and any man under sixty isn't safe on the street."

"Yes, we saw some of his work. Are you Peter's grocer friend?"

"I was. That is, I *was* a grocer, but I closed the shop when I was inducted into the army. I came home only a few months ago, with one hand and one foot missing. Oh, sorry. Oskar Kahl, at your service." He held up his right hand, in polished wood and slightly curved, with fingers a centimeter apart, as if it were about to grip an object but could never close around it. She didn't shake hands with him and he didn't seem to expect it.

The grocer's house was quite far, and it was bright morning when they arrived. The barn was more in the nature of a garage, but with straw and a goat. As soon as the grocer had locked the gate behind them, he called out and Peter appeared from behind the barn door. He ran toward them and embraced them both fervently. "We were sick with worry!" he complained. "You were supposed to come yesterday. What happened?"

"Long story, we'll tell you later," Frederica said, following him back toward the barn. "How's Rudi doing?"

"We got him some civilian clothes so we could get rid of the pajamas, and of course two days' rest has done us both good," Peter said, but a quick glance at Rudi sitting, morose, on a bench, revealed the improvement was only physical. "But I'm afraid we've eaten all Herr Kahl's food. Have you brought anything?" Peter glanced meaningfully at the canvas bag in Katja's cart. The old man had hobbled over, holding his grandchild's hand.

"In fact we have. First of all, we owe your granddaughter this." Katja lifted the tin of oatmeal from under the canvas. "With a little cooking, it should go well with the marmalade she's already earned. But before you open the cereal, why don't we start with some real food."

With a flourish, she brandished three tins of goose-liver pâté. "And to wash it down, we can drink a bottle of this." She pulled out one of the three champagne bottles, by chance, the Veuve Cliquot.

Scarcely taking his eyes from the tins of pâté, Oskar Kahl said, "Everybody get comfortable. I'll be right back with spoons and glasses. Please, don't start without me."

They made themselves comfortable on the barn floor. "So what kept you?" Peter asked.

"Nothing we need to dwell on," Frederica said evasively. "But we were always just one jump ahead of the Russians. We broke into the Jagdschloss during the rainstorm yesterday, or was it two days ago? I can't remember. Anyhow, the Russians arrived there too. Then we took a slight detour to Schwanenwerder, where we got the food. We arrived here yesterday evening and camped out by the station ruins hoping you'd find us."

"That was Herr Kahl's doing, sending out his granddaughter to look for you." Rudi peered into the bag. "What else have you got there?"

"Not all that much, unfortunately. Enough for today and another day on the road. A few packs of cigarettes, to barter with."

The barn door opened and Oskar Kahl came in with five glasses on a pan. His granddaughter followed him, clutching spoons in both hands. After passing around the glasses, Kahl tugged a corkscrew from his back pocket with his good hand and presented it to Peter.

Peter uncorked the champagne with a practiced touch. It frothed over profusely, but Kahl caught the foam in the pan and saved it while Peter poured the rest of the champagne into the glasses.

"Your health," they toasted, and all took a long drink. Kahl then carefully poured the liquid from the catch-pan into his own glass, and drank again.

Frederica opened the three tins of liver paste and handed them around, two persons to a tin. "I think you might all enjoy knowing that you're eating pâté 'organized' from the larder of the recently deceased Reichsminister of Propaganda."

The grocer looked momentarily alarmed, then shrugged. He held up his glass and said, "To the Reichsminister," and then under his breath, "May he rot in hell."

❖

At midday, they began the last, most arduous leg of the journey toward the West. As they expected, the main highway, was a solid column of refugees: families and individuals with enormous bundles on carts or bicycles, or on the back of a staggering horse. What they did not expect, however, was that they would be sharing the road with retreating military, not only Wehrmacht, but Waffen SS.

Whole detachments of soldiers forced their way through the crowds in their military vehicles until the petrol ran out. Then they formed aggressive little bands, marching with the same iron determination to surrender to the Allies as they had shown in their recent campaign to defeat them.

Though Rudi was able to walk for longer stretches, he weakened sooner than the others, so the freight bike that had transported him for three days still proved useful as a sort of wheelchair. But after five hours, his pain and exhaustion began to show, so they stopped for a supper of the remaining paté and the second bottle of champagne. With only a single bottle of champagne and a small inventory of tobacco left, Frederica abandoned the cart and carried their remaining goods in a bag on her shoulder.

Then they resumed the long march, stopping every few hours for short rests by the roadside. The sheer force of numbers of the mass of humanity that plodded inexorably westward kept them moving through the night. But at noon the next day, all four were on the verge of collapse. The day was warm, the ground dry, and the grassy meadow beckoned irresistibly. So they locked their bicycle and huddled together under their coats and, within minutes, slept like animals.

Four hours later, Peter woke to discover that someone had stolen both the bicycle and its lock. Furious, he woke the others.

Everyone blustered for a moment, but Frederica was the voice of consolation. "Think of what we've all lived through for ten years, and now we're only two days away from freedom. Rudi knows we can care for him. We just need to take the hours as they come, and soon it will be over."

"I suppose you're right," Peter said, helping Rudi to his feet. "If you'll excuse us, Rudi and I have some morning business."

A tank crew had pulled up in the meantime along the road, and Peter led Rudi past the huge panzer to find privacy in a patch of trees. Rudi was able to take care of business with one arm, so Peter focused on his own trousers. While he relieved himself, he sensed a tall lanky man come up beside him. One of the panzer fighters. Decorum, and a little fear, kept him from making eye contact. The soldier urinated as well, but when he finished, he didn't step away as decency would have required.

Peter closed his trousers and turned to confront the intruder.

A Wehrmacht major in full field kit locked eyes with him unashamedly and Peter cringed inwardly. In the last days of the war, in full retreat, was this Nazi going to do him in, after everything else?

The major shifted his glance toward Rudi and tilted his head. "Rudi? Rudi Lamm? Is that you?"

"What?" Rudi answered dully. "Do I know you?"

"Richard Koehler," the major said, offering his hand. "We worked together on *Triumph des Willens*, don't you remember? I did the aerial shots. Made me airsick, so when the war broke out, I chose tanks. Of course I've put on a little flesh in eleven years." He patted his midsection.

Memory seemed to dawn and Rudi returned the handshake with his good hand.

The major focused on Peter again. "I'm sorry, I think we might have met too, but I don't remember your name." He offered his hand again.

"Peter Arnhelm. I remember you now too. We had supper together that afternoon in Nuremberg. Strange to meet again this way."

"Yeah. Things sure didn't look like this back in Nuremberg, did they? A hundred and fifty thousand men on the field that day, raring to go. I wonder how many of them made it.

Peter shrugged. "Well, the ones who did are probably on the road just behind us."

Koehler ignored the irony. "What a fuck-up, eh? I lost almost my whole squadron, just east of Berlin. The Reds completely overran us. There's just the five of us now. And the tank, *Panzerkampfwagen* Tiger, Model B. She's a beauty, isn't she?"

Rudi scrutinized the huge panzer that took up most of the road. It looked both formidable and comical, since its entire gun had been blown away. "Not much good for battle any more, is it?"

"Insensitive of you to bring it up," the major said, feigning insult. "She's very self-conscious of her little blemish, you know. But she's still good for running away."

"Where did you get the fuel for it?"

"Stolen, siphoned from derelict vehicles, we collect it liter by liter. Can't be much left now." Koehler glanced down at Rudi's bandages. "You look like you could use a ride?"

"Jesus Christ, yes," Rudi said.

Peter added, "You're not going to believe it, but some others from the film team are here. Frederica Brandt and Katja Sommer."

They strolled together back to where the women stood, and the major nodded recognition. Can I offer you a lift? I think we've got room for four."

Frederica hefted her canvas sack. "Only on the condition that you accept our last bottle of champagne."

"With the greatest pleasure. You all climb on board while I pass this around to my men. They deserve it more than I do."

Peter helped Rudi up onto the panzer dome, and the women clambered up after them, anchoring themselves to various handles and protuberances. In a few minutes, Koehler returned with his men, who waved their thanks and gathered around the tank. Two of the men wore head bandages and so climbed up beside Katja. Major Koehler took the command position while the tank driver dropped inside and started the engine.

With the low afternoon sun in their faces, they rolled due west. The four of them crouched behind the turret with its emasculated cannon. The major rode in front of them, his upper body protruding from the hatchway, and the afternoon sun radiated around his head and shoulders like a halo. It stirred a faint memory in Katja, of another haloed leader who rode triumphantly into the morning light, but this time their man was headed toward sunset.

Chapter Thirty-eight

May 4, 1945
Tangermünde

The Tiger tank lurched once or twice as they began the uphill approach to the bridge abutment, and after some hundred meters, it ground to a halt.

No matter, Katja thought; they had arrived. "So that's it, then," she said, gazing into the gray distance at the Elbe crossing.

"*Jawohl,* Tangermünde, gateway to the West," Major Koehler said. "All you have to do is get across." Sliding his arms through a bulky rucksack, he lifted himself out of the hatchway and dropped to the ground. His soldiers gathered around him, blanket rolls, mess kits, and the like hanging from their shoulders. "Best of luck to you all." The major waved to his civilian passengers, then marched off to surrender with the last four men under his command.

"Unbelievable," Frederica whispered, taking hold of Katja's hand.

The four of them stared, speechless, at the sight. The countless thousands of troops and refugees that poured westward across Germany had met a final obstacle, a demolished bridge. Like any blocked stream, the flow of humanity pooled and grew ever wider until a sea of dark specks covered the marshy meadow at the end.

They clambered down from the dead Tiger tank and braced for the final walk. "How are you holding up, Rudi?" Frederica asked.

"I'll manage," he said, though he looked anxiously at the precipitous drop from the end of the elevated ramp to the water's edge below.

In twenty minutes they were at the height of a five-story building, and below them, Katja could see the blown-up railroad bridge that lay in the Elbe River. On the far side, the superstructure of girders still tilted upward, out of the water, with portions of the rail track just visible.

But on the near side, at the foot of the descent they were about to make, the bridge lay underwater. The Allies had apparently constructed a temporary wooden structure about a meter wide and some ten meters long and connected it to the twisted girders, but to reach it, the refugees had to clamber down from the highway over broken slabs of concrete and debris.

"Let me go first," Peter volunteered. "I can block anyone falling forward. Frederica, why don't you come second, with Rudi leaning against you, and then Katja, hanging on to Rudi from behind."

All agreed, and thus encumbered, they made their way down the fractured concrete and rubble and steel. But the precariousness of the descent merely brought them to the swaying mass at the water's edge—of soldiers, old men, women with children in their arms, and the walking wounded. All waited to cross in single file along the one-meter-wide walkway.

No one could carry anything larger than an infant or a suitcase. Anyone who couldn't walk couldn't cross, and a half-submerged body floating along the current away from the bridge made it clear that the weak would have no help.

The four of them held onto each other, edging ever closer to the wooden planks, and made their way laboriously forward in the mournful, shuffling line.

Midway into the river the footbridge ended. Thereafter, they had to grab hold of the girders and pull themselves along a series of planks laid haphazardly over the remaining railroad ties that still protruded from the water. At the end, the tracks rose up at a nearly 45-degree angle to the shoreline, and the walk became a climb.

All along the way, people slipped to their knees and were cursed by the exhausted people behind them until they could rise again and stagger on.

The steep gradient of broken steel that rose at the end of the bridge was the final obstacle, and the refugees reacted variously. With the end in sight, some seemed to draw strength for the final push. But for others, it was a signal to break down emotionally. One woman leaned over the railing and sobbed, another elderly man stumbled slowly past her mumbling something in Latin. Women urged whimpering, stupefied children ahead of them.

The soldiers, both Wehrmacht and SS, still carried their rifles, and bundles of equipment hung around them. Most of them had grim expressions, a few weak smiles. Katja could not imagine what they were thinking.

Where the bridge touched land, a stocky soldier with MP painted on his helmet and armband was shouting in English trying to separate the soldiers from the civilians and direct them toward internment. He punctuated his orders with occasional blows of his rifle butt across the backs of the Germans, and though they still had their weapons, no soldier dared to resist. This was rescue.

Katja and the others moved toward the left with the noncombatants, but Peter held them back for a moment. "Look," he said in a voice filled with awe.

Just beyond the abusive MP, the German soldiers were surrendering their weapons, and as the GI received each rifle, he tossed it behind him. The mountain of rifles was already high over his head and extended for at least twenty meters. And thousands of soldiers arriving on the other side of the Elbe would bring still more. A gun, it seemed, for every man in Germany.

"There's Major Koehler," Frederica said. They watched as the panzer commander shuffled up to the pile and divested himself of rifle, steel helmet, and sidearm. He made a faint nod of salute to the GI collecting the weapons, then marched with his men into the sea of soldiers penned together in a field. "Poor bastard," Rudi said. "That could be me."

" I guess it's time to get rid of this," Peter said, drawing an SS holster from his rucksack. "Rest in peace, Gearhardt Kramer," he said, and lobbed the holster and gun in an arc onto the pile.

"Let's go." Katja pulled him away from the continuing drama back into the line of civilians.

Some distance along their route, they passed a sign in both Russian and English. Frederica read it out loud, translating it into German for Katja. "'Welcome. The American 102nd division greets the fighters of Russia. One of the United Nations.' I guess this is where the two armies met before the Russians doubled back to finish the job." She thought for a second. "Strange that the Americans stopped their advance. I wonder who decided on that strategy."

Just past the sign, another MP held a clipboard, but otherwise seemed unoccupied. Frederica approached him and spoke in flawless English. "Can you tell us how to reach your commanding officer?"

The MP first registered astonishment at hearing English, then contempt at the request. "Who the hell are you? I don't think Major General Keating is available at the moment."

Frederica persisted. "Is it possible to get a message to him? I, that is, we, are with British Intelligence and would like to give General…Keating did you say…some useful information."

The MP frowned in consternation. "You got any identification papers, Miss?"

Frederica reached into her sweater pocket and produced her Berliner identification papers, which included the stamp from the Ministry of Propaganda. He held them up them, obviously befuddled by the German script.

"But of course it's not going to say 'British Intelligence,' is it?" Frederica said coolly. "British agents don't usually carry their badges while in enemy territory, do they? The only way to check my story is by contacting my superior in London. I believe your commanding officer has the authority to do that."

"Look, don't get smart with me, lady. I've had just about enough with you Krauts coming here and making demands all of a sudden. You've just lost your goddam war and you've surrendered, so get back in line, the four of you."

"Thank you for that lesson, but I'm also British, and if you'd just send a message to General Keating, we can clarify everything. If I'm telling the truth, you will not endear yourself to your superiors by delaying my delivery of the information. You could even be court-martialed," she added softly.

The MP muttered something profane and called over another soldier. "Dugan, go tell the lieutenant we've got someone who claims to be working for the British and who wants to see the general."

"Wait over there." The MP pointed with his clipboard toward a wall where a number of civilians already stood. Frederica led the way and Peter lowered Rudi carefully to the ground.

"So what *are* you going to tell the general, exactly? I mean Rudi and I don't work for British Intelligence. Where does that put us?"

"I can make a strong case for you, Peter, since you were doing active sabotage. That and the fact that you both were persecuted by the Nazis should at least get you refugee status and keep you free."

Rudi shook his head. "I was interned because I'm homosexual. That's still illegal. And the penal regiment. Well, if they learn about that, I'm done for."

Frederica's lips tightened. "I don't know, Rudi. I'll do my best to keep you out of another internment camp." She nodded toward the ever-expanding mass of German soldiers.

They had little left to say and their feet were sore, so they settled down to wait. They were sure the victors would ignore them, but in fact, within fifteen minutes, the private who had delivered the message returned with an officer.

"I'm Lieutenant Forbes. What can I do for you?"

Frederica stood up to meet him eye to eye and offered her hand. "My name is Frederica Brandt. I've been working undercover for British Intelligence since 1935 and for the Special Operations Executive since 1940, code name Caesar. I've reported directly to an agent called Handel and indirectly to Maurice Buckmaster. I wish to come in, along with my colleagues, who have put their lives at risk in collaborating with me: Katja Sommer, Peter Arnhelm, and Rudi Lamm." She gestured toward each one as she named them. "In addition, I have specific information about Adolf Hitler and a letter from Joseph Goebbels. You can obtain confirmation of my identity by contacting Mr. Buckmaster at the SOE in London."

"Code name Caesar, eh?" He looked faintly skeptical. "Very interesting. Unfortunately, we're sort of tied up processing a hundred thousand surrendering troops and civilians, so we're not equipped to hold any conversations with London at the moment. What's your information, specifically?"

"Primarily that as Joseph Goebbels' secretary, I was in the bunker with Adolf Hitler at the time of his suicide, and I would like to provide the details of that event to my superiors."

"You were Goebbels' secretary? In the bunker with Adolf Hitler?" The officer finally seemed impressed. "I see. Well, I know exactly the people you need to talk to. Come with me."

He led them into an open courtyard where a military personnel carrier was waiting with its motor running. At his signal, an MP opened the rear double doors. The carrier was nearly full with other passengers, but there were a few benches in the rear, and the MP helped them climb inside.

"Where are they taking us?" Peter asked nervously, and Katja translated his question into English to the officer, who was just about to turn away.

"To Seventh Army headquarters," the lieutenant said. "They'll know what to do with you there." With that, the MP closed the doors, locking them in the grim yellowish interior lit by a single small bulb at the far end of the truck bed.

"Headquarters? But why are we in a prison truck, with prisoners?" Rudi tilted his head and Katja followed his glance toward the other passengers' hands. They were all shackled.

"Um, good question. Any ideas, Frederica?"

"Will you all stop worrying? I'm sure things will be all right once Handel identifies us. Just be patient." Katja couldn't tell if Frederica's reaction was sincere or simply bravado. It seemed absurd, after surviving two concentration camps and the Führer's bunker, that they would end up being imprisoned by the victorious Allies.

The light went out as the truck began to move and plunged them into darkness.

❖

Dozing fitfully as she had been doing for weeks, it seemed, Katja was awakened often by the jolts and delays from traveling along roads clogged with debris.

An eternity later, the truck halted with a lurch.

The doors opened to a military camp and two MPs in clean white helmets and immaculate spats. With swollen feet and dopey from half sleep, the four clambered down out of the truck. The MPs urged them to one side, then unshackled the other passengers and led them toward a building in the distance.

Left unattended, they waited, nonplussed. Katja rubbed her face and glanced around. Barracks, black against the pre-dawn sky. Scattered among them, small cottages. Like Ravensbrück. A wave of dread washed through her.

In a few minutes another MP appeared. "This way, please," he said, and led them to the nearest building, a long, one-story wooden hut. Inside, clerks were setting up large ledgers and typewriters. One of the clerks had a steaming cup next to his typewriter, and the fragrance of coffee made Katja almost dizzy.

Frederica addressed the first of the clerks. "Where are we?"

The clerk ignored her.

"Is this a POW camp? Have we been arrested?"

"We ask the questions here, you give the answers. But for your information, you're at the interim headquarters of the Seventh Army, 7708 War Crimes Group. Now *you* tell *me* who *you* are."

Frederica repeated what she had said to the lieutenant earlier. The clerk glanced up once, obviously surprised when she said "British Intelligence," but otherwise simply recorded her statement on the typewriter.

On the other side of the room, beyond earshot of Frederica, Katja gave her statement in German, while Rudi and Peter were interviewed in another room.

Then, to Katja's alarm, MPs came from the other room leading Rudi and Peter by the arms. As they passed her and exited through the door of the hut, Rudi looked back, and for the first time, his eyes registered real fear.

"That will be all for now," Katja's interviewer said. "The sergeant will show you to your quarters." An MP stepped forward and, without speaking, escorted both her and Frederica from the building.

Katja glanced sideways at him as they walked and marveled at how muscled he was. What did the Americans eat? For all his bulk, he made no effort to prod or intimidate them, but led them at a moderate pace down the row of barracks. Several small cottages made up the fourth side of the camp, and he led them to one of them, opened the door, and waved them in.

The cottage had a single room with four beds. Real beds, not wooden platforms, and an adjacent toilet, with a door, a small table, four chairs, and a lamp. The cottage was otherwise empty.

"Can you tell us where in Germany we are?" Frederica asked.

"You're in Augsberg, Ma'am. I think they call it *Bärenkeller* here. The Seventh Army has taken over the Wehrmacht barracks for incarceration and questioning of persons like yourselves."

"Why have we been separated from the other prisoners?"

"You're not prisoners, Ma'am," the MP said, managing to be polite and aloof at the same time. "You're not allowed to associate with the other inmates, who are. They'll be going for breakfast shortly, but they're off limits."

"But what about the two men we arrived with?"

The soldier shrugged. "I don't know their status, Ma'am. I think the major will be calling for you shortly. Perhaps you can ask him." He saluted with his immaculately gloved hand and left them alone.

Within minutes, a siren sounded. Katja shuddered, recalling the roll calls at Ravensbrück. To confirm that they were free, they tried the cottage door and, finding it open, went outside to study their surroundings.

They watched as a team of MPs unlocked the doors of the several barracks across the way, and men streamed out. Most of them wore uniforms, and all were officers, some with the insignias of very high rank.

Katja sighed. "No sign of Rudi or Peter, but I see at least two generals. I don't recognize them though."

"Only generals? How about a Reichsmarshall?"

Katja glanced in the direction Frederica pointed. "I don't believe it. Hermann Goering. He looks a wreck. I almost didn't recognize him. I wonder who else is here."

"And who's in the cottage next to us? Come on. We might as well find out." Frederica wandered toward it and knocked.

"Come in," someone said.

Frederica opened the door, took a step forward, then halted so abruptly Katja almost crashed into her. "Traudl Junge!" Frederica exclaimed. "How did you get here so quickly?"

Traudl took her by the arm and drew her into the room. "I left the bunker right after the Führer…died," Traudl said. "And it looked as if I had made it to safety, but I had to show papers at Tangermünde, and I guess the Americans had my name. That's when they picked me up and brought me here."

"So you're a prisoner?" Frederica asked.

"Yes, but they're not treating us like the men. They seem to think we're harmless and just want all the information they can get. They're interrogating us all the time." Traudl's expression changed to cheerful resignation. "Whatever happens, at least they feed us well. I was just about to go for breakfast. There's a place away from the male prisoners where they'll let us eat. Want to come along? Your friend too."

Katja had scarcely been listening, for her eyes were riveted on the other woman, who half sat, half crouched on her bed, her knees drawn up to her chin. Next to her was a battered leather briefcase, which she seemed to be guarding. "No, thank you. We'll keep Frau Riefenstahl company while you're gone."

"Ah, so you know each other. Well, then, until later." Traudl nodded amiably as she passed them and left the cottage.

Katja strode ahead of Frederica toward the bed. "So, we meet again," she said, wishing she had thought of a better greeting. "And once again you are in bed. Were you also running away from the Russians?"

Leni Riefenstahl clutched her knees and rested her chin on her forearms. She was gaunt and appeared ill, but offered a wan smile. "In fact, I was running away from the Americans. They arrested me in Austria and I was put in a camp, but not a very secure one, so I escaped. They caught me and put me in another one in Germany, where I escaped again. They caught me a third time and I escaped yet again. I think they're getting a little irritated."

Her speech was slightly slurred, as if she were drugged.

"Are you all right?" Frederica asked, leaning over her.

"No, of course I'm not all right. I've been sick as a dog off and on for a year, and it was all I could do to keep the pain under control just to keep working. Fortunately, the Amis let me keep my medication when they arrested me. I'm here instead of locked up someplace only because they know I'm too sick to run any more."

"What were you doing in Austria?"

"Filming *Tiefland*. I know it sounds insane to be filming during the last days of the war, but, well, that's the way it was. But at the end, some of my best film friends betrayed me."

"What do you mean?"

"The Schneebergers. They encouraged me to flee with them, when the Russians got close. But when the Führer committed suicide, they suddenly turned against me. They called me a 'Nazi whore.' Can you imagine? Just because I cried hearing about his death."

Katja *could* imagine. Easily. The sexual slur, she knew, was false, but Riefenstahl had been in Hitler's entourage, which was almost as bad.

"Ridiculous. I admit," Riefenstahl said. "I was taken by his powerful personality but never joined the party, and I was never anti-Semitic. None of that was important to me. I was, I still *am,* an artist."

Katja had heard it before and was tired of it. "I'm afraid the Allies won't see it that way. Once they look at *Triumph des Willens*, they'll call it party propaganda. Surely you can't think otherwise."

Riefenstahl shook her head. "That film will finish me. I wish I'd never heard of the damned Nuremberg Party Rally."

"A lot of people are saying that now," Frederica said coldly.

Riefenstahl had obviously already formulated her defense. "I'm sure all of Germany regrets letting things get so out of hand. I certainly do. But I didn't know about the concentration camps."

Frederica frowned her disbelief, and Riefenstahl amended her remark. "I mean I knew there were camps for Hitler's enemies, but I had no idea of the torture and killing on that scale." She seemed to look inwardly for a moment, then added, "Don't you remember? In the beginning, Nazism seemed like a daring, magnificent idea. It went through the German spirit like a force of nature, made the nation into a great, noble beast. But I should have seen how dangerous that was."

Frederica's mouth twisted in contempt. "The Nazis *wanted to be* great, noble beasts, but in fact, they were blustering emotional adolescents, and their followers were sheep. If they thought they were a force of nature, they met a bigger one and now have nothing to complain about."

Katja was more conciliatory. "I'll be happy to speak for you, Frau Riefenstahl. I mean I'll tell them about your rescuing me from Ravensbrück. I have to thank you for that. It's only a pity you couldn't do the same for Rudi. He's survived, but he's a broken man."

"If I *had* saved him, I couldn't have saved you. It was a card I could play only once. People always overestimated my friendship with the Führer, probably because people kept photographing us together. But there was a difference between being a Nazi and making a work of art for them. You know that, even if the Amis don't. And even if they imprison me, it will always be true that I was an artist."

"Yes, you were," Katja said. "The best in your field. I think people will remember that, when all is said and done."

Riefenstahl seemed to warm at the remark. She laid a hand gently on Katja's forearm. "Sweet of you to say that. You know, I still have some of the photos, believe it or not."

She pulled the leather case onto her lap and snapped it open. It held loose papers, undergarments, a camera, and folders of photographs. She leafed through them, smiling to herself as if reminiscing. "Here's my favorite," she said, sliding one of the photos out and handing it to Katja.

"Ah, yes. Your 'Flag' picture. The Hitlerjugend holding up the Nazi flag with the sunlight filtering through it. I remember that Rudi showed it to a friend, a Russian photographer who was very impressed. He said it made him want to go out and make his own flag picture. I wonder if he ever managed it."

Still thumbing through her photos, Riefenstahl seemed not to hear. "I've also got a nice picture of a group of us," she said, and pulled out another from the folder. "Remember? Our last day on the film."

Katja studied the photo with a sudden rush of nostalgia and regret. "I'd forgotten about this one. The thirteen of us at our last supper in Nuremberg."

"I wonder what happened to everyone," Riefenstahl remarked. She tapped her fingers on two of the men. "Allgeier was filming with the Wehrmacht and the last I heard he was alive. Vogel, unfortunately, was killed on the Eastern Front." She moved her finger along the line of faces. "What about Hans Gottschalk?"

"He went down with the *Bismarck*, and Dietrich Kurz fell at Stalingrad," Katja said.

"I'm sorry to hear that," Riefenstahl said with obvious sincerity. Her finger moved to two others. "What about Marti Kraus?"

"In the Volkssturm in Berlin. His son too. I don't think they made it."

"And Erich Prietschke?"

"Dead," Katja said coldly, and offered no detail.

"Are we three the only ones who got out, then?" Riefenstahl asked.

"No. Richard Koehler was in a panzer division and surrendered at Tangermünde. We actually saw him just at the end. Rudi Lamm and his friend Peter also survived—against all odds. They arrived here with us, though I don't know where they're being held."

"Oh, I'm glad to know they made it. Do you think they'll be held as POWs?"

"Not Peter. He's a half Jew and was underground the whole time. But Rudi was on the Eastern Front in a penal SS regiment. It's a complicated case."

"That's what they say about mine. One day I'm just a filmmaker and the next day I'm Hitler's mistress." She shrugged.

Katja had left the cottage door open on entering, and another figure stood in the doorway in a shiny white helmet. He knocked on the doorjamb. "Miss Riefenstahl, I'm to take you to interrogation again."

"Again? This will be the third time," she grumbled. Groaning slightly, she swung her feet over onto the floor and stood upright with effort. "They're convinced I can give them details about Hitler's sex life. So very Hollywood, don't you think?" She emitted a long sigh and hobbled in obvious pain through the doorway to follow the sergeant.

Another white helmet appeared a moment later, the man under it even bulkier than the one before. "There you are. I was looking for you. Miss Brandt, Miss Sommer, I'm to escort you both to interrogation."

Frederica translated to Katja. "Interrogation, just what we want. This is where we get to tell our story to someone other than a GI with a clipboard. Let's hope they'll listen this time."

Chapter Thirty-nine

The corridor outside the interrogation room was empty but for two wooden chairs, and Katja waited on one of them. She supposed the Americans were interrogating Frederica first to make sure they both told the same story, but what was taking so long?

Finally an MP stepped out of the room and came toward her. "Major Bernstein will see you now." This soldier, with light-brown hair tending toward red and a hint of childhood freckles, reminded her for a brief poignant moment of Dietrich, though ten kilos heavier.

The interrogation room was not particularly intimidating. A simple office space with a central aluminum table and wooden chairs on both sides of it. A map of Germany hung on the wall and a shelf nearby held numerous loose-leaf binders. No portrait of the US president, Katja noted. Who *was* the president now? Oh, right. Truman. Too new to have an official portrait, she supposed.

Major Bernstein, a man of about forty-five and trimmer than most of his colleagues, had unmistakably Semitic features. Would he be hostile toward them? Yet a softness in his expression made her want to trust him. He didn't offer his hand but gestured toward the empty chair next to Frederica. "Please take a seat, Miss Sommer," he said in passable German.

Katja sat down next to Frederica, who smiled encouragement at her. The major picked up a fountain pen and glanced down at the open folder in front of him. "You are Katherine Sommer, resident of

Berlin?" His marked American accent made him sound simple, not to say comical, but she reminded herself that he held all their fates in his hands, and she answered respectfully.

"Katherine officially, sir, but I've always only been called Katja."

He noted it down. "Can you describe your relationship to Miss Brandt?"

The question threw her and her heartbeat quickened with fear. Had Frederica confessed their romantic involvement? Should she lie about it? "I…uh…we…"

Apparently noticing her confusion, he amended, "I mean, how did you meet and become involved in her activities?"

Katja relaxed. He meant the espionage. "We were colleagues working on a film back in 1934 and became friends. I had no idea she was working for British Intelligence. After a mutual friend of ours, Rudi Lamm, was sent to Sachsenhausen, I became hostile to the Nazis but didn't know what to do about it. Then one day I saw Frederica make a drop at a kiosk and confronted her, threatening to denounce her if she didn't tell me what she was doing. I was lying, of course. I never would have. But I needed to know. When she told me it was for British intelligence, I asked to join her and we worked together after that. That is, until I was sent to Ravensbrück."

The interrogator scribbled notes while she spoke, but when she said Ravensbrück, he looked up in surprise. "That's a concentration camp?"

"Yes, for women. Near Berlin. But after a few months, Frederica convinced Leni Riefenstahl to use her influence with Hitler to get me released, so I came back to Berlin. I continued working at the Charité hospital and helping Frederica make her information drops, although the locations kept changing."

"Can you tell me more about the organization you worked for?"

"Well, as I understood it, the Special Operations Executive was supposed to assist the resistance in the Nazi-occupied countries and not so much in Germany. But because of Frederica's unique position in the propaganda ministry, our resistance was in the form of furnishing military and political information to Britain."

"And how did you do that?"

"I'm sure that Frederica already told you, she transcribed the journal entries of Joseph Goebbels, the ones he dictated to his stenographer. In the beginning, she made the drops alone, but the risk for her was very great. Since it was easier for me to be anonymous, I began to do them for her."

"What was the nature of Miss Brandt's personal relationship with Joseph Goebbels?"

Alarm bells went off again. Was he trying to make a case for Frederica being Goebbels' mistress? The possibility of losing Frederica to an Allied prison loomed up before her. She tried to calm herself and answer coolly, but heard how tight her voice had become. Could he see how the question terrified her?

"I'm sorry, I don't understand the question. Do you mean did she work closely with him? Yes. She had spent years on winning his trust and finally succeeded to the point that he let her transcribe his personal letters and diaries. He thought she was a good Nazi even at the end, in the Führerbunker. That's how good she was. Is." Katja's face grew warm, but she would not be brought to say more.

Bernstein held up a crumpled and slightly soiled piece of blue paper. "Then she might have come into possession of a final personal document of Dr. Goebbels."

Katja's fear began to subside. He wanted simply to verify the typed note Frederica had brought out of the bunker and carried in her skirt for a week. "More than simply 'come into possession.' Goebbels kept her in the bunker until the very end and, as I understand it, he dictated a final statement to her before committing suicide."

"And what about Rudolf Lamm and Peter Arnhelm?" Bernstein asked, opening another folder.

Exhaling with relief, she hoped not audibly, Katja moved cheerfully onto the next subject. "They were Frederica's friends from a long time ago, but I met them while working on a film. Rudi was a photographer, until he was arrested and sent to Sachsenhausen. Peter was my friend throughout the war. He worked as a costume designer until it was forbidden to employ Jews. Somehow he was able to hide at the zoo, taking care of the animals. I know he was active in sabotage for a few months too, setting fires in factories. He also helped several times on a drop at a hotel, acting as a male escort."

"I see." The major jotted a few notes on paper, then closed his folder. "Thank you very much for your information. Now, if you don't mind, I'd like to show you some footage that was filmed by the British earlier this month. It'll take only a few minutes. Then the sergeant will escort you back to your quarters." He stood up, signaling the end of the interrogation, and led them to an adjoining room, where a projector and portable screen were set up.

Katja recalled a similar scenario eleven years earlier, when Leni Riefenstahl had called the entire camera crew to view a sampling of their ambitious documentary. But this opening scene was not a hymn of praise to the Führer. This scene was his damnation.

In grainy film, a camera held by a shaky hand scans a wide terrain scattered with emaciated corpses. In among them, living skeletons wander, or squat on the ground slack-jawed and stupefied.

"Bergen-Belsen, camp two," Bernstein replied to her unasked question.

Katja watched, hypnotized by horror as female SS guards, plump and sullen are led at rifle point to join their male colleagues. Some of the men are still in uniform, others stripped to filthy undershirts. Trucks arrive, piled high with naked corpses, presumably the ones filmed earlier, and the guards unload them. The camera alternates between their expressionless faces and their awkward gait as they carry or drag the partially decomposed bodies a short distance to the edge of an enormous pit. They drop the bodies, which slide down the side of the pit, already holding what appear to be thousands of cadavers. The camera, mercifully, does not show their faces.

Katja's practiced eye recognizes the panorama shot that follows, not of a stadium of robust young patriots standing at attention, but of an enormous mass grave. The camera pans along all four sides. The female guards stand on one side, the males on the other. All look away from the camera. Nearby, a line of old men in business suits and coats frown in consternation.

"The Burgermeister and other civic leaders," Bernstein explains.

At the far end, two men stand alone. It seems to be a ceremony. The camera comes around behind them, looks over the shoulder of one onto a book from which he reads.

Then a scene almost worse than the sight of the bodies themselves. A bulldozer shoves the walls of excavated material back into the pit over the dead, which twist and tumble helplessly as they are caught in the fall of sand. Again and again, the wide scoop pushes and the bodies tumble, until they are finally covered and the film ends.

Katja sat for a moment, nauseous. When she spoke, her voice was dry. "Why do you show this to us?" she rasped. "We told you, we opposed the Nazis."

Major Bernstein signaled the projectionist, who reversed the reels. Over the whirring sound of the rewinding film, he answered. "I don't doubt it. But that makes no difference. You also said you worked on a party documentary. I don't know when you had your conversion, but I want to make sure that no German can say, 'It didn't happen,' or 'It couldn't have been so bad.' I suspect, in time, we will uncover atrocities on *all* sides, but this one belongs to Germany." He stood up and motioned toward the door. "You can go now. We'll let you know as soon as we hear from our British colleagues."

The redheaded MP was already leading Katja and Frederica back to their quarters when two others escorted Rudi Lamm into the interrogation room. He sat down, gripping his upper left arm, which still rested in a sling. He glanced up nervously at the American major, then down at the folder the major was just opening. He licked his dry lips.

"Your full name is Rudolf Lamm, from Neukölln, Berlin?" Major Bernstein said in German.

"Yes, sir. It is."

"What was your profession?"

"I was a photographer, sir, until I was arrested."

"When was that?

"In 1939. I was sent to Sachsenhausen."

"How long were you there?"

"Until December 1941."

"And then you were released?"

"Uh, not released. Just transferred to a penal regiment."

"What was the name of the regiment?"

Rudi blanched. This was the mortal blow to his freedom. "SS Sonderregiment Dirlewanger."

Major Bernstein nodded and glanced down again at his folder. "That was from December 1941 until August 1944?"

"Yes, sir. May I ask how you know all this?"

"Generally I am the one who asks the questions, but I don't mind telling you that our Soviet allies have been quite thorough in obtaining records from the headquarters that have come under their control. They have unearthed numerous atrocities and war crimes, and it is in their interest as well as ours to identify the perpetrators. So, my next question is, what happened in August 1944?"

Rudi stared up at the ceiling, formulating his response. "I deserted from my unit in Hungary. I was on my own for a while, but the Soviets were everywhere, so I joined a Wehrmacht battalion near Danzig. It was easy to say I lost my paybook, and they issued me an interim ID. They were glad to have another man. Then in April of this year, I was wounded and evacuated back to Berlin. That's how I met up again with Katja and Frederica."

Major Bernstein had not taken his eyes from the report on his desk. "And were you with the SS Sonderregiment in May 1942?"

Rudi swallowed hard. "Yes, sir."

The major held up the paper he had been staring at. "This is a preliminary list of names of SS war-crimes suspects we have been asked to watch out for and apprehend."

"And my name is on that list?" Rudi was ashen.

"Yes. Mr. Lamm, it is. On May 12, 1942, you are accused of participating in the mass murder of the inhabitants of Kliczów in Byelorussia, and of individually burning to death Irenka Kachurin."

Rudi pressed his hand over his eyes, as if to remove the image that was seared in his memory. "That's not true, sir. I did not fire my rifle during the mass execution, and the woman—I didn't know her name—was set on fire by another member of the regiment. I shot her to put her out of her agony."

"Unfortunately, there is a picture, and you and Mrs. Kachurin are the only ones in it." The major slid the photograph across the table toward him. Rudi holding his pistol to the head of the woman whose head and shoulders were in flames.

"I swear to you, I fired only one shot that day, and it was to end that woman's suffering. Why would I shoot her if I wanted her to burn to death?"

"Perhaps so. But in the following two-and-a-half years, you never fired your rifle? You never set fire to anything?"

Rudi let his head fall back against his chair. He was broken. "I shot dozens, maybe hundreds, I don't know any more. At first it was just to keep them from burning, but then I followed orders, the same as everyone else. If I hadn't, I'd have been killed. Doesn't that count for anything?"

"I think that's an argument we're going to hear a lot in the coming months," Major Bernstein said coldly. "Even if you feel you're being made a scapegoat for the crimes of the others, you can't lay claim to being innocent."

"I *was*, in the beginning."

The major was not sympathetic. "Everyone is."

Rudi laid his face in his good hand. "Will I have a trial?"

"At some point. In the meantime, you will be interned. Do you have anything more to add in your defense?"

Rudi's voice had grown soft again. "No, sir. Just the request to speak to my friends."

"In a little while. First I'd like you to watch something. After that I'll allow you fifteen minutes to say your good-byes before transferring you to the war-crimes barracks."

Rudi nodded, resigned, then followed the major into an adjoining room where Peter was already sitting. He sat down, comforted by Peter's presence, and waited. Then the light went out and a grainy film began to flicker on a portable screen.

❖

At ten o'clock the next morning, Katja and Frederica were summoned again to the major's office. The MP admitted them but, to their surprise, only Rudi and Peter were present.

They greeted each other reassuringly and Katja glanced around, puzzled. "Are they going to interrogate us all together now, do you think?"

Rudi was somber. "We're not here for interrogation. It's for us to say good-bye. I've been arrested for war crimes."

Katja sat down, stunned. "Good grief, why? You haven't done anything like that. You were in a concentration camp, for God's sake."

"It's because of the SS regiment I was in. They committed atrocities in Poland and Byelorussia, set fire to villages, killed women and children, that sort of thing."

"But you can't be guilty of that. I know you," Frederica said.

Rudi shook his head. "Guilt's not black and white. Did you see their film about Bergen-Belsen? That was done in our name and nobody in Germany is guiltless now. I started being guilty when I ignored the railing against the Jews and the gypsies, and worked on Riefenstahl's propaganda film. I finally saw the danger when they came for people like me, but by then it was too late. I'd been so concerned with my own survival and success, I'd helped them build their Reich. Joining the regiment to get out of Sachsenhausen was just the next step."

Katja persisted. "But you didn't kill civilians."

Rudi's chest seemed to deflate and he slumped in his chair, disconsolate. "The Nazis changed me, Katja. Peter had made me a loving man, but Sachsenhausen made me a whore. And Russia made me a murderer."

"Prison. My God," Frederica whispered. "And I delivered you to them, like a Judas."

Rudi shook his head. "No, they had my name on a list. They would have caught me eventually. It actually looks better that we came willingly and I didn't lie."

"No, I won't have it." Peter's jaw went tight. "They're making you a scapegoat, sacrificing you because they can't catch any of the others."

"*We* are the others, though," Frederica said solemnly. "We've all killed someone. Two of us with our own hands." She avoided looking at Katja. "Don't you think a few people died in those factory fires you set? Some worker or overseer who wasn't allowed to go to a shelter? And I'm the worst of all. I sent the Allies strategic information and helped kill more than all the rest of you together." She shook her head. "None of us are lambs."

Katja leaned toward Rudi and touched his shoulder. "Did they say you'd have a trial?"

"Yes, the Major promised me at least that. They can't execute every soldier who followed orders on the Eastern Front, so I suppose they'll just give me prison time."

Peter slid closer to him. "Then I'll wait. I've already waited for five years. I'll wait another five. Or ten. Don't let this break you and make you stop loving me."

Rudi threw his free arm around Peter's neck. "I'll never stop loving you," he said, his voice breaking. "I never stopped for a minute in the camp or on the Eastern Front. You're all that kept me going."

"What about you, Peter?" Katja asked. "Where will you stay?"

"Don't worry about me. The major said I automatically have refugee status. I can stay in a camp for a while. Then I'll take things day by day, as I did during the war."

Frederica leaned toward him, laying her arm across his back. I promise I'll send money and packages from London, as soon as possible. To Rudi, too, if I'm allowed. But you'll have to contact us when you're settled and tell us where you are. You'll be able to reach me, I'm sure, through the SOE office, and if you register with the Red Cross, we can find you too. We're family, Peter. We won't leave you."

"Time's up." The MP opened the door and stood waiting. They had just enough time to exchange embraces before a second soldier appeared and the two of them led Rudi and Peter away.

Katja and Frederica sat stunned for a moment, until Major Bernstein entered and reclaimed his desk.

❖

Frederica confronted him. “Major, with all due respect, you can’t just charge Rudi Lamm with war crimes like some big Nazi. He was a victim of war crimes himself and was *forced* to join the penal regiment. Surely you can appreciate that.”

“Oh, I do. But you must also appreciate the magnitude of the crimes. This is not just a single murder, although the charge of immolation is a grave one. We are uncovering widespread civilian massacres and genocides far beyond the bloodshed of the battlefield. Someone must be accountable for these atrocities.”

“Both sides have committed atrocities, Major.” Katja’s face heated with unfocused anger. “Immolation is a grave charge, you say? Do I need to remind you that Hamburg and Dresden were firebombed, that whole cities were set ablaze and their civilian populations burned alive? Who will be accountable for them?”

“There is no point in trading accusations, Miss Sommer. The scale of horrors in this war keeps rising and leaves us all shaken at what men are capable of. All men. The company chaplain keeps praying for a time when the lion will lie down with the lamb. But he doesn’t want to accept the terrible fact that the lion *is* the lamb.”

Someone knocked at the door. “What is it?” he called out.

An MP took one step into the room, his hand still on the door. “Sir, the SOE people have arrived. They said to give you the code name Handel.”

Frederica stood up. “Handel is here?”

“I believe so, Ma’am.”

Chapter Forty

Should we go out to meet them?" Frederica asked, starting toward the door.

Bernstein raised a hand. "That's not necessary. They're probably talking to the duty officer and will be along in just a moment."

Katja also was too impatient to remain seated and went to the window. Outside, an MP stood with the inevitable clipboard next to a dusty car. He was alone, but the ensign that jutted up from the car fender identified it as British.

Katja returned to her seat and Major Bernstein resumed his ruminations on war. "I'm confident that in the years to come, the discussions of this war will continue, that is, unless the greed and stupidities of new wars overshadow them. Time will show whether this one has taught us anything."

Katja was about to respond when the door opened again. A man in his fifties, paunchy and balding, with watery blue eyes, entered and gave a casual salute. Katja glanced at Frederica, disappointed. Was this bland and colorless man the tower of strength they had both depended on?

Frederica didn't wait for introductions and, with a timidity that seemed foreign to her nature, held out her hand to him. "You're Handel?" she asked uncertainly.

"No, my dear. I'm Captain Atkins. That would be Squadron Officer Humboldt." He pointed with his open hand toward the woman who stood just behind him, still framed in the doorway.

The other officer, dark-haired and trim in her WAAF uniform, stepped into the room, then stiffly offered her hand to Major Bernstein. Her mouth suggested an odd mix of sensuality and severity, but both were offset by large brown eyes that she lowered as she turned toward Frederica.

Katja was confused for a moment. Though the man had spoken English, she had definitely understood the names and the gesture. Then two facts struck her at once. The woman, not the man, was Handel, their constant protector in England, and her name was Humboldt. Just like Vera Humboldt. Could it be a coincidence? She glanced quickly at Frederica, whose expression of shock confirmed that it wasn't.

Frederica stood speechless in the middle of a handshake. Then she seemed to force out the unfamiliar word, "Mother?"

"Yes, dear," the squadron officer said, but made no move to embrace her.

"But how…why…" Frederica stammered.

"Of course you have a lot of questions. We can talk about all of that later." Vera Humboldt turned to the major, whose puzzled frown showed that he, too, was trying to make sense of the little drama. Discretion apparently prevented his commenting.

Squadron Officer Humboldt did nothing to enlighten him, declaring merely, "Major Bernstein, I am happy to identify Frederica Brandt and Katja Sommer as having acted as agents for the SOE since 1939. I will have my office supply you with a written statement for your records. As soon as you release them from your custody, we will arrange for their transportation to London."

Major Bernstein, too, was all business. "Thank you, Squadron Officer. I'll see to that procedure immediately, so that you can leave without delay." But he also seemed to grasp the delicacy of the situation for he added, "Perhaps Captain Atkins and I can settle the paperwork while you and your…uh…agents have lunch. I believe Miss Brandt and Miss Sommer know the way to the canteen."

"Very kind of you, Major Bernstein," Squadron Officer Humboldt said, offering her hand again.

A moment later, the three of them were outside, and it was all over. They stood in an awkward group, no one knowing quite how to begin a new conversation. Too many events had occurred that morning: Rudi's arrest, Peter's uncertain fate, their own release, the return of a prodigal mother. The air was warm, a slight breeze caused the American flag over the main barracks to flutter, and the three simply looked out silently onto the prison camp itself.

The prisoners stood under guard on the grassy areas between the barracks, and it was apparently the exercise hour. "Strange how different it looks now that we're free," Katja said finally, feeling a surge of pity for the countrymen she was leaving behind. She felt particular sympathy for the sweet-natured Traudl and for Leni Riefenstahl, who clutched at her artistic identity while surrounded by the ruins of the Reich she had glamorized.

Then, in the distance, she spotted Hermann Goering in conversation with one of the other party bosses, and her pity evaporated. The Luftwaffe head and field marshal, who had promised aid to Stalingrad troops but failed to deliver it, was still fat and still alive. And Dietrich was dead.

Vera Humboldt saw where she stared and remarked, "There you have it, Germany's 'blond beasts.'"

Frederica glanced at Vera from the side. "You've changed a lot. Once you were attracted to that kind of man. You left my father for one."

"For a Communist, not for a Fascist, but I know what you mean. That attraction to the 'beast' cost me my family, and I learned the lesson much too late. So did Germany."

A few steps brought them to the canteen, where they filled their tin trays with scrambled eggs and bacon, which the Americans seemed to have in unlimited quantity. At the table, Vera sat across from them, studying them at discreet intervals.

Frederica chewed a small bite of food then laid down her fork. "Why did you involve me in this espionage in the first place?"

It was strange to hear an English mother and daughter speak to each other in German, and Katja knew it was on her behalf. It reminded her of the linguistic challenge that lay ahead of her.

"I didn't," Vera answered. "Not 'in the first place.' That was your Aunt Claire's idea. When she informed me, I was aghast. I knew I'd thrown away the chance to be a real mother to you, and the thought of risking you that way seemed heartless. But Claire insisted you were simply working in the ministry in all innocence and it wasn't dangerous, so I agreed. It seemed a way to keep an eye on you. But when the war started and you started smuggling out reports, I panicked."

"Really? It's hard to imagine you with that emotion."

"Oh, but I did. I tried to get the prime minister to recall you and offer you the chance to come in, but you were just too valuable. The War Office was not willing to give you up. After we lost Denise and Violette and Cecily, I appealed to them again, but by then the invasion had started and no one had the resources to get our agents out of Berlin."

Frederica had clearly not yet warmed to her mother. "Yes, and whose idea was it to name a female agent Caesar, anyhow? What was I supposed to conquer?"

Vera smiled for the first time. "Conquer? Oh, it had nothing to do with the emperor. I chose the name from Handel's opera. *Guilio Cesare*. They had just performed it at Covent Garden. Caesar is sung by a woman."

"Oh," Frederica said, but would not be drawn away from her offensive. "Well, Britain got its money's worth out of me. Did you know I was in the Führer bunker at the end? I watched Joseph and Magda Goebbels kill themselves and saw the charred remains of Hitler and his wife."

Vera put down her coffee cup. "His wife? What are you talking about?"

"Oh, I've got lots of other things to tell you too. But that's all for later. Thanks for the slightly belated concern for my welfare, and for trying to get me back, but I doubt I would have wanted to come in anyhow. After Katja and I were together, I wouldn't have left her."

Vera studied Katja with obvious interest, though it was impossible to tell if she understood the implication of *together*. "Do you still have family in Germany?" she asked.

"No. My mother died of cancer a few years ago, and my husband fell at Stalingrad."

"And your father?"

"He was killed during the bombing of Berlin." Katja left unspoken that RAF bombs probably did the job.

"I see." Reaching a dead end on that subject, Vera redirected her attention to Frederica.

"Well, you can tell all your stories during the debriefing in London. Everyone will be dying to hear them."

"I'm sure they will," Frederica said dryly.

Katja felt the tension in the air. Obviously mother and daughter had important things to say to each other, and whether it would be in rancor or reconciliation, she had no desire to be in the middle of it. "Will you excuse me? I'm going to the ladies' room and then I'll get a breath of fresh air. Be back in a short while." Frederica nodded gratefully at her as she rose from her chair.

Frederica sat across from her mother in awkward silence. She stared at her empty cup, rolling the corner of her napkin and avoiding eye contact.

Vera, for her part, stared unashamedly. "How beautiful you've become. Much more than your old SOE identification suggested. A bit thin from deprivation, but we'll make sure you get plenty of good food again."

"I don't want anything from you," Frederica said quietly, then sensed how petulant the remark sounded. "I mean, of course we need for you to get us out of Germany, and we could do with some clean clothes. Both Katja and I are wearing sweaters from Magda Goebbels' closet."

"Magda Goebbels? However did you…? Well, I suppose that will be another of the stories you'll tell later."

Frederica nodded, unsure of whether Vera was being sarcastic. Obviously they were going to have to get to know each other all over again. Or maybe for the first time.

Vera's voice softened. "Escaping this way, with someone else's clothes on your back, must be difficult. But don't worry. We'll see to it that you get everything you need. Besides, you've earned the gratitude of the War Office, and you'll receive a substantial pension. Of course, you won't need Handel to look after you any longer, but I hope you'll let *me* help you get started. There'll be so many new things."

Frederica gave an ambiguous shrug, but was silent.

Vera tapped her fingers nervously on the tabletop, then veered away from the personal back into business. "At this point, I suggest you think about what else you want to ask for from the prime minister. The euphoria is running high right now, but we won't have his attention for long."

Frederica replied without hesitation. "I want a passport for Katja. Immigration papers, special status, whatever it takes. She risked her life over and over, and it's the least Britain can do for her."

Vera's fingers stopped drumming. "That should be possible."

"And I want compensation for Peter Arnhelm. He assisted us on several occasions, and if we don't help him, he could easily starve. He's got nothing."

Vera's eyebrows went up. "That might be a little more difficult."

"It can't be too difficult. Everyone here is destitute. Any amount will help him. If necessary, you can take it out of the funds that accrued to me over the years."

"I'm sure we can work that all out. Of course I'll put your three friends in the report and apply for assistance for them."

"They're more than friends; they're family." She emphasized the word 'family,' as if it were a reproach. "Katja especially. We'll live together, of course, wherever that might be."

The announcement caused surprise to flicker for an instant over Vera's face, then neutrality returned. "There's a desperate shortage of housing in London, but Oxfordshire is untouched. Your aunt Claire has a garden cottage she's offering you as long as you need it. She's looking forward to having you around again."

Frederica stared into space for a moment. "Garden cottage. Ah, yes, I remember. Wasn't an old couple living there?"

"They died ages ago. Then the shire used the house for several years to keep children evacuated from London. In any case, it's empty now and waiting for you."

Frederica allowed herself a slight smile. "That's good. Oxfordshire will be a nice place to introduce Katja into British life. She'll like the university."

"You care a lot about Katja," Vera observed cautiously.

"I love her. You have to know that straightaway. She changed my life. I did my job for you there in Berlin, alone, but I was dead inside until Katja joined me. She stayed with me, while she lost everything herself—her family, her house, everything. She was even in a concentration camp. But for all that, *she* saved *me* and then led me out of Germany." Frederica paused for breath, then added, "I want to spend the rest of my life with her."

Vera's eyes clouded momentarily, as if she peered at something mysterious, then she conceded. "It must be wonderful to be so sure of someone."

"I am, Mother, and I want you to be sure of her too."

"Thank you," Vera said, almost under her breath.

"Thank you? For what?"

"For calling me 'Mother' and including me, however vaguely, in your future."

"I didn't mean—"

The redheaded MP appeared again suddenly at their table and saluted Vera. "Ma'am, Major Bernstein said everything is signed and sealed, and you can leave whenever you wish. Captain Atkins and the other young lady are waiting by your car."

"Thank you, Sergeant," Vera said, standing up. As they walked toward the door, Vera's hand touched Frederica's back with the faintest hint of maternal protection.

Katja studied the faces of the two women as they emerged from the barracks and approached the car. Though Frederica seemed slightly dazed, Vera Humboldt, at least, was smiling. A sign that they hadn't quarreled. "Everything settled?" she asked Frederica.

"More or less. Are you ready to go?"

"No baggage to collect, only the clothes on our backs, so yes, I'm ready. I've been ready since 1943."

"Me too," Frederica said, and stepped into the backseat of the SOE car, drawing Katja in after her.

Vera took the wheel, and as soon as Atkins was seated on the passenger side, she started the motor.

Katja fell to brooding as the vehicle swung around past the entrance to the camp. It was full of war criminals, but Rudi was there too, and Leni Riefenstahl, and hundreds of others who hovered in the gray area between innocence and guilt.

Leaving Germany was hard, but the Germany she had believed in had left her long ago. Gone were the soldier heroes of her youth, and even the very idea of military heroism. Now she had to rethink everything—and she'd have to think it in a new language.

Katja peered over Vera's shoulder through the front windshield. The American flag that flew over the barracks was visible just above the little British ensign that fluttered from the right fender of the car. She recalled the blood flag of the Nuremberg ceremony, of Riefenstahl's light-filled Nazi flag held aloft by the Hitlerjugend, and then the brash Soviet flag that waved from the roof of the conquered Reichstag building.

At that moment, Katja hated flags. Each one stood for a nation that had committed atrocities, genocides, rape, and the slaughter of innocents. Katja would never again feel patriotism, for no nation was the repository of virtue and courage. Only individuals were. And those were few.

She grasped Frederica's hand. This is where her sole loyalty lay—not with an idea, but with a stateless woman who had shown courage, heroic persistence, and tenderness.

"I love you," she whispered into Frederica's ear. It was the first sentence in English she had ever uttered.

End

Postscript

No one who has heard about Leni Riefenstahl is indifferent to her. People condemn her as a Nazi—in spirit, if not in name (she never joined the party)—or they acclaim her as a cinematic genius. To some extent, both attributions are true. Her friendship with Adolf Hitler, which caused her to weep openly when he died, and her indifference to his devastation of Europe condemn her unequivocally as morally blind. But her masterpieces, *Triumph des Willens/Triumph of the Will* and *Olympiade/Olympia*, are visible evidence of cinematographic innovation and brilliance. One has to separate the two and to pass two judgments. The novel, which uses large sections from her biography, also tries to do both, that is, to expose her and admire her.

The opening scene of the novel, one of the panoramas of *Triumph des Willens*, typifies the effects she favored: stunning, heroic, and aesthetically satisfying. But she wanted them to be without political consequence, a position that her own behavior belied. Five years later, her witnessing of German soldiers slaughtering Polish civilians did nothing to dampen her enthusiasm for Hitler.

Adolf Hitler needs no explaining, or he needs volumes of explaining, but we learn nothing from history if we see him merely as demonic. His motives were complicated, as were the motives of all the actors in the Nazi madness: the perpetrators, the victims, and the many who were both.

To win most of Germany to his side, he used the familiar theme of heroic victimization, of the pure and good-hearted German Volk beset by Jewish-Bolshevism. The conjoining of Communism and Judaism in the German mind was one of Goebbels' great achievements, though the enemy he propagandized about was, curiously, both primitive and "over-intellectualized" (his own term). It was patriotism raised to the level of religion.

The role of Joseph Goebbels, propaganda minister, cannot be overestimated, for between Hitler's public appearances, Goebbels fanned the ideological flames through regular delivery of his own addresses and articles. He was fixated—even more than Hitler—on what he saw as "judified" culture, i.e., anything modern, abstract, or threatening to the robust simplicity of the German. His diaries, kept obsessively throughout his adult life, were invaluable in shedding light on the inner workings of the Third Reich. He was physically a revolting little man, but after he came to power, he had great success with women. All speeches in the novel attributed to him are authentic, though shortened and, of course, translated.

Nazi genocide of Jews, Communists, Poles, and Gypsies is widely acknowledged and functions occasionally as a shorthand interpretation of Nazism in general. But in a war that cost between sixty and eighty million lives, there were many other victims with stories to tell, so I have focused on homosexuals and the moral deterioration of the "good German."

The Special Operations Executive (SOE) was formed by Winston Churchill in 1940 to aid resistance and conduct guerilla warfare against Germany through espionage, sabotage, and reconnaissance. It employed some 13,000 people, about 3,200 of whom were women. Nearly a dozen of those women died in German concentration camps, some horribly, and three of these are commemorated in this story with their real names. Their fates are poignantly told in Sara Helm's book, *A Life in Secrets*. However, no known agents infiltrated the machinery of the Nazi government, most certainly not the Ministry of Propaganda. Frederica Brandt is a pure fantasy, and her espionage is of a sort that could only be fictional.

A few readers will likely raise an eyebrow at my use of a Last Supper to introduce the main players in the tragedy. I did not attempt to sanctify them, but merely to lay them out visually, as a *dramatis personae*. In moral character, they run the gamut from the vicious Prietschke to the heroic Frederica, though all are tainted by virtue of their participation in the documentary. And in the troubling gray areas of war, even the "lamb" who is martyred becomes a murderer.

Having chosen to start with the Riefenstahl film and end with the fall of Berlin, I was forced to create a narrative arc over a period of eleven years and thus could only briefly mention the major events of World War II. Here I relied on the reader's knowledge (or ability to 'Google') to appreciate the significance of each thumbnail sketch or reference, such as the Führer oath, the fall of Stalingrad, the Invasion at Normandy, the Auschwitz experiments, the surrender at Tangermünde, and the macabre events of the Führerbunker. For the latter, I drew heavily on the excellent German film *Der Untergang*, based on accounts by Hitler's surviving secretary, Traudl Junge. For the fall of Berlin in general and the zoo, I relied on the richly detailed book by Cornelius Ryan, *The Last Battle*.

Less known is the story of Yevgeny Khaldei, the photographer responsible for the iconic photo of the Red flag over the Reichstag. He was also active as a photographer at the Nüremberg trials, and I must add that there is no historical evidence that he was homosexual.

Homosexuality was illegal before and after the Third Reich, due to paragraph 175 of the German Penal Code. This paragraph is responsible for the tragedy of the few homosexuals who survived the camps being immediately rearrested and incarcerated in post-war Germany. Ironically, Ernst Roehm, the head of the SA, was a notorious homosexual, and the early ranks of the Brownshirts were rife with it, until the organization was purged for political expediency.

Another gray area is the role of the prestigious Charité hospital, which was efficient and innovative, treating wounded soldiers drawn right from the Berlin train station. But it was also tainted by several of its Nazi doctors who were involved in or benefitted from medical experiments in the concentration camps.

Sachsenhausen and Ravensbrück were camps near Berlin. I base my portrayal of them on various first-person accounts by homosexual prisoners, particularly *The Men with the Pink Triangle* by Heinz Heger. I could offer only the briefest sketches of camp life, but wanted to show how victims were regularly pressed into being victimizers. Not only was much of the cruelty in the camps meted out by prisoner wardens (Kapos), but the release of prisoners into the SS special regiment under the leadership of Oskar Dirlewanger created one of the most ruthless SS units of the war.

One of the more extraordinary events at the end of the war was the rush toward the West by both civilians and German troops anxious to surrender to the Allies rather than the vengeful Russians. The desperate crossing at Tangermünde over the demolished bridge is poignantly shown on numerous YouTube videos.

In the search for war criminals after the end of the war, a victim-criminal like Rudi would not have been arrested or even identified for months or years afterward, though Dirlewanger himself was already captured and beaten to death by his Polish guards in June 1945.

Leni Riefenstahl, on the other hand, was arrested and escaped multiple times, then eventually tried and found not guilty of war crimes, though her career in filmmaking was over. Years later, she emerged as a still photographer of the Nuba and then an underwater photographer—in her 90s! She died at the age of 101.

And finally, let me address the tiger/tyger motif. Belligerent forces and sports teams love to associate themselves with the big cats for their savage ruthlessness, and Blake, in his poem "Tyger, Tyger" does this as well. Under the influence of Nietzsche, the Nazis went a step further, identifying the "blond beast," with the German Volk. They even had a line of tanks called "Tigers." With our modern appreciation of endangered species, we view the tiger as more victim than savage beast, but in Blake's terms, the tiger forms a useful icon of the ruthless ethic of the Nazi state. An icon that crumbled, of course, when it confronted an even more ferocious force, the Allied armies.

The fact of WWII still puzzles us morally, or should. Was Nazism and its jungle ethic a unique expression of pure evil that came from elsewhere and must be kept outside, or does the tiger sleep within our own civilized consciousness? "Did he who made the lamb, make thee?" Blake certainly intended the answer to be "Yes."

Glossary of German Terms

Alles raus! Schnell!	Everything out, quickly!
Amis	German slang for Americans
Abitur	Final exams taken at the end of secondary school
Anschluss	Annexation of Austria by Nazi Germany, 1938
Arbeit Macht Frei	"Work makes (you) free" Sign over entrance of several German concentration camps
Arbeitsdienst	Labor Service
Aufseherin	Female concentration-camp guard
Blockleiter	Lowest political official of the NSDAP, responsible for the political supervision of a neighborhood or city block
Blockova	(Female) Prisoner in charge of the block or barrack
Bratkartoffeln	Fried potatoes and onions
Brigadeführer	SS rank roughly equivalent to a brigadier general
Brownshirts	The SA, referring to their brown (surplus WWI) shirts.
Bund Deutscher Mädel	German Girl's Federation—female equivalent to the boys' Hitlerjugend
Comintern	Acronym for Communist International. Association of Communist parties of the world, founded by Lenin 1919
Dirlewanger Regiment	SS penal regiment known for ruthlessness beyond that of the usual SS troops

Einsatzgruppe	Ad hoc group/commando dispatched for a specific mission, often execution of civilians: partisans, Jews, commissars, etc.
Einsatzkommando	Same
Feldgendarmerie	German military police until 1945
Feldwebel	German rank equivalent to US staff sergeant
Gau	District/ territories designated uniquely by the NS party and monitored by a party leader. These disappeared with NS.
Gauleiter	Party leader in charge of the Gau
Glühwein	Hot mulled wine
Götterdämmerung	*Twilight of the Gods*. Opera by Wagner
Hauptsturmführer	Mid-grade level SS officer, equivalent to captain
Hausmeister	Superintendent, custodian
Hitlerjugend	Hitler Youth (ages 14–18)
Kachelofen	Tile-enclosed wood-burning stove
Kapo	A prisoner with lower administrative authority
Knödel	Dumplings
Kriegspost	Letter from the front, delivered by the army
Kübelwagen	Volkswagen manufactured for battlefield use
Lagerstrasse	Main avenue running the length of a camp
Lazarettzug	Hospital train

Leibwache	Personal bodyguards of the Führer.
Loden	Sheep's wool used without removing the lanolin.
Mischling	Mixed breed. Person lacking fully Aryan ancestors
NSDAP	Nationalsozialistische Deutsche Arbeiterpartei Ultra-nationalist, fascist political party that originated as a reaction to the conditions of the surrender after WWI
Obergefreiter	Wehrmacht rank equivalent to US senior lance-corporal
Obergruppenführer	Waffen SS rank equivalent to US lieutenant general
Panzerfaust	Explosive anti-tank warhead, operated by a single soldier
Rechts um/Links um	Drill commands for right turn, left turn
Reichsminister	Minister of the Reich (used also as a form of address)
Reichsparteitag	Reich Party Congress/rally
Schutzstaffel (SS)	Protection unit—original function of SS
Scharführer	Squad leader. Equivalent to sergeant or corporal NCO
Schatz	Treasure. Common term of endearment
Schmiss	Dueling scar on the face (usually deliberately inflicted)
Soldbuch	Paybook. Detailed ID and record of service for Wehrmacht soldier
Stahlhelm	Steel (battle) helmet
Staatsoper	State opera
Strassenbahn	Street car/tram

Sturmabteilung (SA)	Storm troopers. Paramilitary of NS party
Sturmbannführer	SS rank equivalent to major
Sturmmann	Trooper
Tafelspitz	Bavarian/Austrian dish. simmered beef with horseradish
Unteroffizier	NCO (occasionally Sergeant)
Volk	Race, tribe, a culturally unified people. Mystical term for Germans as racially distinct from all others
Volkssturm (Volksstürmer)	Civilian home guard
Warmer /Warmer Bruder	"Warm Brother"—Queer
Wehrmacht	Federal military
National Socialist newspapers:	*Der Angriff*, Goebbels' own newspaper *Der Völkische Beobachter* *Das Schwarze Korps* *Der Stürmer*

About the Author

After years of "professing" at universities and writing for international literary journals, Justine Saracen began writing fiction. Trips to the Middle East inspired the Ibis Prophecy books, which move from Ancient Egyptian theology to the Crusades. The playful first novel, *The 100th Generation*, was a finalist in the Queerlit Competition and the Ann Bannon Reader's Choice award. The sequel, *Vulture's Kiss*, focuses on the first Crusade and vividly dramatizes the dangers of militant religion.

Saracen then moved up a few centuries, to the Renaissance and a few kilometers to the north, to Rome. *Sistine Heresy,* which conjures up a thoroughly blasphemic backstory to Michelangelo's Sistine Chapel frescoes, won a 2009 Independent Publisher's Award (IPPY) and was a finalist in the Foreword Book of the Year Award.

Mephisto Aria, a WWII thriller that has one eye on the Faust story and the other on the world of opera, was a finalist in the EPIC award competition, won Rainbow awards for Best Historical Novel and Best Writing Style, and won the 2011 Golden Crown first prize for best historical novel.

Sarah, Son of God appeared in 2011. In the story within a story, a transgendered beauty takes us through Stonewall-rioting New York, Venice under the Inquisition, and Nero's Rome. The novel won the Rainbow Awards First Prize for Best Transgendered Novel.

Beloved Gomorrah, her work in progress, sheds a radical new light on the story of Lot and his daughters, and links it with the discoveries of a young artist and scuba diver in the Red Sea.

Saracen lives in Brussels, a short flight or train ride to the great cities she loves to write about. Her favorite non-literary pursuits are scuba diving and listening to opera. She can be reached through www.justinsaracen.com, through FB justinesaracen, and Twitter as JustSaracen.

Books Available from Bold Strokes Books

Night Hunt by L.L. Raand. When dormant powers ignite, the wolf Were pack is thrown into violent upheaval, and Sylvan's pregnant mate is at the center of the turmoil. A Midnight Hunters novel. (978-1-60282-647-2)

Demons are Forever by Kim Baldwin and Xenia Alexiou. Elite Operative Landis "Chase" Coolidge enlists the help of high-class call girl Heather Snyder to track down a kidnapped colleague embroiled in a global black market organ-harvesting ring. (978-1-60282-648-9)

Runaway by Anne Laughlin. When Jan Roberts is hired to find a teenager who has run away to live with a group of anti-government survivalists, she's forced to return to the life she escaped when she was a teenager herself. (978-1-60282-649-6)

Street Dreams by Tama Wise. Tyson Rua has more than his fair share of problems growing up in New Zealand—he's gay, he's falling in love, and he's run afoul of the local hip-hop crew leader just as he's trying to make it as a graffiti artist. (978-1-60282-650-2)

Women of the Dark Streets: Lesbian Paranormal edited by Radclyffe and Stacia Seaman. Erotic tales of the supernatural—a world of vampires, werewolves, witches, ghosts, and demons—by the authors of Bold Strokes Books. (978-1-60282-651-9)

Tyger, Tyger, Burning Bright by Justine Saracen. Love does not conquer all, but when all of Europe is on fire, it's better than going to hell alone. (978-1-60282-652-6)

Words to Die By by William Holden. Sixteen answers to the question: What causes a mind to curdle? (978-1-60282-653-3)

Haunting Whispers by VK Powell. Detective Rae Butler faces two challenges: a serial attacker who targets attractive women, and

Audrey Everhart, a compelling woman who knows too much about the case and offers too little—professionally and personally. (978-1-60282-593-2)

Wholehearted by Ronica Black. When therapist Madison Clark and attorney Grace Hollings are forced together to help Grace's troubled nephew at Madison's healing ranch, worlds and hearts collide. (978-1-60282-594-9)

Fugitives of Love by Lisa Girolami. Artist Sinclair Grady has an unspeakable secret, but the only chance she has for love with gallery owner Brenna Wright is to reveal the secret and face the potentially devastating consequences. (978-1-60282-595-6)

Derrick Steele: Private Dick The Case of the Hollywood Hustler by Zavo. Derrick Steele, a hard-drinking, lusty private detective, is being framed for the murder of a hustler in downtown Los Angeles. When his best friend Daniel McAllister joins the investigation, their growing attraction might prove to be more explosive than the case. (978-1-60282-596-3)

Nice Butt: Gay Anal Eroticism by Shane Allison. From toys to teasing, spanking to sporting, some of the best gay erotic scribes celebrate the hottest and most creative in new erotica. (978-1-60282-635-9)

Worth the Risk by Karis Walsh. Investment analyst Jamie Callahan and Grand Prix show jumper Kaitlyn Brown are willing to risk it all in their careers—can they face a greater challenge and take a chance on love? (978-1-60282-587-1)

Bloody Claws by Winter Pennington. In the midst of aiding the police, Preternatural Private Investigator Kassandra Lyall finally finds herself at serious odds with Sheila Morris, the local werewolf pack's Alpha female, when Sheila abuses someone Kassandra has sworn to protect. (978-1-60282-588-8)

Awake Unto Me by Kathleen Knowles. In turn of the century San Francisco, two young women fight for love in a world where women are often invisible and passion is the privilege of the powerful. (978-1-60282-589-5)

Initiation by Desire by MJ Williamz. Jaded Sue and innocent Tulley find forbidden love and passion within the inhibiting confines of a sorority house filled with nosy sisters. (978-1-60282-590-1)

Toughskins by William Masswa. John and Bret are two twenty-something athletes who find that love can begin in the most unlikely of places, including a "mom and pop shop" wrestling league. (978-1-60282-591-8)

me@you.com by K.E. Payne. Is it possible to fall in love with someone you've never met? Imogen Summers thinks so because it's happened to her. (978-1-60282-592-5)

High Impact by Kim Baldwin. Thrill seeker Emery Lawson and Adventure Outfitter Pasha Dunn learn you can never truly appreciate what's important and what you're capable of until faced with a sudden and stark reminder of your own mortality. (978-1-60282-580-2)

Snowbound by Cari Hunter. "The policewoman got shot and she's bleeding everywhere. Get someone here in one hour or I'm going to put her out of her misery." It's an ultimatum that will forever change the lives of police officer Sam Lucas and Dr. Kate Myles. (978-1-60282-581-9)

Rescue Me by Julie Cannon. Tyler Logan reluctantly agrees to pose as the girlfriend of her in-the-closet gay BFF at his company's annual retreat, but she didn't count on falling for Kristin, the boss's wife. (978-1-60282-582-6)

Murder in the Irish Channel by Greg Herren. Chanse MacLeod investigates the disappearance of a female activist fighting the Archdiocese of New Orleans and a powerful real estate syndicate. (978-1-60282-584-0)

Franky Gets Real by Mel Bossa. A four day getaway. Five childhood friends. Five shattering confessions…and a forgotten love unearthed. (978-1-60282-585-7)

Riding the Rails: Locomotive Lust and Carnal Cabooses edited by Jerry Wheeler. Some of the hottest writers of gay erotica spin tales of Riding the Rails. (978-1-60282-586-4)

Sheltering Dunes by Radclyffe. The seventh in the award-winning Provincetown Tales. The pasts, presents, and futures of three women collide in a single moment that will alter all their lives forever. (978-1-60282-573-4)

Holy Rollers by Rob Byrnes. Partners in life and crime, Grant Lambert and Chase LaMarca assemble a team of gay and lesbian criminals to steal millions from a right-wing mega-church, but the gang's plans are complicated by an "ex-gay" conference, the FBI, and a corrupt reverend with his own plans for the cash. (978-1-60282-578-9)

History's Passion: Stories of Sex Before Stonewall edited by Richard Labonté. Four acclaimed erotic authors re-imagine the past…Welcome to the hidden queer history of men loving men not so very long—and centuries—ago. (978-1-60282-576-5)